The Adjacent

■

CHRISTOPHER PRIEST

The right of Christopher Priest to be identified as the author
of this work has been asserted by him in accordance with the
Copyright, Designs and Patents Act 1988.

First published in Great Britain in 2013
by Gollancz
An imprint of the Orion Publishing Group
Orion House, 5 Upper St Martin's Lane,
London WC2H 9EA
An Hachette UK Company

This edition published in Great Britain in 2014
by Gollancz

1 3 5 7 9 10 8 6 4 2

A CIP catalogue record for this book
is available from the British Library

ISBN 978 0 575 10538 6

Typeset by Deltatype Ltd, Birkenhead, Merseyside

Printed and bound by CPI Group (UK) Ltd,
Croydon, CR0 4YY

The Orion Publishing Group's policy is to use papers
that are natural, renewable and recyclable products and
made from wood grown in sustainable forests. The logging
and manufacturing processes are expected to conform to
the environmental regulations of the country of origin.

To Nina

Contents

PART 1

IRGB

1

THE PHOTOGRAPHER

Tibor Tarent had been travelling so long, from so far, hustled by officials through borders and zones, treated with deference but nonetheless made to move quickly from one place to the next. And the mix of vehicles: a helicopter, a train with covered windows, a fast-moving boat of some kind, an aircraft, then a Mebsher personnel carrier. Finally, he was taken aboard another ship, a passenger ferry, where a cabin was made ready for him and he slept fitfully through most of the voyage. One of the officials, a woman, travelled with him, but she remained discreetly unapproachable. They were heading up the English Channel under a dark grey sky, the land distantly in view – when he went up to the boat deck the wind was stiff and laced with sleet and he did not stay there for long.

The ship came to a halt about an hour later. From a window in one of the saloons he saw that they were heading not for a port, as he had imagined, but sidling towards a long concrete jetty built out from the shore. While he wondered what was happening, the woman official approached him and told him to collect his luggage. He asked her where they were.

'This is Southampton Water. You're being taken ashore at the town of Hamble, to avoid delays at the main port. There will be a car waiting for you.'

She led him to an assembly area in the lower crew section of the ship. Two more officials came aboard and he was led by them down a temporary ramp and along the windswept open jetty towards land. The woman remained on the ship. No one asked to see his passport. He felt as if he was a prisoner, but the men spoke politely

3

to him. He could only glimpse his surroundings: the river estuary was wide, but both shores had many buildings and industrial sites. The ship he had been on was already moving away from the jetty. He had boarded it during the night, and he was now surprised to see that it was smaller than he imagined.

They passed through Southampton in the car soon afterwards. Tarent began to sense where they were taking him, but after the last three days of intensive travel he had learned not to ask questions of the people assigned to him. They went through countryside and came eventually to a big town, which turned out to be Reading. He was lodged in a large hotel in the city centre. It was a place of stultifying luxury within a cordon of apparently endless levels of security. He stayed only one night, sleepless and disturbed, feeling like a prisoner or at least a temporary captive of some kind. Food and non-alcoholic drinks were brought to the room whenever he asked, but he consumed little of it. He found it hard to breathe in the air-conditioned room, harder still to put his mind at rest, and impossible to sleep. He tried to watch television, but there were no news channels on the hotel system. Nothing else interested him. He dozed on the bed, stiff with fatigue, suffering memories, grieving over the death of his wife Melanie, constantly aware of the sound of the television.

In the morning he tried breakfast but he still had little appetite. The officials returned while he was at the restaurant table and asked him to be ready to leave as soon as possible. The two young men were ones he had not seen before, both wearing pale grey suits. They knew no more about him or what was planned for him than any of the others. They called him Sir, treated him with deference, but Tarent could tell that they were merely carrying out a task to which they had been assigned.

Before they left the hotel one of them asked Tarent for identification, so he produced the diplomatic passport issued to him before he travelled to Turkey. One glance at its distinctive cover was enough to satisfy the enquiry.

He was driven to Bracknell and at last he was sure where he was being taken. Melanie's parents were expecting him at their house on the outskirts of the town. While the official car drove away,

Tarent and his two in-laws embraced on the steps outside their house. Melanie's mother Annie started to cry as soon as he arrived, while Gordon, the father, stayed dry-eyed but at first said nothing. They led him into their house, familiar to him from previous trips, but now it felt cold and remote. Outside, a grey day brought heavy showers of rain.

After routine polite enquiries about his need for the bathroom, drinks, and so on, the three of them sat close together in the long sitting room, the collection of watercolour landscapes, the heavy furniture, all unchanged since his last visit. Melanie had been with him then. Tarent's bag was outside in the hall but he kept his camera equipment beside him, resting on the floor next to his feet.

Then Gordon said, 'Tibor, we have to ask you. Were you with Melanie when she died?'

'Yes. We were together the whole time.'

'Did you see what happened to her?'

'No. Not at that moment. I was still inside the main building at the clinic, but Melanie had walked outside on her own.'

'She was alone?'

'Temporarily. No one knows why she did that, but two of the security guards were on their way to find her.'

'So she was unprotected?'

Annie tried to suppress a sob, turned away, bowed her head.

'Melanie knew the dangers, and you know what she was like. She never took an unnecessary risk. They warned us all the time – no one could be a hundred per cent safe if we left the compound. She was wearing a Kevlar jacket when she left.'

'Why did Melanie go out on her own? Have you any idea?'

'No, I haven't. I was devastated by what happened to her.'

Those were the first questions and they ended like that. Annie and Gordon said they would make some tea or coffee, and they left him alone for a few moments. Tarent sat in the thickly padded armchair, feeling the weight of his camera holdall leaning against his leg. Of course he had intended to visit Melanie's parents, but not as soon as this, the first full day back in England, plus living with the guilt about Melanie's death, the loss of her, the sudden end to their plans.

After the non-stop travel and temporary overnight stays, the familiar house felt to Tarent stable and calming. He consciously relaxed his muscles, realizing that he had been tensed up for days. Everything about the house looked unchanged from before, but it was their house, not his. He had only ever been here as a visitor.

He came awake suddenly, the smell of cooking in the air. There was a mug of tea on the table in front of him, but it had been cold a long time. He glanced at his watch: at least two hours had passed while he slept. Sounds came from the kitchen so he walked in to show them he was awake again.

After lunch he went for a long walk with Gordon, but the subject of Melanie's death was not discussed. Their house was on the Binfield side of the town, close to the old golf course. It was late summer but both men wore thick outer coats. When they left the house they had to bend their heads against the chill blustering wind, but within an hour the weather had changed and both men took off their jackets and suffered the glaring heat of the sun.

Thinking of the heat he had endured while he was at the clinic in Anatolia, Tarent said nothing. It was uncomfortable to be out in the sun, but it was better than the cold wind.

They walked as far as what Gordon described as the decoy site, one of dozens that had been built around London as a fire lure during the Second World War, to try to keep the Luftwaffe bombers away from the city. Bracknell then had been a village three miles away, and the decoy was out in the wild. There was not much to see: the remains of a dugout shelter, bricked up and overgrown with weeds, and some half-visible piping firmly buried in the soil. Gordon said he took an amateur interest in these old decoy sites, and described how they had been used. He sometimes went to look for other sites. Most of the big industrial cities had installed decoys in 1940, but nearly all of the sites had disappeared since. This was one of the less well preserved ones, but some of those up north were in better condition.

Walking back towards the house, Gordon pointed out the hospital where he was a consultant surgeon, and where Melanie had also worked for a while. It was before she and Tarent met. Gordon told Tarent a long story about an operation he had performed several years earlier. Every procedure had gone wrong almost from the start, and although the surgical team did everything possible it was one of those cases where the patient had just died, no matter what they tried. The patient had been on the table for more than eight hours, a young and attractive woman, a dancer with a touring ballet company, apparently healthy, in for minor abdominal surgery, little risk of infection or other complications, no reason to die. That day Melanie had been training as a theatre nurse, on secondment from her ward nursing, and she had been beside him the whole day.

'I love that girl more than I can ever say,' Gordon said, and he and Tarent walked on down the hill in silence. By the time they were approaching the house the cold wind had returned. Gordon's story about the operation was, for the rest of that day, the only mention anyone made of Melanie.

The next morning Tarent awoke in the guest bedroom, refreshed after several hours of deep sleep, but wondering how much longer he was to stay with the Roscoes. From the time he had been evacuated from the clinic in Turkey his life had been taken over by the authorities. The people who accompanied him never said who they were, but Tarent's licence to go abroad had been authorized by OOR, the Office of Overseas Relief, so he assumed the bland young men and women who ushered him around were from there. It was they who had brought him here, and presumably they would collect him. But when? Today? Or the next day?

Gordon was already out of the house, away on call at the hospital. Tarent showered, then went downstairs and saw Annie, so he asked her if it was OOR who had warned them he was being brought to their house – she confirmed that it was, but that they had said nothing about when he would be collected.

After breakfast, feeling that he should, he said, 'Would you like me to talk more about Melanie?'

Without turning towards him, Annie said, 'Not while I am here on my own. May we wait until this evening? Gordon will be back then.' She too had a medical background: she was a midwife who worked in the same teaching hospital where Gordon had trained.

Tarent spent the rest of the morning in the guest room, making a start on the immense task of sorting through the thousands of photographs he had taken during the trip. At this stage he restricted himself to looking for the dud or unfocused shots and erasing them. Fortunately, the signal was strong in the Roscoes' house, so he could access the online library without any problems. He kept all three cameras on recharge, because online editing quickly depleted the batteries.

He took another walk in the afternoon and when he went back to the house Gordon had returned. The three of them sat around the bare pine table in the kitchen, a place of family meals, easy conversation, but today it was different.

Gordon said, 'Don't try to spare us details, Tibor. We are used to details. We need to know how Melanie died.'

Tarent began his account with a white lie: he said that he and Melanie had been happy together. Instantly he regretted it, but it did not seem to him likely to affect what her parents wanted to know. He described the clinic in Eastern Anatolia, situated close to a town but also within reach of four or five villages in the hills. It was one field hospital among several that had been opened in Turkey – they weren't in direct contact with any of the others, except when a Mebsher called with supplies or relief staff, or one of the helicopters came in with extra medicines or food.

He showed them some of his photographs, ones he had found while scanning the mass of others that morning. Mostly he had selected shots of Melanie to show them, but for reasons he was never going to explain to her parents there weren't as many of those as perhaps they expected. There were thousands of others, all without Melanie, many of them duplicating each other, some showing the worst victims of the situation in the region, the children mostly, and the women. There were dozens of amputees because of the land-mines. He had photographed many skeletal bodies, babies with diseased eyes, wasted women, dead men. Because the Roscoes were a medical family he felt no qualms in showing them what he had seen. Gunshot or blast wounds, dehydration, diarrhoea, cholera, typhoid were the most common injuries and diseases, but there were other horrors that seemed untreatable, new strains of

8

virus, different bacteria. In many cases starvation took the victim's life before a more serious disease took hold.

He had taken photographs of water – it was a novelty to come across areas of standing water of any size. He found damp patches under trees, a filthy puddle, a vile swamp littered with abandoned vehicles, rusting oil drums and the corpses of animals. The one river in the area had become a dehydrated track of crazed and hardened mud, with sometimes a trickle of brown water near the centre. Everywhere else for miles around was a continuum of dust, wind and found corpses.

Annie admired one of the photographs he had taken, of Melanie working in the clinic surrounded by desperate people waiting to be treated. Her expression was composed, neutral, intent on what she was doing. The small boy she was treating was lying limp and still while she unwound a long dressing from his head. Tarent remembered the circumstances of taking the picture: it was a day when not much had gone wrong, on the scale of routinely awful events at the clinic. He had stayed inside the building with Melanie because there was a warning from one of the militia groups. It was a disrupted day, men with automatic rifles on the balcony and in the yard outside, alternately threatening the staff and pleading for drinking water. Every now and then a couple of the younger bloods would fire rounds into the air. In the evening a pickup truck arrived, bringing some kind of leader of the militiamen, and there was another volley of bullets, prolonged in welcome. This was towards the end: Tarent had had enough of taking risks for the sake of photographs, of being there, of hearing guns going off and land-mines exploding in the near distance.

He remained silent as Annie held the digital viewer, Gordon at her side, while the pictures flicked past.

On the evening of the day that photograph was taken, he and Melanie fell into another bitter argument. It turned out to be their last row, so everything between them ended in anger. He remembered his frustration, not necessarily with Melanie but focused on her because she was there. He simply wanted to cut loose, head back to England somehow. He could no longer tolerate the endlessly killing heat, the scenes of desperation, the cocksure and unpredictable gunmen, the dying children, the threats and misunderstandings and random beatings, the women with bruised loins and broken limbs, the total lack of any kind of support from the Turkish authorities, if there still were any. Everyone said there was no longer a central government, but the relief charities who sponsored their work should have known what was going on. There was no way he could travel home on his own, so he had to wait until a group of the workers was evacuated, and even then he could not join them unless Melanie decided to leave too. He thought she never would. It depended ultimately on a team of relief volunteers being sent from the north, but there was not even a hint that anyone was coming.

That night, Tarent was convinced they would have to stay at the clinic indefinitely. In one sense he was right, because it was to be their last night together. After Melanie's death the other medical and relief workers were so demoralized that they began to close down the clinic, abandoning the local people to the heat and the drought and the militiamen.

They never found Melanie's body. She walked out in the afternoon of the day after their argument, seething with rage at him, saying she wanted to be alone. He said nothing, let her go. Their rows always hurt them both, because underlying the differences was a genuine bond of love and long-term commitment. For Tarent, one of the most urgent reasons for wanting to escape from the field hospital was his wish to repair the damage the episode was causing them. But that day, knowing he was watching her helplessly, Melanie pulled on the Kevlar vest over her nurse's uniform, packed a rifle, took a canteen of water and a radio, followed the rules, but she was leaving the safety of the compound at one of the most dangerous hours of the day. When the explosion was heard in the near distance there was the usual immediate head-count, and they knew she was missing. No one had actually witnessed the attack, but one of the orderlies said that immediately before the explosion he had noticed a point of light in that direction, something in the air, higher than tree-height, and so bright it had hurt his eyes. All the security guards, and some of the medical team, drove out in reinforced vehicles to investigate. Tarent was in the front vehicle, his gut instinct telling him it had to be Melanie, that it was all over, but because all they could find was a huge triangle of blackened earth and no sign of a body, her death seemed at first to be uncertain. There was just the weirdly regular scar caused by the explosion, three straight sides forming a perfect equilateral triangle, an inexplicable shape for a crater, with no sign of other wreckage, no blood anywhere, no human remains at all.

By the end of the following day Tarent and the others knew she had to be dead. Even if she had somehow survived the explosion, one so powerful that it appeared to have wiped out everything in its immediate vicinity, she would have been morbidly injured. Without medical treatment, without fresh water, without protection from the daytime heat, it was impossible to survive.

2

The OOR people came to collect him the next morning – they telephoned the house thirty minutes before he was to be ready, and arrived at the exact moment they specified. Tarent was still upstairs, carefully packing his cameras, when he saw the car drawing up outside the house.

His farewell to Gordon and Annie Roscoe was more hurried than any of them would have liked. Gordon shook his hand, but then unbowed and gave a hug – Annie held him closely and cried.

'I really am so sorry about Melanie,' Tarent said, again at something of a loss as to know how to say the right or true thing, and settled for the true. 'Melanie and I were still in love,' he said, 'after all these years.'

'I know, Tibor, I believe you,' said Annie softly. 'Melanie always said the same.'

Tarent joined the others in the car. This time his minders were a man and a woman – the man was wearing a grey business suit, the woman a *burqa*. The driver was another woman, glassed off from the main compartment of the car. An attaché case parked on a rack at the back of the passenger seats bore the OOR insignia, but that was the only clue as to the identity of these people.

During the drive that followed neither of the officials said anything casual or unguarded to him, and the woman never spoke at all. She faced Tarent most of the time, regarding him opaquely from within her shroud. Soon after leaving the Roscoes' house the young man spoke to pass on instructions.

He said that they were taking him to London where there was an apartment he could stay in overnight. He gave Tarent a key, and told him where he should return it when he was collected the next day. He would then be driven to a debriefing office in Lincolnshire, where he would be expected to file a detailed report of his experiences in Turkey. This would include him having to hand over the original datafiles of every photograph he had taken. Tarent bridled, as he had a freelance contract with his usual syndicating agency, but he was curtly reminded of the agreement by which he was to be allowed to accompany his wife on her mission. Tarent could retain commercial rights to the pictures, but he would be told if there were any that were not to be published. There would be no argument.

The official then established that Tarent was not carrying a smartphone, so he handed him a new one. The compartment it was removed from at the back of the vehicle contained several more identical handsets. After he had familiarized himself with the phone's most basic features, Tarent stared out of the smoked-glass car window, a dimmed, darkened view of the Thames Valley. There had been storms in Britain while he was away – Gordon and Annie told him about a particularly violent one just over a week earlier that flattened thousands of trees in the east and south of the country. It was known as a temperate storm, the product of a new kind of climatic low-pressure system. The visit to Melanie's parents now felt to him like an isolated snapshot of his life: two snapshots in fact. There was the old past, the first years of the marriage, the conventional visits to see his in-laws and to spend a little time with some of Melanie's old friends and nursing colleagues. Those days were of course gone forever. Then there was the more recent sliver of experience: staying in the Roscoes' house, recounting for them the last few days at the clinic, Melanie's death and his abrupt return to the IRGB. So much had happened in between those two points. Gordon and Annie saw only a part of him, knew little about the rest.

The journey was slow, with several time-consuming diversions into side roads, caused by barricaded sections, and they made two stops. The first was what the male official called a comfort break at a service station. Armed police patrolled. Tarent wanted to buy some food and drink, as he had eaten nothing since a light breakfast at the house, but he was told there was no time. He had no money of his own. The silent woman produced some coins for him, so he went to a kiosk and was able to buy a bottle of water and something wrapped in cellophane that had nuts in it. Another halt was a prolonged one at anonymous buildings that looked like offices but had no identifying signs outside. The woman in the *burqa* left the car here and was replaced by a man. He was older than the other, and by his manner appeared to be his superior. Both men sat away from Tarent, one working on a laptop computer, the other reading slowly through a sheaf of papers.

After about three hours, by which time Tarent felt sure they must be approaching London at last, the older man began making calls on his mobile phone. He spoke in Arabic, a language Tarent did not speak or understand. However, he heard his surname several times, and realized the younger man was regarding him, perhaps to see if Tarent was following what was said.

They passed through increasingly built-up areas, approaching the capital. The younger official leaned forward to the driving compartment, said something quietly to the driver, and almost at once the smoked-glass effect deepened on all the windows as well as the dividing glass, making it impossible to see outside. Two dome lights in the car's roof came on, completing the sense of isolation.

'Why have you done that?' Tarent said.

'It's beyond your security clearance level, sir.'

'Security? Is there something secret out there?'

'We have no secrets. Your status enables you to travel freely on diplomatic business, but national security issues are a matter of internal policy.'

'But I'm a British citizen.'

13

'Indeed.'

The vehicle was moving more slowly now. The road surface was uneven and the vehicle jolted sharply several times. Tarent could see his face reflected in the darkened glass of the window, shuddering as the car rattled along.

'Where are we now?' he said. 'Can you tell me that? And what's the rest of the route?'

'Of course, sir.' The older man consulted his handheld electronic device. 'We are in west London and have just passed through Acton. We are taking you to an apartment situated near Islington, in Canonbury, but we are having to make a slight detour. After that it will be a straight run through. We do not have much time – we have been warned that another storm is likely to affect south-east England later today.'

At that moment his phone rang, an insistent, high-pitched squeal. He took the call, grunted his understanding of something that was said, then spoke in Arabic again. Still holding the instrument to his ear, he nodded to the other man, who tapped again on the pane of glass that divided the driver from the rest of the car. The dome lights went off, the smoked glass lightened. Both men stared out of their side of the car.

Tarent looked out of his own side. For a few seconds he glimpsed the landscape outside the car. It was a blackened plain, flat, featureless, stretching away as far as he could see. There was nothing out there – everything had been levelled, reduced, annihilated. Were it not for the fact that much of the sky was visible and a low sun was glinting, Tarent could have imagined that the windows of the car were still blacked out.

He had seen this before, on a much smaller scale. The place where Melanie was killed had looked just like it.

Tarent turned towards the other men, seeking an explanation, but already the windows were being opaqued again. He briefly saw part of the sky on their side of the car: a deep, threatening purple. The shades were falling out there, while on his side the devastated landscape had been bathed in bright sunlight.

The glass quickly darkened again, cutting off his view.

3

Heavy rain was pouring from a lowering sky when the car came to a halt outside a block of apartments on the Canonbury Road. The large car shook with the impact of the wind. The two men went with him to the main door, but did not enter the building. Tarent stood at the door, watching as the two men hurried back to the car, splashing in the rippling sheets of water blown along the street.

Although the apartment building was an old one the flat itself had been recently modernized. When Tarent turned on the lights he found a clean, livable space, with every modern convenience. He put down his bags, grateful to be on his own for the next few hours. He sank into one of the chairs and picked up the TV remote.

The storm had been dubbed TS Edward Elgar, by the World Meteorological Organization. Tarent discovered this when he turned on the TV, and although outer bands of heavy cloud had already hit London and the south-east of England the full central force of the storm was not due to strike until the early hours of the morning. It was expected to reach Level 3 or 4 at its height. There were repeated warnings to take shelter, and not to venture out in the storm. Hurricane-force winds were expected, with flooding and structural damage almost inevitable. To underline the message, the TV station played footage from an earlier storm, the Level 4 TS Danielle Darrieux. This had struck land in Ireland, crossed over into Wales, then travelled east towards Lincolnshire before moving out into the North Sea. It had eventually blown itself out as it encountered the colder and shallower waters off the coast of Norway. Blizzards had isolated the Norwegian town of Ørsknes. It was the beginning of September in Europe.

He looked in the kitchen: the refrigerator was working, but there was no real food inside. There was a bottle of soured milk, a carton of margarine spread, three eggs, a half-eaten bar of chocolate. Tarent was hungry. When he went to the main window of the apartment, which looked down into Canonbury Road, he discovered it had stopped raining. He decided to see if he could find a restaurant that was open, or at least a grocery where he could buy something to get him through the evening. As soon as he was in the street he realized there were almost no shops open. Most buildings were dark, or shuttered. The only restaurant he could find was closed – two streets away there was a small grocery still open, but three men were hurriedly boarding up the windows. Inside the shop, Tarent found a ready meal he could heat up, but the man who owned the shop warned him that power outages were likely. Thinking his stay would last for one night only, Tarent bought two bread rolls, some processed chicken and a couple of oranges. He remembered too late that he was carrying almost no cash, but the shop owner accepted a card from him.

As he left the shop, the power went off.

The flat was in darkness when he returned, and neither the fridge nor the cooker would work. The power stayed off for most of the remainder of his stay in the flat, which instead of lasting one night only, extended to more than two days. There was no way he could leave. The storm broke in full force, as forecast, during the first night of his stay, at about two-thirty in the morning. The old apartment building was solidly built and was left relatively unscathed by the gales, torrential rain and hurtling pieces of wreckage, but Tarent was cold and hungry. In a small cupboard in the kitchen he found two unopened cans of food (one a mixed fruit salad, the other a supermarket-brand chili con carne), and he eked these out as long as possible. Without electricity he had no radio or television, and the digital network that he used before he went to Anatolia was down. On the second day the battery of his new smartphone became exhausted, and there was no way he could recharge it.

It was impossible to venture out. He spent hour after hour sitting by the window, looking down Canonbury Road, watching fearfully as the violent squalls skirled along the street, carrying water and debris, thrashing against the concrete stanchions that blocked the roadway and shooting cascades of water against the walls of the old buildings. A small office-block directly opposite his apartment window was demolished on the first night, and every scrap of its wreckage and contents was swept away by the gales. Sheets of metal, cables, parts of car bodies, traffic signs, branches of trees, skidded endlessly along the street, adding to the cacophonous racket of the howling gale. The sight of the endless damage was awful but the screeching of the wind was the true terror. It seemed never to let up, never to vary, except, impossibly, to worsen. Tarent had rarely felt more alone or vulnerable than during those two days and night. He was no worse off than anyone else, or so he imagined, and that became a consolation of sorts. For all that he remained uninjured by the violent weather, and indeed safe and dry, he suspected he came through the storm better than many. The building stayed intact, the windows did not blow out, or at least not those in his apartment, and he was too high above street level to be affected by the flooding.

On the second night he slept for a few hours and when he awoke at first light he discovered that by some miracle the electricity supply had returned. He found his mobile phone charging – he had left it plugged into the mains in the eventuality the power might come on again. He cleared all the uneaten food out of the refrigerator and threw it away. He then phoned the number he had been given, and gave the necessary code word.

A Mebsher, he was told, was passing through north London at that moment. It was quickly arranged that it could divert to the Islington area to collect him. His location was known. All he had to do was wait for a coded message on his phone, and he would find the personnel carrier waiting for him in the street outside.

He returned the phone charger to the power source and less than three hours later a message came through. When he went down to the street the Mebsher was waiting. The floodwater was receding, but even so it reached above the axle level of the huge wheels. Tarent waded across to the extensible access steps. Dripping water from his legs and shoes, he clambered inside and took a seat.

4

The Mebsher was originally designed for military use: a means of transporting troops and matériel through hostile territory in a vehicle that could withstand most forms of violent attack, including RPGs and IEDs. As conditions around the world deteriorated, Mebshers were used increasingly by aid agencies and government departments, and civilian variants had been developed.

Tarent was familiar with the Mebsher, because in places like drought-stricken Eastern Anatolia, with insurgent militias roaming the hills, it had become the vehicle of necessity. The interior of a Mebsher was utilitarian, every metal surface painted a drab grey, or left bare. Visibility to the outside was restricted, and the few windowed apertures were made of thick, toughened glass. There were always minor variations in the number or type of seats, the interior fittings usually on a scale from rudimentary to broken or not working.

The seat he took was next to one of these tiny windows. He apologized to the three people already on board as he clambered in, his luggage bag and cases of camera equipment bulking through the narrow doorway, floodwater draining from his legs and pooling around him. The other passengers briefly acknowledged him. The Mebsher was under way almost as soon as he had seated himself. He fidgeted around for a while, stacking his bag in the rack at the rear, placing his cameras close to him and trying to find a spare cushion of some kind – there was nothing to be had, so he took a towel from his luggage and rolled it up to make a head-rest. He leaned his head against the metal wall, closed his eyes and tried to relax. The vehicle rocked and jarred constantly, but there were no extreme movements: the Mebsher was designed for rough terrain. Tarent did not care about the discomfort – he just wanted to be taken to wherever it was intended he should be, and not to think or do anything until he was there. Gradually, his soaked lower legs and feet began to dry out.

It was as usual noisy inside the compartment. The huge turbine engine was in theory surrounded by sound-proofing, but the roaring whine of it could always be heard. The intercom from the driver's compartment, which was hidden away from the passengers in the front of the vehicle, was switched on. The voices of the two drivers could be heard, communicating in Glaswegian accents. From time to time a radio voice from somewhere else burst in, screeching with static.

Tarent let himself doze for about an hour although real sleep was an impossibility. He drifted for a while, but he was constantly aware of his surroundings. When he opened his eyes he regarded the other passengers, looking at them properly for the first time. There were two men and a woman.

One of the men sat alone in the front row of seats, a laptop computer plugged into the cable socket, and various papers spread out on the other seats beside him. He had short grey hair and what looked like a muscular build beneath his clothes. He had a lip-mic clipped somehow to his jaw and as he read data off the computer monitor, which he held at an angle so that no one else could see it, or from some of the papers, he muttered into the mic. He was using the recognition language applied to certain kinds of software, not English nor any spoken Euro language but a kind of machine jargon, a dialect of code.

The other man and the woman appeared to be travelling together: they sat beside each other in the row in front of him. From time to time they spoke quietly to each other. As Tarent stared at them the man turned slightly away from her, pulled on a black sleep mask and screwed in earphones. He let his head droop forward and he relaxed in his seat, rocking with the endless jerking movements of the Mebsher.

Tarent regarded the woman. He had not yet seen her face. It was half shrouded by a scarf or shawl, a concession many Western women made to Islamic convention, but not formally *hijab*. The woman had not yet looked directly back at him, nor even shown any awareness he was in the row of seats behind her, but he sensed that she was as alert to his presence as he was to hers. Her shoulder-length hair, partially revealed where the scarf did not cover her, reminded him of Melanie's.

Inevitably, he started thinking about Melanie again, what the first attraction had been. Her hair, straight and fine, not too long, had framed her face well. He simply liked the way she looked, and on that afternoon in Bracknell, where he had just completed a photo-shoot, he struck up a conversation with her. It was then they discovered the link between them that had created the initial superficial bond: they were both semi-foreigners.

Tibor Tarent – American father, Hungarian mother, born and mostly brought up in England, feeling British, but always with that revealing European first name, and because of his father speaking with an ineradicable sound of East Coast USA. Melanie was more remotely descended from another culture. Her grandfather had moved to Britain from Poland after the Second World War, married a British girl and changed his name from Roszca to Roscoe. His son Gordon had been brought up without any knowledge of his Polish background, and only discovered it from family papers after his father died. Melanie had even less awareness than that of her distant heritage, saw it as amusing and irrelevant, and had never really thought about it until she and Tarent met. Yet he discovered, early on, that some of her friends called her by an affectionate nickname, Malina, or Mally. Malina was a Polish name meaning raspberry, Melanie said, quietly making the rude noise with her mouth. They were married a few months after they met.

Tarent was less comfortable about his background. It led him to the habit of feeling different, an outsider. He had known it all his childhood, and it worsened when his father was killed in Afghanistan, in circumstances never explained, even by the US State Department for whom he had worked. Tibor was a child at the time, only six. The concealed bomb beneath the roadway that destroyed the armoured Jeep in which his father was travelling was in its own way comprehensible through the familiarity of so many other similar incidents, but why his father had been out there at risk in the rugged hills was never established, or at least never made known to his family. Officially his father was a diplomat but clearly he was more than that, or less. Something other than diplomacy was going on, putting him in a role that sent him out there to a mountain road, in the wrong place and at the wrong time.

Tibor's mother, Lucia, also a diplomat, remained in Britain afterwards. She was a cultural attaché at the Hungarian Embassy in London, so never in the same kind of danger as her husband, but she too died a few years later, victim to breast cancer, as Tibor was leaving university.

That sense of foreignness became more remote as he and Melanie began a more or less conventional married life. No children appeared. She worked at a hospital in London, but his freelance photography caused him to travel, took him away from her, sometimes for a week or more at a time. After ten years in London, Melanie found the hard routines of hospital work were telling on her. She enrolled with Médecins Sans Frontières, loved the work, but it took her away too, often for many weeks at a time. Their marriage began to crumble. The expedition to Eastern Anatolia, not with MSF but with a new aid body set up by the British government, had been a last-ditch attempt by them both to try to cement themselves together again.

Tarent looked through the toughened porthole at his side. While he dozed the Mebsher had travelled a fair distance, and there was a glimpse of countryside out there, a hedge beside the road and a grassed area beyond. But his view was restricted – it might have been an urban park. There were two trees in sight. One of them was leaning at an angle, its upper branches entangled with the one next to it. Neither had many leaves.

Pressing his eyes to the glass, Tarent tried to see as much as he could. The more he looked the more he saw that storm damage was apparent everywhere. The soil and subsoil were laid bare where the storm wind had scoured unsheltered fields, a bleak reminder to him of the scorched and desolated landscape of Anatolia. At times the Mebsher drove past houses or larger buildings, and most of these too had suffered damage. They passed teams of rescue workers, tackling the trunks and thick branches of fallen trees, or pieces of masonry that had crashed into the road. The Mebsher slowed to go past these teams, the vehicle lurching over some of the obstructions. There was flooding in most places, by now becoming shallow, but mud was everywhere. The smell of sewage came in through the filters of the Mebsher's air-con.

Tarent reached down to one of the protective cases he had placed on the floor beside his feet and deftly slipped out the Canon. He tried to line it up through the distorting glass, get it to focus. The camera felt natural in his hand, like a thin glove moulded into his grip. He took a couple of shots through the porthole but he knew even as he released the virtual shutter that the pictures would be no good. The cabin was vibrating too much, there were too many imperfections in the thick glass.

As he lowered the camera he saw that the woman in the row of seats in front of him had turned her head to see what he was doing. It was his first glimpse of her face: she looked nothing like Melanie.

'There's a lot of storm damage out there,' he said unnecessarily.

'Do you have a licence for that camera?'

'It's my job.'

'I asked you if you were licensed to carry a camera.' She had an intent, officious look.

'Of course.' He swivelled the camera so that its back was towards her. The LIN was engraved there. He wondered how she had known he was using the camera – she had been facing away from him and the camera operated silently. 'I'm a professional photographer. I'm carrying three cameras, and have three licences.'

'We were told you were a member of the Diplomatic Corps. Attached to OOR.'

'I'm travelling on a diplomatic passport. I've just returned from abroad.' He briefly explained the means by which the OOR had enabled him to travel with Melanie. Non-medical staff were not allowed to travel abroad, not even spouses. They needed Melanie's specialist training and experience, though, and she made it clear she wanted Tarent with her otherwise she would take another posting. The solution was a temporary passport, which to Tarent's quiet satisfaction seemed to open the way to almost anything he needed to do. His swift return to IRGB would have been impossible without the passport and the status it conferred.

'If you're not a diplomat you should hand it in,' the woman said.

'I'm still on government business.'

'You don't need a passport for that. I could cancel it electronically now.'

'Please don't. I might need it to go abroad again. My wife was killed, but her body was never found. It might be necessary for me to identify her.'

'She was the woman killed in Turkey? Nurse Tarent?'

'Yes. How do you know?'

'We heard. She was a civil servant.' She turned away from him again.

He was chilled by her inquisitive manner and irritated by the intrusion, but it was the first time he had been able to take a look at her. She had a strong face, with good features: a firm jaw, wide forehead, dark eyes. He did not like her frown, the humourless sense of authority over him. He thought perhaps she was in the police, but the law required all officers to identify themselves to members of the public. If she was a cop, did his presence in a government Mebsher place him temporarily outside the category of member of the public? Then again, she might not be a cop.

He kept the lightweight camera in his hand, cupping it lightly. The slow journey continued. After a few minutes one of the drivers fed the BBC news bulletin into the passenger compartment, but the storm and its after-damage were hardly mentioned. Most of the bulletin was about an Emirate meeting of heads of state, due to take place in Toronto. Tarent lost interest and continued to peer at what he could see through the small window. After the politics, the news turned at last to the storm.

It sounded bad. Several of the southern English counties had been affected by damage and floods from the storm surge, but most of the water had already soaked away, especially from the towns and along the Channel coast. Essex was worst affected. Inland rivers had swollen and broken through their banks and levees, cutting off towns and villages, bringing down power lines and swamping electricity relay stations. Many wind turbines had been damaged or put out of use. The tidal generators in the Essex archipelago were no longer functioning, or were producing reduced power. Tarent, remembering the country he had just left, one almost without any fresh water at all, imagined the streets of IRGB cities transformed into canals, the quietude that always attended a flood, the slow sound of the water draining away, the stench of mud, sewage, rottenness spread about.

Above everything now, a cleaned and cloudless sky, brilliant blue. The last spiral outriders of the storm system had rolled away eastwards over the North Sea and the hurricane, spawned in the warm Atlantic waters of the Azores, was gone. Officially, IRGB was never at risk from hurricanes, too far to the north, too far east, so they were called Temperate Storms. The news said that Edward Elgar had been less intense than was feared at first, but nevertheless it had caused extensive damage.

Another storm, TS Federico Fellini, was already crossing the Bay of Biscay, gathering intensity, but its likely strength by the time it reached Britain was still not known, nor was its route.

The radio clicked off, with an ear-popping snap of static.

Tarent, growing bored, stared around the compartment he was in. Much of his journey down to Turkey had been inside vehicles like this one: they had been picked up in Paris, travelled down to Italy in a Mebsher, transferred to a train across to Trieste, then another long slow haul in a Mebsher through the Balkans. The tedium of being trapped inside the vehicle was always much the same. You felt safe because of the strength of the armour, but you were always more vulnerable because the sight of a slow moving personnel carrier was often too tempting to be ignored by insurgents. While they were crossing Serbia a pair of youths had loosed off RPGs at them. One had missed but the other struck the armoured side. The noise of the explosion was terrifying, and he was still suffering tinnitus as a result, but there was no serious damage to the Mebsher. The only injuries to the passengers – himself, Melanie and two doctors – were cuts and bruises from being hurled violently around inside the cabin, but nothing more serious had happened. After that, no one was willing to complain about the cramped conditions, the unrelenting heat, the noise, the boring food. Instead, they travelled in tense silence, fearful of another attack.

At least in Britain the armed gangs who controlled some parts of the countryside were carrying mostly automatic weapons, not grenade launchers. And during the summer months in Britain the temperature inside was usually bearable. It was different in hotter climates where the intensity of the sun on the metal skin overcame any attempt to keep the vehicle cool. The other extreme was just as unmanageable – in three more weeks the heating equipment inside the elderly vehicles would barely cope when the first of the big freezes set in. September in southern England was getting to be a problem, the interface between climate upheavals, a delineation of two distinct climate challenges.

They came eventually to Bedford, a cordoned town, a devolved seat of government, or DSG, in case of national crisis. Tarent looked curiously through his distorting window, wondering what the town would look like in its new ascendancy of importance, but it was much as he remembered it from his last visit some years earlier. They had now travelled a good distance away from the footprint of the storm, and no damage to buildings could be seen.

Tarent and the others spent the night in a Home Office hostel, an installation with most of its facilities concealed below ground level. It was somewhere near the railway station, which was apparently still in use. They saw little else of the town before transferring from the Mebsher to the building, stepping through the chill evening air.

He was relieved to be allocated a single room for the night because he was in no mood to have to share with a stranger. Once again his diplomatic ID was invaluable. It was concerning to him that someone like the woman in the seat ahead of him apparently had the ability to disable it remotely, but for the time being at least it went through the swipes and scans without a hitch.

The room he was given in the hostel was little more than a cell, several floors down and therefore deep underground. It was properly ventilated, though, and was kept clean and tidy. The corridor outside smelled of old food, paint, rust and damp. Tarent located the refectory on the same level, ate a large meal, followed it with some fruit, then returned to his room with a carton of chilled fresh milk. He went early to bed but slept badly. There were noises all night: doors slamming, voices passing down the corridor. The ventilator droned constantly, and in the early hours someone went slowly along the corridor with an electric cleaner. He was woken at 7:00 am.

He was first to take his seat in the Mebsher. When the others boarded they barely glanced in his direction but nodded briefly and conventionally towards him. The woman was last to board. As she clambered through the narrow, reinforced hatch her shoulder-bag caught on something. While stretching back to free it she stared directly at Tarent for a moment, but as soon as she had wrenched it from the obstruction she looked away again without saying anything.

'Good morning,' Tarent said as she took her seat in front of him, but she did not reply. She opened her bag, apparently wanting to make sure nothing had been lost from it.

They were soon under way again. As the Mebsher moved slowly out of the town centre one of the crewmen came on the intercom. It was a formula greeting: peace be unto you, Allah is almighty, welcome back aboard, keep your seat-belts fastened, food is available in the galley but remember that no alcohol is allowed aboard, please follow all instructions from the crew in the event of emergencies, Inshallah. There would be a short refuelling stop in about an hour. The crewman added that there could be breaks in the journey for prayer if requested, and these were not only allowed but encouraged. At least one hour's notice would be required, either to travel to the nearest mosque or to locate a suitable halt and to manoeuvre the Mebsher into position.

Tarent had met both of the crew the day before when he boarded. They were young, apparently well trained and efficient NCOs. They were from the Royal Highland Regiment, the Black Watch, courteous and sharp-witted, willing to try to meet the passengers' needs while the long and uncomfortable journey continued.

They drove north out of the town, shortly heading into the flat countryside of Cambridgeshire. Tarent tried to see what he could through the window. After two hours the drivers pulled in at a depot to recharge the vehicle's cells and to take on more biofuel. The woman in the row in front of Tarent climbed down to the tiny service bar beneath the passenger compartment. She brought back two styrofoam cups of coffee, one for herself and one for the man she was travelling with. She did not look in Tarent's direction.

Thinking ahead to the need for food at lunchtime, and like the other passengers rather unwilling to try clambering down the steep steps while the Mebsher was in motion, Tarent went down to the service area and took some sandwiches and a vacuum-sealed salad from the chill box.

He returned to his seat and stared again through the narrow pane of armoured glass. From the position within the recharge dock he could see at least a dozen fallen trees, which must have lined the side of the road before they fell. Maybe they had been struck by the storm Melanie's parents had mentioned. Their root balls stood perpendicular, great ragged discs of soil and root material. There was still a carpet of leaves, smaller shrubs, branches and other debris spreading across the dock forecourt and into the main road. With interest he regarded the many tonnes of timber and vegetation he could see in just this short stretch of the road and from a restricted viewpoint. The whole of southern England must be similarly wreathed in torn and broken vegetation because of the storms. He wondered what would happen to the valuable material when at last it was cleared up.

His interest in the recycling of timber and other vegetation had been sharpened by the last photographic assignment he went on, two weeks before the start of the ill-fated visit to Turkey with Melanie. This had been to central Spain. Here he had covered the PCVE, *Proyecto Carbón Vegetal Españolas*. The Spanish authorities had set up a vast network of carbon-negative power generators based on the bulk creation of charcoaled biomass. The residue, when buried in the ground, restored the waste carbon to the soil, not to the atmosphere. As a long-term measure it would also return fertility to the hundreds of thousands of hectares of the country that had turned to desert since the beginning of the twenty-first century.

At a time of ever-worsening ecological catastrophe, the PCVE had induced in him a feeling of optimism, that something was at last being done. Looking at the fallen trees around him, Tarent hoped and assumed that people in Britain would not be so shortsighted as to incinerate the organic debris from this or any other of the recent storms, or to pile it somewhere to decompose. The Spanish charcoal biomass project was still the only large installation in Western Europe, but immense complexes of biochar electricity generators, coupled with carbon reclaim, had been established in China, Ukraine, Russia, India, Brazil and Australia.

He knew, though, that in many parts of the world the climate was so extreme, and the urgent re-use of waste so little understood, that the old and wasteful methods were still being employed.

He settled down on the thinly padded seat as comfortably as he could to endure the inevitably long hours of travel that must still lie ahead. Boredom was an enemy because of the mental blankness it created, allowing in the thoughts that normally he could guard himself against. It was still only a few days since Melanie had died. They had been together for more than twelve years and in spite of everything that had gone wrong he still did not yet know how he was going to get by without her.

Obviously it had been a mistake to travel with her – from the moment they arrived at the field hospital he realized he was at best superfluous and at worst in the way of the clinical work. He busied himself with his cameras, went out on shoots as often as possible, but the hospital inevitably drew attention to itself, and as the weeks went by it became increasingly dangerous to venture outside. Soon he was more or less confined to the compound, or to the clinical areas inside. Melanie hated that, and his presence became the endless, continuous aggravation that did so much damage to their relationship.

The journey to Anatolia was the first time they travelled abroad together, and at first the experience drew them together. For days they passed through blighted countryside, past barren slopes and dried-up lakes and rivers. They saw striking evidence of the abraded climate: sudden devastating storms that led to flash floods and mud-slides, blinding, airless heat, the fields of burnt crops, the fire-blackened forests. All that was what they saw as they passed through southern France, through Provence, along the Mediterranean coast, as the Mebsher took them slowly to the north of Italy. After a total of more than a month of such travel, Tarent's party had joined up with another OOR medical team in Trieste. They allowed themselves three days' rest. A slow convoy of Mebshers then set off through the perilous mountains of the Balkans. It took another four weeks to reach the hospital compound in Eastern Anatolia, where work was already going on. The people they relieved left immediately in the Mebshers. Backed up by intermittent supplies brought in expensively by privately operated helicopter couriers, the staff managed to keep the hospital running for five months, two more than their original expectations, but towards the end everything about the work was becoming unsustainable.

When the refuelling was complete the Mebsher resumed its journey, but was now moving noticeably more slowly than before. Two more hours passed before another halt. Tarent again scrambled down the steps at the rear of the compartment and took some more food and a cup of coffee. None of the other passengers responded when he offered to bring them drinks, so he silently resumed his seat.

His fellow passengers were quietly aggravating him. They ignored him all the time, although Tarent had to admit they barely spoke amongst themselves. It was still impossible to work out if they were travelling together, although they were apparently of the same background of officialdom, or at least in roughly equivalent positions within those circles. The man who sat alone in the front row either concentrated hard on the screen of his laptop, or dozed for brief periods. Sometimes he spoke on his mobile phone – an indication of his high status since nearly all digital access was forbidden while inside a Mebsher, because of the sophisticated electronic equipment on which it depended for defence. In any event, the thick armour plating normally prevented any signal getting through, but the man had connected his cellphone through a cable of some kind, presumably gaining access to the network. When they had boarded that morning in Bedford, Tarent had glimpsed the flash of a CIA identification chip and briefly heard a New England accent. The man was tall, his close-cut grey hair grew thickly and his face was one of the most humourless Tarent could remember seeing. The man's self-absorption was like a black hole, neutralizing any attempt at contact.

The other two passengers still appeared to Tarent to be together, although today they were sitting slightly more apart. It seemed not to be a personal relationship. The man was older than the woman. All he could see for most of the day was the backs of their heads: the man's dark, almost black hair was thinning over his crown, the woman's brown hair mostly covered by the scarf. There was a gap above her collar, by her left ear, where part of the scarf had lifted away. As the Mebsher lurched along the uneven road surface, their heads shook and moved together. Sometimes she raised a hand and tweaked her fingers through the strands of hair falling behind her ear.

Tarent took a few surreptitious shots of the others. One picture caught the profile of the woman in what he recognized as a typical gesture: her head was tipped forward, her eyes were closed, a finger lifted the side of the scarf to touch her hair.

She still reminded him of Melanie, and he wished she did not. Maybe it was guilt. The sense of the years wasted and his failure to do anything about that. Melanie was thirty-eight now, or had been thirty-eight until the week before last. Memories of her kept returning, maddeningly. Tarent sometimes imagined he could hear her voice, trying to break in over the racket of the Mebsher's engine. Her scent was still on his skin, or so he thought.

The night before she was killed they made love, something they sometimes did after a row. It was unsatisfactory for them both. The bunk they were in was too narrow and the walls of the safehouse were treacherously thin. It was hot. Humidity and heat, endlessly, invariably. They made the effort, an unspoken attempt to try to tell each other they were still together, but they both knew they were not. After those fevered minutes of physical and sexual exertion, the habitual distance spread out again between them, not a real barrier but a painful and familiar reminder of how fragile their marriage had become.

Lying in the dark they riffed a fantasy they both knew well, the one about returning to Britain, taking a vacation, going to a good hotel in London or one of the other cities and spending the back-pay on a few nights of selfish luxury. But it would never happen, they both knew, and even then they had no idea how disastrous the next day was going to be.

She resented him, he resented her. But how can you resent a nurse? Tarent had found several ways, a defence mechanism. His own practical qualification, a degree in environmental sciences, was where there were jobs for the taking. Allegedly. After university, Tarent had found there was no apparent need for an inexperienced pyrologist. After a year's visit to the USA he returned to Britain while the political and social upheaval that accompanied the foundation of the IRGB was still in progress. No jobs were going at all at that time, so he drifted into photography, working first with a friend from uni, later striking out on his own as a freelance. That was what he was doing when he met Melanie.

She once described photography as a passive activity, receptive, non-interventionist. It recorded events but never influenced them. She believed that nothing was worthwhile that was not practical, hands-on, proactive. That was her function, but not his. He defended himself in what he saw as a candid way, but which Melanie described as ineffectual. Photography was a form of art, he said ineffectually. Art had no practical function. It only was. It informed or it showed or it simply existed. But it could move the world. Melanie derided him for that, pulling open the loose neck of her shirt and pulling it down, exposing yet again her shoulder and upper arm. That was where a deranged patient had scraped a soiled needle against her, trying to infect her with whatever it was he had. That was her trophy, the personal reward for proactivity.

'So photograph it, why don't you?' she yelled at him once, during the second week of their transit across Turkey, somewhere in the high arid deserts beyond the coastal strip. That day their Mebsher convoy had run short of water, and they were waiting to be resupplied. Tarent could still remember the grim surroundings of stone and desiccated vegetation, the abandoned town of Hadimá down the hill, the mountains of yellow rock, the distant glimpse of the sea, the blasting hot wind and the cloudless sky.

The resentment hurt, but he still loved her. He remembered what she seemed to have forgotten, their early days, their intensive

31

letters and long phone calls, the excitement of all that, the immense emotional challenge. Love was stronger than resentment.

But now he was to go back to his damned passive photography.

6

He closed his eyes, dozed for a while. Suddenly, a voice came through the intercom, the Glasgwegian accent.

'This is Ibrahim, your second driver. Peace be unto you. There's some kind of fault with our power cells and unfortunately many of the usual recharging points are unavailable. We need to make our overnight stop earlier than planned, so we're going to divert and make an overnight at a place called Long Sutton. They can take us for one night. It means another delay, but that's probably better than running out of energy. We can have replacement cells fitted there, and we'll make up time tomorrow. The weather forecast is good.'

There was a pause. The microphone stayed on. Behind the hiss of the communicator they could hear the two men in the cockpit speaking to each other. The woman in front of Tarent had reacted visibly to the announcement, looking up in surprise. Now she turned her head and spoke quietly to the man beside her. He shook his head, listened to more. Then he silently agreed with her, nodding, eyebrows briefly raised, looked away.

Tarent leaned against the wall of the compartment, peering again through the narrow window. As he did so, two things happened simultaneously. Something was thrust insistently, firmly, inexplicably, into his hand, and he folded his fingers reflexively around it. And a second voice, the other sergeant in the cab, took over the announcement.

'This is Hamid, senior driver.' Tarent recognized Hamid as the young sergeant who had helped him on board, out of the floodwaters of north London, when he joined the Mebsher. 'Peace be unto you. This is to let you know that we have been ordered to port your security clearances ahead, because of where we'll be stopping.

The Long Sutton base is normally off-limits, as you no doubt know. No cause for alarm – just routine. Everyone on board today is cleared to the required MoD level. Just thought we should mention it in case anyone has concerns. You will have to check in with your chips and ID tags, but they'll be handed straight back to you.'

Tarent had distant memories, from years back, of a number of protest demonstrations when the Long Sutton base was opened. In those days it had been operated by the US Air Force as an advance early-warning listening site, but presumably these days, long after the dissolution of NATO, it was being run by the Ministry of Defence. But early warnings? About whom?

He still had trouble recognizing himself in the role of high-ranking official of some kind, one with a security clearance. His past contacts with government departments had usually been intermittent, mostly when he was assigned to some event that needed permission from the Home Office or Emirate Liaison. Even then he was acting only as a freelance photographer, commissioned by a web magazine or a TV channel, needing accreditation.

As the lumbering vehicle continued on along the road, Tarent was working his fingertips around the slip of paper that had been pushed so forcefully into his hand. He twisted it, making it into a tight cone, sharp at one end, for the moment not thinking about how it had come into his possession. Finally he opened it, smoothing it across his thigh.

Written in erratic handwriting, apparently scribbled in haste, were the words: *I am travelling to Hull DSG. Come with me? The Warne's Farm appointment can be skipped.*

It could only have been the woman in front of him. Tarent screwed up the paper and looked again at the back of her covered head, where her hand rested against her neck. While watching her earlier, bored with everything, he had thought those restlessly moving fingers were a mannerism, an uneasy habit, but now he wondered if she might have been sending some kind of unrecognized signal to him.

He remembered the early impression he had had of her, a sense that she was somehow alert to him. There was nothing but coldness in her overt manner towards him, but now this note. His look turned into a stare he found difficult to unlock. Apart from the fretting of her fingers she was making no movement at all, apparently unaware of him.

If he raised his hand he could touch those fingers, feel her neck and hair.

Nothing happened, nothing changed. Soon he was dozing, a dreamless state of near-sleep, half-aware of the reality around him: the movements of the vehicle, the vibration and noise of the engine, the jerking forward or back if there was a gear change. He thought vaguely about the woman, so close to him, so remote. *Come with me?* To what? The question mark made it into an offer, not a command. An offer of Hull? In other circumstances he might see the note as a proposition, but it was the same woman who had brusquely checked his photographer's licence. And the only certainty in his life at that moment was the fact he had been given strict instructions to attend a debriefing at an OOR establishment somewhere in the Lincolnshire Wolds, called Warne's Farm. The woman's note said he could skip it. He did not see how.

He returned to full awareness when the vehicle slowed suddenly and came to a halt, the whine of its engine running down to silence. Through half-open eyes, yawning, Tarent glimpsed a military presence: two young marines stood on guard, clad in low-vis camo fatigues, Kevlar vests and pads, masked into anonymity with automatic rifles at the ready.

He was aware of his fellow passengers shifting in their seats, as keen as he was to be out of the Mebsher at last. Now that the vehicle was silent and stationary, Tarent felt trapped. The air-con was off, the fans were no longer blowing. It looked cold outside.

At the window again, Tarent saw Hamid outside, signing a number of documents. There were arguments going on, but not ill-natured. Something about the vehicle they were in, to judge by the gestures.

After several more minutes two civilian officials wearing protective clothing and breathing apparatus squeezed their way through the entry hatch into the cramped compartment. Sitting close to the narrow hatch, Tarent felt a welcome draught of fresh air. One of the officials was a man, the other was a woman. The woman was wearing *hijab*, so with the oxygen mask and protective glasses nothing at all could be seen of her face. The man was wearing a dark work-jacket, with 'Ministry of Defence' stencilled on the flap of a breast pocket. Both of them were carrying large pressurized cans – the man squirted a fine aerosol into all corners of the compartment itself, while the woman sprayed all four of the passengers with the stuff. Tarent held his breath as soon as he realized what was about to happen, but his immediate concern was to protect his cameras. Inevitably, he soon had to breathe in. The aerosol was powder-dry, tasted vaguely acrid and where it landed on the skin it stung. As he and the others choked and coughed, the woman directed more spray at them.

They were left to recover on their own. Over the intercom, Hamid and Ibrahim could be heard in the control cab, also coughing. Ibrahim pleaded loudly for forgiveness, but for his own angry thoughts, not for the actions of the officials.

They were allowed to disembark. Although he was closest to the hatch, Tarent held back to allow the others out of the vehicle first. The woman stepped past him, without a glance or a word.

7

The Mebsher had halted next to a long building, brick-built with a flat roof. There were trees everywhere, around the buildings and alongside the two or three tracks that could be seen leading to other parts of the compound. A breeze was moving through the trees. Tarent gulped in the fresh air, trying to calm his breathing. His lungs still felt aggravated by the chemical spray. He could smell the stuff on his clothes, in his hair, on his face and lips. It renewed the feeling he had had ever since arriving back in Britain, that other people were taking over his life, determining his actions. Yet he was also convinced that none of the people he had encountered in the last few days had any conception at all of what he had been doing abroad, what the chaos of events there was like, the morbid sights he had witnessed and the terrifying events he had experienced, the parlous state into which so many parts of the world had fallen. Half of Europe was now virtually uninhabitable. Most people who were able to live here in the temperate world, the ever more narrow and meandering strips of livable land in the northern and southern hemispheres, were having to draw back from the rest, hold on to the remains of what they knew. Curiosity about the uninhabitable parts of the world had mostly died, shrouded by the need for self-preservation.

A white geodesic dome, and two vast satellite dishes, could be seen rising up beyond the trees.

The other three people from the Mebsher were walking ahead of him. He followed them in through a door guarded by a police officer, then along a corridor. The woman was lagging behind the others, and she glanced back at him. Her expression was openly enquiring.

Tarent shook his head, then tried to make a noncommittal gesture.

She turned away from him immediately, straightened the pack on her shoulder, and walked more quickly. She pushed past her male companion, leading the way into one of the rooms ahead.

A lengthy induction process followed. Apart from having to produce ID, they were made to sign disclaimers under freedom of movement and freedom of information legislation. The American man objected with formal words, citing a US Supreme Court judgement, but then cooperated without further demur. They were each given a tag to hang around their necks, to be worn at all times, even in bed. Tarent was relieved and surprised when they did not examine or take away his photographic equipment.

It was still the afternoon. The rest of the day loomed ahead with nothing much to do. Tarent knew nobody there, and Long Sutton's own rules about banned activities and closed zones were posted on every door and most of the walls. He was allocated a room in one of the dormitory buildings – it was as sparsely furnished as the underground room in Bedford, but somewhat smaller.

He stripped off his clothes and lay naked on the bed for a while, then took a shower. Afterwards, still naked but for the obligatory identity tag, he lay on the bed with his head tipped back so that he could look up at the trees overhead. It began to feel warm in the room, but there was no way of adjusting the temperature and the windows were sealed.

He watched TV for a few minutes, flicking through the channels to find a news service or current affairs programme. As so often before, channel browsing for more than five minutes in some hotel room or rented accommodation made him feel moronic and annoyed. When he found a news broadcast the main story was again the meeting in Toronto, so Tarent turned the television off.

Looking out of the window he noticed that the sun was lowering, so he dressed again and walked slowly around the immediate area of the dormitory block. No one else was about. He carried his camera on his belt as usual but this time he kept it half-concealed beneath a woollen pullover. In truth he was not particularly interested in the place, but he was relishing the chance to walk around under trees. When the extremes of climate change struck it was the trees which usually disappeared first: by forest fires, by storm damage, by desperate scavenging for fuel. So many landscapes had been denuded. The trees at Long Sutton provided him with a rare, harmless pleasure. With the Canon set for the lighting conditions, Tarent took several shots of the canopy above, nothing special or picturesque, but a record of the leafy ambience.

He kept walking, heading away from the main group of buildings. He conscientiously stayed away from any area marked as a secure zone. He took several more photos of trees, lining up the shots so that some of the buildings were visible in the distance. In several places it was possible to take advantage of the compound's floodlights, which were neither bright nor numerous. The environment was not pictorially stimulating but Tarent enjoyed the feeling of old instincts returning, to shoot foreground and background, frame the pictures, use exposure imaginatively. Now he was out of the Mebsher he had managed to get a digital link to his remote electronic lab, which graded each of the pictures according to his own default settings. He then downloaded back several of the shots and was satisfied by the deep shades of grey and black, the striking greens. There was electronic noise visible in several of the deeper shades, even after the images had been regenerated by the lab. The sun was now close to setting, and finding the right exposure was difficult in the varying light under the trees.

One of the tasks he was anxious to get down to was to go through the thousands of frames he had shot while in Anatolia. There had been only intermittent digital access there. So far there had only been time for the hurried search through the frames for Melanie's parents, the photos he had been able to glimpse as they were uploaded to the lab. It was therefore another small pleasure for him, to work properly with his camera again, shooting, grading, assessing and then archiving. His subjects were elderly government buildings and ordinary trees, but the process was enjoyable. CCTV cameras had been discreetly installed to cover most of the areas where he was walking, so he assumed he was being monitored.

8

Feeling hungry at last, Tarent wandered back to the place where he had been told meals would be provided. He found a large hall, deserted but for one man working in the kitchen at the far end. A choice of two meals was available, next to a microwave oven. Tarent chose the soyaburger. He cracked it out of its recyclable card container, waited while the oven irradiated it then sat alone at one of the tables while he ate. He saw none of the other passengers or crew from the Mebsher. While he was still eating, the man in the kitchen turned out all the lights at the far end of the room and departed.

Tarent walked out again into the cool evening. The place seemed deserted. There were metal-hooded vents in the roofs of some of the buildings, and these whirred and clanged in the darkness. Condensation clouded out of them, soon dispersed by the breeze. He walked a different route this time and eventually reached the perimeter fence, a daunting combination of loops of razor wire, large concrete blocks and randomly electrified sections. Strict warnings to intending intruders were posted prominently, in five languages. Floodlights bathed the fence and the road. Tarent took a few pictures.

A feeling of isolation and loneliness struck him. These trees, that road, this English evening, so familiar in many ways, but he was nowhere near home. He still had that to face up to. His actual home, the large apartment he lived in with Melanie, had formerly lived in with Melanie, was in the London suburbs on the Kent side. It lay directly under what he now knew was the main path of TS Edward Elgar so there would probably be some structural damage to cope with along with everything else. He still had no idea what future plans he should make: the apartment would be too big for him on his own, but it was full of their stuff. Especially, now, Melanie's stuff. In one sense at least this enforced trip to a government debriefing office in Lincolnshire was a way of delaying that inevitability, but he had been away from home too long.

He looked quickly at the graded downloads from the lab of the pictures he had just taken, then made minute adjustments to allow for the colour temperature of the floodlights. He felt paralysed by the sense of isolation, of displacement, of delay which had grown in him during the evening. Melanie's loss was like a constant ache, but without warning it flared up into actual pain at random times. He wished nothing of the last few months had happened at all. He slipped the camera away without taking any more shots.

While he still stood there, wrapped up in his sudden introspection, a woman's voice said, 'You took photographs of me without permission.'

She had approached him soundlessly. Her accent was flat, free of region, educated. Tarent turned towards her. It was the woman who had been in the Mebsher. Light was playing on her from above. She looked tall and aggressive, standing with one leg before the other, resting on the large root of a tree where it rose out of the ground. Her hair was still covered by the scarf but now she was wearing an insulated puffer jacket with the hood pulled up over the scarf. She was holding out her right hand, expecting him to place something in it.

There were human rights laws in the IRGB, protecting members of the public from being photographed without permission. Tarent, like every other photographer in the business, knew this well.

'I took a couple of test shots,' he said, with habitual half-truth. 'It's a new camera and I was trying it out. They will never be published.'

'That's irrelevant.'

'A Mebsher on a diplomatic mission is usually accepted as being outside national boundaries.'

'That's also irrelevant. You didn't have my permission. Please let me have the pictures.'

'They aren't here any more.'

She gestured impatiently. 'I know you've got them. Why do you suppose your cameras weren't confiscated when we checked in here?'

'Was that your doing?'

'I interceded, yes. I need those pictures back from you.'

'Did you write me that note?'

'Yes.'

'Why did you ask me about going to Hull?'

'You don't have to go to Warne's Farm.'

'I've been told I have to be debriefed about my wife's death.'

'I know about that. That's an OOR establishment. I can intercede there too.'

'Why should you?'

She shrugged back the hood of her coat. Although she had been wearing the scarf under the hood she had unknotted it. Her face was uncovered and the long ends of the scarf were hanging loosely down on her shoulders and chest. She saw him looking, so she swept one end of the scarf across her throat, over her shoulder.

Although the camera was out of sight, Tarent surreptitiously pressed the foldaway feature and the instrument silently reduced itself to a wafer-thin sliver of plastic and alloyed metals. He concealed it in the palm of his hand, like an illusionist palming a playing card. In past photo assignments Tarent had had two cameras taken away from him and destroyed: once when he was photographing a crowd of rioters in Belarus, the other time by a plain-clothes policeman in the French city of Lyon. The latest generation of miniature cameras had been developed specifically to meet the needs of photojournalists who had to be able to conceal their equipment quickly and effectively.

The woman stood her ground, disconcerting him again. Her authoritative manner was of someone used to getting her own way, but unexpectedly it also seemed to reveal a kind of physical vulnerability. He knew so little of her, after two days of physical proximity. Just the hand, the hair, the neck.

They continued to stand apart, facing each other in the semi-darkness. She was breathing hard: with anger, fatigue, stress? White clouds from their breath drifted between them.

He said, 'What exactly is it you want?'

She glanced down towards his hand, where the Canon was concealed. He was allowing his arm to swing freely, trying to make it look like a natural gesture.

'The pictures you took. I have to have them. It's a matter of security.'

'I've already told you they're not here any more. All my frames are transmitted to the agency laboratory. That's how the camera works.'

'It's impossible to transmit anything from inside one of those vehicles.'

'The frames were uploaded when we left. Automatically.'

'I don't believe you. The camera has a memory.'

'Yes, but I don't use it. Once the pictures are at the lab the memory is cleared. Anyway, I took no pictures of you.' The camera had been in stealth mode ever since he left Anatolia. There was no way she could have heard it.

'You're not telling the truth.' She raised the left side of the scarf, turned her head and lightly tapped the area immediately behind her ear. 'I know what you did. You took three shots in quick succession. I can give you the timestamp of each exposure, the EXIF data and the exact coordinates of where we were at that moment.'

She turned her face further away from him and lifted her hair. Light from the overhead flood fell on her and Tarent saw the gleam of a metallic implant there, a tiny sliver of chased alloy, with three tactile keys. He instantly felt an irrational urge to cross to her, take hold of her, tip her head tenderly to one side and peer closely at the device. He could imagine how she would feel with her body against him, his hands on her, smelling the skin of her neck, feel the light touch of the hair that fell across her shoulders, see her lips close to his.

The thought dazed him.

She said nothing, but continued to stare at him. She let her hair fall.

He said, 'All right.' He felt as if he were about to faint, that if he stepped forward he would stumble against her. He groped around in his mind, trying to focus on what they had been saying. 'Those shots are at my lab. They've been archived. I have to use the camera's controller to access them. It's in my room, with the rest of my gear. Come with me and I'll download them now.'

He thought of the cramped space in the room, its constricting walls, the airless warmth, the narrow bed.

'That's a Canon S-Lite Concealable, isn't it? The pro model.'

'How do you know that?'

'I told you I have the EXIF data. You don't need a controller with that version.'

'You can view the pictures, but they can't be downloaded.'

'Are you using any other cameras I don't know about?'

'A Nikon and an Olympus. They're in my room too, unless your friend has been in to take them.'

'My friend?'

'The man you're travelling with.'

'He's a security officer from the department I work in. His name is Heydar. His official role is my minder, but they don't call him that.'

'Is he with you now?'

'He's taking an early night. He thinks I'm in my room.' She made it sound like a confidence, then added, 'He won't go to your room unless I call him there.'

They had both already turned by unspoken consent and were walking back in the direction of the accommodation block. She strode ahead of him but as the entrance to the building came in sight she unexpectedly slowed her pace, allowing Tarent to come abreast of her. She walked at his side, looking down at the ground, the scarf hanging beside her face. They went along the disordered gravel path, under the silent trees, through the intermittent spills of light. Tarent's hand, still palming the camera, swung beside hers.

'Will you tell me your name?' he said. He was surprised by the sound of breathlessness in his own voice.

'Why should you need to know?'

'Not need. I should like to know.'

'Maybe later. Which room are you in, Tibor Tarent?'

'So you know my name.'

'I know a lot about you. More than you probably realize.'

'Such as what?'

'That you met Thijs Rietveld.'

Tarent did not understand. He made her repeat what she said.

'Thijs Rietveld,' she said. 'The theoretical physicist. He was Dutch. Apparently you met him about twenty years ago.'

'If that's true I have no memory of it. Twenty years is a long time.'

'Which room is it?' she said, gripping his upper arm with her hand.

They passed through the main entrance to the block. They reached for their ID tags. Tarent found the slot first and swiped the card. He went through ahead of her, but she slipped in behind him before the door could close against her. Again she walked beside him. The corridor was narrow – sometimes they brushed against each other.

There was barely room for two people to stand inside his room. He had let her in first, so now she stood on the narrow strip of carpet, her legs pressing against the bed, her back towards him. The room was hot and airless. The bed was as he had left it, with the clothes he was wearing earlier scattered across it. He allowed the door to close behind him.

She glanced back, turning her head, watching for the tiny scarlet LED that confirmed the door was secure.

She unzipped her puffer jacket and shrugged it off. She slid the scarf away from her shoulders, shook out her hair. The scarf bunched lightly on the floor. Tarent swept his own clothes from the bed. She still had not turned, still presented her back to him.

She tilted her chin down, then lifted the hair away from her neck, exposing the implant. His face was a finger's length away from her. The implant glittered in the light from the overhead bulb. She leaned towards him, pressing her back against him and presenting her bare neck. Tarent leaned into her with his lips parted. He briefly glimpsed a company logo, deeply etched in the metal of the implant shield: it was a tiny letter '**a**', stylized, surrounded by a pentagon. Nothing else. Then the hard shallow dome of the implant was in his mouth, his lips sucking on the skin around it, the metal rough and grainy against his tongue. She yielded, sideways in his arms, as his mouth roamed greedily across her neck, her ear, tasting her, wetting her, feeling the light brushing of her hair against his lips and chin and eyes. In his eagerness his front teeth grated audibly against the hard surface of the implant, and he pulled back from her.

'You can't damage it,' she said, her voice sounding deeper, tremulous.

'What about you?'

'I'm beyond damage. You'll find out.'

9

It was half an hour later. Crushed against her on the narrow bed, slimy with sweat, Tarent reached up and switched off the overhead light under the glare of which they had made love. One of the floodlights outside was close to the window and there was a spill of harsh light glancing through the top of the blinds. He reached across to the cord pull, managed to move the blind to block the worst of the light. Her limbs, her body, radiated heat at him.

She disentangled herself and sat upright, moving away from him along the bed. She faced him with her legs apart. Tarent sat up as well, arranged his own legs so they went around her. The light from outside still pouring in over the top of the blind laid a diagonal line across her, a pale radiance. She too was damp with perspiration – her hair clung wetly to the sides of her face.

Tarent felt his own sweat running through his hairline, down the sides of his face. He caught a bead of it, then smoothed a line of faint dampness across her left breast. He was short of breath in the stuffy room.

'The window won't open,' he said. 'I tried earlier.'

'They've all been sealed. Every window in the building. MoD regulations. Shall we open the door?'

They had been hearing footsteps and voices outside. 'Are you out of your mind?' he said.

'I thought you wanted fresh air.'

He leaned towards her, put his arms around her and they briefly caressed each other. He said, 'I wasn't expecting that. What we did.'

'I was. I thought you knew. I've been waiting two days for you to make a move.'

He shook his head, remembering the hours in the Mebsher, what he had interpreted as the silent cold disdain pouring out of her towards him. Had he totally misunderstood? Well, it no longer mattered.

Now he could look at her directly he saw that she bore no physical resemblance to Melanie, even superficially. She was broader, taller, her breasts were slightly fuller, her waist was narrower. He guessed she was younger than Melanie had been, but it was difficult to tell by how much.

'I still don't know your name. Or who you are.'

'You needn't know.'

'Why do you say that?'

'Because of what I am and why I'm here with you.'

'Then what are you?'

'A woman with physical needs.'

'And why?'

'The same needs.'

'More than that.'

'A woman whose job doesn't allow her a private life, so her physical needs become urgent.'

'So you take what you can.'

'No, I have almost no life outside my work. You have no idea of the arranging I've had to go to for you, tonight. Or the risk I'm running.'

'Please tell me your name,' he said.

She held up her fingers, touched each one with her other hand, as if counting. She smiled. 'Flo,' she said. 'You can call me Flo.'

'Is that your real name?'

'It could be.' She was sitting erect, her back straight, her arms stretched out before her. She touched her fingertips to his chest. Her legs were folded around each other. She held his gaze steadily. It was an unnerving kind of calmness, not created by inner peace but by seeming to use some kind of tight control on herself. Tarent realized it made him tense up in reaction to it, because he did not know what she might do. He knew she was for some reason playing with him. 'Flo was what they called me,' she said. 'Years ago. No one uses that name now, so you can.'

'Is it based on Florence?'

'For a time I was a Florence. But that was never who I was. Nor what I am. Not then, not now.' She was obviously tiring of his questions about her name, and used her fingers to flick his bare shoulder in mock annoyance. 'I still want those pictures you took of me.'

Trying to tease, he said, 'You've gone to a lot of trouble for a couple of photographs, Flo.'

'No. I wanted to fuck you. If you think that was trouble, you should see the trouble I can make for people if I have to. Going after a fuck is not what I call trouble.'

'OK. Shall we have another fuck? Flo?'

'In a while.' She shifted her position, leaning back a little and stretching out her legs in front of her. She pinned them against his sides. 'I'm still too hot.'

She raised herself, reached for the window catch behind Tarent's head. Her breast brushed against his cheek as she strained at the immovable bolt. The window remained sealed up, and she subsided.

'In some of our buildings, a few of the windows still open,' she said.

'Our buildings?'

'The MoD.'

'So that's who you work for.'

'Why are you so curious about me?'

'I like to know who I'm with. All I know about you is that you travel about the country in an armoured Mebsher, with a minder.'

'So do you.'

'I don't have a minder.'

'As it happens, you do. As it happens, it's me. I've been assigned to you.'

'I was told – I'd missed the transport I was supposed to be in. They said there was another Mebsher in the region and it detoured to pick me up. That doesn't sound like you were assigned to anything. You just happened to be aboard.'

'We knew where you were. After the storm had passed a call went out for one of the personnel carriers to collect you. There are four or five Mebshers en route to Hull at the moment – there's a departmental meeting coming up. When I heard it was you, I decided I'd be the one to pick you up.'

'I thought you said you don't go to trouble to get laid.'

'I don't. Trouble is what I do when I'm in the office. I wanted to meet you, not because I wanted to get laid but because of what happened to you in Turkey.'

'So how do you know about me?'

'We have ways. You're at diplomatic level, which means the files are open to our office.' She briefly tossed her head, flicked her hair back. She laid her fingers on the implant, indicating it. 'I knew most things about you before the call, and today I found out the rest. Your wife – Melanie Tarent, I heard what happened to her. I also know where you were until last week, and what happened to Melanie. She was killed in violent circumstances that were never discovered or explained. Well, I can fill you in with a few details about that. We have established that she was killed by a radical wing of the insurgency in Anatolia, and they were using a new kind of weapon. We have people out in Turkey looking into that at the moment. Did you know they caught the people responsible?'

That startled him. 'No, I didn't. When did that happen?'

'The day after you left. We were trying to get them back to IRGB – innocent until proved guilty, of course. We wanted to ask them a few questions first. On the way they were killed by another group of militiamen, who ambushed our convoy. Two of our people were killed too, several more injured. We think it was a local dispute, and there were two militias operating in that area. They were going for each other. But I thought you might like to know.'

'I'm sorry to hear that. I had no idea more people had died.'

'They weren't there for your sake. We wanted to find out where the insurgents were getting their weapons.'

'You said it was a new device. I was there after the explosion and saw the crater. It was obviously some kind of roadside bomb. We saw those all the time.'

'What did you notice about the crater?'

Her tone had been playful – Tarent nearly answered in kind. Instead, he said, 'What should I have noticed?'

'You were there.' She had not changed her manner. 'What did you see?'

'It was a triangle. It had three straight sides, and they made up what looked like a regular triangle.'

'Could you explain it? Did anyone else talk about it?'

'Not that I remember. I wasn't listening to anyone else. I think I was in shock, after Melanie.'

'That's what we are working on now.' She sat forward, looked around the tiny room. 'Do you have any drink in here? I mean, a real drink?'

'Just water. We're in a government building.'

'I could work around that if you'd like to wait here for half an hour. Anyway, not all government buildings are the same.'

'Meaning that the one you work in isn't?'

'No – ours is the same. Alcohol not allowed. But there are ways. Come round to see me one afternoon and I'll introduce you to single malt.' She rolled to the side, climbed off the bed. Tarent stared greedily at her long legs, her toned upper body, the perspiration still shining on her in patches. She filled two plastic cups from the cooler tap, swallowed all the water from one of the cups in three swift gulps, then passed him the other. 'That's enough of a drink for now.'

She filled her cup a second time. She dipped her fingers in

the cold water and flicked droplets across her arms and breasts, smeared a handful of water over her belly. She sat down on the narrow bed again, this time sitting close beside him. Playfully she splashed some drops on him. He wet his hand and slid it gently across her breasts, then let more drops fall around her neck. His fingers brushed against the implant again.

'So we have established that you work for the government,' he said. 'That wasn't difficult. The Ministry of Defence.'

'Something like that.'

'Come on.'

'I'm not formally allowed to say.'

'I don't suppose you're formally allowed to fuck recently widowed freelance photographers. Anyway, you say you know everything about me, so you know my security clearance. What's to lose by telling me where you work?'

'It might lose me the job, for a start. For a woman to get to where I am now wasn't easy.'

'So, let me guess. MoD, Ministry of Defence, we've agreed. Your job is high up? Department head?'

'Permanent Secretary. Private Office.' She turned her face away from him suddenly, almost as if embarrassed by the revelation.

Tarent opened his mouth to say something, then shut it again.

'I'm not making it up,' she said.

He regarded her nakedness, the tangled bedclothes. The hot room was full of her scents. The improbability of it all.

'You're full of surprises,' he said. 'Should I know who you are?'

'I hope not. We don't advertise what we do.'

'You're not a Muslim, is that right?'

'Yes, that's right. I'm not.'

'I thought—'

'You have to be neither male nor a Muslim, although if you saw the civil servants at my rank in other ministries that's what you'd think. But I guessed long ago that being a woman and *not* being a Muslim were balancing opposites, and went for it. I worked hard, got a good degree, was willing to work for a year as an unpaid intern. Then ... I rose through the ranks. I'm ambitious and I climbed quickly. My minister is an enlightened man. He's what used to be called westernized. He likes soccer and cricket and heavy rock, he goes to the theatre when he can. He enjoys having women around him, and he likes non-Muslims working under him. Most of my staff are female.'

'So who is your minister?'

'His Supreme Royal Highness, Prince Ammari.'

In spite of everything she had said in the last two or three minutes, and even though he was expecting to be surprised again, Tarent almost missed a breath. Sheik Muhammad Ammari was Secretary of State for Defence, probably the highest ranking cabinet minister after the PM. This woman with the slim and sweaty body, the calm hands, the disarrayed hair, the candid eyes and the heady perfumes of after-sex, in effect ran the Ministry of Defence. She would be administratively responsible for the armed services, and held extensive delegated powers.

He reached down to the mess of clothes on the floor and disentangled his trousers, the legs turned inside out in his or Flo's haste to remove them. The Canon was inside his belt pouch. He took it out.

'OK, you get the photos,' he said.

He switched on the camera, expanded it, then pressed the GAIN button. The lab was instantly accessible online, so it took only a matter of seconds for him to locate the three pictures he had taken of her. He held the camera for her to see.

'You know, they don't matter any more,' she said, but she leaned against him to look closely at them. She leant a hand on his knee to support herself. Her nipple brushed against his arm. As photographs the three were not at all special: one was blurred, apparently by a sudden movement of the vehicle, the other two were as sharp as glass. They showed the half profile view of her that had become familiar to Tarent throughout the journey, leaning forward in her seat, her left hand raised so that her fingers rested lightly in the area behind her ear. Her face could not be seen clearly in either of the two best pictures. The interior of the Mebsher was in the background, dark and utilitarian.

She was resting the side of her head against his, strands of her hair dangling against his shoulder. He put an arm behind her, rested his hand on her backside. The images on the camera reminded him of her physical paradox: that coldness she seemed to radiate, her physical proximity yet her remoteness from him. Now this: her warm, voluptuous body touching his, her light breath on his face. She had told him to call her Flo.

'No one but me would recognize you,' he said.

Her hand remained on his leg, her fingers lightly wrapped under his thigh, a gentle rhythm of pressure from her fingers.

'I would,' she said. 'And His Royal Highness would too.'

'OK.' He snapped the controller under the thin body of the camera, and waited for the connection to the lab to be confirmed. He selected the three shots and they dissolved into nothingness. 'No copies, no back-ups, no originals – all gone forever.' She made no response. 'Don't you believe me?' he said.

'Yes, I do.' She removed her hand from beneath his leg, lightly tapped the implant behind her ear. 'I felt them go.'

'Is that thing always on?'

'Twenty-four seven, but I can suppress it when I want to sleep.' She reached out to take his camera from him. Reluctantly, he let her hold it. She held it up, as if lining up a shot. 'I don't understand how it can take photographs without a lens.'

'There's a lens, but it's not optical. It's called a quantum lens. I haven't used a camera with an optical lens for more than a year.'

He pointed out where the three tiny shards at the front of the camera were recessed. He touched the release and they rose silently to form a shallow tepee over the microprocessor aperture. He felt in himself the easy pleasure of talking about the one subject he loved. 'These sensors work at particle or sub-particle level. They digitally radicalize the image when the shutter is opened. An electronic lens is more or less automatic: it focuses, sets the aperture, the shutter speed, all in one operation. I can override the settings, but when it's set to auto every shot is always in focus, always correctly exposed. They haven't found a way to stop a Mebsher shaking my camera hand, but that will probably be the next technical upgrade.'

He was speaking lightly, but when he looked up at her he knew something in her had changed – the relaxed playfulness had disappeared.

'Is it your own camera?' she said.

'This one is. I'm evaluating the other two for the manufacturers.'

'Don't you realize it's illegal to use that kind of camera?'

'I told you I had licences.'

'Licences are irrelevant. If that camera is using adjacency technology, then taking photographs with it was banned last year.'

'I never heard about that.'

'Ignorance of the law is no defence—'

'I was away,' Tarent said.

'Yes, you were in Turkey – in fact, there's no law against them there, as it happens. But you can't use them anywhere else in Europe.'

'Why should they be banned? They're just cameras.'

'Quantum technology has been declared toxic. There are known to be occasional health risks for the user, and for anyone else in range. Too many side-effects.'

'I can't believe I'm hearing this. How can a camera have side-effects? And what kind of illness am I supposed to have suffered? I've been using these cameras for more than a year.'

'I don't remember all the technical arguments. There was an advisory committee, and when the results of the tests were confirmed the Kalifate passed an emergency Act. There is a risk in using them, intermittent but apparently serious.'

'What harm can they do? They've had no adverse effect on me.'

'How do you know? Anyway, you should hand them in.'

'These are how I make my living. There must be a way round this law for professional photographers.'

Flo touched the implant on her neck. 'Want me to find out for sure? I can do it now.'

'No, because then you'll pull rank on me and I'll have to give them up. Let me get this debriefing out of the way, then when I'm back in London I'll talk to the people I work with. If necessary I'll change the cameras then.'

'They'll tell you the same as me.'

'Maybe so. Come on, Flo – you're not in the office now.'

Flo reached out to take the camera from him again, but he swung away from her and placed it back in its case. He plugged it into the recharger. He put all three of the cameras into the tiny closet. She watched him, and as he closed the closet door he looked enquiringly at her, wondering if she was going to keep arguing with him. Instead, her mood had changed abruptly again. She was sitting across from him on the bed, leaning back in a relaxed way on her elbows.

'So, we agreed we'd like another fuck?' she said.

Her mood change made him incredulous. 'I thought after that you might be about to put on your clothes and leave me.'

'No – you're right. I'm not at work now. Ignore what I said about the damned cameras. I forget myself, sometimes. I don't know when to switch off. I'm really sorry.'

'I've been a freelance for long enough to know that the last thing to do is flout the law. If there's a problem I'll deal with it later.'

'I know, I know, let's forget it.'

'Forget everything?'

'No, I've switched off now. Let's just do what we came in here to do.'

10

She pressed him down on the bed. He was uneasy at first, chilled by her mood swings, but they did it all again and this time their lovemaking took longer and was sweatier than before. The heating vent blew unwanted warmth on them as they slowly, pleasurably regained their breath. The physical act purged him of the irritation she had brought on, but now he was wary of her. He lay above her, his chest pressing down on her breasts, one leg trailing away towards the floor to try to find cool air, but he was exhausted, drained, sweltering, fulfilled, exhilarated by her. Flo seemed to be asleep – she was unmoving with her face buried against his shoulder, her breathing slow and steady, but after a few minutes she suddenly tensed up and tried to roll out from under him. He shifted to make a space for her, so she levered herself up and away from him. She left the bed, took a brief shower in the cubicle behind him, then dried with his towel and began putting on her clothes. Tarent watched her dressing, already feeling regrets that it was over, wishing she would spend the remainder of the night with him. The thin shaft of light was still the only source of illumination in the room. He watched as she pulled on her pants over her neat, exercise-toned buttocks, then lifted the ankle-length skirt, and retained it at her waist with a clip.

'Shall we meet again tomorrow?' he said.

'Not possible. Unless you want to give Warne's Farm a miss and travel with me to Hull.'

'I'm under orders. You know that. Why on earth do you need to go to Hull?'

Now that she had most of her clothes back on, she was assertive again. 'It's a DSG, devolved seat of government. I have meetings with the Joint Chiefs of Staff. I've several regional committees to get through, two advisory panels, a meeting with chief constables, applications from the town council, and the rest. Staffing and provisioning arrangements. Mostly routine, but time-consuming. I warned you – I don't have a private life. But I can hide you in my hotel room, and see you after work, at night.'

'I'm not sure—'

'I'm having to deal with a never-ending series of problems.'

'Not on your own.'

'No – the whole department is involved, of course. But there's a state of emergency, because of what happened in London. Everything is a crisis at the moment.'

'What happened in London?'

'You must have heard.'

'I've been cut off from the news for several months.'

'There was a terrorist attack on London. Just over four months ago. It was as devastating as a small nuclear weapon. It was contained in some way that we're still trying to understand. But an area of west London was completely destroyed.'

He stared at her, trying to form a reaction.

'You really hadn't heard about this, had you?' she said.

'That's incredible. There must have been thousands of casualties. It's incredible!' He realized that in the shock of hearing what she had told him he was repeating himself. He suddenly remembered the scenes he had glimpsed from the car window as the officials drove him into London: the blackened, flattened landscape they did not want him to see, the way they had darkened the glass to restrict his view. 'This really happened?' he said, insensibly. 'A nuclear attack, against London?'

'It's known as May 10, the date it happened. Not a nuke, in the way it's usually meant. It was probably a larger version of the thing they turned on your wife. Unfortunately, that kind of device is in use more and more. What happened to her was one of several similar attacks in the last month. But London was the biggest and worst incident yet. We've been able to study it, which isn't true of most of them, because of where they are used. But, well, west London makes a forensic examination much more straightforward.'

'You say there have been a lot of these?'

'At least fifteen in the last four weeks. Most of them in places like Anatolia, but there have been two similar small incidents in Britain. Three in the USA, one in Sweden. Like most people, you probably don't realize that we are at war, and this is one we're not going to win. We've already lost the war against climate change – now there's this. It's the old cliché – the war to end wars. This time it's literally true. If another major city is hit, there won't be another war after this.'

'Tell me what happened in London.'

'On May 10, in the middle of the day, there was an unexplained event just to the south-west of Maida Vale. Mostly in Bayswater. Not an explosion, but it had the same sort of impact. For now it is being treated as a conventional weapon, because radiation readings are so low as to be unexceptional. And the damage was not the type of thing you expect after a nuke. But even so the damage was too great to have been caused by a conventional weapon. There's still a mystery about what exactly it was.'

'What were the casualties?' he said, aghast at this appalling news.

'Over a hundred thousand, at a minimum. The final figure could be as high as twice that, maybe more. It's a version of the Hiroshima Effect: not only were people killed, but many of the records of their lives were also destroyed, and almost everyone who knew them was killed too. Everything was annihilated – that's the word the press has been using. Annihilated. There were no human remains, so it's a question of tracing relatives, or people who had friends or acquaintances at ground zero. The latest count was just over a hundred and twenty thousand people. They are described as missing, but not yet posted as dead. We suspect those figures will turn out to be the tip of the iceberg.'

'I don't understand how we never got to hear about this.' From this perspective it was frankly unbelievable, but for many weeks at the field hospital their only contact with the outside world was the occasional airlift of supplies, brought in by MSF helicopters. Because of the dangers of ground fire, the choppers only came in at night and never landed. The drugs, medical supplies, food and water were either dropped or lowered, before the helicopters soared away again.

And of course his mind was racing, trying to remember anyone he knew who might have been living in west London at that time.

'I was in London two days ago.' He told her what he had seen from the car, and she confirmed that the damaged zone was probably part of the affected area: Bayswater Road, a large part of Notting Hill, an area as far north as West Kilburn, almost as far as Maida Vale in the east. 'I was taken to an apartment after that, somewhere near Islington. The only damage I saw there was caused by the storm.'

'The explosion was contained. The charge was shaped in some way that none of the blast specialists can understand, let alone explain.'

'What do you mean by contained?'

'The blast area was restricted to defined limits. An exact triangle.' She was looking steadily at him, to see his reaction. 'It's a regular triangle, straight-edged, not aligned to north and south.'

Tarent closed his eyes, remembering the day in Anatolia.

'That's what happened to your wife, isn't it?'

Tarent said, 'Why a triangle?'

'We don't know.'

'Is it exact?'

'Was the crater you saw exact?'

'And what is inside the triangle?'

'Nothing. Everything has been destroyed. Annihilated.'

'Who the hell could have done that?' Tarent said.

'We don't know that, either.'

'You said they had been caught.'

'We never found out who they were working for, but there is some new intelligence material we're working on. Our main concern at present is to maintain a defensive posture. We can't let it happen again. All the security measures have been in place for about a month, at the highest level of preparedness – west London is more or less locked down. But what we are having to do now is to set up precautionary arrangements in case there's another attack. That's the answer to what I'm going to be doing in Hull.'

Flo had stopped dressing herself. She sat on the side of the bed next to Tarent, resting a hand on his knee.

She said, 'Shall I stay with you for a while?'

'Please.'

He moved to the cubicle and used the toilet. Then he showered. When he went back into the room Flo had finished dressing. She sat on the side of the bed, her thick outer jacket resting on her lap. He sat down next to her. He was still stunned by the news. He realized the shock that must have run through the country, indeed throughout the world, and that what he was experiencing now was probably a lesser version. At the time it happened there would have been not just the shock, but extreme concern for anyone who was affected, fear that it might happen again, anger, resentment, worry –

At least he had learned about it so long after the event that he knew there had not been a second outrage, or not yet. Or not one as big.

He remembered the unexplained glimpse he had had, as the car slowed down and the men he was with spoke to one another with concern about the coming storm. Because he had not known what he was looking at, all he had gained in those two or three seconds was an impression: blackness, no visible wreckage, a violent levelling.

Whenever there is a major terrorist attack, most people not

directly involved take the news quietly: they learn about it through endless TV coverage, or through the internet, they keep their thoughts to themselves but inside they feel an imagined sharing of the experience: the confusion in the streets, the fright about what might be next, guilty relief that they themselves were not directly affected, wondering endlessly what had really happened. They listen to the accounts of witnesses, survivors, then come the experts, the politicians, the spokespeople, the protesters against government policy. Everything at the time of the attack would have been explained, described, yet would somehow still remain inexplicable. Four months after it happened it was already different: the event itself was clear, known, to some extent understood, but new mystery surrounded it. Even within four months, something as immensely shocking as this moves back into shared experience, history.

Eventually Flo stood up, and said, 'It's time.' He knew it was impossible for her to stay with him, but also he did not want to be alone. It was now long after midnight. She added, 'Have you decided what to do tomorrow? Are you coming to Hull with me? I need to know.'

'I'll go to my debriefing,' Tarent said. The idea of being a sort of sexual plaything for her, hanging around in a hotel bedroom in Hull while she consorted with executives, soldiers and princes, did not appeal. 'I want to get home as soon as I can. Anyway, you have a country to run.'

She did not react to that.

'There's a regular helicopter supply service between Warne's Farm and the DSG compound in Hull,' she said. 'If your debriefing follows the usual format – the one the OOR uses for diplomats returning from overseas postings – it shouldn't last more than a day or two. I have to be in Hull for at least four days. Want to give it a try? I want you there, you know.'

'OK,' he said, but his mind was already full of too many things. The liaison with Flo had not changed anything of his life, except briefly and temporarily. Suddenly it was over. He did not want her to leave.

Now something extra had been added to his grief about Melanie:

the guilt that he had fallen into bed with this woman. It was the first time he had been unfaithful to his wife, or so it unmistakably felt. Even so, he felt an urge to cling to Flo. There was no one else, and she wanted him. She said. His life ahead would be vacant, purposeless without her. He felt an overwhelming but irrational urge to keep her with him, or at least to postpone the moment when she walked out of the door. He had not known this feeling for years. A teenage crush, infatuation for a pretty girl in the town who had said she liked him. 'So will I see you in the Mebsher tomorrow?'

'You'll see me.'

'I want to be with you, Flo,' he said. 'Please stay.'

'Goodnight, Tibor.' She leaned towards him, offered herself for a chaste kiss.

There was something else, something unfinished. As their brief kiss ended, and she began to turn away from him, he said, 'Who was that man you asked me about? You said he was a Dutch scientist.'

'His name was Thijs Rietveld, but he was not a scientist. Not in the sense you probably mean. He was an academic, a theoretical physicist.'

'And you say I met him?'

'That's what it says in your file.'

'Must be a mistake. The name means nothing to me.'

'That's not what the file says. It was some time ago. But if you've forgotten—'

'I just would never come across someone like that.'

'All right.' She was by the door, working the release. The LED on the lock turned green. 'I can't make you come to the DSG meeting with me, but when you're finished at Warne's Farm, come and see me. You were present when your wife was killed, you met Rietveld. To me that's a link in a chain I'm trying to connect. Rietveld discovered adjacency. Does that mean anything to you?'

'No.'

'That's what we're working on. And a bright light in the sky. What about that? Did you see that?'

'Someone at the hospital said he saw one, just before the explosion.'

'It's another link, Tibor. We know about the bright lights,

overhead at the point of the explosion, but we don't know what they are. They're not UFOs. They're something to do with adjacency.'

'I wasn't the one who saw it.'

'You were there. That's enough.' She pulled the door open. 'Anyway, I want to see you again. You know where to find me.'

'But how do I contact you if things go wrong?' The door had closed. 'You never even told me your surname,' he said, into the silence.

A shadow moved across the rumpled surface of the bed, a waving branch, leaves bending to the wind, caught in the thin shaft of light that angled in. She had left her fragrance behind, in the stuffy air of the room, on the bed sheet, in his thoughts. He should have known that her exit from his concerns would be as sudden as her entry into them: on her terms, for her needs. Shared, though. There she was, there she no longer was. He could still hear her footsteps outside, receding from him down the corridor. He was physically exhausted: the lurching travel, the talking, the sex, but he was alert and awake, unready for sleep. He went across to the window and cranked up the blind to let in more of the artificial light from outside. He pulled at the window catch and to his surprise, after being eased against the paint that had sealed it, the handle suddenly moved in his hand and the window could be opened. A delicious, icy draught curled in through the narrow aperture. Outside, a wind had sprung up, blustering coldly between the low buildings. It blew through the canopy of the trees, making the sound of leaves that Tarent had thought he might never hear again in his lifetime. He unexpectedly remembered moments of his childhood, of playing in woods where bluebells grew and where his mother waited, of another teen romance which had involved lengthy and earnest walks in the countryside, of a long holiday in the forests of northern Germany, all conducted to the background hiss and rustle of green broad leaves and a giving wind. He pressed his face to the cold glass, staring out beyond the floodlights at the high foliage of the trees, unlit from below but moving darkly against the sky. He felt the welcome chill of the draught on his neck and shoulders, thinking of cold days, dark nights, life's past prospects. He tried to remember other things as they once had been, not so long ago and within his lifetime, but now that Flo had left him alone in his room all he could think of were the hot and deadly days in Anatolia, the despairing, endless heat, the treeless hills and the arid land, the noise of children crying, the intermittent boom of land-mines and the racket of arrogant gunfire, the broken, mutilated limbs, the sounds and smells of human death.

PART 2

La rue des bêtes

1

The Visionary

Le Havre was some way ahead but the ship cut its engines and slowed to a halt, heaving in the dark swell. I had left the noisy below-decks area after a difficult hour in the main saloon, surrounded by many seasick men, and trying to breathe the stuffy, smoke-thick air. I had just discovered that my rank, Lieutenant-Commander (Acting), came with privileges, one of which was that I could take refuge outside on this windy boat deck. It was late at night in a chill November and a stiff wind was blowing from the south-west, but I stood in the dark just outside the door, gratefully breathing the clean, cold air. Few of us on that ship were natural sailors, and the choppy sea had come as a disagreeable surprise. The *mal de mer* had not as such affected me, but the sights and sounds in the saloon were increasingly difficult to live with.

I moved away from the door, feeling my way in the dark, holding on to a handrail. The only light on the deck was from a quarter moon, and that intermittently because thick clouds were racing along with the wind. I supposed that once there might have been seats or deck-chairs here for passengers, but all of them had been removed. The deck now was stacked with military equipment, which I had glimpsed by daylight in Folkestone, when we boarded: trucks, carts, large crates, unidentified pieces secured beneath tarpaulins. Even in the daytime it had been impossible to work out what most of the matériel might be. I fervently hoped that it was not ammunition.

A fellow naval officer had warned me against leaving the saloons, but I was one of the few passengers who had the choice. I was a civilian, or a civilian officer, but the newly tailored uniform neither fit me properly nor suited me. I felt I was an impostor, that the men around me, especially the crew of this ship, would not be taken in by it.

I worked my way forward to the prow of the ship, hoping that I might be able from there to glimpse the harbour, or at least something of the land. I was eager to leave the boat as soon as possible and start the next leg of the journey. The companionway I was groping my way along was stacked with packages and crates, and I barked my shins a couple of times. The quartermaster had issued me a greatcoat which I was now wearing, grateful for its deadweight feeling of comfort.

There was nothing of the land of France to be seen forward of the ship so I made my way carefully down towards the stern, hoping for a final, dark glimpse of England. I had no idea when I might return, if ever. Again I clouted my shins. I encountered a set of steep metal steps, but I did not like the idea of clambering down them in the dark, not knowing what was beneath me. I paused at the top, thinking I might be able to see something of England from there. The breeze was blowing stiffly against the unprotected deck in that part of the ship, loaded with spots of rain or spray from the bitter-cold fetch of the English Channel. Never before had I left the shores of my native country, so thoughts of the likely dangers ahead were on my mind.

I walked back slowly towards the bow of the ship, because I had noticed a place to stand where I would be at least partly out of the wind.

The black-out on the ship was total, but my eyes were growing accustomed to seeing in the dim moonlight. When I found my way back someone else was standing where I had been, huddled like me in a large outer coat, appearing from his hunched stance to be just as cold and miserable as I was. He must have heard me coming, because as I walked up to him he extended a friendly hand to take mine.

We shook hands in the dark, muttering conventional greetings. The words were swept away by the wind. I felt rather than heard our leather gloves squeaking against each other.

'Have you any idea what's going on?' I said loudly. 'Do you know why the ship has stopped?'

He leaned towards me, lifting his face towards mine, raising his voice.

'I heard some of the crew talking about another ship going down,' he said. 'It was outside the harbour at Dieppe. The captain told me it was thought to be a hospital ship. He said he and the other officers of the watch saw a flash in the east and heard an explosion.' He paused, clearly appalled, as I was, at the consequences of that possibility. 'The captain said he had been intending to divert to Dieppe, but had changed his mind.'

'Was it a submarine? A U-boat?'

'What else might it have been? A mine, possibly, but the approaches to the French Channel ports were swept recently. There are other ships in the area, so it might have been one of those that was sunk.'

'A hospital ship! Good heavens.' I was shocked by the news, the stark reminder yet again that we were involved in a desperate war. 'I can't imagine it. What a disaster that would be, if it were true.'

'I know exactly how you feel.'

'Is this your first time out of England since the war began?' I said.

'No, it's my second. I was in France a few weeks ago, just briefly. What about you?'

'My first time,' I said.

I fell silent for a moment, because when I accepted this commission I had been expressly warned not to discuss anything about it with anyone. The work in which I was going to be engaged was deemed to be of the highest secrecy, although until I reached my destination in France even I was not to know any advance details. For the last two weeks, as I prepared to leave home and tried to understand how I could conceivably make a worthwhile contribution to the war effort, I had developed an inner guard against talking. I was in my middle fifties, far too old to be of any use to the army or navy, or so I had thought, but my name had been put forward. The call of loyalty to my country in times of war made me feel I should have to respond.

I sensed from his general bearing that my companion was the

same sort of age as myself, and therefore not likely to be an officer on active duty. We stood together in awkward silence for a few more minutes, when suddenly we heard the ship's telegraph and almost at once there was a burst of sparks and smoke from the stack. The great engine began to throb once more and a familiar vibration ran through the superstructure. From the saloons below there came the loud sound of ironic cheering as the troops realized the ship was getting under way again. They, like me, probably felt an irrational sense of greater safety, as if movement alone would protect us. While the ship was immobile I could never quite throw off the fear that a pack of German U-boats must be speeding towards us, lining up their torpedo tubes. Our ship was so small, over-loaded, thin-hulled, seeming to me vulnerable to almost anything while it floated on this troubled sea.

My companion evidently felt the same as me because with the returning sound of the engine he said, 'That's much better. We'll be disembarking soon. Even if we have to detour through Calais it won't be a long journey. Let's stand out of the wind for a while. Where are you heading, if I might ask?'

'I'm not able to say. I'm travelling under orders.'

'Let me think. Are you a co-opted civvy?'

'Yes,' I said. 'I've been authorized to describe myself as a tactical consultant.'

'Splendid! That's exactly what I am too. Our missions to France are apparently alike, although no doubt not in detail. We have to keep our traps shut. The greater good they call it. German spies everywhere. But I suppose there would be no harm in exchanging names.'

'Well—'

Now that I was up close to him and my eyes had adjusted to the night-time gloom I was able to make him out more clearly. He was shorter than me, stockily built, and whenever he spoke he bobbed around in an uncommon but attractive way. We were strangers making acquaintance in a tense situation, but I could detect he had a sense of fun, that he was not likely to take me or our situation all that seriously. Even though I took seriously the warnings about remaining tight-lipped, I could hardly imagine a more unlikely German spy.

Part of my professional stage act includes a presentation of mind-reading, which has required me to develop a fine ear for the different accents of English. This chap was well spoken but somewhere in his vowels, his intonation, was a trace of London Cockney, modified by class awareness and the influence of college education. I imagined him living in a well-appointed London suburb or in a prosperous market town somewhere in the south-east of the country. An interesting social mixture. From such fragments of intuition, and in my case years of practice of studying the ways of strangers, we form our early impressions. At that moment, with the lights of the port at Le Havre rising towards us in the distance, I was cold, travel-weary and extremely hungry. It was the sort of physical condition in which I have often found my mental senses to be best attuned. I was eager for intelligent talk to while away the rest of the journey. I wished to like him because I wanted his company.

After a moment's reflection, following his suggestion that we introduce ourselves, I said, 'I suppose you could call me Tom.'

'Tom! I'm glad to meet you.'

We shook hands again. 'And you are?' I said.

'Let me see. You may if you wish call me ... Bert.'

Our handshake now was firmer than before, more open to friendship. Tom and Bert, Bert and Tom. Two middle-aged Englishmen on a boat heading to war.

We remained standing together in that half-sheltered spot near the bow. About ten minutes later the ship navigated slowly between two huge walls to enter the harbour space. We barely spoke, each of us eager to see what we could of the place. The telegraph bells kept clanging and the engine changed note several times. Someone on the shore shouted up to the bridge and our ship let off a couple of siren blasts. Ropes were thrown and secured, the engine idled back and there was a series of mild, slow bumps as the hull settled against the wharf.

We could also detect noises and movement coming from the decks below.

'I must collect my luggage,' Bert said in a moment. 'I imagine there will be a fearful scrap to board the train. I assume you too are travelling on by train?'

'I have a warrant to travel first class,' I said.

'As have I,' said Bert. 'I don't suppose a first-class ticket will make much difference on a troop train, but it might entitle us to seats.'

We made a quick and informal agreement to reunite, if we could, in the first-class carriage of whichever train we were told to board. Just in case we were not to meet again we said our farewells, wished each other a good journey, and then plunged down in search of our luggage, into the hot, odorous and still smoke-filled lower decks.

2

Some time later I was off the ship, had crossed the wide apron and after a certain amount of shoving and squeezing I was sitting on a train. I was beginning to lose track of the time – I felt as if I was enduring a night of never-ending delays, fatigue, noise, with my hands, face and feet freezing to death.

It must have been coming up to midnight. I had been travelling, if that is the word to describe what I had been doing, since just after an early breakfast.

The easiest part by far had been getting from my home in Bayswater to Charing Cross Station, as I had called a cab which carried me and my luggage speedily and in some comfort. Thereafter everything degenerated and the rest of the day had been a particular kind of hell. My first-class warrant duly allowed me into the first-class carriage, but it was a mere technicality. I shared my compartment with what felt like two dozen ridiculously young soldiers, pink of face and shiny of expression, most of them with deep regional accents, all buckled up in khaki and webbing, weighed down with huge packs and strapped-on equipment. They were in good spirits, though, invariably addressed me as Sir, and all in all were a good crowd to be with. We were nonetheless crammed uncomfortably together.

Our slow journey to the port at Folkestone was torture: the train rarely travelled above walking speed and stopped, or so it seemed, at every signal between London and the Kent coast. When we finally reached the harbour station there was a mad scramble first to find a toilet, then to get in line for a mug of tea and some bread and butter. We embarked on the ship, but far from taking a relieved step into comparative comfort I discovered the ship was already crowded with soldiery who had arrived before us. Our own arrival vastly increased the confusion. I stuck it for a long time, knowing that these young men needed to be fed and watered as much as I did, and to stay in the ruck was probably my only chance of finding something to eat.

Once the ship was under way, instead of sailing across towards Boulogne it headed for the more distant Le Havre. It was when the choppy waves brought on the many cases of *mal de mer* and I escaped to the open boat deck that I encountered my new friend Bert.

I could not find Bert when I joined the train at Le Havre – perhaps I was too eager to gain myself a seat. However, I did manage to save a place beside me in case he should come along. The carriage filled up quickly, so I could not keep the seat next to me indefinitely. Soon a young private from the Lancashire Fusiliers thrust his weight down beside me. He offered me a cigarette and a swig from his bottle. His name was Frank Butler, he was nineteen years old and he was from Rochdale. It was his first time away from home. He talked enthusiastically about walking in the Pennine Hills, calling me Sir three times in every sentence. I started to doze in spite of Pvt. Butler's constant chatter. Time began to pass more easefully than before.

Then my arm was shaken.

'Lieutenant-Commander Trent, sir?'

I opened my eyes and saw a tall army lance-corporal standing over me, leaning down at an angle through the crush of bodies.

'Are you Commander Trent, sir? The scientist?'

'I'm Mr Trent, that's right. But—'

'I've been hunting all along the train for you, sir. I'm ordered to look after you as my responsibility, and you're in the wrong seat, sir, if I may say so. If I don't get you where you ought to be I'm in big trouble and no mistake.'

His manner was respectful and his tone was polite. I did not want to get him into trouble, so with a great deal of difficulty and the cheerful help of some of the soldiers I removed my two large cases from the overhead rack. The train still had not moved from the harbour station. The lance-corporal and I forced the compartment door open and we half jumped, half fell to the platform.

'They was holding the train up until I found you, sir,' he shouted back over his shoulder at me.

He took the larger of my two cases and we walked quickly along the side of the train. The troops appeared to have filled every carriage to the point of bursting open the doors and windows.

'Just along here, sir. Much more comfortable than what you was putting up with back there. And the other gentleman's already waiting for you.'

We came to the carriage at the back of the train, a box car with only two or three small windows. The lance-corporal led me up some narrow wooden steps, urging me to hurry. I was still trying to push my case up in front of me when I felt the train lurch and we began moving.

The carriage was the guard's van: a large space with a caged storage area, and a multitude of flags and lanterns for use by *le chef de train*. It was warm in there, lit by lanterns. Sitting alone on a wooden chair inside the caged area was my friend Bert. He was upright but relaxed. He had folded both his hands over a walking cane and his chin was resting on those. A second chair had been placed next to his.

The lance-corporal politely saw me into the cage, put down my bags and made sure I would be comfortable. The train was already gathering a little speed, and knowing that there was no corridor I was growing worried for the able young man. Unconcerned, he showed me a cabinet where there was a flagon of fresh water and some glasses, two long loaves of French bread wrapped in white tissue paper, some cheese and a bottle of red wine. 'I think the bread might be a little dry now, sir, but probably tasty enough.' Indeed, it all looked extremely appetizing.

Not a moment too soon the lance-corporal bade me goodnight, and said he would look out for me and the captain when the train reached Béthune. As he began to clamber down the steps I could see the platform moving by. Then, as if his departure were a signal, the train stopped suddenly with a great squealing of brakes.

While this was going on Bert had roused. He was sitting fully upright, regarding me with his eyes blinking. We greeted each other.

'So pleased you made it here,' Bert said. 'I was beginning to think you had gone on another train.'

I told him what had happened, then, because my stomach was rumbling, I said, 'Would you care for some bread and water?'

'Since we have been put inside a cage, it's an appropriate choice of food.' He crinkled his blue eyes in an amused way and we both went across to the cabinet. 'But perhaps instead of water, a little wine?'

'Yes indeed!'

We broke the bread, took a chunk of cheese each and filled two glasses from the wine bottle. We resumed our seats.

'Did I hear the lance-corporal say you are a captain?'

'Most certainly. I wouldn't abandon my home and family, and suffer a French train, for anything less. You too? I see you are a Navy man.'

He was glancing at my uniform.

'Not a captain. A lieutenant-commander.'

'Aren't you going a rather long way inland to join your ship?'

'It's a land-based installation, I believe.' Again I felt the weight of necessary silence on me, so I prevaricated. 'It was all a little unclear. You are in the army, I see?'

'That's right.' He crunched on the bread, spilling large brown flakes of the crust on the carriage floor. 'I insisted on being a general, thinking I could be negotiated down to colonel, but they would not go above captain. It's more than a little ridiculous, in my view, but then the whole blessed war is ridiculous. I tried to tell them that two years ago, when it all got going.'

'I don't suppose the young men we're travelling with think it's ridiculous.'

'That's right. They're just boys – the eternal tragedy of war and those who become its warriors. I've two boys of my own. Thankfully, they're still at school, so with any luck they'll be spared the appalling mess in France and Belgium. Have you any idea what the young men on this train are going to have to go through? Or how many of them will not be going home again?'

'It's going to get worse.'

'I agree. Things are warming up in worrying ways, but I think this is where you and I come into the picture. They want ideas, fresh ideas.'

He said nothing more to enlarge on that. For a while we sat silently together, enjoying the delicious cheese and sipping the wine. Fatigue was rising in me, though. I looked around the compartment but there was nothing that might be used as a mattress or a bunk. Just our two wooden chairs, side by side.

Bert had obviously cottoned on to what I was thinking.

'Seems to me,' he said, 'that this train isn't likely to move off for a while.' The train still had not departed. 'I was starting to think, just before you arrived, that I might open up my luggage, see if I can find some clothes I could spread out on the floor, up against the wall over there. I'm feeling wiped out. Need to put my head down.'

'Have you travelled far today?'

'Only from Essex. Not a bad trip until the train to Folkestone. How about you?'

'Near the centre of London,' I said. 'Bayswater Road. Towards Notting Hill.'

'I know the area a little. I lived for a while not far away. In Mornington Place, near Camden Town.'

'Ah yes.'

'I still have a small flat in London, but I spend most of my time out in the country.'

Bert's suggestion of trying to bed down was a good one, so we drained our glasses, recorked the bottle and then began searching through our luggage. I was already thinking of my cloak, which was in the case with the other apparatus. It was just about the last thing I had packed: however hard I tried I could not think of a single practical use for it where I was going, but it was so much a part of my normal work that it seemed inconceivable to leave it at home. As chance would have it, it now became ideal for my immediate needs.

The cloak had been made to exacting specifications and at the time had cost me a great deal of money. It is made of purple satin on the outside, warm black corduroy on the inside, and because of the number of hidden layers and pockets stitched into it there is a thick lining.

I tugged it out of the case, spread it out and folded it in four, making a long makeshift mattress several layers deep. Bert watched with interest but said nothing. He spread a couple of coats and some woollen pullovers on the floor for himself. I was dizzy with fatigue. The air was warm in the carriage and the distant sound of the troops in the next car was almost soothing. I crawled on to my satin robe, tugged my greatcoat across me and was asleep within a few seconds.

3

The train was moving when I awoke, but it must have been travelling slowly because there was hardly any noise from the wheels and the only rocking motion was gentle. Sunlight poured in from a small window in the opposite wall. My companion Bert had moved his chair across to it and was staring out.

A railway official had joined us – *le chef de train*. He wore a dark jacket and cap and was sitting on a stool in a corner at the back of the compartment. He took no notice of either of us and was also staring out of the train through a small window beside him. I was impressed by his full but drooping moustache. As he noticed me rousing he acknowledged me with a raised hand.

'*Bonjour!*' I said.

'*Bonjour, monsieur!*'

That exchange more or less exhausted my knowledge of the French language so without wishing to seem unfriendly I nodded to him in a companionable way, stood up, straightened my clothes and went across to where Bert was sitting. He greeted me with his customary informal friendliness, told me the lance-corporal had been in earlier and that there was a promise of food to come. He also pointed out a cubicle in the corner of the van where, he said, the usual offices would be found.

The physical relief that immediately followed was only marginally spoiled by the primitive arrangements: for a toilet there was a circular hole in the floor above the track sleepers, which I could see moving slowly beneath the train, the low morning sunlight angling across them. There was however a cold-water tap over a crude basin, so I was glad to wash my face and hands, even without a towel.

As I returned to our cage, shaking the drops from my hands, the lance-corporal appeared at a narrow door that connected with the next carriage, presumably across the open couplings.

'Morning, sirs!' he said politely. 'Captain Wells, Lieutenant Trent, sir!' He saluted. 'I thought you'd like some good old British bully to help you through the day. No expense spared by His Majesty.' He was carrying a couple of opened cans of the beef, wrapped in a cloth, and laid them out for us. 'We'll be making a halt later, to give the lads a break. So there will be a mug of tea for you with everyone, and some hot food. A tot of rum too, no doubt, seeing as you're a naval gentleman, sir.'

I was glad to be offered something other than bread, but we ate the rest of that too, Bert and I, sitting side by side in our cage.

Afterwards, wiping his mouth, Bert said to me, 'Lieutenant-Commander Trent, is it?' I confirmed that. 'Tom Trent? Thomas Trent? Sounds familiar. Should I know that name?'

'You might,' I said, still feeling the need to be guarded. 'I'm best known as Tommy Trent.'

'It rings a bell,' he said.

'Look, I don't think we should speak too freely—'

'You're worried about our friend over there.' Bert turned around and acknowledged *le chef* with a quick wave of the hand. 'I tried to have a chat with him before you woke up. I found he speaks no more English than you speak French. Somewhat less, I suspect.'

'Hardly possible,' I said.

'I doubt it. Now then, Lieutenant-Commander Tommy Trent, I'm not the sort of chap who likes being secretive. Nor inquisitive for that matter. If I've got the measure of you right you feel much the same. But I think we have a bit of finding out to do about each other.'

'All right.'

'All right, indeed. Let me start by asking you something. Have you visited the British lines before? Out at the front line, I mean, which is where I assume we are both headed?'

'No,' I said. 'Have you?'

'Yes, I told you I had been to France, but in fact I went up to the lines near Ypres, which is in Belgium. I suppose you know what the conditions are like at the front?'

'Well, yes. The newspapers don't tell the whole story, but I think I understand the trenches have become a hell.'

'Hell is an understatement. The trenches are unspeakable, and unspeakably dangerous. So here is my next question, Lieutenant Trent. If you are going to the Western Front as a naval officer, and you have no illusions about what things are like, what the devil do you need with a satin cloak?'

He was in earnest, but he had a merry look in his pale blue eyes.

'I was intending to explain—'

'And, while I am on the subject, why is it a satin cloak with silver and gold stars sewn into it?'

The garment in question was still where I had left it, pressed up in something of a heap against the carriage wall. When I put it down I had deliberately folded it so that the satin side with the stars was not uppermost, but I must have moved around while I slept, exposing the gaudier side of the garment.

I was embarrassed by Bert's question. Now that I was here, really here, in a theatre of war, or at least in its imminence, I saw everything in a new light. At home I had assumed I was being summoned to the front lines to entertain the troops. Entertainment is my job, my career, my vocation. I knew of music hall artistes, singers, dancers and comedians, who had already travelled out to perform for the soldiers at the Front. If I was to perform my act I would need my usual apparatus and props, and that included my cloak.

After searching around for adequate words I finally said, 'You told me you thought my name was familiar.'

'I can't say more than that.'

'Then the situation is this. Tommy Trent is my real name, but I also used it for a long time as a stage name. I am a music hall artiste, an entertainer. Does that help?' He shook his head. 'These days I am billed as *The Lord of Mystery*, but until two years ago I performed as *Tommy Trent, Mysterioso*.'

'You are a magician?'

'I prefer to be known as a conjuror. Or as an illusionist. But yes.'

'If I may say so it explains everything, and nothing at all.'

'Then we are in accord,' I said. 'I know almost nothing about why I am here, dressed up in the uniform of a naval officer, heading for the Western Front.'

I briefly related my story, such as it was. About five weeks earlier I had been performing at the Lyric Theatre in Hammersmith, in west London. After the Saturday night show I was relaxing in my dressing room when one of the theatre staff brought a visitor to see me.

His name was Flight Lieutenant Simeon Bartlett, a serving officer of the Royal Navy. He complimented me on my performance, saying he was much impressed by one particular illusion. This was the trick with which I normally brought my act to a finale. In it I made a pretty young woman (it was my niece Clarice, who regularly worked with me) disappear into thin air.

Backstage visitors usually arrive with compliments, but their real purpose, I often find, is to try to elicit my secrets from me. All magicians are bound by a professional code of honour not to give anything away. In fact, the trick that had so impressed the young lieutenant looked complicated on the stage, because of the apparatus that was needed, but its secret was simple. Sometimes the most impressive illusions are based on tricks or procedures that are so elementary that the audience would not believe what had in reality taken place.

But that is the case. So it had been that evening at the Lyric Theatre. My guard was up, and in spite of the young officer's pleasant demeanour, and his increasingly determined efforts to have the method explained to him, I stood my ground.

Finally, Lieutenant Bartlett said to me, 'Do I have your assurance that you are using a practical or scientific method, and that you are not going in for that sorcery business?' Of course, I had no hesitation in confirming that was so. 'Then I think there is small doubt you shall be hearing from us soon.'

What he meant, as it turned out, was that the following week I received an official letter from the Admiralty offering me a short-term commission, in order, in their words, 'to aid the war effort.'

At a subsequent interview with senior naval officers I was again questioned closely about my secret method, but to honour the magicians' code all I could say was to repeat my assurance that it was, in their word, scientific.

The more they interrogated me, the less I felt confident in the science involved in some strategically positioned lights and a pane of glass.

'So you are going to a shore-based naval unit,' Bert said thought-fully. 'That can mean only one of two things. Balloons or aero-planes. Both are being operated by the Royal Naval Air Service. I still don't understand why you need your cloak, though.'

I said, 'I brought it with me because it is so much a part of my act that I would feel naked without it. But I do see what you mean about the inappropriateness. As for balloons, or whatever, I imag-ine I'll discover what's going on as soon as I am there. What about you?'

'Me? I have nothing to do with balloons.'

'I meant the finding out. I should be interested to know more about you.'

'Oh, much the same,' he said, and I realized it was his turn to feel discomfited, although I could not see why.

'Are you a magician too?'

'No, not at all. Well, maybe some people would like me to be, but I'm much more humble.' He was bracing himself with his cane, because the train was at last moving more quickly and the van was rocking from side to side. 'I think I might be described as a meddler, which is what some of my accusers call me. That about sums me up. I can't seem to stop myself from pointing things out to people who are going about something the wrong way. The trouble is that no one listens! And it's even more irritating when they carry on, then they get everything wrong just as I warned them, and afterwards they turn round and blame *me* for not warning them more forcefully. So the next time I change my tack, try other arguments, but in the end the same thing happens. I try to keep calm, I try always to appeal to their reason. But I go on, because what they call meddling is what I call the declaration of ideas. I am a believer in the human mind and ideas are my profession. I suppose that belief is why I have ended up on this train with you, Lieutenant Tommy Trent, Lord of Magic, Mystery, whatever you said you called yourself. It's my reward for being a busybody and a meddler, and no doubt deserved.'

'Deserved reward?' I said. 'You make it sound like a punishment.'

'I speak ironically, of course. You know, Tom, back in the days when this blessed war broke out, I wrote a series of little articles for a newspaper. I am known for having Opinions, and I had several of those about this war. Afterwards those articles came out in a book. When I get steamed up about something, writing about it is my only way of releasing the energy. I saw this war coming, saw it years ago.

'Now, I have a horror of war, you understand, but I'm not completely opposed to this one, either. I have nothing against the German people, but they have allowed twin evils to arise. They are ruled by Prussian imperialism, and their economy is dominated by Krupp, the maker of armaments. Krupp and the Kaiser stand side by side. It has become an inhuman system. We must raise a sword against it, a sword raised for peace. I don't want to destroy Germany, just do enough to change the so-called minds who are running the place at the moment. When the war is won what we must aim to do is re-draw the map of Europe, form some kind of league of all nations, one where ordinary people have a say.'

I was staring at him in excitement and recognition.

'That was *The War That Will End War*,' I said.

Bert grunted his agreement.

'I read that!' I went on. 'I have a copy of the book at home. It made cracking good sense to me.'

'I'm no longer so sure about it, now I've seen some of what's really going on—'

'But you couldn't have written that book. It was by H. G. Wells!'

Captain Wells nodded again. I stood up in astonishment, then sat down again suddenly, because the carriage was rocking. I gripped the edge of my seat.

'Then you are ...?' I said.

'Please – go on calling me Bert,' said the great man. 'Safer that way all round, I think. Do you suppose we'll be stopping soon? I could make short work of a nice cup of tea.'

4

All day the train slowly crossed northern France. We glimpsed the farmland, flat scenery, peasants working by hand, distant church spires. The only trees we saw were tall poplars. Bert and I had much to talk about, but we took it in turns to rise to the window to see what was out there. It was never much.

The train stopped twice during the day and these halts were greeted with quiet relief by us, and by loud cheers sounding from the body of the train. Hot food was on offer both times and Bert and I mucked in with the troops, rather enjoying the good-natured scrum to try to get the first cup of tea, the biggest bowl of soup, the meatiest serving. In spite of the unrelieved crowding on the train everyone managed to remain in a good mood. There was pushing and shoving to get to the latrines, or to try for a second helping, but it was always comradely in a way I found heartening.

The lance-corporal was waiting for us both times as we clambered down, endlessly civil to us and always keen to provide some little extra, should we want it. Hot water appeared miraculously at the first stop, with shaving cream, soap and clean towels. Bert and I felt spoiled by having the spacious compartment to ourselves, with all our basic needs adequately met. Knowing what the cramped conditions were like elsewhere I was reluctant to ask for anything more.

Meanwhile, I was overawed by my illustrious travelling companion and greatly enjoyed the conversation that took us through most of the journey.

Our second halt, towards the end of the afternoon, was at a small country station, anonymous, unremarkable. As we stepped down from the carriage, the lance-corporal greeting us as usual, we were both aware of a thundering rumble, dimly but continuously heard in the distance.

Bert, looking serious, said, 'Not far to go now.'

My heart sank. 'We'll be there tonight, I suppose,' I said.

'There's one small mercy. At least it is not raining now and seems not to have been for some time. The mud won't be any worse than it already was. You'll soon learn everything there is to know about mud. So will these boys, alas.'

They were already swarming across the wooden platform towards a mess tent. Steam arose around it and on the cool air we could sense the comforting smell of fried bacon. We wandered over, took our places at the end of the shorter of the two queues, and waited our turn.

The distant thunder of artillery continued, but now we were further away from the train I could hear the sound of birds. In a field next to the mess tent two farming men were speaking slowly in French.

Taking our baguettes with great greasy slices of bacon bulging out of the middle we walked back to the train and resumed our private compartment.

It was becoming increasingly difficult to think of my companion as 'Bert', now I knew his true identity. I tackled him about this as my confidence grew – he told me he had been flummoxed when we exchanged names. He said everyone in his family, and close friends, knew him as Bertie, but that didn't feel appropriate as we were so close to the front. I said I'd be happy to address him as 'HG', which was how he was known to the public. He said he would answer to that, and seemed amused.

No matter what we called each other, to be spending the day in the exclusive company of one of the great visionary thinkers of our time was a privilege beyond estimation. HG himself was a modest man, always seeming to self-deprecate, but at the same time he was sure of his opinions. Every now and again he would start ranting in an entertaining way against what he saw as the forces of dullness, or those who were in power, or those who under-rated the questing spirit of ordinary people. His periwinkle-blue eyes would glitter with dedication, or amusement, or rancour, and he waved his hands expressively, making him impossible to ignore. He was brimming with ideas and opinions and had ingenious answers or suggestions for almost any problem I suggested.

Then he would suddenly stop, apologize to me for dominating the conversation and ask me some disarming questions about myself.

He was one of the few people I have ever met with whom I was happy to discuss the principles and techniques of magic. The old habit of protecting secrets still had me in its grip, but I saw no harm in teaching him some simple methods. I showed him how to palm a playing card, or how to force one on someone, or how to make a cigarette double itself or disappear. All this evoked an almost childish delight in HG. For a few minutes we played around with some of my props, to the evident interest of *le chef de train*, who sat silently in his corner with his flags, fingering his moustache and watching us with grave eyes.

But magic was my bread and butter and was no novelty to me. I found HG's conversation more engaging and challenging.

He asked me, for instance, if I knew what 'telpherage' was. I said no, and asked for more details. Instead of telling me he asked me another question: had I ever worked in a department store? No, I said again.

This immediately provoked an apparently irrelevant and emotional reminiscence of his life as a young man, when his mother had indented him to a drapery store in Southsea. A series of horrifying or amusing anecdotes followed: the cruelly long hours, the dreadful food, tedium beyond endurance, the company of dullards. I was soon reminded of a novel of his I had read a few years earlier: *Kipps*.

'That's the one!' he cried, his voice chirping with excitement. 'All of it was true!'

More stories about crooked cashiers, inept apprentices and eccentric customers flowed out. Most of them were amusing to hear. The French farmland passed by at a snail's pace, unseen by us, as the afternoon began to fail, the evening closed in and we lurched towards the war. *Le chef* lighted some lamps in the van.

Eventually, HG returned to the subject of telpherage.

'It's a system they use in some of the big shops,' he said. 'When you come to pay for your roll of cotton or your lengths of yarn, the assistant puts your money and his chitty in a little metal container, hooks it up to an overhead ropeway, pulls a handle, and the thing rushes across the ceiling of the shop to the cashier's desk. A few moments later it comes whizzing back with your change and a receipt, and that's the end of the business.'

I said that of course I had seen this happen dozens of times.

'The little metal container is correctly called a telpher,' HG said. 'And the ropeway is called telpherage.'

I waited for more but he looked away vacantly, perhaps remembering some incident from his days in a Southsea drapery establishment. Eventually I prompted him to continue.

'Well, it's all about mud, you see.' He was concentrating again, and I realized that his constant harping on about mud meant it must be a favourite subject. 'You've no idea how much mud there is in those front-line trenches until you experience it yourself. And it's everywhere else, come to that. Worst in the trenches, but just everywhere! Some of it is above your knees, filthy, runny muck, stinking and sloshing everywhere you go. Until I visited the Ypres Salient I had no conception of how bad it was. And the worst of it is, mud can be a killer. Our troops have to carry most of their own ammunition as well as their packs, the rifle, a lot of other stuff. They wear this device called a Christmas Tree. That's a belt which is supposed to allow them to carry everything, but it's always full up, can't get any more on it, so they carry other equipment in their arms. It was the ammunition that bothered me. It's fiendishly heavy. It means that most of the soldiers who report for active duty are already half worn out before they start. Some of them have to walk more than a mile, carrying pounds and pounds of extra weight, and for most of the way they have to wade through mud. If you fall face-down in the mud while hauling that lot, the chances are you won't be able to struggle up in time. While I was in Ypres I was told that on average three British soldiers a week were dying in that sort of accident. Drowning in mud! It's disgusting. We can't have that.'

HG had saved part of his bacon baguette from earlier, but now he broke off the end and chewed on it thoughtfully.

'So, what happened next was when I was back in London. I was having dinner with Winston Churchill. He asked me—'

'Did you say Churchill? The politician? First Lord of the Admiralty?'

'Now you're in the Navy he's your commanding officer. That's right – the First Lord. He's not actually a close friend of mine. Far from it, I would say. I don't want to give the wrong impression. He's a politician and it behoves one to sup with a long spoon when you dine with politicians. Out for themselves, the whole lot of them. But they can be useful to someone like me, especially a keenly ambitious man like Mr Churchill. He's still a Young Turk who doesn't mind bending a few rules from time to time. He doesn't think much of me – he was in fact one of the first people to call me a meddler. He put me in one of his newspaper articles, you know, back when I published a book about—'

'You were telling me about the telpherage,' I said.

'Quite so. Winston Churchill happens to be the cousin of a young woman sculptor, a good and intimate friend of mine. You wouldn't expect me to name her, I know. Well, I was having supper with her one evening and Mr Churchill turned up unexpectedly and joined us at the table. The subject came up of the troops having to carry ammunition to the front. Churchill knew all about that and shared some of my concerns. He told me he had spent some time in the trenches himself and knew at first hand the problem of the mud.

'Sitting there with him I had an inspiration. I suddenly thought of telpherage – if you could put in a big telpherage system, with ropes strong enough to carry boxes of ammunition, perhaps even two or three soldiers as well, power it with the engine of a truck, everything would be a lot quicker, save a lot of blood and sweat and floundering in the mud, and the whole thing would put our lads in less danger. I was awake all night thinking about how to make it work. A few days later I put in my plans to the Admiralty, Churchill took a personal interest, a few strings were pulled with the Chiefs of Staff, and here I am. On my way to put my experience as a draper's assistant to good use.'

He went into more details of how it would work, how it could be made portable, who would operate it, and so on, and although I listened carefully I must admit my own mind was racing on all sorts of adjacent subjects. For instance, it occurred to me that the very fact HG and I were travelling together suggested that I was on a similar mission to his. But unlike him I had not the least idea what mine would be, nor why I had been summoned.

I was dazzled by HG's company. Intelligence and commitment radiated from him, making everything seem possible. He was at this time probably the single most famous writer in the country, perhaps even in the world. I, on the other hand, although enjoying a certain amount of celebrity in a small theatrical circle, was less a man of creative inspiration and more a careful follower of procedures. That was the difference between us.

What I do on the stage is contrived to look like a series of miracles, but in reality the preparation of a magical illusion is a prosaic matter. Few people realize the amount of rehearsal conjurors have to put in, nor what goes on in the background. A trick often requires technical assistants, who will help design and build the apparatus. The movements a magician makes on stage are the result of long and patient rehearsal, while still having to look natural and spontaneous to the audience. It is an acquired practical skill, in other words. Only while in performance, in the glare of the limelight, can magic look like inspiration. Even at best it is never more than an illusion. Things are never what they seem.

I felt humbled by the great man's infectious energy. His imagination was like a torch burning brightly in that shabby old railway carriage. The war was about to be won! Germany would be defeated and Britain would be triumphant! Thousands of lives saved! Prosperity for everyone. A democracy for all men. Science would lead progress and progress would change society.

5

The train pulled into the town of Béthune just as daylight was a last gleam in the western sky. Lights were showing in the streets but not many of them and they were shaded so as not to shine too brightly. As we rattled slowly through the edge of town both HG and I pressed our eyes to the tiny windows to see what we could. At first there did not appear to be too much damage to the buildings, but as the train slowed to walking pace and we approached the station in the centre of the town it was clear that artillery shells had landed in many places.

It was being borne in on me that the life I had been leading in London was based on a false understanding of this war. News of it came in regularly, perhaps every day, but it was usually portrayed as a distant affair conducted in a foreign country, not something that might threaten the daily lives of ordinary Britons. But the foreign country was France, a short sea crossing away, and battles lost in France would almost certainly lead to invasion and occupation of our country by a hostile foreign power.

Everyone remarked on the increasing absence of our young menfolk, everyone had a son or a brother or a lover in the army, or at least knew of a close friend who did, yet the connection of that with an imminent threat never seemed to be made. Shortages in the shops were annoying but they did not indicate a crisis. There were rumours that Zeppelins, gas-borne monsters of the skies, were about to let go a thousand bombs on our homes, but they had not appeared. Music hall comedians made fun of them, while the threat remained just a threat.

That imprecise feeling of worry was now behind me, and reality was around me. I could see in the dark countryside beyond the edge of town that the sky was lit up by a constant, endless display of flashes. The unarguable evidence of the wrecked buildings, seen in every part of Béthune, and the many large piles of uncleared rubble, underlined how immediate and close this war really was.

When the train finally came to a halt, and the crowds of soldiers spilled out tiredly on to the platform, HG and I hesitated before joining them. We had re-packed our luggage, but half-expected the lance-corporal to turn up and tell us what was to happen next.

The troops were being lined up on the platform in squads, helmets on their heads, packs on their backs, rifles held smartly against their shoulders. A shouted order echoed around the vaulted roof of the station and the first squad of young men marched away with impressive discipline. We had a good idea how tired they must have been after so long on the crowded train, but they gave no sign of it.

After the third troop marched away the platform was clear. *Le chef de train* had left us as soon as the train halted, and HG and I were alone. There was no sign of the lance-corporal.

'This is where we must go our separate ways, I believe,' HG said to me. 'I am being met here, or so I was told. How about you?'

'I suppose someone will be here to meet me too,' I replied, but uncertainly. I had no information about that.

'Good! All will be arranged, I'm sure. Let us take leave of each other. We have been travelling a long time and I am fair done for.'

We shook hands in a firm and friendly way, then HG went down the outer steps to the platform. My bags were still on the floor behind me, so I collected them and went to follow him. From the top of the steps I saw the back of my distinguished friend as he walked slowly towards the distant exit. I was suddenly struck by the idea that he was someone I might never see again. Extreme dangers lay ahead.

On an impulse, I called after him.

'Mr Wells!'

He heard me somehow, glanced back, then returned at a slow step. I clambered down with my bulky luggage.

I said, 'I'm sorry to detain you again, Mr Wells, I mean ... HG. I merely wanted to say what a thrill and a pleasure it has been to meet you, and to have enjoyed your company today.'

He shrugged away the compliment, but he was smiling in a merry way.

'It has been a pleasure for me too, I assure you. I shall remember everything you told me about your secret methods. I do not often meet a Lord who can swallow a lighted cigarette.'

6

Again, HG walked on ahead of me. I was having trouble with my luggage, hoping in vain to see a porter. A few minutes later, when I had struggled out of the exit from the station, HG had gone. I was standing beside a broad road. The rhythmic sound of the soldiers' marching was already fading into the distance. I imagined some swift and efficient welcoming patrol had been waiting for HG, and swept him away.

Over the dark silhouettes of the buildings the bright flashes of the artillery gave a sense of foreboding. Some of these buildings had been damaged – I saw a broken sky-line, parts of roofs and walls, wooden joists sticking up. A deep growl, like thunder, rolled across the streets.

I was already bracing myself for a spell in the trenches. Wells's vivid descriptions had horrified me, but it was too late to do anything about it. I had volunteered for this.

Alone, I wondered what I should do next. In my pocket I had the only written orders I had been sent, so I took out the sheet of paper and unfolded it in the dim light spilling out from the station.

Beneath the printed letterhead used by the Admiralty, someone had written, '17 Sqn, La rue des bêtes, Béthune.'

Road of the beasts? I had no idea how to begin a search for such a street. I spoke no French, had no map of the town, and in any case the whole place was quiet. Few lights showed in the buildings I could see. I was starting to feel a little frightened by my situation.

'Lieutenant-Commander Trent, sir!'

I turned sharply. A young Royal Navy officer had appeared behind me, standing to attention, saluting.

'I apologize for not being here to meet the train, sir!'

I said, 'Thank you. Please ... um, stand at ease.' I returned his salute, feeling clumsy and self-conscious. In the dim light I saw that he was wearing a uniform similar to mine.

'Flight Lieutenant Simeon Bartlett, sir.'

'How do you do?'

'We have met before. I hope you remember me? We met in

89

London, when you allowed me backstage. Your performance in Hammersmith.'

'Yes, yes of course,' I said. 'Good to see you again.'

'I have brought the squadron van with me, so there's no problem with your luggage. Did you have a good journey from England?'

I was charmed by his easy good manners, and his casual but courteous and entirely proper way with me. Carrying the larger of my two cases he led me to a brown-painted motorized vehicle, which I had noticed standing outside the station but which I had not imagined was there to transport me.

'Have you had something to eat on the train, sir?'

'I'm not especially hungry at the moment,' I said.

'Good, because I have been directed to take you straight to our base, where there will be dinner available in the wardroom. It's not quite the Café Royal, but we do receive much better food than the poor chaps in the trenches.'

Once I was installed inside the vehicle he made a few energetic swings on the starting handle and after a moment the engine clattered into noisy life. He leapt into the driver's seat and we were off. He chatted informatively as he drove us out of the town, the engine coughing and wheezing noisily. A cold draught blew in on me through a window that was impossible to close. He made remarks about various landmarks as we passed through the town, but depressingly several of them were of the sort that said: 'That's where the market used to be.' Many buildings had been damaged by shellfire, or were simply indistinct in the darkness. We had to shout to make ourselves heard over the racket of the engine. He told me that most of the inhabitants of Béthune had fled: at first they stayed on and braved the occasional bouts of German shelling, but a few weeks ago the position of the front had moved closer to the town and now the explosions were more frequent. The town was becoming more or less impossible to live in, or at least to live normally.

I said, 'Whereabouts is *La rue des bêtes*? My orders were to report there.'

'That's where I'm taking you.'

It seemed to me we had left most of the town behind and were now passing through countryside. It was too dark to be sure of anything. The vehicle jerked and lurched constantly on the uneven road, but whenever we slowed to pass a column of men making their way on foot I knew which method I preferred for moving around.

At first I was confused by the young lieutenant's casual language, which half the time seemed to be referring to ships. As HG had pointed out we were well landlocked. I said nothing about this, not wanting to appear ignorant of Navy ways and assumed that all would become clear in the end. Instead, I raised a subject that had been puzzling me.

'If I might ask,' I said, loudly over the sound of the engine, 'you say you are a lieutenant?'

'A flight lieutenant, sir. Same rank as my colleagues who are posted to ships. I am an officer in the RNAS.'

'Then how many Royal Navy lieutenants have the authority to pluck middle-aged civilians from their peace-loving lives, and drag them across to the Western Front?'

He laughed aloud.

'None of us have that power, sir. I am no different from any of the others of my rank, but I do have an uncle who is a staff officer in Western Approaches HQ. Vice Admiral Sir Timothy Bartlett-Reardon, of whom you might have heard?' I shook my head in the dark, a response he did not see. 'The admiral and I have had many informal discussions about naval strategy, strictly unofficially of course. He is an open-minded and adventurous man, superbly equipped to manage the fighting of this war. But, like me, he some-times feels frustrated by the lack of progress against the Boche, and likes to consider new ways of prosecuting our war. He and I have talked about several ideas, and after I saw your stage act I talked to him about one of my own. He arranged your commission.'

I stared at the muddy road ahead, distractedly imagining HG wading along it.

'So I have you to thank for this.'

'I believe it will be the whole country that will be thanking you soon, sir.'

'It would help immeasurably,' I said, 'if I knew what you want of me. I thought you merely wanted me to entertain the troops.'

'Oh no. I have something more useful in mind.'

Lieutenant Bartlett explained that we were going to the airfield where he was based, operated by the RNAS. It was a good safe distance back from the lines, out of range of the enemy's artillery.

'We keep a weather eye open for it, though,' he said, his voice only just audible over the racket from the engine. 'We keep hearing rumours about some ruddy great Krupp cannon that can lay waste to Paris. If they've got one they'll probably practise on people like us first. They don't like what we get up to.'

'And what's that?' I shouted.

He jammed on the brakes, and skewed the van towards the side of the road. A spray of mud was thrown up at the front. He allowed the engine to turn over quietly.

'I don't want you to miss what I'm saying, and no one can hear us here.' He spoke in a normal voice. The night was dark around us, and still. 'Our squadron serves as aerial observers,' he went on. 'We fly low and slow above the enemy trenches. The idea is to build up a picture of what the Boche are up to, report back while we can still remember what we've seen, and describe it to the people who keep the trench maps up to date. We mostly do the observing with the naked eye, but a few of our kites have been fitted with photographic cameras. If you ask me the cameras are more trouble than they're worth. They're heavy and bulky and they take up the rear cockpit, which is where the other crew-member normally sits. The pilot has to go it alone, which means not only does he have to fly one-handed while he's operating the camera, he has no one sitting behind him to defend the plane with a machine-gun. And the results are always a bit unsatisfactory. It takes a couple of days to have the pictures produced, by which time everything will probably have changed down there. And there's too much blurring caused by the engine's vibrations, or just by the movement. We're always trying to find ways of flying more slowly.'

'Wouldn't it be safer if you went faster?'

'Of course – but then we wouldn't see anything at all.'

'I assume the Germans shoot at you.'

'Yes, and they're pretty damned good shots. Small-arms fire mostly, but bigger stuff too. We call it archie, or ack-ack. Firing from the ground. We're losing a lot of machines that way. More importantly we're losing men – pilots are valuable, and of course so are the other crew. That's the problem in a nutshell, yes. If we go too fast or too high we can't see anything, but whenever we fly at the right altitude and speed for observing they zero in on us straight away.'

'So what's the answer?'

'This is where you come in. I've seen the way you make people disappear.'

'Yes,' I said. 'But—'

'I know, professional ethics. I understand you won't tell me how. And I know you can't make things disappear, *actually* disappear. But you do know how to make them invisible. That's all we want. We need you to show us how to make our aircraft invisible.'

I said, 'But that's just an illusion. I can't really—'

At that moment another vehicle came roaring along the road towards us, its bright lights illuminating the spray of mud it was throwing up. Lieutenant Bartlett immediately made our van move again, shouting to me that unless we were going at speed our lights didn't work. This turned out to be true – we safely passed the other vehicle without a collision. I held on as we swayed along the un-even road once more.

Soon after passing the other vehicle, our van abruptly came across a huge crater in the road and Lieutenant Bartlett had to take extreme avoiding action. I was thrown from side to side in the uncomfortable cab.

'That was a new one,' he said. 'It wasn't there when I drove out to meet you. Must have been a stray shell. You should be wearing a tin helmet.'

'I haven't been issued with one.'

'Draw one from the stores. Once the German guns open up you never know where the next piece of sharp metal is coming from.'

But I noticed, without commenting, that he was still wearing just his naval cap, set back on his head at a rakish angle.

We drove on, no longer trying to make conversation over the noise from the engine. I was fairly relieved, as the talk had been veering too close to a subject that was difficult for me.

The illusion I performed on the night Lieutenant Bartlett came to the Gaiety Theatre was one I frequently used to bring my act to its conclusion. My niece Clarice, whose life appears to be in great danger, is shockingly and inexplicably made to vanish into thin air. The stage is to all intents and purposes bare. The audience sees that I am nowhere near her at the moment in which it all happens. It looks like a marvel, a miracle. But it is no more than a stage illusion, and not one that is especially complex. It requires the apparatus to be set up correctly, and there is an exact lighting cue which has to be rehearsed with the technical crew at the theatre, but it uses nothing more than standard magicians' techniques. The same methods are used every week in dozens of theatres by many other conjurors. For that reason the secret is not mine to give away.

Was it the right moment, while I was being driven through the French night to an operational fighting squadron, to tell this pleasant and intelligent young man that he had been duped? That he had not seen my lovely niece disappear, or become invisible, but that she had simply become lost to his sight?

I could not in reality make her disappear, and I certainly had no idea how I could make one of the Royal Navy's observer aircraft invisible.

My mood became increasingly introspective, a feeling I knew was familiar to other magicians. Sometimes we are credited with greater powers than we have. Usually, the misconception is something that can be explained away, or treated without seriousness, but I was getting into hot water.

After what felt like a long drive along the uneven road, more or less doubling back over the way the train had travelled, Lieutenant Bartlett suddenly slowed the van down, turned the steering wheel sharply and drove with a violent lurching motion across rough ground. Low buildings lay ahead, picked out fitfully by our light. After another turning lunge we came to an abrupt halt and the engine died.

'Here we are at last,' Bartlett said. 'Royal Naval Air Service Squadron No.17 – or as we call it, *La rue des bêtes.*'

'Why do you call it that?'

'We've taken over a tract of farmland. What's now our landing strip used to be a place where cows grazed. It was someone's joke at first. The farmer wasn't in the habit of closing gates so the cows sometimes wandered back when we were landing or taking off, but since then it's become semi-official. And we've fixed the gates.'

We went to the back of the van and pulled out my two bags. I stretched my arms and back, sucking in the calm air. After the din from the engine I relished the quietness of the night. We had travelled far enough to the west, away from the lines, for the flashes in the night to be distant, unthreatening. The display was like the last flickering glimpse of a storm as it moved away out to sea. The sound of the guns rumbled on but the horrors of war remained distant.

'You won't get to see much of the base tonight, sir,' Lieutenant Bartlett said. 'But let's find you a berth, somewhere to sleep, and then we can grab a meal. At least the wine here is good. I'll show you around the airfield tomorrow.'

The night was cold and bright with stars. I followed the young officer towards the smaller of the two buildings, only just visible in the dark.

7

I was billeted in a room alone. There was a narrow single bunk, a small cupboard beside the bed, a wooden chair squeezed in between the bed and the wall and a few hooks where I could hang my clothes. The ceiling sloped down sharply over the bed, as my room was at the end of the hut. Once I had dragged my two cases into the room I could barely move. I re-packed as well as I could, moving everything I thought I would not need immediately to the larger of the two, then, after emptying the smaller case and hanging up some of the clothes, putting out my toothbrush, and so on, I managed to squeeze the larger case out of the way under the bed. The room was unheated so I undressed quickly and crawled into bed.

My mind was racing with memories of everything I had seen

and experienced, and especially with my conversation with H. G. Wells. I was dog-tired after the day, though, and although I was cold and uncomfortable I fell asleep almost at once.

I awoke while it was still dark. After the first moments of confusion about where I was I felt nervous, in danger, frightened. Everything around me was unseen and silent, and although I quickly remembered where I was, and how I had got there, I felt terrified of the unknown.

All through my life I have suffered these night fears. I know I am not alone, that psychological experts have described the pre-dawn period as the time when the intellect and emotions are at their lowest ebb. Fears and regrets come easily and quickly, seem real and immediate and awful. They retreat somewhat when the new day dawns, becoming easier to bear, but all that changes is the context. Fears in the night are not imaginary or exaggerated, they are merely at the forefront of your mind.

There I was in rural northern France, alone in a mean room, lying on a bed with inadequate covers, in the dark, a war in progress a few miles away. I remembered what Simeon Bartlett had said about the giant Krupp cannon. Was it real? Would they really target bases like this one before turning it on Paris? I also remembered what H. G. Wells had prophetically written about the power and influence of the Krupp company. I was wide awake and completely at the mercy of my fears. I turned over twice, trying to relax, trying to slip back into that blissful sleep, but it proved impossible.

I sat up, plumped the pillow, lay down again. Many thoughts were circling, all of them painful. My conversation with H. G. Wells – I realized that he must have found me dull and politically naïve, and had only spoken to me at all because there was no one else around. I recalled the haste with which he was so keen to leave me at Béthune station. I should have talked more intently to the famous author about his books. I should have shown some interest in the subjects which were his passion. Instead, I showed this brilliant man, a confidant of people like Winston Churchill, how to shuffle a deck of cards and make a cigarette disappear. What a fool he must have thought me. Then there was the lance-corporal – I had taken his good nature for granted, but said nothing as a compliment, or thanks. And how seriously I had taken Lieutenant Bartlett's little joke about the road of beasts!

Worst of all, there was his misunderstanding about what my supposed magical powers were.

I concealed my young niece by the use of conjuring techniques, but Lieutenant Bartlett thought I could make her actually and really invisible. Would that I had that or any other power! My niece does not become invisible – to think otherwise is madness, yet at every performance, with a planned use of well-positioned lights, a strategically placed sheet of glass, a bang from a gun that fires blanks, and general hocus-pocus, I can make it seem that way.

I mislead and deceive. That is what I do.

Squatting uncomfortably in the cold and narrow bunk I remembered the wave of spurious patriotism and gallantry that swept over me that evening at the theatre in Hammersmith, when Lieutenant Bartlett found his way backstage. I suddenly saw myself as making a contribution to the struggle against Germany, using my skills to amaze and encourage the brave young men who were doing the fighting.

That was my misunderstanding, perhaps the lesser of the two. The reality of the war was becoming all too clear. My misunderstanding ended there, in that bed, while I tossed and turned, waiting for the day to start.

But then there was the larger misconception. I was going to have to do something!

Surely Lieutenant Bartlett must have understood the true nature of my work? A concealment from the audience was relatively easy to contrive in the controlled circumstances of a theatre stage, where the performer knows how to dazzle or confuse or obstruct. The sordid reality of war, with real aircraft, real guns, real shellfire, young men risking their lives every day – an impossible challenge.

I tried to be calm. The room was bare, cold, inhospitable. It had the feeling of a barrack room, of temporary occupation by others who had used it before me. What had become of them? In the return to darkness I could at least put those unwelcome thoughts aside. I saw at the small window that there was now a faint greyness in the sky as dawn approached. I made myself breathe calmly, a relaxation technique I sometimes employed before going on stage. Still my mind turned restlessly.

I remembered HG's stories about his Kipps-style experiences when he was a youth. Years afterwards, when he was no longer a disaffected sales clerk on starvation wages, he had seen the potential, writ large, of the telpherage system that was still in use in many British emporia. As an author, H. G. Wells had always inspired me – could my meeting with him now prompt me to conceive of thrilling new possibilities?

I began to wonder if there was something I might know about magic that could provide Lieutenant Bartlett with the camouflage he wanted. I forced myself to think practically about the techniques I took for granted.

Many times in my stage career I have had to think up some new trick for my act. I sit at home, sometimes in a semi-darkened room, planning how to pull it off, thinking about how I want it to appear when on stage, and working out what material or apparatus I might need. Sometimes I would chat obliquely to other magicians – never was anything directly said, because in my profession secrecy is everything, as is respect for the secrets of others. But it always helped to talk over the general principles, without giving away too much about what I was planning. The principles of magic are much simpler than most people think – concealment, production, and so on. They apply to every illusion ever performed. What often looks like a new trick to the audience is a variation on one of these principles: a new way of performing a familiar card trick, a surprise production of a dove or a rabbit, a modified cabinet inside which my compliant niece would seem to be transformed.

Here in France they wanted me to make an entire aircraft invisible, to try to protect the young airmen flying it, to help them elude the enemy, to make the prosecution of the war more effective. Was that possible?

Fighting back my fears of inadequacy, I went through the possibilities. The most obvious, and probably the cheapest and simplest, would be to change the colour or appearance of the aircraft so that it merged with the sky in some way. Paint it silver or pale blue?

Would it work? My experience suggested it probably would not.

A few years earlier I had tried to design a new and, I thought, clever way of creating a disappearance on stage. I persuaded my then assistant to wear a costume that was made in the same colour, and of the same material, as the curtain backdrop. It turned out to be one of those ideas that are better in theory than practice. No matter what I tried, with movements or lights, she remained as visible to the audience as she would have been dressed all in white, or black, or indeed normally.

What if it was applied to an aircraft, though? I tried to imagine how a camouflaged plane might look while it was overhead. Like most people I had not seen many aircraft close to, although I did go to an exhibition flight by the famous French aviator, Louis Blériot. At one point in his display he zoomed slowly and blackly over the heads of the spectators. *Blackly* – that is the key word. On that sunny day on the South Downs near Brighton, his fragile little machine looked from our position below like a dark bird of prey. But if it had been painted the same colour as the sky? Would we have seen it then?

Assuming it was possible to find the right shade or tone of a silvery blue, and assuming the sky was bright, with high cloud coverage ... what then? I closed my eyes, trying to visualize the result.

Doubts arose almost at once. An aircraft is not a smoothly contoured object. It has wings and an engine and struts and wires and wheels below and a pilot and observer sitting in their cockpits above. It also carries identifying marks.

Under certain highly controlled circumstances, and with ideal sky conditions, it might be possible to contrive that a warplane was less noticeable. It would only work if the plane remained in the right environment: it might become indistinct when crossing the glowing sky, but how would it look from the side, or from above? How would it blend in against a background of trees, grass, concrete, mud?

Flying in the air was a far from ideal circumstance. The aircraft would dodge and weave, its propeller would spin, the engine would make a racket and, no doubt, a trail of exhaust smoke would follow it.

Skies are bright. Paint is a medium that reflects light – the sky is a source of illumination. If my camouflaged plane were to fly between the enemy and a brilliant sky, the aircraft would show up as a black silhouette, just as Monsieur Blériot's had. It was an object that would block light, not reflect it. And, as contrary case, what if the sky were not bright, but a lowering cloud base presaging rain? What if my pilot, departing on a daytime sortie in a bright blue-and-silver craft, was forced to return in a gathering dusk?

My mind first shied away from these thoughts, then re-circled around them.

I knew only a little about the science of camouflage and wished I had had the wit to learn more about it before I left London. I did know why the British Army clad its soldiers in khaki – that was an inheritance from the Mutiny in India. Then the troops' fighting gear had been dyed a dull yellow-brown colour, so that their uniforms would tend to merge with the dusty landscape. Until then it was the custom of armies to kit out their soldiers in bright primary colours, reds and blues and whites – this was partly to impress and intimidate the foe, but also to allow easy recognition for troops on the same side. That had to change in the Indian campaign. It was a mobile, unstructured war that put a formal army at a disadvantage. There the British had an enemy who ran and hid, and laid traps, who melted into the back streets when chased, who knew the terrain intimately and used it unscrupulously. The khaki fatigues were an attempt to fight back on something like the same terms.

I had heard that a new kind of camouflage was being used experimentally on ships: it was a painted design that did not attempt to hide the ship, or make it blend into the background, but which used dazzle techniques. This made it difficult for an enemy to determine in which direction the target might be heading. British merchantmen had been attacked by German submarines from almost the first days of the war. The U-boats scanned their targets and took aim from beneath the surface, using the periscope. When the bulky optical gear broke the surface, a sharp-eyed lookout on a British escort warship might quickly spot the presence of a submarine, so the German raiders could only raise it for a few seconds at a time. The idea of the dazzle was that the asymmetrical outline would confuse the U-boat captain when aiming his torpedoes.

It appeared to be a successful tactic, because the tonnage of lost ships had been significantly reduced since the dazzle paint was introduced. It gave me a few thoughts, a few ideas, a possible way of trying that technique with the British observer aircraft.

One of the classic disappearance techniques used by illusionists is placing a carefully angled mirror between the object that is to vanish and the audience looking at it. For example, a mirror placed beneath a four-legged table along the cross diagonal will not only give the illusion that the table is just like every other table (that is, supported on all four legs, one in each corner), but will create a space behind it within which something, or someone, may easily be concealed.

More can be done with half-silvered mirrors, and even more with plain glass. This, lit appropriately with a dark space behind, will make a completely convincing mirror when the lights are shining from one direction, and become transparent if the lights are suddenly, or even gradually, made to shine from another.

It was difficult to imagine how mirrors might be used to hide an aircraft, though. The problems appeared insurmountable. Glass is heavy and to try to conceal an airplane with a mirror would require one as big as the craft itself. I had no idea of the lifting strength of modern warplanes, but I seriously doubted if Lieutenant Bartlett and his fellow airmen would want to go to war lugging a huge mirror beneath them, even if they were able in the first place to take off with one.

And of course this did nothing to address the essential question of the disguising angle, how to calculate it and how to achieve the desired effect. A mirror carried horizontally beneath the aircraft, assuming it could be done at all, would merely reflect the ground back to itself.

I wondered briefly if there were some other reflective material available, a lightweight fabric perhaps, the sort of thin outer skin used on gas-filled dirigibles. If something like that could be coated with a silver reflecting paint, then held tautly enough to create a true and steady reflection …?

Perhaps if two airplanes were to fly side by side, navigating carefully to maintain a steady distance between them, and stretching the silvered cloth between them. How might that disguise their presence?

I tossed. I turned. I was getting nowhere.

I looked towards the small, unwashed window, where the faint glow of pre-dawn showed. I desperately wanted this long and painful night to end. Lying still, trying to control my breathing, I listened for the dreadful but strangely hypnotic sound of the distant war, but either I was now too far away or the guns had at last fallen silent. It was a moment of peace, or at least of a temporary cessation of violence. I could imagine those wretched men in the front line, huddling in their earth trenches, deep in mud and filth, able at last to snatch a little sleep.

I knew that this small sign of quietude meant I should try to catch a couple more hours of sleep before having to rise, but there was another thought nagging at me.

There is one more method magicians use to make something seem to disappear. It is in fact one of the main techniques of stage magic and is employed in almost every trick you ever see performed. It is the art of misdirecting the audience.

Misdirection can take two forms. The first is to manipulate the audience's expectations, to allow them to recognize their own knowledge of the world of normality, and from there allow them to assume that those rules will still apply to what they are watching when a trick is in progress.

Let us say that the magician begins to do something with a hen's egg. Most people will assume that the egg they are seeing is entirely normal, not 'prepared' in any special way. A good magician will reinforce the assumption by, for example, handling the egg gently so as not to crack or break it, or will make a little joke about what would happen if he were clumsy enough to drop it. This helps allay private suspicions about any possible preparation, and will increase the audience's instinctive belief in the normality of what they are seeing. The illusionist does not have to state explicitly what he is doing, nor should he try to tell the audience anything about the egg. The simple, familiar appearance of it is his subterfuge. Having established and reinforced the assumption he may then proceed to do something unexpected with the object he is holding. It *looks* like an egg, it is *shaped* like an egg, everyone *thinks* it is an egg, but then he makes the seeming egg perform in some way that would be impossible.

No doubt at the end of the trick he will deftly make a quick substitution and crack a genuine egg into a bowl, to suggest to the audience they were right all along. It really was a normal egg! The trick he just performed looks even more mysterious.

The other way to misdirect is to play against the audience's expectations. In other words, to distract them momentarily, to disarm them with an unexpected pleasantry, to make them look at the wrong object on a table, or to watch an unimportant movement of a hand, or to look in the wrong direction – all of these create brief instances when the illusionist may quickly do something to another object, or move his other hand, or place something in view that won't be noticed immediately.

Audiences who go to magic shows often see themselves as engaging in a kind of undeclared contest with the performer, constantly seeking to spot what he is 'really' doing. These audiences are, paradoxically, amongst the easiest to misdirect because in their eagerness to catch the magician out they concentrate on all the wrong actions.

Distraction can be achieved in many ways. A surprising costume change, a sudden bang or a flash of light, an alteration to the lighting or the backdrop, a witty remark, something that buzzes or vibrates unexpectedly, an apparent mistake by the conjuror. All of these are in the standard repertoire of magic.

I realized that there was potential in this, as an approach to Lieutenant Bartlett's problem. When I had a little more experience of how the aircraft operated from this base, what they looked like and what size they were, and if I was able to find out exactly what they do and how they fly when on an operation, then I might well be able to think up some misdirection that would be useful in the heat of battle.

Another kind of misdirection is in the use of adjacency. The magician places two objects close together, or connects them in some way, but one is made to be more interesting (or intriguing, or amusing) to the audience. It might have an odd or suggestive shape, or it appears to have something inside it, or it suddenly starts doing something the magician seems not to have noticed. The actual set-up is unimportant – what matters is that the audience, however briefly, should become interested and look away in the wrong direction.

An adept conjuror knows exactly how to create an adjacent distraction, and also knows when to make use of the invisibility it temporarily creates. An old colleague of mine used to perform a routine in which he spun a china plate on the end of a cane, then mounted the cane upright on his table and left the plate to spin there. As it slowed down and began to wobble increasingly, threatening to fall off and smash at any moment, hardly anyone in the audience was looking at anything else. For several seconds my friend was in effect invisible on the stage and he made good use of those seconds.

Then I had it! Simeon Bartlett's problem, and potentially a solution to it, fell into place.

One aircraft, two aircraft. One adjacent to the other. Or maybe a third: two aircraft, apparently in formation together, while the third is adjacent to the other two. If I could make the extra aircraft interesting in some unexpected way the Germans would be distracted by it – they would fire their guns in the wrong direction. If the distraction were somehow illusory they would be shooting at something that did not matter, or at something that only looked as if it were there. It would be the wrong aircraft, or even not an aircraft at all. They would not be able tear their gaze away from it, but at the same time they would not be able to see it properly.

It was not going to be easy arranging that sort of misdirection, but it was in fact just a larger version of the kind of thing I did every time I went on stage. I could make it work, but I realized that Lieutenant Bartlett and his fellow pilots would have to put in training. That was something I would have no say about. Would the Royal Navy be willing to divert warplane pilots to extra training in the middle of a war?

Well, the best I could do would be to present my solution, and it would be up to them to implement it. In the meantime, I felt I needed to learn more about the actual aircraft and try to find out what resources would be available to me to build the necessary kit.

I was excited by these thoughts, but I was no longer churning mentally. I felt calm because I believed I had thought up an effective way of deceiving the German enemy, saving British lives and helping the progress of the war.

I turned over, punched the hard and horrible pillow a few times, and moments later I drifted back to sleep.

8

I awoke to the sound of an engine, repeatedly speeding up and slowing down, something that I had learned from Lieutenant Bartlett the night before was called revving. I had heard it several times in the streets of London, made by automobiles. I often felt annoyed by it, but had never known what it was called. This particular revving engine sounded to me unhealthy, because it was coughing and stuttering and the noise it made was erratic. When a second motor started up a minute or two later, closer to my window, I pulled myself from the bed and went to have a look.

It was a bright, sunny morning, the sky white and dazzling with a high layer of light cloud. At first I had to narrow my eyes protectively against the glare. There was a large area of grass spreading out and away from my window, a whole field, leading to some leafless trees so distant they looked tiny and half shrouded in the early haze. Five aircraft were parked directly in my view. They must have stood there all night as I slept, but now there were many men in service fatigues working around the little craft. A miasma of smoke drifted in front of my window but the blast of air from the speeding propeller of one of the machines soon swept it away.

I stared in fascination at these small but deadly-looking craft so close to me. I had seen Monsieur Blériot's frail little plane as it flew over, and pictures of others in magazines and newspapers. Once, at my local picture house, I had seen moving film of an aeroplane flying along a stretch of coastline. But suddenly to be so close to these warplanes, with five of them immediately in front of me, was an astonishing experience. I felt I was being allowed a glimpse into some terrible future, the sort of thing H. G. Wells wrote about, in which everyone would be flying in all directions, in constant peril of falling, being held aloft by these assemblages of wire and canvas and wood. It was a frightening thought, but to be candid it was one I also found enthralling.

In the closer of the two planes which had their engines running, the man I knew would be the pilot was already sitting in the forward of the two cockpits. Most of his body was out of sight inside the plane, but his head and shoulders were above the rim. He was wearing a leather helmet with glass goggles resting on his brow. In the cockpit behind him was an enormous box device, unfamiliar to me.

The other aircraft had a man in each seat, with the second crewman lowering himself into his cockpit. While the engine roared with increasing energy, and at last started to sound smoother and more powerful, two of the men in fatigues carried over and mounted a large gun on a rack at his side. When they had backed away the observer practised rotating the gun, up and down and from side to side. He sighted it through a cross-hatched circle made of wire, mounted vertically above the barrel.

Wanting to watch these two warplanes take off on their mission, I dressed hurriedly and went outside. As soon as I appeared several of the men stood up from their tasks and saluted me. I was still not sure of my status on this operational base so I smiled and nodded, half raising my hand to my brow in an awkward response. The two aircraft were already moving away towards the centre of the field, their wings dipping and rocking alarmingly as they traversed the uneven grass.

One of the pilots signalled to the other plane with a wave of his gloved hand. All three of the men now pulled their goggles down to protect their eyes, and hunched themselves inside the cockpits. The two aircraft, running abreast of each other, accelerated away in the direction of the still-low sun. After a remarkably short run on the grass they lifted away. With their wings still rocking uncertainly they climbed slowly, leaving two faint trails of grey-blue exhaust smoke in the clear air behind them.

The ground crew had already moved away towards the other standing aircraft, but I remained where I was, wanting to watch the two aircraft until they were out of sight. I heard someone walking up behind me. It was Lieutenant Bartlett, with a leather helmet and darkened goggles dangling from his hand.

He greeted me with a salute, which I returned.

'Good morning, sir. I haven't had breakfast yet. I was wondering if you would care to join me? Breakfast here isn't quite the same as dinner, but it's still not too bad.'

We walked together to the wardroom – in reality it was a partitioned area of the aircraft shed, with a handwritten sign on the door: *Officers Only* – where a welcome breakfast was available. It was scrambled eggs ('yet again,' said Simeon Bartlett with a groan, but they tasted good to me) and unlimited supplies of toast, with a large mug of tea. He asked me what I thought of *la rue des bêtes*, but I said I had only been up a few minutes before he found me and had not yet had a look around the airfield.

'I'll give you a tour later,' he said. 'There are some good people here you will be working with.'

As we finished our tea, Simeon Bartlett told me a little about himself. He had joined the Royal Navy before the war began – it was a manly family tradition, and love of the sea and sailing were part of his nature. He served on a minesweeper as a junior officer, then a destroyer, but after that he had been posted to a land-based establishment in Portsmouth. When the war broke out in the summer of 1914 he was still there. It soon became clear that the Germans were using aeroplanes to threaten our army. A naval air wing was promptly set up. Frustrated by not being at sea and not receiving a posting to a ship of the line, Bartlett volunteered for the new service, learnt to fly and after a few adventures he did not describe in detail ended up here on the Western Front, keen to shoot down as many Huns as possible. He said he had been married for a year and that his wife had recently given birth to twin baby girls. He told me how fearful he was of being killed or seriously injured, but that because of his young family he was now ever more committed to the struggle. He found the consequences of a possible German victory unimaginable.

As we left the wardroom, Lieutenant Bartlett introduced me to three of the other pilot officers, but their aura of easy camaraderie and flyers' slang, their familiar joshing with each other and a kind of reckless acknowledgement of the dangers of their job, made me feel more than ever an interloper. The four young men chatted together for a few minutes, discussing the weather report for the day, including the wind direction. Everyone always paid attention to the forecasts, because of the risk that the Germans might release poison gas. Under suitable wind circumstances, tendrils of the gas could reach even as far as this airfield. In fact the forecast for later that day was a light south-westerly breeze, so those fears at least were allayed for a while.

Lieutenant Bartlett led me back out to the field and across to where one of the warplanes was waiting. Most of the other aircraft were gone – I had heard planes taking off while we were eating breakfast. As we approached the aircraft, an airman standing beside it, who had been leaning over to speak to one of the mechanics working on the underside of the wing, spotted us and immediately straightened. He stiffened to attention, then saluted us both. Bartlett responded automatically – I saluted a second or two later.

'This is my crewman,' Bartlett said, as we all relaxed our manner. 'Observer Sub-Lieutenant Astrum. Astrum, this is Lieutenant-Commander Trent, who has come to work with the squadron as an adviser on camouflage.'

'Good morning, sir,' Astrum said, showing no apparent surprise at my appearance. He had a pleasant West Country accent. I was at least twice the age of everyone I had so far seen on the base, adding to my sense of being an outsider. But Sub-Lieutenant Astrum was smiling and he extended his hand in a friendly way. 'Welcome aboard.'

'Mr Astrum flies with me as observer and gunner,' Lieutenant Bartlett said. 'This morning we plan to carry out one of our regular recces of the German lines, which are to the north-east of here. It's a particular area called Bois Bailleu. No trees there now, unfortunately. It's a sector where the archie is usually pretty fierce. We think there might be something going on there they don't want us to know about, because they make it so hot for us. Of course, that makes it all the more interesting, so we keep having to go back for another look and each time the ack-ack is a bit worse.'

Sub-Lieutenant Astrum pointed out an area of the tailplane, near to where he was standing. I could see that the fabric had been patched in several places, then roughly repainted.

'That happened two days ago, sir,' he said. 'Right over where Bailleu Wood used to be. It wasn't too serious – not the closest they've come to shooting us down, but pretty bad.'

'You came back all right?'

'We made it home,' said Bartlett, and he glanced at his wristwatch. 'We're going to have to take off in a few minutes for a proving flight, but before we do I want to show you the problem we need you to work on. Let's take a look at the underside.'

He threw aside his flying jacket and indicated I should remove my tunic too. He lay down on his back in the long grass and signalled me to join him. Together we wriggled until we were beneath the lower of the two wing planes. It was of course the closest I had ever been to an aircraft of any kind, let alone a fully armed and fuelled warplane. With the wing surface just a few inches above my face, I suddenly felt terrified of the machine. The pungent smell from the varnish they had used to tighten the wing fabric, obviously high in ether or alcohol, wafted around us. Lieutenant Bartlett must have detected my reaction.

'You'll get used to the smell in a day or two, sir,' he said. 'Try not to inhale it directly. But these kites wouldn't stay in the air without it.'

I made no reply. I used a similar-smelling liquid in one of my illusions, in which a spectacular burst of flame appeared (or seemed to appear) from nowhere. I was always nervous of the volatile, highly inflammable liquid, treating it with respect, yet these aircraft were coated in it or something very like it. It was all too easy to imagine what would happen if an ack-ack shell were to explode close to the aircraft, or even if a hot bullet were to pass through the fabric.

Bartlett was indicating the canvas under the wing, drumming his fingertips on it to show how tautly it was stretched. It was painted silvery blue. They had clearly been thinking about the same camouflage ideas as me.

'You see what we're trying?'

'Yes, I do. Does it help? Is the plane less easy to see?'

'Not that we would ever know. They still keep shooting at us. The problem is, we can't go on experimenting with different colours. Every coat of paint increases the weight of the plane, and it tends to soften the dope we've used on the canvas. Maybe one more coat would be possible. What do you think?'

'I'm not sure paint is the answer,' I said. 'It's a first step, but I think I might know a better way.'

'Can you tell me what it is?'

'Not yet. I need to carry out some research.'

'Every day counts, sir.'

'I know. I can work quickly.'

We pulled ourselves out from under the wing and stood up. The heady feeling induced by the dope fumes began to dispel. Bartlett scanned the sky and in a moment pointed out an aircraft flying low in the distance, away from the German lines.

'I think that might be Mr Jenkinson,' he said. 'Flight Lieutenant Jenkinson. He's been out on a gunnery test and will be passing overhead in a minute. You can see for yourself the effect the silver paint has.'

Sure enough the aircraft tipped its wings and turned towards the airfield. We shaded our eyes with our hands as he flew towards us. He went into a shallow climb and passed at some height above us. Even before he was directly overhead I could see for myself that the silver paint idea was never going to work. Irrespective of the underside colour, his aircraft was a black silhouette against the sky.

'The Germans don't even go to the trouble of camouflaging themselves any more,' Simeon Bartlett said, as Lieutenant Jenkinson went into a steep turn then lined up on the airfield to make a land-ing. 'They paint their crates every colour you can think of.'

'Presumably they're not trying to observe our lines without being noticed?'

'No, the ones I'm talking about are their fighters. They're the real danger to us. No one likes ack-ack but when the Hun sends up a school of fighters then it's every man for himself. We can cope with that. It's an equal fight. We give as good as we get, but unless we're on the ball they can come at us without warning. We usually get a hint that they're around if the guns on the ground stop firing at us. What we have to do then is stop looking down and start looking up.'

'Have you been in any battles yourself?'

The young officer looked uneasy, and glanced around to see if we were being overheard. 'That would be over-stating it a bit, you know. Not battles. If we were in the infantry we would describe what we get involved with as skirmishes. Here we call them dog-fights, because that's what they are like. A lot of scrapping, barging around, chasing our tails, trying to get off a squirt of ammo at them before they get one off at us. Camouflage doesn't matter a damn then, because we're all up in the sky and the odds are the same for both sides.'

'So what am I to do?' I said.

'Surveying the German lines is our main job, the big effort. We're here in support of the ground troops, because in the end they are the ones who will have to win the war for us. But it's getting dangerous and we need effective camouflage.'

As if to underline what he said, another of the squadron's planes flew across the airfield, this time waggling its wings as a signal. As it approached the centre of the airfield, roughly above where Lieutenant Bartlett and I were standing beside his plane, it climbed steeply before levelling off, its engine coughing. Puffs of black smoke blew out of the engine exhausts. The display of high spirits by the pilot served once again to show how distinct a plane's outline was when seen from the ground.

'You know, part of the problem is the shadow,' I said.

'Shadow?'

'Not on the ground, but the shadow on the underside of the plane. It strikes me that could be changed by putting a light on the aircraft.' I was thinking quickly, if not all that appropriately. 'One light in the belly of the plane, and a couple more along the leading edge of each lower wing. That would fix it. No more shadow, and you'd be difficult to see.'

Lieutenant Bartlett looked aghast. 'Go into battle carrying lights?' he said.

'Well, yes.'

'I think not.'

'But if they—'

Embarrassed, I let the matter drop as suddenly as it had arisen. The challenge of solving a problem had carried me away, making me forget this was not just a technical issue, a puzzle to be solved, but involved the lives of these young men who were risking everything.

9

Lieutenant Bartlett turned away from me and walked across to where Astrum was pulling on his heavy leather flying jacket. They spoke quietly for a moment, with Simeon Bartlett looking back at me more than once. It was a moment of real impasse, which made me realize how serious the problems were, and that my foolish suggestion had probably undermined his confidence in me.

At that moment, to make me feel even worse, another officer came striding across the grass towards me. He was clearly more senior than any of the airmen I had so far met. The ground crew around me stiffened, and saluted.

He ignored them and came directly to me.

'I want a word with you,' he said to me without preamble, jabbing a finger aggressively.

'Yes, sir,' I said.

We stepped a distance away from Lieutenant Bartlett's aircraft, and stood with our backs to the other men.

'I think I know who you are, Mr Trent,' he said, his voice an authoritarian treble. 'You're a civvy, I believe.'

'Well, yes—'

'I don't know how you came to my station, or into my command, or what your orders are. But there's no room for civilians on this base.'

'I'm on a temporary commission, sir, and I am carrying written orders from the Admiral of the Fleet's office at the Admiralty.' I had the orders somewhere inside my luggage, and in fact I had transferred them from one bag to the other when I arrived. I realized I should have sought out this commanding officer as soon as I arrived and presented him with my orders. They had emphasized at the Admiralty that that was what I had to do, but Lieutenant Bartlett's informal greeting at the station had made me overlook this service nicety. 'I apologize, sir,' I said inadequately. 'This is my first posting. I have been sent as a special consultancy detachment.'

'Not at my request.'

'May I provide you with my orders, sir?'

'Later. I only found out this morning you were here. Just do what you came here to do, don't make a nuisance of yourself, then clear out. These boys are exposed to danger every day, and they don't need to be distracted from their duties by some damned illusionist who thinks he can win the war single-handed. You clear on that? You understand?'

'Yes, sir.'

But he was already striding across the grass, saluting in an absent-minded way as he passed other young pilot officers heading out to the airstrip, ready for the next sortie.

While this brief and unpleasant exchange was going on, Lieutenant Bartlett had climbed into the cockpit of his plane, with Astrum in the observer's seat behind. They had pulled on their helmets. A mechanic stood by to swing the propeller, while two others waited for the order to remove the wheel chocks. I walked across to the aircraft. Simeon Bartlett inclined his head towards me.

'We have to make a couple of circuits on a test flight – just checking a problem with the controls. Then I thought you might like to come up with me instead of Astrum here, and have a good close look at the German lines. See what we have to put up with.'

Something lurched horribly inside me. 'Today? This morning?'

'No time like the present. The need is urgent.'

'Are you sure that would be all right with the commanding officer?'

'What did Henry say to you?'

'Henry?'

'The C.O. – Lieutenant-Commander Montacute.'

'He told me to make myself scarce. He said I was not welcome.'

'Then he can hardly complain if I take you into the line of fire!' Simeon Bartlett laughed cynically. 'Don't worry about what he said. I had a strip torn off me before you arrived yesterday, because he thought I had gone to the Admiralty behind his back. Well, in fact I did, because it was my Uncle Timothy who decided you should be brought out here. So I did go behind Henry's back, or over his head, and he doesn't like it. But because the Admiralty has already approved you there's nothing he can do. Hand him your written orders as soon as possible and if he says anything more about it I'll speak up for you. The simple fact is that I have family in the Navy and he hasn't.' He leaned away from me, peering along the cowl of the front-mounted engine. He shouted to the mechanic. 'All right, Seaman Walters!'

The young man standing at the front pulled down hard on the two-bladed propeller, stepping back in the same instant. The prop went through half a turn, then bounced back with what sounded like a wheezing noise from the engine. The effort was repeated several times, until finally the engine took. With a great bursting cloud of blue smoke, pouring out from everywhere around the engine, the propeller began to spin.

Lieutenant Bartlett turned towards me again, just as I was about to back away.

'Get yourself into a flying suit, sir!' he shouted over the racket. 'There are several in one of the huts over there. I'll see you back here in about ten minutes, and I'll take you for a good close look at the Germans.'

One of the mechanics stepped forward, and produced a hand-pistol with a thick barrel. He moved in front of Lieutenant Bartlett's aircraft, looked around in all directions, then took the pistol in both hands. Pointing it into the sky he fired a single shot. A bright red light went shooting upwards, arcing through the sunshine. At the top of its flight it emitted a brilliant red flare, then began to fall slowly towards the ground.

The young man then went quickly to the side of Bartlett's aircraft.

'All clear, sir!' he shouted.

Lieutenant Bartlett waved his hand to acknowledge. The engine note was rising from a slow clattering noise to a lusty roar. Around the plane the grass was pressed into rippling flatness by the stream of air. Lieutenant Bartlett shouted something to the men standing around, waving both his hands. Two of the seamen tugged away the wooden chocks which were restraining the wheels.

The plane started moving forward at once, bumping on the grassy surface of the field. The rudder at the back swung from side to side, as Simeon Bartlett tried to keep the plane heading in a straight line. He directed the plane towards the eastern edge, following the direction of the light wind. When they were about halfway towards the far side the plane turned back on itself and without a pause accelerated into the wind, bouncing and leaping on the uneven ground. As they passed our little group we could see that both men were hunched forward against the slipstream – Astrum's gun was prodding above the cockpit edge, the barrel pointing skywards. The aircraft soon reached enough speed to take off and it rose steeply towards the clouds, leaving a trail of thin blue smoke in its wake.

As soon as it was against the sky the plane assumed the black silhouette I now knew was normal. Once again, the part of my mind that tried to manufacture mysteries knew that a certain amount of carefully angled lighting on the underside would change the apparent shape when viewed from the ground, and would probably confuse the enemy gunners at least long enough to get the crew past them in relative safety. But then of course I could not discount Simeon Bartlett's total rejection of the idea. There had to be another way. I was learning about the limits of possibility in this war, but at least I had a few more ideas about adjacency and distraction.

Over the far end of the airfield Lieutenant Bartlett's plane was turning steeply, heading back over the strip and climbing.

One of the ground crew standing with me suddenly yelled something, but I could not make out what he said. He was pointing upwards to Lieutenant Bartlett's airplane. It had started climbing noticeably more steeply.

Someone else shouted, 'There's something wrong! He'll stall if he doesn't level out!'

The plane was now climbing almost vertically and was starting to rotate beneath its propeller. It was almost exactly above us. Everyone around me was staring up at the little plane, pointing, shouting, yelling for help.

'He'll over-choke it at that angle!'

'Put the nose down!'

'He'll never make it!'

Puffs of dark black smoke appeared around the nose of the aircraft, instantly thrust away by the stream of air from the propeller. But the plane was floundering – it dropped backwards, and there was another burst of thick smoke from the engine. For a moment the plane looked normal, as the nose came down, seeming to correct the fall, but almost at once it began to spin. It was out of control, plummeting with ever-increasing speed towards the ground, the smoke forming a horrific black spiral behind it.

It was falling towards us. Everyone in our group began to run, stumbling frantically on the bumpy ground, trying to get clear, looking up and back.

Somehow the falling aircraft missed us. It hit the ground at an immense speed no more than twenty-five yards from where we had been standing. There was an immediate flash and a loud explosion. The pressure wave from it felt like a kick against my body. White, red and orange flames burst out in all directions. A huge cloud of smoke, streaked with flames, billowed up.

I ran towards the crashed plane with the other men, desperately trying to reach the wreckage before the fire took hold, but the closer we approached the more obvious it was that the fuel tank must have burst open on impact. Tongues of burning fuel ran out across the grass, brilliant orange in the daylight, crowned with a dense rush of smoke. The other airmen ran on but I came to a halt. I was stricken with terror, not of the burning, nor of the fear of a second explosion like the first, but because of a dread of what I might witness.

In fact a second explosion did follow, smaller than the first. The men who were running ahead of me took some of the heat blast. They fell or scrambled away from the inferno.

I, staring ahead in mute horror, saw through the smoke and

116

flames a sight that I knew I would never be able to eradicate from my mind. I saw the shape of a man struggling to stand up and free himself from the broken remains of the aircraft. He was waving his arms in a frantic fashion, screaming with every breath, but I could see that most of the clothes he was wearing had already been blown or burnt from his body. His flesh was exposed, black and burning as I watched. He seemed molten, waxen, burnt not to a crisp but to a soft, pliable mass, melting down. I have no idea if the man I saw was Simeon Bartlett, or his crewman, Astrum.

He folded, bent, leaned forward, flowed downwards into the inferno.

I shrank away in horror as a third explosion occurred, the smallest of the three. I heard the sound of another engine and a fire appliance came bouncing and lurching over the grass. I sat down weakly, in the sun, in the light wind, with the smell of burning fuel and the highly flammable spirit that had been applied to the wings, and the crackle of burning wood and now the sound of water being pumped on the burning wreckage. Thick smoke billowed past me. The smell of it made me want to throw up.

I was still there, in the middle of the field, after the other men had dispersed. I watched the firemen working on extinguishing the rest of the fire. I turned away, not wanting to see as an ambulance crew came to collect what they could of the crewmen's remains. They drove back towards the camp buildings, leaving the wreck a small, smouldering heap of indistinguishable shapes and spars.

Only when a young officer I had not met before walked across to me did I at last leave the scene of the accident. Speaking considerately and gently he told me I was in the centre of the airstrip path. Many more aircraft were waiting to take off on their next missions. Other planes were expected back at any time, and they would need to land.

The war was still going on.

10

So what was I to do?

I returned in a state of shock to the grim little room where I had passed my restless night, sat on the side of the bunk and tried to think. I had achieved nothing at all, and had only the vaguest, most provisional idea of what I could do to put that right. A glimmer of an idea about some kind of adjacency misdirection, a sleight of hand against the German Army, one of the best-led and most highly trained military forces in the world. I proposed to defeat them with legerdemain. What Lieutenant-Commander Montacute had said about an illusionist who thought he could win the war single-handed was some way from the truth but it had nonetheless hurt. All my ideas would probably have turned out to be unworkable. Even to try the simplest sleights would have required much friendly help and cooperation from the pilots of the RNAS, and of course I had been depending totally on my young friend Simeon Bartlett, the only one who appeared to have any faith at all in me. I hardly knew him, but his sudden and horrifying death was the worst blow I could imagine: he was so young, so full of energy and brimming with a loyal intent to fight a brave and honourable war. Gone.

Without him, my place on this airfield was, to say the least, uncertain. I already knew that the commanding officer wanted me off the place. With Simeon Bartlett dead the attitude of Lieutenant-Commander Montacute only reinforced my own sense of insecurity about the value of anything I might be able to offer.

So every nerve in my body urged me simply to pack my bags, get off this base, return home. But I had become a commissioned officer in the Royal Navy, acting under orders, in the midst of an aggressive war. How could I just walk away? Would I be treated as a deserter? Hunted, captured, court-martialled, shot?

After a few minutes of such worry about my own fate, a greater sadness grew in me. I thought of the waste of Simeon Bartlett's life, and that of his crewman. The suddenness of the accident and my shock of witnessing it at such close quarters were reactions that were fading slightly, but they were more than replaced by a feeling of human loss. I started shaking, and did not know how to stop. To see two healthy, intelligent, highly trained and above all *young* men killed like that was more than I could cope with. I do not cry often, but I sat there inconsolably on the dismal bed in that dismal room, weeping without shame.

Beyond the window I could hear the sound of aero engines, starting, revving up, clattering down to silence. I did not look, could not face the idea of seeing any more planes taking off or landing.

When I had at last been able to compose myself I left the room, and bracing myself against another unpleasant interview I went in search of Lieutenant-Commander Montacute. I eventually discovered he was currently leading a mission.

I returned to my room. I located my written orders then penned a polite note to Lieutenant-Commander Montacute. In it I said that I was obeying his personal order to leave the base now that my work was complete, and that I would resign my temporary commission the moment I returned to London. I added a short tribute to the life of Simeon Bartlett as I knew him. I closed with what I hoped the commanding officer would accept as a courteous acknowledgement of the dangerous and worthwhile work he and his pilots were doing. I walked over to the C.O.'s office and left the papers in the charge of his orderly rating.

I packed my bags, having decided to be well away from the airfield by the time the C.O. returned. I found my way down to the guarded main gate, steeling myself for an interrogation about where I might be going and why, but the seaman on duty simply pushed open the barrier when he saw my uniform and stripes. We saluted each other.

Once in the road I turned and looked back. Behind the gate, facing out towards the road, a wooden sign had been erected. Across the top, in neatly printed formal letters, were the words: *Royal Naval Air Service, Squadron No. 17, Béthune*. Beneath was a rather well executed painting of a rural view: cows grazing in a lush field, surrounded by mature trees. Three tiny aircraft circled overhead. And at the bottom, again well printed but in a more informal style: *La rue des bêtes*. Beneath that, smaller still: *Entrée interdite – s'il vous plaît rapportez à l'officier de service.*

I strode down the road, determined, if necessary, to walk the whole way to Béthune, but after a few minutes an army truck appeared on the road and the driver stopped to offer me a lift. I tossed my bags into the back, then sat next to him in the cab as he drove along. He asked several innocent and therefore harmless questions about my war experiences, which I answered in as noncommittal a way as possible. He told me he was a sapper, involved in a difficult project to dig deep tunnels under the German lines, with the intention of placing huge mines beneath their trenches. He said they had never yet been able to detonate their explosives, because the lines of the trenches kept moving to and fro. They were currently working on a new tunnel, much longer and more ambitious, and –

I stared ahead at the rough surface of the road, thinking of war's futility and the death of young men. I saw a flight of British warplanes heading east away from the airfield, holding a tight diamond formation. They flew beneath the high bright clouds, black against the early winter sky.

11

At Béthune I narrowly missed the Calais train and had to wait until the evening for the next. There were few signs of British military activity and the station had a reassuringly civilian look. There was even repair work being carried out on some of the buildings opposite the station – workmen were putting up scaffolding around the main station building. I was able to deposit my luggage in a lock-up in the station hall before I walked into the town to find a meal.

I went through the afternoon and evening in a state of suspense, holding on, waiting, eating a little, drinking a little. The only money I had on me was British, but the shopkeepers had become familiar with that and were willing to accept it, albeit at an outrageous exchange rate. My nerves were constantly on edge in case someone from the British command might notice me and ask what I was doing. I could not eradicate the idea that by walking away from the RNAS base I had become a deserter. The ambiguity of the contact I had had with the commanding officer was no help. Whenever I saw men in British military uniforms I tensed up with apprehension. However, no one seemed in the least interested in me.

When I returned to the station I was informed that all trains were cancelled – *c'est la guerre, mon capitaine*, said the clerk in the ticket office, who was in the process of closing down for the rest of the day. I trudged around the town once more until I found a hotel with a vacant room.

In the morning: good news. The trains were running once more. I bought a ticket for the first one. It left punctually, travelled quickly, and was in Calais in good time for me to catch a ferry to Dover. Boarding was delayed because there were reports of a German U-boat in the Channel, but finally the passengers were allowed aboard. The boat was not crowded. I found a quiet corner of the saloon, wrapped myself up in my coat and tried to blank my mind. There was a short delay outside Dover Harbour and it was late afternoon before we docked. Once on land I found again that there were problems with trains. Controlling my impatience I located a harbourside hotel where I then spent the night, and the next morning was able to catch the first train to London.

Eventually, around two in the afternoon, after an uneventful journey through the Kentish countryside, the train rumbled across the long iron bridge over the Thames and arrived at Charing Cross Station.

I disembarked to the platform with a feeling of immense relief. All I wanted was to get home to my flat as soon as possible, read whatever mail might have been delivered while I was gone, sit quietly and untroubled in my own room. The station was the familiar bedlam of incontinently released steam and distant unidentifiable thuds. Whistles blew shrilly. The railway workers communicated by loud shouts. Pigeons fluttered across the joists of the high, glassed-in roof and strutted erratically across the platform floor. It was undeniably good to be back in London. The problem of whether or not I was a deserter from His Majesty's Royal Navy was something I would resolve in due course, and anyway my position as a commissioned officer felt increasingly academic. They had not wanted me there.

I had to wait on the platform for a porter, but soon enough I was heading along towards the wide concourse of the terminus.

Then, ahead of me on the platform, and also moving towards the taxi rank outside, I saw the short figure of another officer. He was fussing alongside a porter whose trolley was laden with a large suitcase and several small packages. From behind the man himself looked little different from other serving officers, of whom many were passing through the station, but what I could not fail to notice was that his uniform trousers were streaked and coated with mud.

I overtook him just as I crossed with my porter into the main concourse.

'HG?' I said, when I was sure it was he.

He stared straight ahead, a lack of response I took to be deliberate.

I tried again. 'HG?' I said. 'Mr Wells?'

He turned towards me this time, but there was the strain of a dark mood on his brow. He was not pleased to be accosted. But then he recognized me.

'Oh yes,' he said. He frowned again, narrowing his eyes. He smiled, but only briefly, a conventional courtesy, a man who was used to being recognized in the street. 'The magician with the wizard's cloak.'

'I wondered if I should see you again,' I said.

'Times like this, when we are eager to be back where we started!' he said, not explaining anything.

'I don't intend to delay you, HG,' I said. 'If you are hurrying home, I certainly understand—'

'Yes, well.'

We had temporarily ceased our progress and were facing out across the station yard, where horse cabriolets and motor taxis were in competition for our business. There was always a noisy scramble outside London's main termini, the horses which drew the Hansom cabs restive and alarmed by having to wait in close contact with the noisy and smelly motor taxis. I glimpsed the familiar sight of London's traffic, moving slowly out of Trafalgar Square and into the Strand, and the pavements crammed with pedestrians. The indescribable but unequalled smell of London's streets: that unmistakable blend of coal smoke, horse droppings, dust, sweat, food, petrol engines. Queen Eleanor's famous cross rose high above us.

Our two porters had come to a halt a short distance beyond us, waiting for our decisions about which of the taxis we wished to hire.

'I'm glad to be home,' I said.

'I echo that,' HG replied, glancing around at the welcome chaos of our capital city. 'Did you reach the Western Front?'

'Yes. And you?'

Briefly, the look of irritation I had seen as we met flickered across his face again.

'That is what I was there to do,' he said. 'But having finished, or at least having been informed in no uncertain terms that I had finished, I took a quick look-around at the sector I was in and then came home. In short, I was told to push off, and none too politely, either.'

'That's more or less what happened to me.'

'You don't surprise me. It was not what I hoped for, nor even expected. So – there is no call for a magician in the trenches, then?'

'Sadly not.'

'You have come away empty-handed,' he said.

'I am simply glad to be out of it, and on my way home. The same for you, I suppose?'

'Well, because of past experiences, I always make sure that I travel with more than one commission. This time I had two, or three if you count my temporary induction into the British Army.'

'You told me about your system of communication,' I said.

HG glanced around us in a warning sort of way and in particular towards our two porters, who were it not for the constant hubbub of noise from the yard and the street would certainly have been within earshot.

'You and I know nothing of that,' he said, and the frown was back, creasing his high forehead. 'Military secret.'

'What do you mean?'

'I mean no one would tell me anything about it. Not if it had been tried out, not even if they had built the rig. The chap assigned to me pretended he had heard nothing about it, and yet he was the officer named in my orders.' HG was leaning towards me, a fierce expression on his face, and his words came quietly but insistently. 'There was I, inventor of the blessed thing, given the ear of no less a personage than Mr Churchill, and no one in the trenches was prepared to say anything about it. The whole business was fishy, if you ask me. I went as far up the ranks as I could, but none of those officers would say anything to me either. Except to give me strong advice to catch the next train home and not mention anything to anybody at any time.'

'Did you see any evidence of it?'

'That's what I found fishy. The whole front is a mess of mud and cables and holes and dumps of things. The Germans don't help by sending over artillery shells every five minutes, blowing everything up and making an even bigger mess. It's impossible to make sense of what's going on until you've been there a while. But right in the middle of it I noticed an elevated wire strung out on big strong poles, and it looked close to the device I had drawn and sent in. It was still clean, as if it had been there only a few days. But when I asked what it was the chap told me it was a kind of field telephone, or a warning cable, or something like that.'

'So nothing was being carried on it?'

'Not a damned thing.'

'I thought you had been invited out to the front to inspect it and make recommendations.'

'That is what I thought too,' said H. G. Wells. 'But either some Higher Up has decided my idea was not worth the scrap of paper on which I drew it, or they have sold it to the Germans, or, well . . . I am furious with them. I think the truth is that when they saw me they decided not to trust me. Me! My idea, my plan.'

'I'm really sorry to hear this,' I said.

'You're right. I should not say these things. Nor even think them. I have no right to question the leaders of those unfortunate young men in the trenches.'

The expression of despair was slow to leave his face, though. Looking at him I felt that his experiences and mine had mirrored each other.

'You said you had more than one commission,' I said.

'I'm a writer, Mr Trent. It's hard enough making a steady income, even for one such as myself, who has had a few popular successes in the past. And in time of war the climate is even tougher for writers. So these days I cannot afford to go anywhere unless I first secure an agreement from a newspaper, or sometimes a publisher. This time I was travelling as an *ex officio* representative of the *Daily Mail*, and my experiences will now amount to an Opinion. I told you some people think I'm a meddler, but in fact I am much sought for my Opinions. They sometimes amount to the same thing. So, I shall write this new Opinion for the many hundreds of thousands of intelligent readers of that organ, and then, I dare say, I shall later transfer that Opinion to the pages of a new book. There I shall find another audience. In the process I will no doubt offer a Suggestion or two. That is my only true constituency: the interest and common sense of the ordinary man or woman. If my lifesaving idea has no influence on the military or their political bosses, and I am forbidden to discuss it between now and the end of time, at least I hold a strong Opinion on everything else I have seen. I also have the means to express it, and a public who will benefit from reading about it. That is anyway my belief and intention.'

I nodded dumbly. I was of course one of those many readers who would welcome anything he could write that would enlighten us about the war. In spite of my brief visit to *la rue des bêtes* I was feeling less informed about the war than I had been before I left home.

While HG and I continued to talk on the side of the station yard, many other passengers were pushing past us. Our porters were still waiting, but they had let go the handles of their trolleys and were standing together, smoking cigarettes.

'What about you, Tommy?' HG said. 'Do you feel as I do now, that this war is unwinnable? That the just cause we thought we had at the beginning has already been lost?'

'I was most struck by the quality of the men I met in France.

They are a generation who are doomed, which they know full well but they go on with it. Their bravery leaves me speechless. My experience of the fighting was minimal. Not even a skirmish or a dogfight, in the words of one of the people I met. Even so, I have been pitched into gloom by the whole experience. The war is a monstrosity!'

I knew my words probably sounded over-excited, but they poured out before I could think how they might sound.

'I believe we both travelled to France bearing ideas,' HG said. 'We have been disillusioned about the worth of those ideas. War is no place for ideas. It is about armies, fighting, determination and gallantry. Would that sum it up for you?'

'Yes.'

'Then that adds to the horror. When the imagination dies, so does hope.'

We fell into silence then, avoiding each other's eyes. HG was staring down at the stone pavement.

'Did you see anything of the trenches?' he said suddenly.

'No – I saw hardly anything. I was at an airfield, a way back from the line.'

'Just as well, perhaps. Enough, though?'

'Enough, and more,' I confirmed.

HG stuck out his hand and we shook again. This time our gaze met. Those memorable blue eyes, that open expression!

'It seems we have both come home with an Opinion. I at least have somewhere I might express mine. I presume you do not.'

'No,' I said.

'I shall think of you as I write.'

We parted then, our porters hauling their trolleys to the cab rank. H. G. Wells took the first of the motorized taxis, while I selected one of the Hansoms. We drove off into the London streets, never again to meet.

PART 3

Warne's Farm

1

THE TEACHER

Tibor Tarent was standing outside the Mebsher, the great armoured bulk high and dark beside him, the turbine idling but still screeching and the exhaust gases washing across the long grasses, battering them into constantly shifting patterns. The vehicle had halted on the side of a bracken-covered hillock. It stood at an angle, the right side higher than the left, which made clambering down to the ground without falling more a matter of luck than judgement.

While he protected his cameras from knocking against the sides of the metal stairs, Tarent gashed the heel of his hand on one of the sharply jutting catches that held the hydraulically operated door to the shell of the main hull. Pressing the wound to his mouth, Tarent looked to see what it was that had snagged him – it was not the catch itself, but part of the metal cover of one of the clasps which had been torn back somehow, with a jagged edge curling nastily down.

Beset by a blustering wind charged with tiny particles of ice, he had to stand by and watch as the co-driver Ibrahim struggled to find and extract his bag from the space beneath the passenger compartment. The soldier was working hard against the steep gradient inside the vehicle, caused by the angle at which the Mebsher had come to rest.

Finally the bag was found and Ibrahim placed it outside on the uneven ground. He made what looked to Tarent like a perfunctory semi-military salute, but said correctly and courteously enough, 'Inshallah, Mr Tarent.'

'Upon you too be peace,' he replied, with the automatic response.

The crewman operated the door mechanism and they both watched as the integrated steps folded up and out of sight, and the door swung down into place. Tarent noticed that the jagged piece was forced in by the weight of the door, but after a moment it jerked back out. He wondered whether he should point it out to the crewman but he already knew from experience of the Mebshers that the driving crew were normally not willing to service or repair the vehicles.

Ibrahim turned to clamber back towards the drive compartment.

Tarent said, 'Just a minute, Ibrahim. Where is the place I'm supposed to be going?'

'You have global positioning software on your smartphone?'

'Yes.'

'Then the coordinates will already be filed.'

'But which direction is it from here?'

'Along this ridge,' the driver said, gesturing with his hand. There was a trace of an old footpath leading away. 'Parts of it are too narrow for this vehicle. You'll have to walk the rest of the way. Sorry about that but it's not far. This is as close to the place as we could take you, and this diversion means we are now running late.'

'All right.'

Ibrahim moved back towards the drive compartment. Tarent knew that it would take about two minutes for the crew to run through the cockpit checklist, ensuring all systems were running, then power up again to drive speed. Tarent saw it as two more minutes in which he might still change his mind.

He looked around at the terrain where the Mebsher had halted. There was little or no shelter where he was standing: the vehicle had halted close to the crest of a ridge, beneath which a stretch of cultivated land spread out, undulating intermittently. There were few hedges and almost no trees. Lightly dressed because of the heating inside the Mebsher passenger compartment, and not having been given enough time to put on his outer clothing, Tarent now felt chilled and exposed. He found the coat where he last placed it, between the handles of his case, and he struggled quickly to put it on. The whining of the Mebsher turbine remained at idling speed, showing that the cockpit checks were still not complete.

That afternoon, as they travelled inside the Mebsher, Flo had quietly passed him a second handwritten note. It came as almost as much of a surprise as the first, the day before. He had not seen her alone again after their liaison at Long Sutton, not even at breakfast in the small canteen. She was already seated in the Mebsher when he boarded, apparently deep in the study of her laptop, speaking quietly into a headset. She repeatedly tapped the area behind her ear, a code of intermittent but systematic beats, the fingers touching the sensor area at different angles. Tarent tried several times to make eye contact with her, but failed. After that, he slowly reverted to the state of uncomfortable introspection that had been with him the day before.

Then the handwritten note: *Change your plans? Skip Warne's Farm and come with me. I can tell you something about your wife.*

The paper had been torn from some kind of official document, because in the top corner there was a small segment of an embossed seal. All that was legible was the end of an internet or electronic address: *fice.gov.eng.irgb*

He thought for a few moments, staring once more at the back of her head. What could she tell him now about Melanie that she had not been able to tell him the evening before? Would this information explain the activity that was going to and fro in her digital implant? But for him the only thing that would matter now about Melanie would be the news that she had been found alive and well. His loss of her was still a poignant pain. He knew beyond doubt that she was dead. Assuming Flo had some new information, it could only be some extra detail about the way she was killed, or something about the people or group who had killed her. Tarent was not sure he wanted or needed any more of that kind of information.

Maybe Annie and Gordon Roscoe would welcome more facts about what happened to their daughter, but he was still too much in a state of torpid confusion: regrets, guilt, missing her, wanting her, remembering the best of her, loving her, wishing they had not argued so violently that last day together, feeling inadequate. Above all guilt and love intermingled, because he was certain she would not have left the comparative safety of the field hospital compound if had not been for him. Flo could hardly tell him anything more about that.

Once he had agreed to be repatriated from the Anatolian base by the OOR, he had yielded to the temptation to allow other people to make decisions for him. There was apparently an itinerary, a plan someone had worked out, a structure: the swift return to IRGB, the private meeting with Melanie's parents, then a debriefing session at this place called Warne's Farm, and finally he would be turned free to live his life once more.

What that would entail was something Tarent did not fully know and so far had barely had a chance to think about: their flat in south-east London, Melanie's property and personal possessions to be sorted out. At least she had made a will. Then afterwards, what? He could resume his freelance career, perhaps travel across to North America again, find some work there?

It did not feel like much but it had the attractions of a plan, of a practical way forward, even if the prospects for it were largely unknown. But also largely unknown was the alternative: Flo wanted him with her. There was no plan, no itinerary for that.

After a few minutes he wrote an answer on the back of the slip of paper: *Still thinking about it. I want to be with you. But if I go to Warne's how would I contact you later?*

When he saw her left hand dangling over the rear of her seat he passed the slip back to her. She showed no reaction and indeed continued to sit there in front of him for many more minutes, the paper resting loosely in her fingers. She did this for so long that Tarent began to wonder if she was even aware of it, but finally she shifted position and moved her hand into her lap. Tarent was reminded irresistibly of note-passing in school, when the teacher was thought not to be looking. In spite of all this digital technology, people sometimes still preferred to scribble private messages on paper. She spoke to her male colleague about something, and laughed lightly and shortly at something he said. Moments later the hand that had been holding the slip went up to the implant behind her ear. If there was any sign that she had read the note, Tarent never saw it.

Tarent later drifted back into his reverie, an uncomfortable half-sleep, trying to doze but always aware of his surroundings. He was fully roused only when the Mebsher halted and the driver shouted his name on the intercom. He heard the turbine winding down. While he moved hastily to pick up his cameras and his shoulder bag, Flo leaned back towards him as if to help him with his stuff. Her hand touched his and briefly squeezed it. She said nothing, and nothing was pressed into his hand. The other two passengers showed no sign of having noticed this.

Then he was outside on the windy hill, shivering, nursing the gash in his hand and waiting for the Mebsher to power up and drive away.

He felt tormented by his indecision. Maybe Flo really did have some new information about Melanie? He was only going to this Warne's Farm place because someone at OOR had told him to. He stepped forward, raised a hand, but he heard a change in the note of the turbine. Tarent moved quickly, clambering up the uneven slope to a point where he was sure he could be seen by the drivers, but it was already too late.

The turbine began to turn more quickly and a cloud of black smoke belched away from the outlet. Tarent had to step back to avoid being anywhere near the exhaust if the vehicle made a turn. The Mebsher first climbed at an even more extreme angle, because of the rise of the hill where it had stopped, but then it swung around and the vehicle levelled with a downward lurch. The programed reactive suspension system anticipated much of the weight of the movement, but from long experience Tarent could easily imagine the effect on the passengers inside.

He had lost his chance. The Mebsher went slowly down the trackless hill, rocking from side to side and leaving behind it two huge scars in the soft earth. Gases from its exhaust swept past him, with a smell of kerosene, burning oil, hot metal, scorched plastics or other synthetic materials. The noise was terrible, but within seconds the heavy machine had moved down across the edge of the escarpment and the sound level diminished at once. The only wind now assaulting him was the one blowing from the north, with its load of stinging ice pellets.

He shifted his shoulder bag so that the strap ran across his chest, freeing both hands. He carried the camera holdall in one hand, then hefted his suitcase in the other. Treading carefully but heavily, trying to maintain his balance, he set off along the footpath that Ibrahim had indicated. After a few steps, though, he paused and put down his bag again.

He dug out the cellphone he had been given and selected the GPS feature. As it loaded the address appeared as text: *The Paddock, Warne's Farm, nr. Tealby, Lincolnshire.*

The simple Englishness of the address brought a wave of brief and unfocused nostalgia to Tarent: a sudden memory of a time when there were still farms with paddocks. Indeed, when there was still a county properly called Lincolnshire. And further behind that, to a time when England was the place of his childhood, or some of it. He glanced around ruefully at the landscape, almost entirely devoid of trees.

The electronic map loaded and an indicator instantly showed his position in relation to the target address – as Ibrahim had implied it did not look as if it would be too far to walk, but he still had to carry his luggage over the uneven ground. He picked everything up again and continued. Having to hold the cameras separately made the weight of his luggage unbalanced and it was soon weighing heavily on his arm. The handle of the case cut into his fingers and palm. He was anyway out of condition after the long stay at the field hospital and the weeks of enforced idleness while he was there. For a short time at the beginning he had tried taking exercise at night outside the compound, when it was supposed to be cooler and in general safer. But he found the air temperature at night was still stifling, and the darkness of the bare hills seemed to make them into places of greater danger than they were in daylight.

The path unexpectedly led to a steep decline, with taller grasses and shrubs leaning across it and bushes on either side. The GPS display went blank, but he carried on. Satellite gain must be weak here, but at least in this lee the wind lessened a little. He walked another hundred metres or so, climbing uphill again, then came to a high metal fence, expertly and stoutly built, with blanking panels to above head height, wire mesh above that, then two counter-spiralling coils of razor wire. He could not see much ahead of him through the fence, but there was a small familiar symbol mounted on a metal plate: the skull-and-crossbones mortality warning, plus the international trefoil symbol of radiation hazard.

To his left, the fence followed the contour of the hill, moving up through the trees – to the right, the fence ran down into an area of rough brambles and undergrowth. He set off to the left, up the hill, moving away from the fence. After a while he came to another path, slightly wider than the first. He crossed this and continued climbing the slope, and not long afterwards came to the edge of the hilly ridge. Tarent put down his luggage for a moment, to rest his arms.

He looked away down the slope to the west, the direction taken by the Mebsher. The large personnel carrier had returned to his view and was now moving slowly away from him across a wide, roughly rectangular field. The Mebsher appeared to be heading towards a road, whose position was shown by a long sequence of high steel poles, with mesh laid between them, often seen along roadsides in areas where farming still continued and trees could no longer be relied upon to provide a wind-break. He glimpsed a village beyond the screen of poles. From this height and position the Mebsher looked a lumbering, difficult vehicle, anomalous in this familiar English landscape, making a heavy business of cross-ing the soft earth, tearing up whatever crops there might or might not be in the ground. The icy wind sent veils of cold precipitation across the view.

As he watched it the machine halted abruptly, swivelling around slightly to the side, as if coming to a skidding halt, something of which Tarent knew the vehicle was incapable. Almost at once, a point of brilliant blue-white light, small but intensely bright and threatening, appeared in the air directly above the Mebsher. It was impossible to say from where it had come, but it was a glint of sinister, painful luminance, against the dark rain-clouds scudding swiftly above.

The light grew even more intense. Tarent was already lowering his eyes, looking away, looking back quickly, fearing some kind of blinding laser beam, but now he raised his hand to his eyes, tried to watch from between his fingers. The light-point suddenly exploded like a firework, shooting three angled white shafts of light directly down to the ground. They surrounded the Mebsher, one each of the light shafts striking the ground a short distance away from the wheels. A skeletal pyramid of white light surmounted the Mebsher, a perfect tetrahedron, and moments after it had formed it solidified into pure light.

There was a huge concussion, an explosive blast. Tarent was thrown violently backwards, and he tumbled helplessly through the rough bushes and weeds on the level ground immediately below the edge of the ridge. The shock and sheer shattering noise of the explosion stunned him, made him incapable of motion or even thought. All he knew was that he was still alive, because he could feel movement around him, branches and pieces of vegetation and earth falling to the ground. The immediate memory of the explosion kept returning, terrifying and paralysing him.

Gradually a sense of normal life began to return. He moved his limbs tentatively, scared of discovering serious injuries, but apart from a feeling of having been assaulted and bruised by the wall of blast, there seemed to be nothing broken. None of his body felt as if it had been burned, not even his face and hands, unprotected at the moment of the blast. It was more difficult to breathe than normal because his chest was hurting. He had taken the concussion full-on. He rolled over, pressed down with his hands, brought up one knee, then the other, tried to shift his weight. He made himself breathe regularly, but his chest was in agony. Beyond that there was little pain as such in his limbs but a sensation of overall stiffness, a shocking feeling of having been dealt a physical hammer-blow of vast pressure. He raised himself more, so that he was crouching, balancing on his hands and knees, deep in the tangle of vegetation where he had fallen.

Half crawling, half walking, he worked his way back towards the edge of the ridge, to where he had been when the Mebsher was attacked. He became aware that he had been thrown back much further than he had realized. He passed his luggage, dislodged by the blast, but apparently undamaged. His suitcase had not burst open, and when he anxiously examined his camera cases he found those too appeared intact. All three cameras responded normally when he briefly switched them on and off.

Carrying the Nikon he at last regained the ridge. There had not been many trees along it when he was there before, but now none remained.

A drift of grey smoke rose from where the Mebsher had been when it was attacked, but in the time it had taken for him to recover, most of it had dispersed. If there had been a mushroom cloud after the moment of explosion, it too had either blended with the rain-clouds or been spread out by the wind.

Nothing was burning on the ground.

There was no sign of the Mebsher. Where it had been travelling there was now an immense black impact crater.

The sides of the crater formed a perfect equilateral triangle

2

He took many photographs of the crater, but he did not feel it was safe to walk down to inspect it closely. His hands were shaking, and for a while he had to lie flat against the ground to steady himself. He returned to his cameras, changed over to the Canon, then took some more pictures, taking advantage of its slightly greater focal length. While he was still shooting he heard the sound of emergency sirens and saw vehicles hurrying along the road that ran alongside the field where the explosion had occurred.

Tarent sat down on the ground, staring at the inexplicable shape of the huge crater, charred into blackness, a triangle carved into the ground as if with a precision instrument. It was identical to the trace of the explosion that had killed Melanie in Anatolia. It terrified him, the enigma of it, yet also the familiarity, the sense that both had happened so close to him.

But what had happened to the Mebsher? It had been destroyed in the explosion – not just badly damaged, not blown apart by the detonation, not even smashed into small or unidentifiable pieces of wreckage, but utterly obliterated. Flo had used the word annihilated. There was no trace of it at all. And what of the people inside? Just about everyone he had encountered since returning from Anatolia had been in that vehicle. Like the first blast of the explosion, the realization that those five lives had been wiped out was a stunning shock, one that kept replaying itself in his mind.

Above all, Flo. What of her? What had he discovered about the woman other than the fact that he should call her Flo? He had known her physically and sexually, but only briefly. Any deeper knowledge of her still lay mainly in questions. Now, those would never be answered.

Down at the site of the crater a number of uniformed men and women had arrived, with more vehicles turning up every minute or so. A group of armed soldiers in full combat gear had debarked from five huge armoured personnel carriers and were now fanning out slowly across the field, inspecting the ground, but also looking about in every direction. Several of them were moving towards the ridge where Tarent was crouching. He decided that he did not wish to be found, treated perhaps as a witness, taken in and interrogated about what had happened, or what they might think had happened. How could he answer a single question about it? He had seen it occur, but he would have found it almost impossible to describe it or attempt to explain it.

He backed away so that he could not be seen from below, packed his cameras securely, then hefted his heavy bags again and set off in what he hoped was the general direction of the place he was supposed to be going to.

The freezing wind was still blowing but at last the sleet had turned to rain. He barely noticed the cold as he struggled along through the tangle of undergrowth and broken vegetation. He reached the path. Two helicopters, their markings invisible because the machines were black against the sky, swept past swiftly and at a low altitude, heading towards the scene of the explosion. They descended rapidly and soon Tarent lost sight of them.

He started to run, responding to a feeling of growing panic. All that was around him seemed threatening, inexplicable, out of control. He felt himself to be somehow responsible, for the destruction of the Mebsher, for the end of Flo's life, for the end of Melanie's, everything. He was haunted by the image of the triangular crater, whose shape had no logic other than the fact that it existed and he had seen it happen. Weighed down by his luggage, feeling the bulk of his case bashing against his knees and sides as he ran, Tarent sensed that this was the end, that his life was over, with nothing left for him.

He did not have far to go. In this state of mental fear and confusion, close to panic, not paying much attention to his surroundings, and when he had lost hope of finding any kind of refuge, he glimpsed the roof of a large building, made of grey metal. Behind it was another, then a space, and beyond that a third tall building, this one with a high chimney. Several big trees, stripped of most of their leaves but still standing, surrounded the buildings. With no expectation of what the buildings might be Tarent came to a halt, put down his bag and stood still, trying to recover his breath and to become calm. His heart was pounding. He waited a few minutes, hoping that someone might appear, or that there would be some outer indication that he was in the right place. He checked the GPS display, which had started working again, and it confirmed that his position coincided with Warne's Farm.

He flexed his body, collected up his bag and cameras, then hastened further along the path towards the nearest of the buildings. He encountered the fence again, just as forbidding, but at least at this point there was a gate. A stand, made of concrete and steel, was next to the entry, with an electronic reader built into its upper surface. The familiar logo for the OOR was engraved on the surround. Tarent had to put down his bag once again to retrieve his security card from an inside pocket, was relieved to find it, and more so when the gate swung swiftly open. It began to close again just as quickly so he hurried through, dragging his property.

He went along a made path towards the building. It was much larger than he had thought at first sight. There were several wings and extensions, all apparently built at different times and now extending behind the main block. The original building appeared to be a nondescript twentieth-century farmhouse, but any character it might once have had was concealed by a number of alterations. Most of the extensions, flat-roofed and lined with monotonous rows of windows, were constructed of concrete panels and sheets, but these were cracked in many places. A zigzagging line was etched across the main wall facing him, from the ground to roof level, with mosses and other plants prodding through. The windows were metal-framed and looked as if they had not been cleaned in years, although lights were glowing behind some of them. The overall impression was that the building was being clamped to the ground: numerous wide straps, some made of metal, others of thick ropes, had been thrown over the roofs and secured firmly in the concrete like a huge restraining web.

There was no sign of a paddock, Tarent noted as he walked across to the building: just a large yard with a rough concrete floor where several vehicles were parked. As he approached the main door he could smell woodsmoke and something being cooked. He began to think of Flo, then in agony thrust memories of her from his mind.

3

A woman in a *burqa* checked him in, quietly scanning his body and baggage with electronic analysis equipment, then efficiently, and apparently knowledgeably, examining all three of his cameras and the other photographic equipment he was carrying. Throughout this she said nothing. When Tarent volunteered his name she gave no sign that he was expected.

Two or three printed lists of statements and instructions were mounted on the desk between them, under a protective sheet of thick but transparent plastic. She led him silently to the positive result of each examination with a point of a gloved finger to the relevant words. Her pale skin showed through tiny ventilation holes in the glove, the only glimpse possible of any part of her body. There were four columns of text: Arabic, Spanish, Russian and English. She guided him to the column of English phrases. He glimpsed, or at least sensed by the motions of her head, the quick movement of eyes beyond the veiled aperture of her shroud. There was no discernible eye-contact with him. Tarent knew what she and other security officers would be on the look-out for, and like most people who travelled frequently he did not object to being searched, but he was always anxious when anyone handled his cameras. The woman held them delicately, though, then passed them back to him.

The reception area was an untidy, unclean passageway, unlit except by what daylight came through a window set into one of the two doors. The woman worked at a large, low and untidy desk, but there seemed to be no seat for her and she stood behind it. The corridor floor appeared not to have been swept for several weeks – there were many small chunks of broken masonry and cement powder, mixed in with the more expectable rubbish of packages, pieces of paper, small forgotten possessions dropped in passing. The environment of the place reminded Tarent of one of his photographic projects from years before: a pictorial essay for a magazine, about a failing sink estate in a town in Hertfordshire, where the interiors and public areas of the buildings had been and continued to be trashed by dysfunctional youths.

'Is this Warne's Farm?' Tarent said. The woman gave no hint that she had even heard the question. 'An office of the OOR?'

She pointed with a gloved finger to a list of phrases held beneath the plastic sheet. Tarent read: 'You are in the Intelligence and Funding Department of the Office of Overseas Relief, in the Eastern Kalifate of IRGB.' A website address followed, as it did after almost every other piece of text. The finger moved to another line. 'Your request will be dealt with by one of our officers when available. In the meantime, please wait.'

'I have been ordered to report here,' Tarent said.

No hint of understanding came from the woman as she went through his papers and plastic identifiers. After the first minute or two of her impassive silence, Tarent, craving human contact following the trauma of what he had just witnessed, tried to make conversation. Either the woman ignored him, or she touched a finger to another line of text: 'I am engaged in a decision-making process – please wait', or 'If you have a complaint, please communicate with my supervising officer', and so on.

Finally she handed over a plastic key card, then pointed to a chart of a floor-plan of an annexed building and indicated the room which had been allocated to him. He thanked her, praised Allah and averted his eyes. He struggled with his luggage along a short corridor, went outside to cross an open yard, then into a second building, unheated. He located the door to his room without trouble.

As he pushed the door open with his back, dragging in his luggage behind him, he was assailed by warmed air and the smell of food. The room was in darkness. He switched on the overhead light. The room was obviously already occupied: a notepad computer was open on the desk, with a screen saver moving to and fro, used cooking pans were stacked chaotically inside a small sink in one corner and a plate with yellowish curry smears was on the table. Discarded clothes were everywhere, and they were all women's. Tarent glanced around, took in the fact that the room had two beds, one with just a bare mattress, but immediately backed away.

He left his luggage on the floor inside the room and returned to the other building. The woman in the *burqa* was standing behind her desk. She did not respond as he approached.

'Peace be unto you,' he started. The hidden head nodded a slow reaction. 'Do you speak English?'

She leaned forward and removed a white card from a drawer in her desk. She slid it under the plastic sheet and indicated it with a finger. Tarent leaned forward to read what it said.

'I have vowed to be silent during the hours of daylight, and request all visitors not to expect a verbal response from me.' The words were repeated in the three other languages. The handwriting was open, broad, using a thick or soft pencil. The lead had apparently broken while she wrote, as the last three words were written with a ballpoint pen.

Tarent glanced back through the window – although the sky was still overcast and the day was gloomy, there were probably at least two more hours before nightfall.

She removed the card, but the others remained.

He said, 'I respect your vows, begum, but I need your help. Please tell me what you can. The most trivial problem, but the one I want to resolve quickly, is that you have allocated me a room which appears to be occupied by someone else, a woman. Unless there is an extreme shortage of accommodation here, I believe it would be wrong for me to move into that room without her knowledge or permission.' The woman made no apparent response. 'I must also meet the person in charge of this place as soon as possible, because I have been brought here to be debriefed by the OOR after a journey abroad. But more important than any of this, there has been some kind of insurgent attack outside, not far from here, just below the ridge. Less than an hour ago. You must have heard the explosion. I think several people were killed. One of them is a close friend of mine, and I am desperate for more information about what happened.'

The woman opened the drawer again, produced another sheet of paper and slipped it under the sheet for him to see.

It said in printed letters: '*Mr Tibor Tarent, IRGB citizen, seconded to OOR at diplomatic status, priority high, M. Bertrand Lepuits to interview.*'

'Yes, that's me!' Tarent said, greatly relieved to discover that he was known, expected, part of the system or structure of this place. 'May I see Monsieur Lepuits straight away?'

The gloved finger went to: 'What is the number of the room you are disputing?'

He found the key card in his pocket but it was electronically encrypted and no number was printed on it. He remembered that at the same time as she gave him the key card, the woman had passed him a slip of paper. He found that in his pocket.

'It's G27,' he said.

The finger: 'There is a state of emergency at present. Please consult your supervisor.'

'My supervisor – is that Monsieur Lepuits? May I see him? I can't be expected to share a room with someone I do not know. Can he give me more information?'

The finger again, more emphatically: 'There is a state of emergency at present. Please consult your supervisor.'

'Is there another room I could use?' Tarent said. 'One on my own – or perhaps I could share with another man, if there are no single rooms?'

Quickly: 'No.'

'Are any other rooms likely to come free?'

'No.' The gloved finger tapped three times against the printed word.

'Then who is the woman who is already in G27?'

'I am not allowed to answer that question.' The plastic that lay immediately over these words was scuffed and semi-opaque, as if it were referred to more than any other answer.

Tarent thought for a moment. 'I haven't been able to eat any food all day. Is there a canteen, or a refectory, or somewhere I can find a meal?'

The finger pointed to another well-used line: 'Our restaurant is situated on the first floor of the Paddock Building. Staff may not entertain guests without prior permission. Dishes are restricted to available ingredients on a day-by-day basis. The opening hours are from—'

'Thank you.'

4

The restaurant turned out to be a vending machine, placed in a bare room overlooking the central yard. It required coins which Tarent did not have, but there was a slot for his security card. This made the machine display a list of choices, of which there was only one actually available: a Spanish omelette. It was delivered a minute later: it was so hot Tarent could barely handle it in its cardboard sleeve, but tough and tasteless when it was cool enough to be eaten. He sat at a wooden chair and table by the window, picking at the food, both hungry and repelled.

He looked down at the abandoned cars and trucks, which had been pushed together into a rusting group. Beyond them was a cleared area, illuminated by floodlights, presumably in anticipation of the gathering twilight. It was to this pad that a helicopter circled in, hovered, then landed. It was a small machine with closed sides and no identifying marks, but it was expected – on its arrival several men hurried out from one of the buildings alongside the apron and unloaded crates and packages. The helicopter kept its vanes rotating while this was happening. As soon as the last load had been taken off, the aircraft lifted away, already turning as it climbed rapidly. Tarent was reminded of the almost frantic haste displayed by the supply helicopters which had visited the field hospital during those sweltering, unbreathable nights in eastern Turkey.

He was still eating when a second helicopter arrived. It approached through the darkness, lowered its tail, swung around dramatically, then landed in the glare of the floodlights. It appeared to be a military aircraft, the same general type as the ones Tarent had seen hastening towards the triangular scar in the field, but this one carried the shield of the British Army: a scimitar and rifle crossed, with the *Shahada* beneath. This time the men who ran forward to unload it appeared from a smaller building on the far side of the compound. They were soldiers in standard fatigues, with orange hi-vis jackets glaring in the bright lights of the helipad. They formed up efficiently into squads. They had brought with them half-a-dozen glistening metal trolleys. With the help of crewmen who had arrived in the aircraft they carefully and slowly unloaded many small and unidentifiable items, which were placed in a truck, then long stretchers bearing human shapes were brought out, hidden beneath thick blankets and securing webbing. Because of the darkness and the movement, Tarent could not see how many stretchers appeared, but there were at least four or five. They were each placed gently on to one of the metal trolleys, drip feeds and oxygen were quickly but deftly hooked up, and the casualties were wheeled away at fast walking speed to the building from which the soldiers had emerged.

Thinking of course of Flo, Tarent stood up as soon as he realized what was going on, pressing up closely to the window. He leaned against the glass, cupping his hands about his eyes. After the trolleys had been trundled out of sight the helicopter restarted its engine and prepared for take-off. The crewmen who had helped with the casualties now stood outside the aircraft, while the pre-flight checks were carried out. They were armed with automatic rifles. As the engine fired and the blades began to move at full speed, the soldiers leapt back on to the floor of the machine, each squatting beside the open side hatches, feet dangling into space, their weapons pointing at the ground. Within a few seconds the helicopter was out of sight.

Tarent left the Paddock building and returned to the accommodation block. He went to find the room to which he had been allocated. As he approached the door he saw that his large bag had been put outside in the hall.

When he slipped the key card into the slot, the red signal stayed stubbornly on. He pulled out the card, reversed it, tried again. The door remained locked. He thumped on it with his fist.

There was no response, so after a few seconds he hammered again. This time, after a short wait, he heard the lock being turned from inside, then the door eased open and was held by a security chain. A face moved into view, partly shaded by the light behind. It was a woman with untidy hair framing her face. He glimpsed baggy, shapeless clothes. She was wearing half-moon spectacles and she raised her chin to peer at him through them.

'I know what you want. You can't come in.'

'This is my room. I've been given the key.'

'No, it's my room. I was given an undertaking I would not have to share with anyone.'

'They said we had to share.'

'Bad luck. I want to be alone.'

'So do I,' Tarent said, beginning to feel desperate. 'They said they didn't have another available room so I would have to share. I don't want this any more than you do, but I've nowhere else to go.' He sensed that she was about to slam the door closed. 'Maybe another room will become vacant tomorrow. Couldn't I just sleep on your floor tonight? Or in the spare bed. I know there's one there.'

'There are usually other rooms they keep free. Go to one of those.'

She was pushing the door against him, but Tarent, anxious to make his point, held it open with his weight. 'They said there is nowhere else available. Look, I'm exhausted. I've been travelling all day, and I was caught up in that attack.'

'What attack?'

'You must have heard the explosion. A Mebsher was destroyed, or maybe damaged badly.' Because he had just seen casualties being brought in he was no longer so sure of the real extent or seriousness of the damage, or if the injuries had been fatal, as he first assumed. 'I was out there when it happened. I was lucky to escape, because I was about to get back on it when it was leaving. I'm at my wits' end. I just need a place to sleep tonight.' She said nothing, but continued to regard him through her low spectacles. Tarent could see she was not tall, fair-haired, nice to look at, but her expression was implacably hostile, unyielding. 'Please may I come in?'

'No. Allow me to close the door or I'll call security.'

'I won't go anywhere near you.'

'You won't get the chance.'

She shoved the door hard and Tarent yielded. The door closed noisily against him and beyond it he heard the locks turning, then the clattering of two bolts.

5

With nowhere else to go Tarent walked back through the buildings to the corridor where he had met the woman in the *burqa*. He was dragging his bag, holding his cameras. His back was aching, his arms and legs were tired, he was still finding it painful to breathe and his mind was starting to feel numb. He simply craved a place to rest and sleep – even a chair would do.

There was no one in the corridor. The desk had been cleared of papers. The drawers were locked. A notice on the wall gave a number to call out of hours, but someone had scored a red ballpoint line through it. Tarent had no idea what to do next, but he was now in need of a lavatory. He walked the length of the corridor but the few doors were all locked. The further end was unlighted.

His last, dismal chance was to return to the room, and try for a second time to get the woman to admit him, so he started back that way. Then a door in the corridor opened behind him, one of the doors he had found locked a few moments before. A man emerged.

'I thought I heard someone moving around,' he said. 'May I help?'

'I can't get into my room,' Tarent said. 'Are you the manager here?'

'Tonight I am acting duty officer, but these buildings are on Threat Level Red because of an insurgency attack earlier.' His English was excellent, but he spoke with a faint French accent. 'My name is Bertrand Lepuits. First, I have to ask you: how did you gain entry to this site?'

'I was ordered to report here. I believe you are the person I am meant to contact, Monsieur Lepuits. I arrived just after the attack on the Mebsher, which was the one I had been travelling on. The gate opened for me. I am Tibor Tarent, and I understand you are my supervising officer.'

'Yes, Mr Tarent. We were expecting you, but we received an electronic message that you were going on to Hull DSG instead, so the officers who were deputed to debrief you are no longer available.'

'No, I never intended to go to Hull.' Tarent had let go of the handles of his bag, which now stood leaning at an angle on the floor. 'That message was sent by mistake. If I had stayed on the Mebsher I suppose I would have been among those who have been killed or injured. Monsieur Lepuits, I beg you, at the moment all I want to do is find a room, somewhere I can rest. There is someone already using the room I was sent to.'

'I can't offer any help with that,' the other man said. 'You would have to see if the other person is willing to share with you.'

'No, I've been through that,' Tarent said.

'My best advice, sir, would be for you try again. I have no access to the residential side of this establishment. I am so sorry. As far as the OOR is concerned, your case has been taken over by the MoD and you should be in Hull.'

He was already moving back towards the door he had appeared from.

Tarent said, 'Is there anything else you can tell me? Is this place likely to be attacked? Is it safe here?'

'It is as safe as anywhere, and nowhere. We are at Level Red, which is all I can tell you. We are at maximum level of security.

Be alert to danger, Mr Tarent, and if the alarm sounds you must assemble with everyone else outside. There are instructions posted in every room.'

He nodded politely, then withdrew through the door and closed it behind him.

6

Tarent returned to the other building and once again found room G27. He leaned his bag against the corridor wall, made sure his cameras were securely stowed away, then squared up to the door. He was determined that this time the woman in the room should not force the door closed against him.

There was a hand-shaped tactile pad by the side of the door, which he had not noticed before. He pushed his palm against it, feeling the familiar sensation of the reading of sensory information, and waited. A minute passed, then another. Tarent remained braced against the door, hoping it would open, ready to block it with his weight if she tried to close it against him again.

He heard the lock turning, and the security chain rattled. This time the door opened slowly, revealing her face, much as before.

'I told you to bugger off,' she said.

'I'm appealing to you. It's not my fault they've given me the wrong room. I've nowhere to sleep. That's all I want. Please let me in?'

'Try your key card in one of the other doors. That sometimes works.'

'And go through all this with someone else who doesn't want me?'

'Several of the rooms are vacant. Since the May 10 attack this building has been half empty. They are transferring operations out of here to the DSGs. Just walk along and try some of the other doors. I don't want you in here, you don't really need to be in here, admin has fucked up and double-booked you. You'll find another room if you look. I've got work to do.'

'I have diplomatic status.'

'Yes, and we both know that's bullshit. I've seen what the data-bank holds about you. Your security clearance is OK, but you're not a diplomat.'

Still she did not push the door against him. He had his hand raised and his foot placed hard against the base of the floor, in case she did.

He said, 'If you've read the output from my tactile profile, you know I am who I say I am.'

'It makes no difference.'

He stared through the narrow gap at her. She was deliberately keeping her expression neutral, but she was no longer trying to force the door closed. For several long seconds they both held the gaze. Nothing more was said.

He drew back and Tarent thought he saw, for an instant, a small smile dash across her face. What she meant by it he did not know and did not care. He stepped back further, picked up his luggage. She was still there at the door, having moved to peer out at him through the chained gap. He ignored her and walked off down the long corridor.

Putting to the test what she had said he slipped the key card into the reader of the first door he came to. The red locked light glowed instantly, so he withdrew the card at once, not wanting a confrontation with whoever might be inside. The same thing happened at the next door, and the one after, and at all the doors along the corridor. He climbed a staircase to the second storey and at the first door he tried on that floor he was rewarded with a green glow from the LED and the clunk of a released lock.

Hardly believing his luck had changed, Tarent went swiftly inside and slammed the door behind him. The room was not only vacant, it was clean and everything had been arranged tidily. It looked at first sight as if it had barely been used. Every domestic utility was in place – kitchen and cooking equipment, a working shower and toilet, a closet for his clothes, two large beds with bedding folded neatly on top of both of them. There was a desk with a tablet computer, a scanner/printer, instructions for wifi usage and satellite connections printed on a card lying beside them. There was another small room adjacent to this, with a couch and two comfortable chairs, a TV, shelves for books, and more. The rooms were moderately heated.

He left most of his luggage where he had first dumped it as he entered the room, threw off his clothes and luxuriated in a hot shower.

He went to bed.

Tarent was woken in the morning by the unnerving feeling that he was not alone. He sensed a presence in the room, a movement of the air, a subtle variation in light, the sound of quiet footsteps. He half-opened an eye, reacted to the glare of daylight from an uncurtained window. He closed the eye again.

He lay still, waking quickly but not yet turning or sitting up, knowing someone was in the room with him. It was obviously some new problem that would have to be dealt with. The many events of the day before were still fresh in him – sleep had not alleviated his memories of them. He imagined an intrusion from the officials who ran this place, someone else whose room it was intended to be, instructions to vacate.

Then a female voice said, 'I can make you some coffee if you would like it.'

He turned over and levered himself with his elbows into a half-sitting position. It was the woman from Room G27. She was standing away from his bed, next to the alcove where the cooking equipment had been positioned. A cupboard door was open. Her stance was neutral, unthreatening. The offer of coffee was tentative, almost a pre-negotiation.

'How did you get in?'

'The usual way. I'll drink some coffee too, if you will have one.'

'Black, please. Without sugar.' She took down the coffee filter machine that was on a ledge. 'How did you get into my room?' Tarent said again.

'The same way you opened my door.' She raised an arm and presented the palm of a hand towards him.

'So how did you know which room I'm in?'

'You're carrying a signal emitter.'

'My camera?'

151

'Whatever.'

'Do you mind if I get out of bed? I need to use the bathroom.'

'Help yourself,' she said, without turning. Tarent, seeing no alternative, rolled naked out of the bed, took a moment to find his balance and catch his breath, then walked across to the bathroom. His chest was still painful. He emerged a few minutes later with a towel wrapped around him – the woman was now seated in one of the chairs, but she turned away while he pulled on some clothes.

'You might want to read this,' she said. Gripping it lightly between two of her fingers, she held out a security card for him to take. With a cup of coffee scalding his fingers, Tarent walked across to the reader installed on the wall next to the door and downloaded the ID information about her. She sat silently while he read the screen, watching him, sipping her own drink. He made a hard copy of what he found.

She was called Marie-Louise Pejman, born of Anglo-Iranian parents, both now deceased. Her father had been a government scientist in Teheran, her mother a teacher at the English school in the city. Their deaths were recorded as natural causes, but both had been in their forties at the time of death. Teheran was heavily shelled by anti-republican forces when régime change took place – from the dates it seemed likely they had been caught up in that. After their deaths she was evacuated to IRGB and after leaving school she changed her name to Louise Paladin. She was known to friends and some of her colleagues as Lou. She was now 39. She lived in London with a partner, but all references to the partner were greyed out on the screen and did not print in the hard copy. This was the convention used by the databank for information thought to be inaccurate or out of date.

Her profession was described as a supply teacher, English, Art, Design and Farsi, for students of either sex in the age group 11–18 years. She had become a full-time teacher in recent months, and was described as having been seconded to OOR.

Tarent had read many of these print-outs in the past and like most people had learned to try to see past the bureaucratic annotations and interpretations. In Lou Paladin's case, there were not many of these, although her matter of secondment to the OOR had been annotated as 'provisional'. As well as all this, there were the usual extra factual details of no great interest to Tarent: her place of birth, education, security rating, address, and so on.

The working protocol of tactile or card ID was that users were able to access data at equivalence levels – this meant that the lower of the two was usually the level at which information would be available to read or be exchanged. It followed that Lou Paladin had learned as much about him as he had learned about her, or could do if he took an interest and read through to the end.

He handed her back her ID card.

'Do you normally share this sort of thing with strangers?'

'No. But because you palmed my door, I was able to read what they have on the record about you. Isn't it fair that you should read mine?'

'I suppose. Is that normal in this place?'

'I don't think so.'

'So you are a teacher. Does that mean there are children on this base?'

'Not now. I'm waiting for a ride out of here, but my manager is not sure where I should go. London is off-limits at the moment and the DSGs are spread about, so no schools have been set up yet.'

'Why not London?'

'It depends if I want to go on working for the Office. If I do that I have to wait until a school is ready, which means staying here. If I hand in my resignation I could go back to London any time I like. But you know what happened in London.'

'Yes, but I only heard about it yesterday. I've been abroad, out of contact with what happened. Were you living in London?'

'I was in a flat in Notting Hill.'

'That was under the—?'

'The May 10 attack. Yes. I'd also have to find my own way back to London, and I'm not sure I'd know how to do that.'

'Things are that bad?' Tarent said.

'Private travel has become almost impossible because of the restrictions. There have been insurgent attacks all over the country, so it's risky to drive anywhere, even when the roads are opened. Trains were in use until recently, provided you could put up with the security measures, but the last storm did a lot of damage to bridges and embankments. I suppose you're sorry you came back from wherever it was.'

'I was in Turkey.'

'Yes, of course. I read that. You were in Anatolia. And I know your wife died. I'm sorry.'

She glanced away. The wind was high again and rain was slanting down the window glass. There was a cold draught from the window.

'Why did you come to my room?' Tarent said.

'Well, I thought I should apologize for last night. There was no way I was going to let you in, but I think I could have handled it more gently.'

'It worked out all right,' Tarent said, looking around at the satisfactory room where he had ended up. 'I think I might have done the same if it was the other way around. I'm no longer sure why I'm here. There was supposed to be some kind of debriefing interview about what happened to me in Anatolia, but that seems to have been abandoned by the people here. Like you, I'm going to have to decide what to do next.'

She leaned towards him intently.

'When you arrived back in Britain, did you travel through London?'

'Yes.'

'Did you go anywhere near May 10? In west London? Did you go through Notting Hill?'

'We passed close to that part of London, but I saw nothing,' he said. 'I was not allowed to see. I was in a car but they dimmed the windows. There was a brief glimpse: I just saw blackened ground.'

'Before I came here,' she said, 'I lived in Notting Hill. That was more or less the epicentre of the May 10 incident. I lived there for more than ten years. Please, tell me anything I saw. I need to know!'

'Do you have friends there?'

'My whole life was there!'

She was crying. She raised an arm against her mouth and face, wiped it roughly over her eyes, turned away, looked around. She went to the kitchenette, found a roll of paper towels, wadded two of them up and held them to her face. She was sobbing, saying words in such misery that Tarent could no longer make them out.

We are both casualties, he thought, watching her, this stranger, but because she was a stranger he was thinking about himself, thinking about what she had described as a whole life. Her whole life, but his too.

What did he have left of that life? His parents now gone, no sisters or brothers. No roots, just endless travel as a child and temporary stays in towns whose names he never discovered, a series of schools where he eventually learned to read and write English. That was his liberation, an escape into the world of words. By the time he was ten he was more or less settled and the distractions of journeys were behind him. From there he finished school, passed through university, started work, moved into freelance photography, a further escape into the world of images. That was his career, but what had his life been? What was the whole life of which he had just become aware? Everything focused on Melanie, that relationship, all the good years, a few of the bad periods, the times of mute anger and difficult silences, the contented memories that filled in. The first romantic years, then later the rows, the tears, the sexy reconciliations, the brief holidays. No children, but they had tried for a while. Long worries about money: everyone knew how badly nurses were paid and his own income was intermittent and dependent on others hiring him and paying him. Then the trips abroad – first his, then hers. They disrupted everything, although they provided a gloss of achievement, a sense that something was actually being done, but in reality the foreign visits made them foreigners to each other. Finally Anatolia and the disaster. Since then, a return to the world of sanity he had left and once understood, only to discover everything in that was breaking down too, the peace, the society, the weather, the economy, law and order, even the stabilizing forces of consensus government, a civilian police force, a free press. Nothing was as it had been, nothing was safe. The world was being marked illogically with small triangular areas of destruction, like patches of amnesia which could never be penetrated or cured.

What could he tell this woman about her home, her past whole life, that had existed somewhere in Notting Hill, now an illogical black scar on the face of London?

She was sitting between him and the window, her head bent forward. She was hiding her face – perhaps she did not want him to see her crying. She threw aside the paper towels, which had become a sodden pulp, tore off two more. Behind her head was the square of sky revealed by the window. It was still early in the morning, yet there was hardly any light coming down from the sky. A great blackness of cloud obscured everything. The wind was rising, and every now and then the building shook as a stronger than usual gust impacted against the outer walls.

The woman moved across to him, and sat on the floor beside his legs.

'You're crying,' she said, and rested a hand on his arm.

'You are too.'

'I—'

Tarent folded himself sideways to reach towards her, letting an arm rest on her shoulders. He clamped his eyes closed, trying to hold back the tears. When he breathed in he had to sob because he could not help it, but his chest was still stiff after receiving the blast and the irregularity of trying to breathe through sobs made him cough and gasp aloud with pain. He slid further forward in the chair and down, so that he landed on the floor beside her.

She was holding his head now, gently brushing his hair. They were acting as lovers who did not know each other, who had no love, just need – she pulled his face so that it rested on her breast while he tried to control his breathing, tried to remember what it was she had asked him.

When he moved suddenly her spectacles fell from her nose, knocked against his face, slid down his arm and landed on the floor. She made no move to recover them. He could see their half-moon shapes beside her legs. They were stained with tears. He remembered the hard, level look those lenses had given to her eyes as she slammed the door against him the night before, but now she was caressing his head and neck, trying to calm him with a compassionate touch. Her chest was heaving.

She said, 'I'm sorry, Tibor. I don't know what we can do.'

So he closed his eyes and waited for his breathing to subside, feeling once again that he was cracking out of the hardened carapace of his past, sliding vulnerably into an unknown future. The reality of the present moment was temporary, incomprehensible. Behind him was loss, ahead danger, and nothing that followed would be as it should be, and nothing was certain any more.

Feeling her hand on the side of his head, one of her fingers resting on his cheek, the rest of them reaching down tenderly towards his lips, he said, 'I've forgotten your name.'

'Louise. Lou Paladin.'

'Oh yes. Did I tell you mine?'

'Of course.'

The darkness outside increased. They could hear the roof above them creaking and groaning as the gale swept roughly against it. The time went by while they pressed against each other, no longer speaking, just holding and touching, waiting for something to change. Hailstones rattled against the window.

PART 4

East Sussex

1

My name is Jane Flockhart and for most of my career I worked as a feature journalist for a web-based newspaper. I was one of the last people to see Professor Thijs Rietveld alive. He committed suicide during the evening of the day on which I interviewed him.

Colleagues and friends have sometimes asked me how I feel about that, their implication being, I suppose, that it was my line of questioning or my aggressive or confrontational stance that tipped the great man over. He was widely perceived to be undergoing a period of deep disillusionment, self-absorption and depression, answering no letters or emails, never agreeing to meet journalists or fellow researchers, and had famously buried himself in a small village somewhere in the English countryside, living under an assumed name. There were reported to be MI5 operatives monitoring his activities, and keeping all strangers away.

Almost none of this was in fact the case. It was true that he was living alone in a quiet village, but it was an open secret to the people who lived there who he was. The place was, incidentally, not at all an obscure hamlet concealed from the world, but a fairly large village in a popular area, much favoured by City workers who commuted to their jobs in London. There was a mainline station there, with trains every half-hour into Charing Cross Station. Rietveld's house was on the main street of the village, although not close to where the shops were. There were no secret agents anywhere near him and probably never had been. As for him not speaking to journalists: I contacted him from the office of my newspaper in London, made no secret of who I worked for and requested an interview and photographs. He agreed at once, and I travelled down to meet him early the following week.

I went by train because I wanted to see for myself what the village was like from his point of view – he did not drive and was known to dislike cars. I planned to walk around the village before approaching his house: to see where the nearest shops were, how far it was to walk to the station, and so on. The photographer was planning to drive down and would meet me at the house later, towards the end of my interview.

I had interviewed a Nobel laureate before – the writer, philosopher and pacifist Bai Kuang Han, who was awarded the Peace Price in 2023 – but Thijs Rietveld was a much more formidable challenge for a non-specialist journalist. Until about twenty years earlier he had been working at the Rutherford Appleton Laboratory in Oxfordshire, engaged in theoretical physics. It was for this work in sub-particulate dynamics that he was belatedly awarded the Nobel Prize for Physics, but the making of the award coincided with the first results of his more recent work. This had the unfortunate effect, for Rietveld, of drawing attention to it. Working with a team of quantum field theorists Rietveld's analytical research work into the so-called Perturbative Adjacent Field had been until then shrouded in secrecy and high-level security.

At the time the Nobel was announced, few people had heard of him – he emerged from the obscurity of the closed unit where the PAF was being developed, flew to Oslo, made a short, gracious speech of acceptance in Dutch, then returned to Strasbourg, the location of the laboratory. It was only then that the public became aware of the PAF in the most general of terms – the popular press, guessing and simplifying, immediately described it as an infallible weapon of passive defence. It was soon known as The Weapon That Will End War. Within a year, though, the wider scientific community had been informed of the result of the PAF research, and not long afterwards it was universally understood in those circles. Rietveld modestly shared the credit for the development with the other scientists, but because he was a Nobel laureate he was assumed to be the team leader. It was in fact his theoretical work that led to the development of a practical application.

The PAF was for a while known as the adjacency defence. As originally conceived it had no aggressive function, being in every respect a passive reactant. Using what quantum physicists sometimes call annihilation operators, an adjacency field could be created to divert physical matter into a different, or adjacent, realm. An incoming missile, to use the famous example described by Professor Rietveld, need not be intercepted or diverted or destroyed – it could be moved to an adjacent quantum dimension, so that to all intents and purposes it would cease to exist. In its early working models, adjacency consumed a huge amount of energy, but it was in its nature that it could be minimized, maximized, deployed again and again. Subsequent development of the technique concentrated on reducing the energy load, of making the defence system a more practical device. Professor Rietveld once optimistically described the potential for an ideative future world in which every city, every scientific installation, every home, perhaps even every individual person, might one day be permanently protected from physical assault by a localized field of adjacency.

Drawing on the lessons of history, in particular the experiences of their forebears who had worked on the Manhattan Project, the theoretical work which led directly to the first nuclear weapons, Rietveld and his colleagues produced an extensive and formal rationale in defence of their theoretical work. The Perturbative Adjacent Field had no possible application as an aggressive weapon, they explained in their apologia. Its function was wholly peaceful. It could not destabilize the world, or in any way affect the balance of power between east and west, south and north. Ideologies, economic systems, religious beliefs, political movements, would remain intact because they were immune from its effect. Adjacency could not kill, could not poison, would not pollute, did not spill radioactive waste, could not become corrupted by falling into the wrong hands.

It was what followed that sent Professor Rietveld into his self-imposed exile from the world. Within two years the first test of an adjacency weapon took place in the Gobi Desert – naturally, it was 'under the strictest of scientific and moral controls'. The use of the word annihilation was picked up by a journalist from a scientific paper, and thence into popular understanding. Proliferation followed, as was inevitable, as Rietveld and the others had feared and tried to prevent, and soon every major or expansionist power had one form or another of the device. No one threatened to use it – it was simply enough to possess the capability. There was no talk any more of its role as a passively reactant defence.

I had heard that Professor Rietveld was not well, that he had been diagnosed with some unspecified but degenerative condition, and that he was now eighty-two. I tried a long shot, made contact, asked for my interview, and that was how it began.

2

In the event I never wrote or published the interview based on our meeting. I had proposed it for my own reasons: I was working on the Society page for the newspaper, and felt I was in a journalistic dead end. My editor agreed that I could try writing serious profiles of famous or celebrated personalities in the arts or sciences.

Professor Rietveld was my first project: I heard a mention of his work on adjacency defence on a late-night television programme, and I made contact with him the next day after a lead from a friendly official at the Foreign Office. I knew little about Rietveld, I had no background in physics, certainly had no grasp at all of quantum field theory, and was as ill-prepared for a serious interview as ever I had been. I spent the weekend browsing through the newspaper's database, but without learning much about him in any depth, or anything closely relevant to his work.

His early life was in the Netherlands, then latterly in Germany, the USA and the UK – all this was adequately covered but it had little directly to do with the discoveries of his later career. There was extensive reporting of his Nobel prize and his speech, and the Science & Technology page of the newspaper ran a long and detailed essay by an outside contributor, an academic at Cambridge University. This was an account of the theoretical basis of parity-symmetry, weak interactions and particles with significant masses. After his outburst against the President of the USA at a White House dinner in his honour, and his subsequent disappearance from public life, Professor Rietveld became a different kind of celebrity: an exile from a body of thought, a political protester, a scientist who was trying to repudiate his own discoveries, someone who shunned not only publicity but contact with other researchers in his field. As often happens with people in public life, after intense initial media curiosity, interest about his possible whereabouts or activities was almost non-existent.

I don't know what I expected to find on arrival: maybe a physically handicapped old man struggling against cancer. Or an embittered reject from the body scientific. Or perhaps even a senile, shrunken figure, lost in disconcerting mental fragments of despair, anger and misremembered details.

In person he looked many years younger than his actual age. He walked with a slight limp, blaming osteoarthritis. He spoke excellent, almost unaccented English, but many of the books on his shelves were in Dutch or German. He spoke in a wry, serious voice, and made no jokes or self-effacing remarks. He told me he had a housekeeper, whom I did not meet as it was her day off. A nurse visited him once a week and collected his prescription medication for him. He showed me his garden, which he said he felt obliged to keep tidy, and he showed me round his house, which he said he loved and felt no such obligation to tidiness – it was in fact not at all a cluttered or unclean house, but had the cosy feel of a place well lived in. He said he knew none of his neighbours by name, but always greeted them in a friendly way. He told me his wife was dead and that they had had one daughter, but she too had died a few years before.

He was neither sad, bitter, secretive nor particularly outgoing. He answered my questions with apparent truth and sincerity, but because the questions I was asking were general in nature, so too were his replies.

Eventually he asked me if I understood quantum theory, or quantified field theory. I told him I did not and he looked relieved. He said he was tired of trying to explain it to non-physicists. Then he asked me why I had approached him for the interview. By this time I felt there was nothing to lose by honesty, so I told him I was looking for a better position on the newspaper I worked for. He told me that if in fact I had turned up at his house armed with detailed questions about bosons, gravitons or superstrings, he would not have had much to say because he was now many years behind and would not have wanted to risk being quoted in the scientific press, revealing how out of date he had become on quantum theory.

We were interrupted by the arrival of the photographer, who had driven down from London. He was exactly on time, which surprised me, as photographers normally turned up either late or early at interviews like this. He was someone I had not worked with before, a young man who spoke with an American accent, apparently on his first freelance commission for the newspaper. He proved to be a careful and imaginative worker. With the professor's permission he went through the various rooms in the house on his own, then walked slowly around the garden, seeking angles or positions from which to take his pictures.

When he was ready he led Professor Rietveld into his garden. The professor paused only to pick up a pink-and-amber coloured conch shell I had noticed earlier, sitting on a shelf near the window. He nodded to me with a faint smile as he followed the photographer into the garden, but gave no hint about what was amusing him. I was left alone in the large kitchen-diner. This was where the professor told me he took all his meals: the sink was piled up with unwashed dishes, but otherwise it was a clean, comfortable room with a view down the garden.

I watched the young man working with his subject, asking him to stand in the shade beneath a large tree, to walk past the beds of roses, to sit in the rustic seat on the side of the slightly overgrown lawn. It was high summer: flowers were everywhere, and honey bees were hovering around the dog roses and buddleia that were growing beside the small patio.

The professor looked relaxed and cooperative, and as I watched him chatting to the photographer I began to think that I might after all be able to write an intriguing or interesting portrait of the man, even if I understood little about his work. It was a human story, perhaps: one of the world's great scientists, living out his years in the green Sussex countryside, feeling behind the times he had help explicate, beyond all ambition or regret or pride.

The two men were speaking intently to each other, but from where I was standing at the window I could not hear a word. The professor pointed up towards the sky – the American guy looked where he was indicating. Then the professor walked to the side of the garden, where he had laid the conch shell on the edge of the lawn. He moved to the centre of the grass, holding the large shell in one hand. He posed like that: both hands extended, the left empty, the right balancing the beautiful shell with its subtle colours and the fascinating spiral construction.

The photographer took many shots of him: from different angles, close up, and from as far across the garden as he could back away to. He finished with a series of shots from middle range, presumably capturing full-length images.

Finally, the young American appeared to be satisfied he had enough shots. Both men shook hands amiably. They walked back towards the house, the professor carrying his shell in one hand. The photographer halted and raised his camera to take a picture of something above his head. The professor immediately restrained him, swiftly pulling down the other man's arms to prevent any pictures being taken.

They entered the kitchen together, apparently still cordial, and the professor put the conch shell back on the shelf.

I said to the photographer, 'Do you have everything you need?'

'Yes.' He fished into an inner pocket then handed me his card. I glanced at it, because I liked the way he worked and I wanted to remember his name if future work opportunities arose. He was called Tibor Tarent, a freelance with membership of a couple of professional organizations, an address and contact details in London. 'I'll see you at the newspaper office tomorrow,' he said. 'I'll bring some prints in, and we can have a look at them.'

All this was the sort of practical conversation I usually had with photographers sent to work with me on an assignment. The next day's meeting would probably include the pictures editor as well as my boss.

But then Tibor Tarent said, 'Would you help me get my stuff

back in the car?' He led me outside – his car was parked opposite the house. As soon as we were away from the house he said, 'That is one of the most amazing men I have ever met. I'll never forget what happened. Did you see what he was doing while I was taking pictures of him?'

'I was in the kitchen – I couldn't see too well.'

'It's impossible to describe. I'll show you the photos tomorrow. He was like a magician – he could make that big shell appear and disappear. I couldn't see how he was doing it.'

'I was watching from the window, but there was a trellis in the way. He didn't seem to be moving about.'

'That was it. He didn't move a muscle, but something weird was happening. I took pictures of it all. You'll see tomorrow.'

While we were speaking he had opened the car and placed his camera equipment carefully inside. Then we shook hands, he climbed into the car and drove away.

I returned to the house.

The professor was sitting at his scrubbed pine table in the kitchen-diner, resting his head on his hands. He looked up, and his eyes looked redder than they had been before, his complexion more sallow.

He said, 'I'm afraid that young man has tired me out. That's not a criticism of him – he has a job to do, but sometimes it is a real effort to keep up an appearance of normality.'

'Professor Rietveld, just before the photographer arrived you were talking about physics.'

'Was I really? I didn't think you would be interested.'

'I said I didn't understand quantum physics, but that doesn't mean I'm not interested in what your work meant to you.'

'My work was my life.'

'That's what I thought.'

'And in some ways my life ended after I was given that prize, because after that it was impossible to keep Perturbative Adjacency secret. Of course the media was interested in what I was doing, but so too were my colleagues and rivals. We were forced to declare our hand long before we were ready. What we had discovered was more shocking, more devastating in theory than splitting the

168

atom. What we wanted to do before we announced our findings was either to find some way of controlling it, putting it to passive use only, or, much more difficult, we wanted to try and close the Pandora's box.'

'I always thought adjacency could only be used passively.'

'That is what we said then. Of course, we should have known, and we did know, that once our papers were open to review it was only a matter of time before some other group discovered the whole truth.'

'I understood that the balance of power had not destabilized.'

'The major powers, yes. How we trust them! Look, I must show you what I tried to show that young man with the camera. Please, come into the garden with me.'

I helped him out of his chair. He picked up a small scrap of card that was lying next to some books on a shelf, then gave me his arm so I could support him. We walked together into the sun-drenched garden.

'You obviously now realize what happened to me a few years ago when I was in Strasbourg. We were naïve, all of us but especially me – we thought we were making a breakthrough into something that would neutralize weapons. It would always be safe to use, non-aggressive in nature, harmless because it would remove harm. But what we all feared soon came to pass: minds other than ours worked out how to make quantum adjacency into a weapon of war. It's now too late to regret that. We can't change history. What we most dreaded, though, was that sooner or later the process would become devolved, if you see what I mean. Small groups, terrorists, insurgents, private militias, might be able to get hold of smaller, more portable forms of adjacency generator. With people like that, even the false responsibility of the major powers would be gone.'

'I understand,' I said.

'I want you to look at what I have had built above this garden.'

He pointed upwards. I saw now that a small metal contrivance, not in any way streamlined or given the sheen of professional manufacture, hung directly above the lawn. It was held up by three strong wires, which ran from narrow metal poles, two placed in the far corners of the garden, and the third close to the house.

The object suspended at the centre had various metal and plastic components, but the centrepiece was a dull grey sphere, rather like the side of an old aluminium kettle. It was about half a metre in diameter.

'Now let me ask you if you know what a tetrahedron is?'

I said, 'It's a geometric form of some kind, isn't it?'

He brandished the piece of card he had picked up. It was in the shape of a parallelogram, and had three creases scored though it. It had obviously been folded and unfolded many times.

'This is called a net,' he said, meaning the card. He quickly folded it to form a solid triangle. 'You see, a tetrahedron is a triangular shape with four sides and four vertices. It is physically very stable, very strong – it always takes the same form, no matter which side is down. This is similar to what some physicists call an interaction, in this case a strong interaction. We can only break it down by a process of theoretical annihilation, using what we call a bosonic field annihilation operator. Am I explaining too much?'

I was scribbling as much as I could into my notebook, from which I am now transcribing what the professor told me that summer's day, but in fact he was, as he said, explaining too much and too quickly.

'This card model is just a symbol, a way to explain,' he said. He unfolded it and slipped it into his pocket. 'The quantum adjacency we created can be considered as a tetrahedron of particles.' He pointed up to the globe above our heads. 'Think of that as the apex, the strong constant point. Beneath it is a virtual tetrahedron, so where we are standing is in the centre of a triangle imprinted on the ground.'

I could not help glancing down. Beneath me was a lawn in need of mowing.

Professor Rietveld said, 'I need you to understand what I say, because I want you to write about it in your article. What you see here is not a weapon. This is an experimental piece, one I adjust and calibrate for scientific purposes. But a portable adjacency weapon, much cruder than anything ever worked on in laboratory conditions, operates from above, just as this experimental model does. It has to be directly above whatever the target is. In practice, in anger, it may be dropped from a plane, fired from a mortar or a large gun, fired in a missile. It may even be thrown from a high building. In fact, one already has been used in that way: the disaster in Godhra two years ago – you will remember that?'

I did: a mysterious explosion had destroyed a part of that Indian city. The attack had eventually been blamed on Islamic separatists, but there was no certainty about that and many of the details about what really happened were still obscure.

'When adjacency is used as a weapon it creates a tetrahedron of quantum annihilation: a three-sided pyramid of equilateral triangles, with a fourth triangle as its base. Anything beneath it, anything within that triangle, is vulnerable.' He was speaking breathlessly, and he was resting his hand on my arm for support. 'That is all, Mrs Flockhart. The technology has fallen into the wrong hands, and if it is ever used it will become a most terrible threat to peace. I am largely responsible for it.'

3

That night, when I was at home with my family, the children in bed, my husband working in his study on the top floor of the house, the news of Thijs Rietveld's death was announced on television news. At first there was no information about the cause of his death, and in the shock of my sudden grief I assumed that the life of the man with whom I had spent much of the day had simply come to a natural end. He had certainly looked tired at the end of my interview. The old man I said farewell to as I left his house barely resembled the sprightly and energetic octogenarian who had greeted me on arrival.

When I went into the newspaper office the next morning the truth was coming in from the police in East Sussex. Professor Rietveld had injected himself with a huge overdose of a prescribed painkiller, then drunk at least one glass of scotch whisky. His body had been found in his garden, lying in the centre of the lawn.

The house and garden were cordoned off, apparently by the

police, although confidential sources in the newspaper office suggested that security forces had actually ordered the closure of his house.

In the afternoon, Tibor Tarent, the young American photographer, came into the office as planned. He had of course heard the news. He brought with him several large prints of the photographs he had taken the day before.

All my plans to write a profile of the professor were put on hold, permanently as it turned out. The paper ran a long obituary written by one of his former colleagues, published several private tributes from friends and other colleagues, and within a few days the death of one of the greatest physicists of our era had passed into history.

But on that awful day of grief, Tibor Tarent gave me a large photographic print, based on shots he had taken during the last afternoon of Thijs Rietveld's life. It consisted of four separate frames, placed in a rectangle together.

He said, 'You were there, Jane. You saw me taking these photographs. You could see what he and I were doing from where you were standing, couldn't you?'

'I could.'

'And you saw him take that conch, hold it out in his right hand, and stand calmly there on the lawn while I took these shots?'

'That's right.'

We were both staring at the print as it lay on my desk.

'He never put down the conch? You agree?'

'Yes.'

'Did you see him pass it from hand to hand?'

'No.'

'I took these frames one after the other, just a few seconds apart. What the hell happened?'

I said I didn't know. We talked about it for a while, but afterwards Tarent and I went downstairs to a local bar and split a bottle of red wine between us. We drank to the memory of the intriguing old man we had met so briefly. We did not stay long – Tibor had another assignment to go to, and I had work to do back in the office.

I still have the print of the photographs he took that day, of

Professor Rietveld standing in the centre of his lawn, holding the beautiful conch. I have the print framed behind glass, and it hangs on the wall above my desk. I am dimly visible in all four of the separate photographs: slightly out of focus beyond the clump of bee-heavy buddleia, but clearly standing inside the house, watching from the window that overlooked the lawn.

The four shots form a rectangle. In the frame at the top left, he is holding the pink-and-amber shell in his right hand. In the picture next to it, he is standing in an almost identical pose, but now the conch has moved to his left hand. Below the first frame, Professor Rietveld is shown holding two identical conch shells, one in each outstretched hand. In the fourth picture, both his hands are empty.

Only in the fourth picture is the old man smiling at the camera.

PART 5

Tealby Moor

1

THE INSTRUMENT BASHER

For Mike Torrance, Aircraftman First Class, known to the others in his crew as 'Floody' Torrance, the sight of a Lancaster flying low in daylight was always a moment of beauty. He and the other members of the ground crew had little time for looking around, but whenever a Lanc landed they almost always raised their heads from what they were doing. The engines would be heard before the plane itself came into sight, which would then pass low in the near distance across the Lincolnshire farmland. When it turned in for its approach to the airfield, the dark green and brown upper camouflage was briefly visible as it banked. As it headed down towards the runway, nose raised slightly for the landing, the aircraft appeared all black, painted to blend with the night sky in which it flew. At night over Germany it would become invisible, or at least difficult to see, from below.

The beauty of the machine lay in its rough, purposeful and utilitarian shape. Every part of a heavy bomber was there to function as it should, without streamlining or any other flourishes of style. The gun turrets, in the nose and between the tail fins and in the upper part of the main fuselage, were made of bulbous perspex, there were observation bubbles at the sides of the cockpit and long bombing doors in the base, the engines were huge Merlins, their cowlings painted as black as the rest of the aircraft, the wings, with a span of more than a hundred feet were thick and round-tipped, holding tanks that would carry enough fuel for up to twelve hours at cruising speed.

Inside there were no comforts for the aircrew, nor for Mike

Torrance and the others when they went aboard to service the plane. The seats were barely padded, the interior was only intermittently heated, the long fuselage was narrow and jammed with equipment. Jagged edges and unshielded metal corners protruded from several places. The aircrew in their bulky flying suits, worn over layer after layer of woollen clothing, could barely move about inside. Things were much worse if they had to put on their parachutes. The mental image of the desperate scramble for the escape hatch inside a stricken Lanc tumbling towards the ground, perhaps engulfed in flames, was something on which none of the ground crew could dwell.

There was no sound insulation, so the roar of the unsilenced Merlins was constant and deafening. In flight, thin cold air jetted in through a dozen cracks and apertures. The airframe itself was barbed on the outside with sensors, aerials, ports, access hatches. There was nothing about a Lancaster that did not have to be there, and there was no attempt to conceal what did.

It was nonetheless a thing of beauty for Torrance, because he considered it the best plane in the world to make the long flight across the North Sea, and then to bomb the German cities to hell. It was winter in early 1943. That was what they had to do, then.

2

148 Squadron, Bomber Command No. 5 Group, based at RAF Tealby Moor, was still new to Lancs, having been operational with the two-engined, obsolescent Wellingtons until just before Christmas. Mike Torrance had joined the squadron at about the same time, after training on the Lancaster instrumentation. A few operations had already been launched: they were known as 'gardening', mine-laying in the Danish narrows against the movements of the German U-boats into and out of the Baltic. It was hazardous work – 148 Squadron had already lost two of their Lancasters and their aircrews.

The new and replacement Lancasters came in from the factories, ferried by the pilots of the ATA, the Air Transport Auxiliary. They arrived one by one, two or three aircraft a week. Few of the ground crews had ever been close to a Lancaster before the first ones were delivered, although all were trained in their particular area of speciality.

Mike Torrance was an instrument mechanic, invariably known to the other aircraftmen as an instrument basher. His domain was the Lancasters' oxygen supply, bomb sight, gun sights, the DR compass, altimeter, artificial horizon – the instruments that were used to operate any part of the machine that was not the main airframe, engines or undercarriage. There were other teams for those. They were called the airframe bods, the engine wallahs. And the armourers who loaded the bombs and ammunition. The bowser operators, the refuellers. Maintenance was constant as soon as the aircraft arrived – repairs were necessary almost from the moment the planes started ops.

Before he was posted to Bomber Command, Torrance had been attached to Coastal Command, servicing the instruments on seaplanes. Seasickness, and tools dropped irrecoverably into the sea, were the daily hazards of his life. After retraining for the Lanc he was relieved to be transferred to a land-based squadron.

In charge of the Instrument Section of the squadron was Flight-Sergeant Jack Winslow, an RAF regular who had joined up in 1935, and who seemed to the new recruits almost omniscient about the aircraft they serviced. Two corporals, 'Steve' Stevenson and Al Harrison, worked under him. They knew what they were doing but the rest of the erks were a motley crowd, doing their bit in the air war, secretly never as confident of their skills as they tried to make out.

Mike Torrance, who felt himself typical of the young crewmen around him, had joined the RAF because he wanted to fly. He was a gangly six foot three, so he discovered he was too tall to fit usefully into any operational aircraft. He never proceeded beyond the first medical for the aircrew volunteers, for that reason. In civilian life he had been training as an architect after leaving school, but at eighteen he was already restless. He was good at drawing, but he loved books and music, had tried writing stories and poems. When the architecture firm moved over to war work he was out of a job, and he went immediately to join up. Months later he was a trained mechanic.

The first Lanc that arrived at Tealby Moor was for one of the squadron's most experienced pilots, Squadron Leader 'JL' Sawyer and his crew. The captain was already the veteran of one completed tour of operations and was a third of the way through a second. He and his crew took the new plane up for a flight test the day it arrived, and afterwards Torrance and many of the others watched with ill-concealed envy as the ground crew assigned to that flight went to work, checking it out after it landed.

3

Within two weeks of the first Lancaster delivery, 148 Squadron was fully equipped and after a few days of gunnery testing, familiarization flights and general preparations it became operational. The war was showing no sign of coming to an end. Most of the ground fighting was in Russia, following the end of the siege of Stalingrad. Stalin was demanding that Britain and the USA should open a second front to relieve the pressure on the Soviet Union, but few people thought that was possible. The best the Allies could come up with was an unrelenting bombing campaign against the German homeland. The American Eighth Air Force was now based in Britain and had started daylight raids, but the Yanks were suffering terrible losses of aircraft and men.

The night campaign was what 148 Squadron was drawn into. In the annals of the RAF the period is known as the Battle of the Ruhr: a series of heavy raids on the complex of industrial cities in the north-west of Germany. Two or three times a week, from the middle of March of that year, the squadron's Lancasters flew off into the ever-shortening nights to join the bomber stream heading out across the North Sea. Naturally, the squadron began to sustain serious damage to the aircraft and many actual losses.

The Lancaster captained by Flight Lieutenant Andy Everett was lost at the end of March. This was 'E Easy', the aircraft Torrance worked on every day. Everett and his crew disappeared over Duisburg, presumed shot down. It was only several weeks later that the people at Tealby Moor learnt that of the crew of seven aboard Everett's plane, all but one had survived: the dorsal gunner, a Canadian called Ken Accent, was trapped inside the burning plane as it crashed. The rest of the crew managed to parachute to the ground and were taken prisoner. This welcome news was still unknown to Torrance and the others three days later, when in a grim mood they took delivery of the replacement Lanc. The call sign on this was 'D Digger'.

D Digger was delivered in the late afternoon, so it was taxied to dispersal and the ground crew did not start checking it over until the following morning. It was a grey, rainy day, the few trees on the perimeter of the airfield bending under a stiff wind from the North Sea, not far away to the east. Mike Torrance's D.I. – Daily Inspection – was the first he had carried out without supervision. There were already several other erks at work. Because the aircraft were delivered by civilian pilots none of the gun turrets was armed, so one of the first jobs for the armourers was to fit and install the machine guns. It was noisy work, and with the perspex cowls thrown open the interior of the plane was especially cold and draughty.

Torrance made his way to the cockpit, because the delivery pilot had reported that the altimeter was not working properly. Warned in advance of this, he had obtained a replacement altimeter from the stores. Removing the faulty instrument and fitting and connecting the replacement was a relatively straightforward job. The only difficulty was the usual one: the cramped space behind the instrument panel, which meant he had to lie down and reach awkwardly upwards behind the panel. Torrance's fingers and knuckles permanently bore grazes from these tricky jobs.

With this completed, he looked again at the pilot's sign-off to check nothing else had been reported. He stayed where he was on the floor, the rudder pedals pressing against his back. Getting in and out of this position was clumsy and sometimes painful, and he did not want to do it more often than necessary. However, there was just the one line: 'Altmeter u/s.'

The handwriting was stiff and rounded, rather like a child's, but the spelling mistake was not unusual. These reports were often filled in hastily by the pilots, or while still taxiing.

Torrance was levering himself up from the prone position, so that he could move on to the rest of the D.I., when he noticed something colourful and flat had become wedged between the base of the pilot's seat and the floor. He reached over, jiggled it free, and stood up.

It was a wallet of some kind, but it was made of stiff fabric rather than leather. He could tell it contained papers that crackled when he pressed the sides. There were also a few coins somewhere inside. The wallet was sealed in a way he had never seen before: two leather strings or cords were wrapped several times around the wallet and tied together in a slip-knot. It was obviously a personal possession, probably highly valued by whoever owned it – standing there in the cold cockpit with it in his hand, Torrance felt as guilty as if he had stolen it.

Torrance well knew the regulations: any personal possession found in an aircraft had to be reported immediately. He looked around for the duty sergeant, but he was nowhere to be seen. Everyone else in and around the aircraft was working hard, pre-occupied with what they were doing.

Intending to hand it in as soon as he came off duty he slipped it into his breast pocket, buttoned it down, then continued with the D.I.

He had soon forgotten about it and it remained hidden in his pocket until the evening. He was about to walk over to the canteen block for supper, but as soon as he made the discovery he let the other lads go on ahead. When he was alone in the hut he took it from his pocket and looked at it properly for the first time.

The wallet, or purse, or whatever it was he had found, shone with colours: bright yellow and orange circles, green stripes woven through and round them, a brilliant red piping stitched along the sides. There was something about the colours that induced in him a heavy nostalgic pang for his past life, not so long ago but feel-ing unreachably distant: long days of childhood, toys he had once had, memories of a garden full of flowers, living at home with his parents and his little sister. He was now in a world where colours were drab or virtually non-existent. Wartime Britain was a country of unlit streets, blacked-out windows, unilluminated signs. On the base he and the other crew wore faded blue fatigues and jackets, beige or grey shirts, grey pullovers, navy forage caps. The planes were black or dark brown. The airfield was grassy but also covered in muddy patches and streaks. The concrete runways were long dull strips of concrete. The skies seemed permanently full of heavy clouds. The place where he lived and slept was a Nissen hut of unpainted metal, the hangars were darkly camouflaged, the main squadron buildings were plain brick and also painted with green-and-brown camouflage.

A sense of sharp and unexpected melancholy swept over him as he sat on the side of his bunk, staring at the coloured purse. It was a realization of the unrecoverable loss of something abstract and barely remembered, a feeling of how bad things had become for him, for everyone in the country, and an unwelcome reminder that the grim daily drabness of war was something he would have to bear and try to survive.

For a few moments Mike Torrance was stalled by these feel-ings. He was still only twenty-one years old – the life he had been hoping to find was slipping away somewhere. He turned the firm, slightly cushioned object around in his fingers, feeling once again the stiffness of the paper that was inside and the round weight of the coins. He drew on one of the laces, unwound them both and the wallet gaped open. A part of him was appalled by what he was doing: intruding, interfering with something private, but he thought that if he could find out who the thing belonged to then he could hand it back without going through the bull of RAF regulations.

He reached in with two fingers, deliberately trying not to look too closely at what was inside. He touched two small, stiff pieces of card, which felt as if they might be photographs: he glanced in, saw a blur of black and white, a smooth coating, looked no more. Beneath those were the coins: there were about five but he could not tell if they amounted to much. It was unlikely. No one in the forces ever had much money.

The rest of the purse's contents were pieces of paper or light card, some of them folded. He shrank from prying any further but he still needed to find out, if he could, the owner's name.

Then he noticed that on one side of the main part of the wallet there was a small compartment closed with a zip. Inside was a piece of white card. He guessed it was a service card or a pay chit, but this was different. On the card was an insignia in dark blue ink, made up of two stylized wings. They were similar to, but certainly not the same as, those worn on their chests by serving pilots on the squadron. Between the two wings, circled, were the letters ATA, the two As nestling beneath the top stroke of the T.

He recognized the insignia at once: the initials stood for Air Transport Auxiliary, the civilian organization of pilots which ferried aircraft from the factories to operational bases. Some of the other fitters said the initials stood for 'Ancient and Tattered Airmen', because many of the pilots were veterans of the 1914–18 war and several of them were handicapped in some way. Torrance had heard stories about planes being flown in by pilots with a missing limb or with an eye gone. Some of the pilots were rumoured to be women. Many of the volunteers had escaped to Britain when the war started and barely spoke English.

They had a mixed reputation amongst the operational pilots, who were instinctively sceptical about civilians getting their hands on warplanes. However, the four-engined Lancasters, which normally carried a crew of seven men, were flown single-handed by ATA pilots, and without the aid of radio or maps. That earned them the respect of other pilots, no matter what their background. The ground crews rarely had any contact with the ATA. On arrival the planes were always taxied to a special dispersal point on the far side of the airfield, and then the pilot presumably departed the base by some other means. The new aircraft were later hauled over to the flight stands by tractor.

Beneath the insignia was a name, *Second Officer K. Roszca, ATA*, and the address of the ATA headquarters in London. At the bottom was a telephone number, on the Hamble exchange. The handwriting was the same as Torrance had seen on the sign-off form: clear, round, almost childish letters.

He stopped thinking, stopped wondering what to do. He decided to act immediately. He took one of the bicycles that was leaning against the wall outside and pedalled quickly across to the NAAFI hut, in the admin area of the airfield. There was a public call-box outside the main door.

Darkness had fallen and it was raining hard – cold drops stung Torrance's eyes, and wetted and chilled his hands and face.

He had never made a long-distance call before and asked the operator what he should do. Presumably used to the young airmen posted to this area, she explained how much it would cost and warned him to have the right change ready. She told him he would not be able to speak for longer than three minutes unless he had more money ready.

Torrance put down the telephone. He went into the building and braced himself with a half-pint of beer from the bar inside the NAAFI, partly to work up some Dutch courage, but also because he needed extra coins. He paid for the drink with the only ten-shilling note he had, which he had been saving for his next period of leave, then carefully counted some of the change into the amount he would need. It was going to cost him a big chunk of the weekly pay the RAF gave him.

4

'When the number you are calling replies, press button A to be heard.' Torrance muttered a thank-you to the operator. He could already hear the phone ringing at the other end. Then it clicked, and a woman's voice said, 'Hello?'

He pressed the button and heard the coins clatter down into the box.

'Hello!' he said, a bit too loudly.

'Hamble 423. Who are you calling?'

'I want to speak to Second Officer Roszca,' he said, guessing at the pronunciation. 'K. Roszca. It's urgent.'

'Who are you, and what is it you want?' She had an accent of some kind, pronouncing 'what' and 'want' with a long *a*.

'This is Mike Torr – I mean, I am Aircraftman Mike Torrance, attached to 148 Squadron, RAF Tealby Moor. I need to speak to Mr Roszca urgently.'

'You can tell me,' she said. 'What is it?'

'Um – Mr Roszca left a wallet inside a Lancaster that was delivered to our airfield. I have found—'

'You have my purse?' There was a silence he did not know how to fill. Then she said with her voice rising, 'My God! You *found* it?'

'It belongs to a pilot,' he said, confused in his shyness by her response. 'An ATA pilot. The wallet is safe. I'm looking after it.'

'I must have it back! I have been searching everywhere for it! Who are you?'

'I told you my name.'

'Say it again. You are in the RAF?'

Her insistent voice, her strange accent – it all added to his confusion. The call was not going as he expected. He repeated his name, then the squadron and airfield. He had no idea how much of his time he had already used, but three minutes felt frighteningly brief. He wished now that he had found the duty sergeant and handed the wallet in, but it was already too late for that.

'Is Mr Roszca there, and please may I speak to him?' he said, knowing he was sounding stupid, but the call was completely disorienting him. The fingers of his free hand were clenched immovably into a fist.

'I am Roszca.' She pronounced the name *rozh-ska*. 'It is my purse you have.'

'You were the pilot?'

'Yes. I must get my purse back as soon as possible. How can I find you?'

'I thought I could post it to you if I had an address, or if I knew the airfield where you are based—'

'No, it might be lost. Or someone would steal it. I cannot risk that. Which airfield do you say you are at?'

'Tealby Moor. In Lincolnshire.'

'I was there. Yesterday. I flew a Lancaster to Tealby.'

'That's right,' he said. 'I found the wallet in the cockpit.'

'Thank you, thank you! Oh my God, I cannot thank you enough!' He heard her draw a deep intake of breath. 'I'll come to Tealby, soon. How will we meet?'

'I work on "A" flight. The instrument section.'

'You are not a pilot?'

'No, I'm a fitter.'

Three interruptive pips sounded, over her voice and his. The operator came on: 'Your time is up, caller. Do you wish to insert more money?'

'No!' he said loudly. He shouted to the woman called Roszca, 'I'll watch out for you!', but only silence followed.

He put down the receiver. He was in the gloomy semi-darkness of the telephone box, while the rain fell unrelentingly on the concrete path outside. Another erk was standing a short distance away, waiting for the call box to come free and sheltering under the guttering of the building. Telephone numbers were scratched or written on the metal pane next to the telephone, where instructions about emergency calls were printed. The kiosk smelled of old tobacco smoke, unwashed clothes and something else – the vague but familiar background smell of a wartime RAF base. He could hear the sound of voices inside the NAAFI, coming through an efficiently blacked-out window. He stood there for a few more moments, feeling the chill, holding the slim purse in his hand.

'Hurry up, mate!' said the man waiting outside.

Torrance tried to look apologetic as he dodged out of the telephone box into the rain. He hurried along the short path beside the building. He went inside, succumbed to the noise of voices and the music from the piano. As he passed through the door he glanced once more at the wallet tucked into his breast pocket, briefly rejoicing again at the glimpse of its glowing colours. He was giddy with excitement.

Four nights later 148 Squadron lost two more Lancasters while on a raid over the German town of Essen. Both were known to be destroyed because other aircraft reported seeing them crash. They were crewed by men Torrance had often seen around the base, and he knew one or two of them by their first names. He grieved silently with everyone else, continued with his work.

A week after that a German Junkers 88, a night intruder, shot down 'H Henry', the Lancaster of Pilot Officer Will Seward and his crew as it was returning to Tealby Moor from a 'gardening' raid, mine-laying in the Baltic narrows. The Lanc was on its final approach to the main runway, no more than half a minute before touching down, when the night fighter opened fire. Witnesses said that although the remaining fuel in the plane was ignited, the pilot managed to keep the plane level and above the runway. An explosion immediately followed. The crippled plane overshot the runway and crashed down on the farmland beneath the ridge. All seven men on board were killed.

The next morning, Torrance volunteered to join a work party to visit the wreck and try to recover personal items belonging to the crew. By the time they arrived the fires had been put out and the bodies removed, but the remains of the broken aircraft were heaped more or less where it had landed. One of the wings had broken on impact, and was folded over and across the crushed fuselage. The tailplane had also broken off, and had swung around. The effect, seen from above as they were driven down the ridge in the squadron van, was that the stricken aircraft had ended up in the centre of the field in an almost perfect triangle of blackened wreckage. The six men of the work party completed their grisly job in less than an hour, and returned to their normal duties.

Three nights later, yet another Lancaster was lost, this one on a raid against Krefeld, in the Ruhr.

Nothing could numb the upset feelings of the people who worked in the squadron, who had to cope with these regular shocks, but the pressure of work meant that there was little time to reflect. Death became a part of normal life. Mike Torrance was no different, feeling the loss of each man as an acute tragedy, but since the phone call he could not help but think beyond the individual disasters. Every Lancaster lost meant that another would have to replace it, which in turn meant that he might be able to meet the owner of the lost wallet.

In due course the lost aircraft were replaced. However, when the new Lancs landed, presumably flown in by members of the ATA, they were immediately taxied away to the usual distant dispersal. No contact was made. Torrance still had the wallet, concealed as securely as possible whenever he was in the hut, where privacy was almost non-existent. When he was moving about the base, or at work, he carried it inside the breast pocket of his tunic, buttoned tightly.

His turn came round for a week's leave, so he headed home to his parents' house in Hastings, on the coast of East Sussex. The visit reminded him that this war was not confined to actual combatants: the town was a regular victim of hit-and-run air raids from Luftwaffe bases across the English Channel in northern France, and his parents were at real risk. Two houses in their street had already been bombed out, no more than a hundred yards from where they lived. His father was away from home several nights of the week as he was having to work shifts at a factory which built engines for patrol boats. One morning his mother told him how frightened and lonely she felt whenever his father was away. Ellie, his sister, had been evacuated with her school to Wiltshire, but she was in her final term and would soon be returning home. His mother was torn between wanting Ellie to stay away in safety and having her back.

The days at home gave him a period of calm. He worked in his parents' garden, cutting back the weeds so the flowers could bloom. As a child he had spent many happy hours playing in the garden. The work gave him time in which to think about what he should do about the wallet. He knew he had not acted sensibly, but he had meant well. He also knew the woman who owned the wallet was anxious to have it returned. It was a huge dilemma for him, but by the end of his week's leave he had decided the best thing to do was to hand it in.

He set off on the slow journey back to the base in Lincolnshire. He travelled all day across England, struggling with his heavy kit, invariably having to take slow-moving trains that halted at every station. He was crammed into overcrowded compartments, found little to eat or drink on the way except whatever could be grabbed at brief station stops. As usual after a period of leave he made it back to the base with aching shoulders and arms, and feeling hungry, parched and footsore.

This time, though, as he walked into the smoke-filled hut a ragged cheer went up.

'Here he is!'

'C'mon, basher!'

'Copped it this time, Floody!'

'What's up?' he said guardedly when the hubbub died down, knowing all too well how easy it was to transgress some simple RAF regulation while away from the base.

'Chiefy was looking for you just now,' said Jake, the chap who slept in the bunk above his. Chiefy was Flight Sergeant Winslow, who ran the Instruments Section. He never came looking for any of the erks unless it meant trouble.

'Did he say what it was?'

'You must report to him before eight o'clock, and if you're not back by then, first thing in the morning.'

It was just after half-past seven. Torrance threw his kit on his bunk, then borrowed one of the bikes and rode at high speed across to the Sergeants' Mess. Chief Winslow was playing darts and made him wait until his game was finished. He won, which briefly seemed to Torrance to be a good thing.

'Aircraftman Torrance,' he said. 'You are relieved of duties tomorrow until eighteen hundred hours.'

'What have I done, Sarge?'

'Nothing I know of. You're to report to Dispersal 11 before nine hundred hours tomorrow. Know where that is?'

'Yes, Sarge.' In fact he did not, but was not about to reveal that. He could ask one of the others or find his way somehow. 'Can you tell me what it's about, Chief?'

'Search me. Orders from Group. Passed on by the Station

Commander. Do what you're told, then back to normal duties after that. Got it?'

'Yes, Sarge.'

'Go on – get on with it.'

Torrance went to the canteen to try to scrounge a late meal before heading back to the hut.

6

The morning was bright. Warm early sunshine flooded across the runways. He was already halfway across the airfield, following someone's imprecise directions, when Torrance realized that Dispersal 11 was the part of the base where the arriving ATA pilots parked the new aircraft. There was not much to see: just a couple of familiar-looking single-storey brick buildings with flat roofs, square windows, a couple of doors each. A twin-engined Avro Anson was parked on the concrete apron in front of the buildings.

He left his borrowed bicycle leaning on the wall somewhere around the back of the building, and walked out to the apron. He stood close to the Anson, professionally aware of the smells and sounds of the workhorse plane. The engines were making noises as they cooled down. The entrance to the cockpit bore many scuffs from people climbing in and out – the sun on the perspex canopy was reflected by the myriad of tiny scratches on the surface, testament to hundreds of hours of flying time. It was a bright, warm morning and the early mist had lifted. The sky was cloudless. Somewhere on the other side of the airfield he could hear the familiar sound of a Lancaster's Merlin engines being run up on test. He found it easy to imagine the scene of activity as the crews went to work on the various aircraft: the engine nacelles open, the bomb bay doors hanging down, the ladders and the trolleys and the equipment dollies scattered all about.

He noticed a car driving at a moderate speed along the perimeter road, approaching the dispersal where he was waiting. A shift in the direction of the wind made the sound of the Lanc's engines louder, purer, wafting across the flat airfield. Because he was away from his usual work area, Torrance's senses were more acute. He was aware of the smell of cut grass, and of wild flowers. There was a banked hedge behind the buildings, a haze of white and yellow blooms – this was a part of the perimeter he did not know. The sense of the open countryside out there, beyond the edge of the airfield, away from the war, hit him hard, another reminder of past years, imprecise but potent.

The car curved around and halted outside the building. A WAAF was driving. A young woman in a smart dark-blue uniform stepped out of the passenger seat at the rear. She put on a forage cap and walked towards him. The WAAF driver moved off immediately, turning the car around and back to the perimeter road, accelerating away.

He thought the young woman was about to salute him, or was expecting him to salute her, such was the ingrained ritual of RAF life, but she came to a halt a short distance away from him. Her stance was completely informal. She seemed transfixed by his appearance, staring towards him with a smile of recognition. Then she sagged expressively, bending her knees, thrusting out her arms towards him. Torrance assumed she recognized him, as if she was expecting him to know her too. She tore off her cap and threw it on the ground, then walked quickly towards him. Both her arms were raised to greet him.

But she did not embrace him. She said something aloud, a stream of foreign words. He caught only the first, or thought he did. It sounded like 'Thomas!', or perhaps 'Torrance!'

Then she was standing right before him, her hands reaching up to rest on his shoulders, beaming at him, her face raised as if for a kiss. Torrance froze with embarrassment, not resisting or backing away from her but amazed by her behaviour.

The moment died. Only a second or two passed before she lowered her hands, took a step back, turned her face away.

In English she said, 'You are Mike Torrance?'

'Yes.'

'I am Krystyna. Krystyna Roszca. I am so sorry – I am here to meet you, but the moment I saw you I thought a miracle had happened. I thought you were someone else. You look so like him—'

'I heard you say "Thomas".'

'Tomasz.' The long *o* and the soft consonants at the end gave the name a foreign sound. She said, 'It is almost the same name, I think, in Polish. I was ... surprised when I saw you. I hope you did not think that I—' She stepped back from him, leaned down to retrieve her cap from where it had landed on the grass. She brushed it with the edge of her hand. 'You see, there is someone I know, still in Poland, a good friend, a close friend. His name is Tomasz. You look so like him. It is astonishing to me! Your hair, your eyes! I could not believe it when I saw you. I am sorry – I should not say these things. You must be wondering what I was doing.' She held out her hand. 'I have come for my purse, that you telephoned me about. Do you still have it?'

'You mean the wallet? Of course.' He fumbled with the buttoned flap of his breast pocket, found the treasured, safeguarded thing, slipped it out and held it towards her. The bright colours shone in the sunlight. It was the moment of transaction he had been imagining and dreaming about for nearly five weeks, and now it was all but over.

She took it from him, held it briefly against her breast.

'Thank you again! I do not know what I would have done if it was truly lost.' She was unwinding the leather laces, her face shining with eagerness. As soon as it was open she slipped her hand inside and pulled out the two photographs he had touched with his fingertips, yet had never actually looked at.

She glanced quickly at them both, then held one of them out for him to see.

'This is Tomasz,' she said. 'You see how much alike you are? You are like brothers, like twins!'

He took the fragile square of card carefully and peered at it. The picture had apparently been cut from a larger photograph, because as well as a head-and-shoulders shot of a young man, there were partial glimpses of other men he was standing among: he was part of a sports team, or a group of friends, or perhaps a squadron like the one he was himself a part of. There was a diagonal crease across one corner. The photo was not sharply in focus but Torrance could see that the young man had an open, good-looking face, high cheekbones, a long forehead, curly hair, dark brown or black. It was difficult for him to tell if there really was a resemblance, but he appeared to be roughly the same age, seemed to be tall, and his hair was a little like Torrance's, a dark, unruly tangle.

'You see?'

'Well, yes.' He handed the photograph back to her. She glanced quickly at it again, then slipped it inside the wallet once more. 'I assume he is –?'

'He is Tomasz, my fiancé. We were planning to be married four years ago, but there were problems. I could explain if we had more time. Tomasz and I had been meeting for a long time and trying to move away from Kraków, where we both lived, and it seemed at last we would be able to, but then the Nazis – ' Suddenly she stopped. 'You do not wish to know any of this.'

'I do,' he said, because he had realized that now he had handed back her purse there was no more excuse or reason to stay there and talk. Soon she would leave. He did not want her to go. No matter what she was saying about her fiancé he wanted to be with her. He was trying to appraise her without appearing to do so, without staring obviously at her, but he found it almost impossible to take his eyes away from her. He could not think of any other young woman he had ever known who was so interesting, so astonishingly attractive. He thought her devastating in her dark-blue uniform, which looked smarter and more assertive than the standard grey-blue RAF uniform he was so familiar with. On the left side of her chest, above the pocket, the double-wing ATA pilot insignia was sewn in place.

While they had been talking the distant engines on the Lancaster had continued to roar, a familiar accompaniment to his day's work out there in the flights, but now, unexpectedly, they fell silent. He and the woman were standing next to the Anson, and they were both resting their hands lightly on the leading edge of the wing.

'Do you like to fly?' she said.

'Of course I do! But I'm not allowed, unless—'

'I have the use of this Anson all day. Would you like me to take you on a flight? I want to show you how grateful I am to you, how much it meant to me when you found my purse. We don't need permission. It is all taken care of.'

7

They flew across the country to an airstrip she told him was a satellite field, only used in cases of returning night-time emergencies or diversions because of bad weather. She said she had learned about it when she was forced to make a landing when fog closed in on her destination. It was in the low-lying country between Shropshire and the hilly Welsh interior.

She made Torrance sit in the co-pilot's seat on the right-hand side, the starboard, beside her in the cockpit. On a Lancaster this was where the flight engineer sat and was considered by all to be a privileged position. Torrance was familiar with the cramped cockpit in the Lancs, but the Anson's felt about half the size. When he squeezed himself on to the hard metal seat his shoulders were pressing against hers. She seemed not to mind. She pulled on a flying helmet, then gave him a pair of brown Bakelite headphones so they could communicate with each other in flight. He discovered how close and intimate her voice sounded in his ears, but it also lost direction and gained a tinny, almost mechanical quality. When he replied to something she said, he felt her reacting.

'No need to shout!' she said, emphasizing the point with a friendly nudge of her elbow.

He sat back and tried to relax, determined to enjoy the flight. At first he assumed she would be going to do a few circuits of the airfield, the sort of short test flight on which the airmen sometimes took a few of the ground crew as a favour, but it was soon clear she had other plans. After running rapidly through the pre-flight check, and a brief radio-telephone conversation with one of the controllers she taxied the Anson to the end of the relief runway, then without any delay opened the throttles. With a roar the plane rolled down the concrete. They were in the air in what seemed like moments. She banked steeply and turned towards the west.

'Are you sure we should be doing this?' he said, suddenly nervous of what might happen if any of the NCOs in the Instruments Section should find out where he was.

'I told you not to worry. I have this aircraft for today.'

'But you can't just borrow RAF planes when you feel like it.'

'Sometimes I can. Later I will tell you how.'

She levelled the plane out, not at a great altitude. He could easily pick out houses and fields, roads and woodlands. At first Torrance was so enthralled by what they were doing that he could barely take in what he was seeing. He felt hypnotized by the movement, the sensation of height, the oily smell inside the plane, the noise and the vibration. As soon as they were in the air it was much colder inside the cockpit, but the sun dazzled down through the canopy. When he asked her about their height she pointed to the altimeter on the instrument panel in front of them – it was of course an instrument he had fitted or adjusted many times, but it had not occurred to him to look at it in flight. It showed they were at just over 2,000 feet.

The Anson was a famously slow aircraft but they were in the air for less than an hour. She carried no maps, and navigated by constantly watching the ground as she flew. She told him that all the ATA pilots had learned to memorize landmarks: mainly canals, rivers and railway lines. She said she had a route-map of England in her head. She spoke from time to time on the radio-telephone, obtaining permission to cross from one control sector to another, reading from a series of codes which were scribbled in an exercise book, folded open at the page and strapped to her right leg just above her knee. It was the same open handwriting he had seen before. The casual way she pulled back the hem of her skirt, or moved her leg against his to read the codes, had a perturbing effect on him.

All too soon she told him on the intercom that the airfield she was heading for was in sight. She pointed down and to the left, but because of where he was sitting he could not see the ground ahead. She throttled the engines back, making the plane seem to brake in the air, then went into a steep turn. The sky, now scattered with a handful of bright-white cumulus clouds, deep blue above, circled around them. The steeply inclined glimpse of the ground made it feel as if they were about to tip right over. He was terrified and thrilled by the sensation, somewhere between soaring and tumbling. The turn caused him to lean against her, but she did not seem to mind. Soon she levelled the plane out and he could see a long section of yellowing grass mowed flat to form a landing strip in a field ahead.

The plane landed, bumping and rocking on the turf. She was calm, matter-of-fact, taxiing the plane across the uneven ground. As the plane swayed from side to side, his arms and shoulders bounced against hers.

8

There were formalities. A solitary RAF warrant officer was on duty, in a caravan parked on the side of the field. He accepted her inward flight plan. Something written on it made him start with surprise – he immediately began addressing her as 'Ma'am'. There was no problem with the return plan, which he filed with obvious haste. He asked if she would need a car placed at her disposal, or would be requiring lunch. She politely turned down both offers, and the W.O. looked disappointed. She asked if the airstrip was on emergency stand-by that night, and he confirmed that it was.

'Ma'am, I have to be sure to clear your Anson for take-off well before nightfall.'

'It will be,' she said.

'Does it require refuelling?'

'No, thank you.'

Torrance's ears were ringing from the endless racket of the Anson's engines, heard inside the cockpit. He followed her as she walked away along the path behind the warrant officer's caravan, through a wooden gate and out into a narrow country road. She was carrying a canvas bag, which she had slung over her shoulder. The lane ran parallel with the edge of the small airfield, but as soon as they had passed through the gate it was almost as if the airstrip was not there. Tall hedges grew on both sides, and a calm silence rested on the land. A haze of light scents drifted through the air. The sun shone down on them and Torrance unbuttoned his jacket.

'You are not a curious person, are you?' she said.

'What do you mean?'

'Ah, now then, you have asked a question. I thought you would not. But you ask no others.'

'I don't like to,' he said. 'I mean, I have nothing to ask.'

'Yes, you have. You want to know why I have taken you for a flight, and where we will be going now. You want to know why I am Polish and what I am doing here in England. And most of all you are wanting me to tell you how I can borrow an aircraft from the RAF and fly it about wherever I please, all day. Is that not true?'

'Well, I was wondering – should I call you "Ma'am"?'

She laughed. 'No, you must please call me Krystyna. I am not a senior officer. I am not even in the RAF. And you, Mike Torrance – I wish to call you by your first name. Is that right? Mike?'

'Mike, or Michael. Since I've been in the RAF everyone I work with calls me Floody.'

'Floody?'

'Floody Torrance.' She was looking puzzled, so he added, 'It's a nickname. Flood, Torrents. Torrance.'

'No, I do not understand. I will call you Michael.' She pronounced it *Mee-chyal*.

'But why did that warrant officer call you Ma'am?'

'I showed him my orders and he saw who had signed them.' She pulled some papers from inside her jacket. 'Do you recognize the name?'

The orders were typewritten. At the bottom was a large rubber stamp, showing that the orders had come from *No.1 Site, Bomber Command HQ, High Wycombe*. The signature was an indecipherable scribble, but beneath it was typed *AVM Hon T. L. A. Rearden (Bart)*. Torrance stared at the name, aware that it was familiar, but at that moment, as he walked slowly along the sunlit lane with this amazing young woman, it was impossible to make sense of it.

'Air Vice Marshal Rearden,' she said. 'Does that help you with the recognizing?'

'Rearden! He's Harris's second-in-command!' Torrance said. 'How on earth did you get Rearden to sign this?'

She was laughing again, but it seemed to him that it was with the delight of surprising him, not from making fun of him.

'His name is Timothy, or as I know him, Tim. I have a room-mate where I am living, Lisbeth. She is in the ATA as well. We share a house in Hamble. That is where our ferry pool is based, close to one of the aircraft factories. I'm not allowed to tell anyone what kind of aircraft they build there, but that's why we stay where we do. My room-mate's name is Rearden, Lisbeth Rearden ... her father is the Vice Marshal. Sometimes she takes me home at weekends, and once or twice the Marshal has been there and we played cards and we drank gin and whisky and he would tease me and once he made me sing for him, and he always tells me long stories about flying in the last war.'

'You know Rearden?' Torrance said, stunned by this news.

'I know Rearden, yes. So sometimes, if I do not do it too often, I can ask Lisbeth's father if he will do me a big, big favour. And for today I asked him if I could borrow one of his training aircraft for a few hours. I did not tell him why and he did not ask. So here I am and as long as I return the aircraft to Hamble by nineteen hundred hours, I can go where I wish and take who I like with me.'

'May I remove my jacket?' Torrance said to her. 'I'm feeling awfully warm.'

'Yes, Michael. If I may also remove mine.'

9

They came shortly to a village. They walked past a row of terraced cottages and small shops, then at the point where the lane joined a wider road she took him through a lych gate and into a churchyard. Torrance had noticed a pub in the village and would have liked a beer, but she said she never touched alcohol when she was flying.

The churchyard was shaded, with bright patches of sunlight where it broke through the shadowing trees. Many of the old gravestones were overgrown with bushes or weeds. Birds sang, insects flitted about. There was no one else in sight.

'I discovered this place last summer,' she said. 'I come here whenever I can, which is not often. I like it because it is so beautiful and it reminds me of a place in the hills near Kraków which I knew when I was a child. It was somewhere I liked to walk by myself, then later I would go there sometimes with Tomasz.'

'You say Tomasz is still in Poland?' Torrance said. He felt a stirring of quiet jealousy whenever she mentioned him.

'I will tell you about Tomasz soon, but before that I must have something to eat. I did not have any breakfast. I brought a little food with me, which we can share. Are you hungry too?'

They walked through to the far side of the churchyard, where there was a small cleared space between three raised, ancient catafalques, the engraved names and tributes long blurred away by time or the elements. A low bench was here, facing back towards the grey walls and tower of the church. Cows were grazing in the field behind. Torrance stood beside her as she sat on the bench and pulled two or three packages and a bottle from her bag.

'You like cheese?' she said. 'Hard-boiled eggs? I have brought some very English sandwiches for us.' She also produced a glass jar of pickled cucumbers, which Torrance had never seen or tasted before.

They sat side by side, eating in silence, then shared the bottle, which contained lemonade squash. Now that the flight was over and he was alone with her, sitting quietly in the peaceful churchyard, Torrance felt tongue-tied. He did not want to hear any more about Tomasz, the newly discovered rival. Yet he hardly knew anything else about her: how could he claim anyone to be his rival for a young woman he had met barely more than an hour ago? And he was acutely aware that her work in the war, ferrying operational aircraft all over the country, was far more interesting and daring than his own modest job, adjusting compasses, cleaning out Pitot tubes and replacing faulty instruments. What could he tell her about himself that would interest her?

She kept glancing sideways at him while she ate – once he caught her eye, and she smiled.

As she screwed up the paper food bags she had brought, and stuffed them back into her bag, she said, 'You will never know what this has meant to me, Michael. I know you are not Tomasz, I know it is a big mistake to think the way I am thinking, but I was so shocked to see you.'

'How long is it since you last saw him?'

'Four years ago, in 1939. You are what, twenty-two?'

'Twenty-one.'

'Tomasz was about that age when I last saw him. You look exactly as I remember him – it's uncanny to see you. But of course I don't know what has happened in four years. He will be different now.'

'Have you heard from him?'

She said, 'Not since the Nazis invaded. I must tell you. Today – I wanted only to meet you, only to ask for my purse back, and I thought I would take you for a short flight to show how grateful I am to you. I brought food because I would be hungry, and I brought enough for you too. That was all that I intended: a short flight around your airfield, some sandwiches to share, maybe a little walk and some conversation. Very British, just as I like it. But until I saw you I had no idea the effect you would have on me. I have to tell you.'

10

Michael Torrance writes: It is 1953, ten years since I met Krystyna Roszca. The Second World War is long over, the past has gone, everything is different in the world, in my life, in everybody's lives. I am no longer, I hope, the callow young man I was then. But on that warm day in the early summer of 1943, Krystyna told me the story of how she travelled to Britain and became a pilot for the ATA. Of course, she told me in her own way, in her lovely, accented English. I cannot reproduce that, but I was so infatuated with her that everything she told me burned into my consciousness. I have never forgotten her story. It is of course not so different from many stories from that time: a lot of young people met each other briefly during the war, but were then roughly parted in some final, often distressing way. As soon afterwards as I could I jotted down a few notes on what she had told me, but in fact her story was vivid in my memory. I remembered, or I believed I remembered, everything. I have always intended to write down what she said, and at last I have done it. It is as true as I can make it. I have tried to write it in her words, although all I can do is offer my remembered version.

I still hope and believe that one day Krystyna might read this, and will then understand that there was not one tragic wartime parting in her life, but two.

11

THE PILOT

I was born on a small farm in Kraków Province, the województwo of Kraków, about twenty kilometres to the east of the city. It was open farmland all around, although there was a village close by called Pobiednik. I had three brothers and a sister. My father was called Gwidon Roszca, my mother Joanna. Our family was poor and I was often hungry as I grew up. My parents always made sure I attended school, which I enjoyed.

When I was aged eleven my father succeeded in selling a large number of his herd of cattle to a man he knew only as a local landowner. The money briefly made a great deal of difference to my parents, but for me the sale had a much more important impact. It turned out that the landowner was an important aristocrat and legislator, and during the transaction he must have noticed me. After the sale of the animals, I discovered to my shock that I too had been sold, and that I was to move in with his family as a companion for his own child. Can you imagine how horrible that felt? I believed I had been rejected by my parents, discarded as unwanted. I had failed in everything. My mother cried for three days and nights, and my father would not speak to me. Later, I was to discover that it was not a form of slavery but a voluntary arrangement that might be brought to an end at any time, and that the intentions of all the adults were good, if misguided. I was not to know that at the time.

One day, not long after, I was dressed up and driven to the centre of Kraków itself, where I was deposited at the rear entrance to a large and beautiful house in the Old Town, not far from St Florian's Gate and overlooking part of the Rynek.

That house was to become my permanent home. I was just a girl from a poor farm so I was overwhelmed and intimidated by the family's wealth: there were dozens of servants, and the house was opulently furnished and richly decorated. My re-education and new upbringing began on that day, and one of the first things drilled into me was a need to be circumspect about the family and their ways. That discretion is still with me, but I can tell you that Rafal Grudzinski, Count of Lowicz, was one of the most wealthy and influential men in Kraków. Apart from the fact that he owned great stretches of farmland, and several manufacturing companies in the north of Poland, there is little I am able to say about him. I have no idea what has happened to him or his wife since the Nazis and Soviets invaded our country.

I was educated, I was groomed in the courtesies and manners of the class I had joined, I grew up. I spent the years 1928 to 1939 with the Grudzinski family, fulfilling the role that had been created for me when I was given up by my parents. That role was something I did not understand at first, but eventually I learned that Madame the Countess had become unable to bear more children after the birth of her only son, Tomasz.

I was eleven when I was taken to the Grudzinski household and by the time I was sixteen I had become, as I thought, a full member of the family. In my heart I knew I was still just a little peasant girl, but the grooming had given me a superficial sheen acceptable to this important and socially prominent family.

The count was a renowned and enthusiastic sportsman: he was a swimmer, a horseman, a shooter, a sailor and a climber. He went in for all of these activities in a wholehearted way, competing whenever competition could be found. Poland was mostly a poor country, but the count was rich beyond anything I could imagine. In 1934, just after my seventeenth birthday, he developed an interest in aviation, bought a small and fast aircraft, learnt to fly it, and within a year was competing at international level in several European countries: the south of France, along the Baltic coasts of Germany and Poland, in Austria, Sweden and Estonia. At first he would disappear from Kraków for a week or two at a time, then return either jubilant or dispirited, but it was not long before he was expecting the family to follow him to these events. The countess showed no interest in any of this, so it meant that Tomasz and I, and a retinue of servants, were the recruited support team.

I should describe what was developing between Tomasz and me. At first I had been completely in awe of him – he was the same age as me, just a few weeks older, but he had been born into an easy and affluent way of life. I found him difficult and arrogant. I think it is true to say that for some time we wholeheartedly loathed each other.

But within a few years, around the time we started accompanying Count Lowicz to his sporting events, matters became rather different. I found I was only happy when I was with Tomasz, and whenever we were separated, such as the weeks we spent at our different schools, I pined for him and dreamed up a hundred schemes for escaping somehow from where I was so that I could be with him. I knew without being told that he was feeling the same about me. For both of us the count's long trips to flying competitions were a chance to be together for several days at a time.

During the first two trips to air races – one was in Monte Carlo, the other on the Adriatic coast of Italy – I barely registered what was happening, so full of joy was I to be with Tomasz. Both meetings were a cheerful chaos of boats, crowds, hot sunshine and annoyingly noisy aircraft. But then we travelled to Tallinn in Estonia, where the race itself was just a part of a much larger festival of sailing and flying. Although it was high summer it was cooler than it had been in the other places, there were not the same crowds and people were much more interested in the actual flying. For me, during the first day and a half, it meant that while the count was busy with his mechanics and his plane Tomasz and I had plenty of time together alone.

Then it happened. One of the count's racing friends asked Tomasz if he would like a flight in an aeroplane. Tomasz agreed, climbed into the spare seat at the rear and was flown around the harbour and along the coast before returning. Then it was my turn.

We took off and within the space of a few seconds everything in my life simply changed.

I wanted to be, *I had to be*, a flier. I pleaded with the man for another flight, but that was not possible for some reason. I had to be content watching the count and his twenty-odd friends and competitors roaring past at what looked like immense speed. Tomasz too seemed keen to learn to fly, and while we watched the long race we talked excitedly of how we could arrange some lessons.

A few weeks later, while we were still taking lessons at an airfield near Kraków, the count presented Tomasz with a little two-seat RWD-3 high-wing monoplane.

I qualified as a solo pilot within three weeks.

Two months after that, at the end of yet another week of extended lessons with his tutor, Tomasz confessed to me that he was not a natural pilot, that he usually felt sick in the air, that the movements of the plane frightened him, and that whenever he took the controls he felt paralysed by terror. He said he knew he was never going to be able to fly solo.

But he agreed that I had taken to the air as if it were my natural element. From that day, with Tomasz's encouragement, the RWD-3 became in effect my own plane, although I never flew anywhere without Tomasz in the seat behind me.

Flying became our lives together. A private airstrip was carved out of a long piece of the count's estate a few kilometres to the north-east of the city. We were free to fly as often as we liked. We took advantage of that freedom. At first I was guiltily conscious of what had happened, that I had leapt ahead of Tomasz. I did not know of any other woman pilot, in Poland or elsewhere. Flying was a man's sport, and to be a pilot was a male prerogative. One day I confessed these feelings to Tomasz, but he immediately told me not to be foolish. He told me he loved to fly with me, that the feelings of fear and sickness had left him, and that he saw our flying as a way of our being alone together.

I was in love with Tomasz, but I was passionate about flying, obsessed with it. Every time I took off that passion increased.

Money partly insulates the wealthy from the perils of history, so while we were falling in love with each other, and flitting about the Polish skies, we were to some extent immune from the large and dangerous political changes that were taking place in other European countries. Not that we were blind to them. In fact, it was soon impossible to ignore them because the rise of fascism and communism in countries bordering ours was a real concern.

Much against my private wishes, though not in fact Tomasz's, the count bought his son a reservist commission in the Polish Army, and he joined the Poznań Uhlan Regiment. It meant that Tomasz was often away, but somehow I managed to shut out the realities and our loving friendship continued whenever he was at home.

In the following summer I entered my first air race: the Challenge Tourist Trophy, flown on a course above the dykes bordering the Zuider Zee in the Netherlands. I came sixteenth. At the next race two weeks later, in a valley in Austria, my little aircraft suffered engine trouble and I was forced to land early. I damaged the undercarriage when I made a sudden landing in a field.

Two weeks later, with the plane repaired, I entered another race in Pomerania: the IG Farben Classic Cup. I came in fifth. After this race I started to become recognized. I was not just the only woman pilot taking part, I was actually beating most of the men. A newspaper published my photograph and a magazine interviewed me. Tomasz said he had never felt so proud of me.

Later that week Tomasz asked me to marry him.

It was almost as if this simple act of love set in train the upheaval that was to drive us apart. At the same time as Tomasz proposed to me, the Nazis in Germany were making an endless stream of demands on the Polish government, and issuing threats against the Polish people. A strip of our territory lay between Germany and the

German-speaking port of Gdańsk – Hitler wanted it removed. The noises from the east were no more reassuring, with Stalin's avowed aim of collectivizing by force the whole of Europe. He intended to start with those countries lying immediately to the west of the Soviet Union.

So we were in no doubt about what was going on in the world around us. However, for Tomasz and myself there were many more problems on our minds. When we broke our news to the family, expecting a joyous response, we were appalled when we discovered how hostile his parents were. Madame the Countess, in particular, said immediately that she would disallow it. She was abusive to me, calling me a semi-literate peasant and a parasite, and accusing me of trying to get my hands on their money.

It was a shocking end to an illusion. For the second time in my life I felt rejected by people I thought I could trust. The illusion of happiness ended, but the practical form of it continued in an unnervingly undefined way. Tomasz and I went on living in the family house in Kraków, with nothing more being said aloud, but the atmosphere was thick with unstated resentments. He and I escaped to go flying together whenever we could, but even that was becoming more difficult because of the threats of war.

We knew how dangerous the situation was becoming when Tomasz was called up from the reserve. He left immediately and I did not see him again for nearly two weeks. It was a nervous time for me, because with Tomasz gone my position in the household was ambiguous and tenuous. Then he returned, striding sensationally into the house in full uniform. He had never in the past disguised his admiration for the valorous traditions of the Polish Cavalry Brigades, and as a first-class horseman and the son of a count he was ideal officer material. He had joined the Uhlans, and was now a First Hussar in charge of a cavalry troop of more than a hundred men.

My heart melted to see him in his splendid uniform, but I was full of dread and fear. The Germans had fleets of warplanes and hundreds of battle tanks – I could not imagine how brave horsemen armed only with sabres and revolvers could put up any resistance at all, should it come to that.

Tomasz returned to Poznań, and I was alone again. I flew my plane whenever I could, but the emptiness of the seat behind me kept acting as a reminder of my increasing isolation.

One day, towards the end of August, I landed at the count's private airstrip to be greeted by a man who had often visited the Grudzinski family house as a guest. I now discovered he was a senior staff officer, dressed in the uniform of the Polish Air Force: Major General Zaremski. My heart started thudding: I assumed immediately that he was waiting for me with bad news about Tomasz, but those fears were soon allayed.

The general explained what he wanted. The Polish government was facing the overwhelming might of the German Luftwaffe and was redeploying every fighting aircraft and every trained pilot. An invasion by the German Army appeared to be inevitable. At the same time, the government was rapidly moving offices and key staff out of Warsaw and into smaller regional cities and towns. They were recruiting civilians to perform passenger, courier or delivery flights across Poland. I was by this time one of the most prominent aviators in the country and the Lieutenant General of the Air Force, the commander in chief, had personally ordered that I be approached.

Naturally, when General Zaremski told me why he was there I agreed at once.

It was then I noticed a larger plane parked alongside the hangar at the end of the strip. This was to be my first assignment as a courier: I was to transport General Zaremski back to Warsaw as a passenger. As we walked across to the plane he told me not to ask how he and the aircraft had arrived at the airstrip, because the new emergency regulations forbade high-ranking officers from piloting themselves. I guessed the answer and said no more.

While the engines were warming up I pushed my little RWD-3 into the hangar, disabled it by detaching several control wires and removing the magneto cables, then locked it away. I wondered if I should ever fly it or even see it again.

A few minutes later I took off in the Air Force plane, and flew to Warsaw. The major general acted as my navigator. I did not mention that I had never flown a two-engined aircraft before.

A hectic week followed. I flew across Poland in a variety of different aircraft, some ancient, some modern, all of them unfamiliar to me. I flew single- and double-engined planes, and for one journey even a Junkers Ju-52 trimotor. I learnt as I flew. Staff meetings and defence strategy conferences were daily events. I frequently carried confidential documents in sealed bags. I have never been so excited in my life! On September 1, the sixth day of my unexpected recruitment into the air force, the Nazis invaded our country, crossing the border in huge numbers at many different points. Although it was mainly a land attack the Luftwaffe was active too, using dive-bombers to attack Warsaw and other major cities, and also attempting, with terrifying success, to put our own air force out of action.

I flew every day, and sometimes at night, frequently seeing German tanks roaming across our countryside and farmland. Sometimes I came under fire from the ground. Once I saw a squad of three Luftwaffe fighters high in the sky to the south of me – that morning I was carrying six army nurses to the town of Bydgoszcz, where the hospital had been damaged by bombing but was still functioning. They were critically short of nurses. To avoid those fighters I dived steeply towards the ground, seeking cover, but the Luftwaffe fliers did not spot me and an hour later I landed the aircraft safely. That afternoon I was back in Warsaw, ferrying a group of senior staff officers for an aerial view of the fighting.

I slept when and where I could, ate whenever I had the chance. The work was exhausting but exhilarating. I felt I was doing something practical to defend my country from invasion, even though every day brought more evidence that we were losing the war. One morning I was given a two-seat RWD-14 Czapla, and instructed to ferry a senior officer from Warsaw to Kielce. During the flight he told me that the German Army was advancing on Kraków from the west. After I had safely delivered him I immediately flew further south to Kraków, heading for the count's airstrip. From the air there appeared to be no sign of the enemy, but I circled around three times until I was certain it was safe to land.

I taxied the plane to a large copse of trees growing on the side of the field. I parked it there, knowing there was no way of hiding the large and cumbersome aircraft from anyone on the ground, but hoping it would not be spotted from the air.

The car I had used to reach the airstrip was still where I had left it, on the day the major general commissioned me. I started it up without difficulty and drove at breakneck speed into Kraków. As I passed through the outer areas of the city I could see that something terrible was already going on. Four columns of dark, roiling smoke were rising in the distance, on the western side. I saw several straggling lines of people, heading away in the direction from which I had come. They looked to be in a frightful and pathetic state.

I drove towards the centre of the city – I could see St Florian's Gate, high and clean against the sky, but there were several fires close to it. The air was full of smoke.

The road that I was driving along towards the Rynek was unexpectedly blocked – a large house had collapsed across the street, and pieces of burning timber were falling from the two buildings that had been on each side of it. I slowed the car, appalled by the sight. I had never before seen such destruction, such evidence of human loss and tragedy: wallpapered rooms were exposed, pieces of furniture hung from the broken floors, flames licked at the huge pile of bricks and other debris into which the building had fallen, beams and rafters rested on the ground at crazy angles, some of them charred and smoking. The remains of children's toys, clothes, fabrics, hung dankly like dead leaves.

I tried to drive past but the road was impassable for a vehicle. I backed away, parked the car, then continued on foot.

I had still not reached the Rynek when I came across a troop of Polish soldiers attempting to put out a fire that had started inside a shop. I knew the shop: I had visited it many times. I went around the men, keeping my distance, covering my mouth and nose with a part of my sleeve, but then suddenly a familiar voice shouted, 'Krystyna!'

It was Tomasz, his hair tousled and his face and arms blackened by the smoke. He was in his army uniform, but he had removed his jacket and was working in his shirt sleeves with the other men. Of course I rushed to him and we embraced as if we had not seen each other in years. I could hardly believe my luck in finding him here, so close to the house where we had lived. We had to raise our voices to make ourselves heard, because of the many different noises around us: distant and near-distant explosions, bells ringing, people shouting, the roar of flames and, all too often, the horrible, hollow fracturing noise as yet another of Kraków's old wooden-framed buildings collapsed when the fires ate away at the interiors. The fires were spreading, apparently unstoppably, all along the street.

He shouted, 'Krystyna, it's not safe for you. The Germans are already entering the city.'

'If it's not safe for me it's not safe for you.'

'I have to be here. I'm under orders. You must get out immediately. Do you still have the car?' I waved back vaguely in the direction of where I had left it. The street now was choked with smoke. 'Then use it. Warsaw has already fallen to the Germans. They'll have Kraków before today is out. Do you have enough fuel in the car to get to Tarnów? The Germans have not reached there yet. My parents and some of the servants have already gone to Tarnów.'

'I want to be with you, Tomasz. Not with them.'

'I know, I understand. But my father is well known there. You'll be able to buy petrol in Tarnów. I've heard some of the senior officers saying that there is going to be a Polish government in exile in Romania, and there will be transport from Lwów. So you must get to Lwów as quickly as you can.'

'Not without you,' I said.

'I'll come later. We will be withdrawing soon.'

'Come now!' I said loudly, desperately, against the racket of a fire appliance rushing past.

'You can see I can't!' he shouted, indicating his squad of men. 'I have a duty. But there's a plan – tonight our brigades are going to regroup and head south. Mine is one of them, so I will meet you in Lwów. Not straight away, but in a few days. Use the people you know in the Air Force.'

'Tomasz, my love! What is happening here? Have you been to your house?'

'The house has been abandoned for now. Three of the servants

211

stayed to try to take care of the place, but I told them this morning to flee – the rest have gone to Lublin. Everyone else is in Tarnów. They should be safe there.'

He kept glancing across to the blaze while he spoke, obviously torn between talking to me and carrying out his duty.

There were two more gigantic explosions, somewhere behind us, in the next street, terrifyingly close to where we were standing. Glass in many windows burst out and cascaded down into the street. I was left breathless and frightened by the sheer violence of the explosions.

'Those bombs landed in Floriańska!' Tomasz shouted hoarsely – Floriańska was the name of the main street leading from the Gate to the Rynek, where his parents' house was situated. 'I'll have to take the men over there!'

He left me, clambered back over the rubble to the blazing shop and gave hurried orders to the two NCOs working with the troops. Then Tomasz grabbed my hand and we ran through the plumes of swirling smoke, hindered by the piles of rubble on the road, much of which was still burning. I realized we had reached the Rynek, the market-place in the centre of the Old Town. Miraculously, the beautiful Cloth Hall, the Sukiennice, was not damaged, although thick smoke was surging around it. We hurried past the medieval building, looking for the count's house. Then we halted.

Tomasz stood beside me, staring forward.

In all the chaos there was a moment of seeming stillness. Across the Rynek, on the far side, three houses were burning out of control. The one in the centre of the three was the count's house: the glorious townhouse, with its ancient windows, carved gables, timbered walls, built at least three hundred years before, was engulfed. There was something unreal, grotesque about the sight – I looked away, glanced at the sky, so blue and clear beyond the thick coils of smoke rising from all parts of the city. My eyes were streaming with tears, and I could barely breathe.

'It's gone,' Tomasz said.

'Your home.' It was all I could manage to say.

'No!' He turned towards me and placed both his arms around me, pulling me against his chest. 'Not my home. The place I lived.

The place you lived. Ever since you were there with me I have wanted only one thing and that is to be able to leave that house.'

Part of the roof collapsed down into the flames below, sending up a huge display of sparks and a thick burst of grey smoke.

'It's over, Tomasz.'

'I love my parents but I loathed the life they led.'

'Their way of life brought us together,' I said.

'Yes, of course. They meant well then, but I hated what they said to you.'

'Are you sure there's no one trapped inside there?' I said, watching the flames grow higher. The building next door to it looked as if it too were about to collapse.

'I searched the place this morning. No one was inside and all the rooms were closed.' He was already stepping back, away from the blaze. A loud explosion went off in the street beyond the count's house, making us both turn away instinctively, throwing our hands up to protect our heads, but although we saw pieces of wreckage flying in the air, and a rising ball of fire, the blast somehow did not strike us. 'It's the end, Krystyna. That life we had has gone. As soon as this war is over we will be together.'

A formation of German aircraft appeared overhead, high and silhouetted black against the afternoon sky. They were Junkers Ju-87 Stukas, the Nazis' dreaded dive-bombers. They appeared to be circling. Their engines throbbed above the sounds of the inferno in the town. One by one the aircraft turned away from the formation, went into a steep dive and flew at a horrible speed directly towards the ground. There were sirens on each aircraft, set to howl – an unspeakable wailing noise which added an element of deliberate and sadistic terrorizing. The dive-bombers were aiming themselves at the buildings by the river, half a kilometre away from where we were standing. No one on the ground was firing back at them. The lovely old city was at their mercy, and they had none of that.

Tomasz seized my wrist and we began running, retracing our steps. Broken glass and shattered masonry was all around. Within a minute we reached the place where the shop had been, but in the short time we were away the building had been almost completely destroyed. The squad of soldiers had disappeared.

Tomasz looked alarmed.

'I have to find them,' he said.

'They could be anywhere,' I said, because I had a sudden irrational urge to make him flee with me.

'No – we have orders. This street, and the one beyond.'

'Come with me, Tomasz. This is hell.'

'I can't abandon my men!'

'Yes, you can. The Polish cause is lost. There's nothing to fight for any more. The Nazis will move in and round up everyone who has been in the army.'

'We fight to the end.'

Another explosion, somewhere at the far side of the Rynek, made Tomasz take me in his arms and we kissed deeply for the first time since we had met that day. For a few seconds, in that closed world of love, it felt bizarrely as if life was about to revert to normal. Everything receded. But moments later we heard again the sound of German aero engines. Another flight of dive-bombers appeared above us, now only intermittently visible through the thickening columns of smoke. They were already circling, preparing another deadly attack.

'Quickly, Krystyna!' Tomasz shouted, thrusting me away from him. 'Go now!'

'What about you?'

'We'll meet in Lwów. Just get there as soon as you can!'

So we parted. My last glimpse of Tomasz was as he ran in search of his troop, keeping his head down, along the ruined street, zigzagging around the heaps of wreckage. The howling of the dive-bombers was closer now so I ran too, away from the Old Town and towards where I had left the car. Rubble from a building collapse had crashed over the engine compartment, and the front windshield was cracked, but otherwise it seemed to be more or less undamaged. I pushed away what rubble I could with my hands. The engine started at the first attempt. I had to drive forward through a mess of broken glass. I ignored it, swung the steering wheel around then accelerated away. A heavy door frame had been blown into the street, and I did not notice it until too late. The car shook violently as I drove across it. A horrible scraping noise sounded from beneath the car, then stopped. The car lurched on. There was an explosion somewhere close, but I could not see where it was – almost immediately a Stuka passed directly above my car, low and close, at the bottom of its dive as it levelled out and climbed away. It passed so near me that I could see, as in a still photograph, the metal rack where the bomb had been carried, the black of the tyres in their streamlined covers, the mottled green camouflage and a glimpse of the swastika on the fin as the plane turned sharply and banked low across the town. It headed towards the west.

I leaned away from my steering wheel to stare at the aircraft, not watching where I was driving. It was suddenly no longer an enemy aircraft, but just an aircraft. The fascination I always felt for planes gripped me. I wondered what it was like to fly a Stuka, how it might feel to peel away from a formation, aim down at some target on the ground, dive headlong at full speed, the siren screaming, the aircraft shaking with the stress of the dive——

The car had started to veer. It banged and swerved as it collided with the paving stones at the side of the road. I wrenched the steering wheel, straightening the car. I drove with no direction in mind, only to escape the worst of the bombing. The steering was heavy and sluggish and the ride of the car was unstable – I assumed at least one of the tyres had been punctured. I checked the fuel gauge: only a few litres remained. I had no idea how far it was to Tarnów, nor even if the roads were safe to drive on.

When I saw some German battle tanks to the south of me, arrayed in a broad flank, heading towards the city with their peculiar and threatening motion, I swung away from them as quickly as I could.

I continued to skirt around the city, but now I had changed my mind. It made no sense to drive to another city, when I had an aircraft that I could use. I headed for the airstrip, trusting that the Germans would not yet be there. The car's engine was making a loud clattering sound, presumably because of the damage I caused when I drove across the door frame. It was difficult to keep the car headed straight forward. I saw no point in halting to try to find out what was wrong.

There was hardly any other traffic on the road. I saw one column of Polish army trucks, but they took no notice of me.

I reached the airstrip. As soon as I drove in from the road, turned into the familiar field, I was struck by how normal it felt. Everything was just as I had left it. I went straight to the Czapla I had been flying earlier in the day, started the engine and taxied it back to the hangar. Here I filled the petrol tank to the top, then made everything as secure as I could. I wasted no time. As soon as the aircraft was fuelled I searched in the tiny office for every map of Poland I could find, filled a bottle with water for myself and then took off.

The aircraft was equipped with a radio so when I was in the air I switched on, scanning for incoming signals. The usual frequencies were silent, an ominous sign. Knowing that I should at least inform my superior officer I used the standard communication channel and filed my flight plan. No response.

The day was coming to an end and it was dusk by the time I reached the Lwów sector. I located the military airfield, radioed down for permission to land and received it at once. The controller's voice on the radio-telephone was professional, calm. He courteously repeated the identification signals that I would see displayed on the runway approach, then signed off.

That, I think, was for me the last reminder of the order and peace that had once existed in my home country. I landed the Czapla, taxied it as instructed to an air force hangar. When I climbed out of the cockpit, shaking out my hair from under the leather flying helmet, the maintenance men working there stared at me in surprise. Where I normally flew, people were used to me. Here I was among strangers.

I was by this time tired and hungry, not having had any kind of break since the morning. When I had made sure the plane was secure, the wheels chocked, the engine correctly closed down, the controls equalized, I went to the duty office to report in.

Here I learned several alarming facts, the first of which was that late in the day several divisions of the German Army had made a lightning attack, moving in on Lwów from the south and setting up a cordon around the southern limits. A full attack was expected before first light the next day – there were no Polish ground troops anywhere near to repulse them. The tentative plans to set up a rendezvous point in Lwów for the government in exile had been abandoned.

All service personnel and members of the civil service and diplomatic corps were to be evacuated even further to the south and east, initially to Czernowice, in the shadow of the Karpathian mountains.

But – Lwów was where Tomasz and I had planned to meet! I felt panic rising. He was still somewhere in Kraków Province, with the Nazis sweeping all before them.

As if all this were not upheaval enough there were many reports that the Soviet Union had invaded Poland in the north. Some rumours said that the Russians had invaded on 'our side', to fight the Germans on our behalf. That idea was dismissed with the cynical distrust that Poles have always held for both Russians and Germans: if the Soviet Union was invading, they were not going to do us any favours. Events of course were to prove us right.

While I was still trying to absorb this welter of unwelcome information I was suddenly informed that because of the emergency I had ceased to be a civilian and was now commissioned as a Flying Officer in the Polish Air Force. This meant I was under direct orders from any superior officer, not just the informal 'requests' I had been receiving from the top brass I had been ferrying around.

The first such order I received came from the duty officer who broke the news to me. He said I was to fly immediately to Czernowice in a two-engined plane, carrying several diplomats as passengers, then return to Lwów before daybreak to collect more.

It was impossible. I was practically in a state of physical collapse. I pleaded to be allowed a few hours' sleep. The officer then insinuated that if I had problems with night flying then he would understand, and transfer me to clerical ground duties for which I would be more suitable. I angrily brandished my log book in his face, showing the dozens of flights I had carried out in the past few days. I said I could not fly safely, day or night, on the ragged edge of exhaustion, but that I would be back at the airfield at least an hour before dawn.

I did not tell him that I had never in my life taken off in a plane in the dark.

217

I stumbled off to find something to eat and a bunk I could borrow for a few hours.

I was awake by 4:00 am and reported back to the airfield. While I had been sleeping the place had been transformed. All semblance of order was gone. The control tower radio-telephone was not responding and the illuminated flares along the sides of the runway had been extinguished. I could find no officers, or at least any officers who either knew what was going on or who were prepared to give me orders. Artillery was firing in the distance, but no shells were landing anywhere near the airfield. I began to think nervously of the Stukas, but I assumed they would not attack until after sunrise. In the time I was walking around trying to find out what I was supposed to do, three clearly overloaded Polish aircraft taxied down at short intervals to the unlighted runway, took off after an agonizingly slow run and flew precariously towards the south.

I made a decision to act on my own initiative. I thought it might be safe to make one flight, then return to Lwów to try to locate Tomasz. I went through to the assembly area and discovered a large group of civilians clustered miserably together, surrounded by many bags and cases of their belongings. They pressed around me, demanding to know when they would be evacuated. Most of them had been waiting all night. Some were holding official-looking identity cards or letters. There was no point my reading them, but to try to take control of the situation I took two of the letters and skimmed through them. Both of those men were from the French embassy.

Out on the apron I found a LW6 Żubr – an obsolete two-engined plane with the reputation of being loathed by every pilot who had to fly it, but it was the only machine available. It had cargo space behind the pilot's seat. I managed to locate one of the engineers. He confirmed the plane was airworthy, but not fuelled. I searched for and found a working bowser and moved the aircraft across to it. I refuelled it myself, clambering nervously on top of the wing.

The sky in the east was lightening quickly.

We took off after the sun had just started to appear. I managed to cram five of the civilians into the cargo space, but only on the condition that they took none of their baggage. They resisted at first and seemed reluctant to take orders from a woman, whether she was in air force uniform or not. I made it clear that I was about to fly the plane away, with or without any of them, but I could take five passengers. I returned to the aircraft to wait. A minute later five men walked out sheepishly and jammed themselves into the cargo space. When I taxied out to the runway the airfield was still in semi-darkness, and shrouded in morning mist, but either my instincts took over or we were lucky. We lifted away from the ground without trouble, although the plane was horrible to handle.

I climbed the Żubr at the steepest angle it was capable of, because I suspected the enemy lines could not be far below us. In fact I saw no sign of the Germans, either in ground formations or in the air.

The few hours' sleep had revived me. Personal priorities were now dominant. I maintained the plane's altitude at about a thousand metres above the ground, the morning air cool and calm, the very best of weather in which to fly. The plane was painfully slow and every movement of the stick was a physical struggle. While I kept an eye on the ground I was thinking about Tomasz and how we might make contact with each other again. When I thought rationally I realized that our meeting in Lwów could not now happen – everything I had seen there told me that the Germans would be in control of the city before nightfall. There was hardly a trace of military resistance from the Poles. If it was true that the Russians had also invaded then it was only a matter of a few hours before the whole country capitulated.

I found Czernowice by map-reading and dead-reckoning and landed the plane safely, albeit with a bone-jarring crunch when I misjudged the height above the runway. My cramped passengers untangled themselves from the hold and limped away to whatever their destinies might be. I secured the unlovely plane, then went in search of more information.

I quickly realized that even this remote town, in the far south-eastern corner of Poland, was not a safe haven for anyone, military or civilian. Here in Czernowice the talk was all of the Russians: they were fifty kilometres away, perhaps a hundred, only twenty-five. Three Red Army divisions were marching in our direction, fifteen, maybe twenty divisions. I disliked rumours – they always frightened me. My country was being overrun and destroyed. My life was in danger, but so too, I knew, was Tomasz's. I had achieved a measure of self-determination, but Tomasz was trapped in an outdated and under-equipped army, confronted by two of the most aggressive military powers in the world.

Unexpectedly, Major General Zaremski arrived in another plane half an hour after I landed. From the main building on the airfield I saw him striding across the apron, the junior officers around him apparently bringing him up to date on the invasions. I went out to meet him but he brushed past without recognizing me. Later, when I attended a briefing for all air force pilots who had success- fully reached Czernowice, Zaremski finally realized I was there.

We were to evacuate again, he announced, this time towards Bucharest. No civilians would be transported – priority would be given to air force personnel. The intention was to regroup and form an independent detachment of the Polish Air Force. We would then launch guerrilla air raids on the occupying armies of the homeland. Zaremski named an air base in the north of Romania where we had permission to land and where there would be all the facilities we needed. It sounded impractical to me but Zaremski's manner was calm and plausible. I listened to him with the other pilots, but I was aware that of all those present I was the only one who was not combat-trained.

He sought me out afterwards and took me aside.

'I want you to be my personal pilot again,' he said at once. 'You will not be expected to take part in the action. But I will be in effect the commanding officer of this strike force, so you will be in danger because of that. Are you prepared to serve me once more?'

'Yes, sir,' I said, even though I was starting to think that he and everyone I was with was descending into a kind of madness. How long could Polish warplanes operate from a base inside Romania without the Germans or Russians retaliating? What then? Would Romania too be dragged into the war? It was hard for me to think clearly: I had not eaten since the night before, I had slept only a few hours, I had been flying for most of the day.

Within an hour we were in the air again, but this time I was in a new aircraft, a twin-engined PZL.37 Łoś. General Zaremski was the only passenger. He sat beside me in the cockpit, never commenting on the way I was flying, even though I suspected he was more familiar with the aircraft than I was. I was too tired to care, which probably made me a better, more instinctive pilot. He acted as my navigator.

We crossed the Karpathians, we flew above the rugged and broken terrain to the south-west of the range, we droned low across an apparently empty landscape of farmland and small settlements. Towards the end of the day we approached the designated airfield. I was once again on the point of exhaustion. Zaremski guided me towards the landing-path. I went into the final approach with the feeling that I was dreaming, but we settled safely on the runway. I taxied the plane as directed to a certain part of the base.

And there the adventure abruptly ended.

All our plans collapsed in a moment. It was instantly apparent that the Romanian government, presumably under pressure from the Germans, had lured us to this place. The intention was to take as much of the Polish Air Force as possible out of the reckoning. Armed troops arrested us as soon as we climbed down from the aircraft. We were driven away as prisoners of the Romanian government – 'internees' was the word they used, but it amounted to the same thing.

I spent the winter months billeted in the house of two Romanian schoolteachers, living with them and their two children. I spoke no Romanian, they spoke only a few words of Polish. We managed to communicate with a few scraps of English and German. They obtained for me an English-language textbook from their school and I spent the long idle hours learning this language. That at least was of benefit to me.

It was more or less impossible to obtain information about the progress of the war, and in particular news of what was happening inside Poland. I knew that the fighting had ceased within a day or two of my escape, and that the country was now occupied by both the Germans and the Soviets. No news at all of Tomasz, although there were disturbing rumours I heard from other Polish exiles that many of the officers in the forces who had remained in Poland had been rounded up and interned. I listened anxiously to the broadcasts from the BBC – they were often jammed, but about twice a week it was possible to hear most of their bulletins. They rarely if ever said anything about Poland: it was as if my country had ceased to exist. The British had gone to war in our cause but now they ignored us. For me, the main benefit of the broadcasts was that they gave me a chance to listen to English being spoken. I repeated the words aloud, learning and learning.

The winter passed slowly. I thought longingly about Tomasz every day, but it was an agony of longing. I wrote to him care of every address I could think of, but no reply ever came.

At the beginning of March 1940, a middle-aged army staff officer in his Polish uniform turned up unexpectedly at the house and told me that we were going to be evacuated to France, where a Polish government in exile had been set up by Władysław Sikorski. We were not allowed to fly – all our aircraft had been impounded, and, we later discovered, put into service by the Romanians. An overland journey lay ahead: through the Balkan countries, the north of Italy, most of France.

The following few weeks are now a blurred and unpleasant memory of endless travel and delays, rough sleeping and only occasional meals, but I and many others arrived in Paris in the last week of April. Most of the Poles who had been interned in Romania did manage to complete the journey, but by the time we climbed down from the last train at Gare de Lyon in Paris we were hungry, bedraggled, homesick and frightened.

My own experiences are little different from those of the others. We were housed well in Paris and began to regain some health and confidence, but it was only a few days after our arrival that the news came that the Germans had invaded the Low Countries and were advancing on Paris. The consequences were not lost on any of us. Sikorski's government hastily relocated to London and as the sole remaining representatives of Poland's free military forces we had to move there too.

Three days later I was in London and once again billeted with a family. This time I was in the west London suburb of Ealing, living with expatriate Poles who had moved to England about ten years before. I was in London all through that summer and the following winter, while fears of a German invasion were on everybody's mind. Because I was a foreign national, and a woman, I was not allowed to do anything practical to defend the city beyond fire-watching at night. I was obsessed with the idea that if only they would allow me an armed aircraft I could rid the skies of the German menace. Instead, I was instructed to take high vantage points and from church towers and the roofs of office blocks I watched for fires. People in Ealing suffered like the other Londoners under the nightly air-raid alarms, but because we were far to the west of the city, in reality the number of bombs that actually fell during the Blitz on London were few in comparison with other parts of the city.

I continued to be frustrated by my position. Many of the Polish men with whom I had escaped to Britain were allowed to re-train with the RAF, and soon joined fighter or bomber squadrons, but there was nothing for me to do. I was a fully qualified pilot with more hours of solo flying time than most of the men I knew, and certainly a more diverse experience of different types of aircraft, but the operational RAF was a strictly male-only force. The best they could offer me was a job as a liaison officer in the WAAF, working with Polish airmen on bomber bases. I was about to accept this posting, thinking it would be better than nothing, when I heard about the Air Transport Auxiliary.

I assumed at first that the ATA would be open to men only, but I soon discovered that a women's wing had been formed, as there was a critical shortage of civilian male pilots. I applied immediately, waited for what felt like an eternity, I was eventually interviewed, complimented on my command of English, but then I was sent away to improve it. Never was anyone so motivated as me, to master a new language.

I began flying with the ATA in the spring of 1941. It was a dream come true, and I imagine I shall be doing the same job until the end of this war. Only one thing would make life better, and that would be to have firm news of Tomasz, or to see him again.

THE INSTRUMENT BASHER (cont'd)

Krystyna finished her story. She and Mike Torrance sat side by side on the churchyard's wooden bench, leaning against the hard raised back, their shoulders resting companionably together. Torrance was intoxicated by the warm feeling of her arm against his, and as she waved her hands about to express herself the movement made him tingle with an inner excitement. Sometimes she pressed her fingers to part of his leg, or then she would move slightly away and turn to face him directly to say something with extra conviction or sincerity, but she would return and fold her body affably against his once more. Once, when she told him of her last glimpse of Tomasz in the ruins of Kraków, she paused, her breathing shuddering, her hand suddenly hot on his. He put his arm around her then, as she cried.

Torrance was lost in his own feelings, an astonishing surge of love and affection for the young woman he had met only a few hours before, not only a stranger to him but in fact the first person he had encountered in his life who had not been born in Britain. He was confused by the intensity of his feelings: why it had happened, what she might want from him, what they should do next. Above all, he was wondering how he could ensure that this would not be the last time he saw her.

He felt the minutes ticking by, the afternoon slipping inexorably away from him. So she spoke, softly, intently, telling him of her lost lover in Poland, her life in the sky and her passion for flying, the planes and the flights, the dangers, the long struggle to escape from the Germans.

He knew that all too soon they would have to part, that he was inevitably destined to return to the reality of his life on the Tealby Moor base. He knew that Krystyna was also aware of that, because he saw her glancing at her wristwatch, the reminder of time running over, or in this case out.

When he dared, he said, 'How long do we have before we must return?'

'Maybe half an hour.'

It was no time at all! 'Can we meet like this again?' he said.

No answer to that came. She turned away sharply, looked down at the grass. 'Don't say any more.'

He obeyed, biting back the words he wanted to declare, words he already knew would be pointless: a plea for more time with her, much more time, a frantic plan to run away together. She was half-turned from him, her shoulders hunched over, her dark hair tipping forward to obscure most of her face, but her left hand held his tightly and soon her other hand crept across and held it too. She would not look at him.

Then he heard her say, quietly, as she turned to look at him again, 'I know you are not Tomasz, that you could not be him, that it is not fair of me to hope you might be him, that you only remind me of him because you are so tall and your hair is the same. I am lonely and desperate, all alone in this country, but you are here and Tomasz is not. You give me hope about him, you help me imagine him, you help me remember him. You know nothing about any of that, but you are all I have today and all I have ever had since I left my home. Dear Michael, suddenly you are so precious to me. I know one day we can and will meet without Tomasz here too, seeming never to leave me, but today you must let me keep the pretence. I am so happy to be with you, even though what you make me remember and wish for is only a memory of memories, the times before everything went wrong. My life has been inter-rupted. Do you possibly understand that?'

'Yes,' he said, thinking how inadequate that single word must sound. 'All I want to know is that we will meet again soon.'

'I will try.'

'No – I'll go crazy unless you promise.'

She was silent again. Then she said, 'I don't want you to be crazy. I promise you.'

'Will it be soon?'

'If I am sent to Tealby Moor it could be tomorrow,' she said. 'Or the next day. As soon as I can.'

But even as she said this he realized that it meant they would not meet that way. She could deliver a dozen Lancasters to the airfield, but he would never know it, and nor would he be able to take time off to see her.

The sun had moved across the sky while they sat there, and now they were pleasantly in the shade of one of the taller trees to their side. Her hands were still holding his.

'I would like to give you something, Michael. Something that not even Tomasz had. Would that make you believe I will see you again?'

'What is it?'

'I have no money, nothing I can give you to keep, but I can tell you a secret. When I was a little girl, my mother had a special name for me. I mean my real mother, the one I have not seen again since I was eleven. It was what we call at home a love-name, a child's name. My *matka* called me Malina. It's an old Polish name. It's based on the name of a fruit, a malina. My mama was very fond of malinas. When I was little my hair grew long. She used to put me on her lap and brush my hair and kiss me, and call me Malina. Not even Tomasz knows that. I never told him, never told anyone.'

'You want me to call you Malina?'

'I want you to know that is my private name, a secret between us. Say it again.'

'Malina.'

'Good.' She moved her wrist deliberately, looked at her watch. 'Now we have to fly back to your airfield.'

13

They walked under the lych gate and followed the straight lane through the village. Torrance tried to take her hand as they went along but the moment he touched her she swung away from him. They were carrying their uniform jackets slung over their shoulders, and as he walked close beside her they sometimes brushed against each other. She did not seem to mind that.

'I can take a weekend's leave soon,' he said. 'Can we meet then?'

'I am never given leave. I'm a civilian. Sometimes I fly, sometimes I do not. Leave is for airmen, for soldiers.'

'But you must have time off. Can't we arrange something?'

'I will try,' she said.

'What is it you really want, Krystyna?'

'I have given you a promise, Michael. What I want is the same as what you want, but it is not easy to arrange. I am happy doing what we are doing now.'

'Then how are we going to meet?'

'We will find a way.'

They had reached the part of the lane that ran alongside the perimeter fence of the airstrip. It was another reminder that this unique time of privacy with her was coming to a real end, and in one sense almost at once. It would be too noisy inside the Anson for more than basic communications through the intercom. As soon as they landed back at Tealby Moor then of course they would have to part immediately. Everything about the war, and life in the war, lay like a barrier between them.

'You asked me what I want,' she said suddenly. 'Would you really like to know?'

'I assume it is Tomasz,' he said miserably, already wishing he had not asked the question.

'Yes, of course. You know that now. But it is also you, Michael.' Her hand found his and quickly squeezed it. 'You are – suddenly, so important to me. The dread that I carry in me is that Tomasz has been killed and I do not know. Today, meeting you, being with you, for the first time I have been able to think of what might have happened to Tomasz as a reality. Whatever the truth, I can never go back to the life I had before the war began. Poland has been destroyed. The privileged life of Tomasz's family will never come back, and I would not want it even if it were possible. Anyway, there are other wishes.'

She laughed unexpectedly, let go his hand and plucked a long shoot from the bank beside them. She swung it from side to side, ruffling the grasses, and insects rose around them.

'Other wishes, such as?'

'Don't you have ambitions? Even small ones, things you want to do? Not just feelings?'

'Yes.'

'I do too. I have dreams, but I have never told anyone. So I will tell you, but you will laugh at me. I am serious, though. My god I am serious! I want one day to be given the job of flying a Spitfire. It is the most beautiful aircraft ever made.'

She raised the shoot she was still holding and threw it away from her like a dart, towards the top of the bank. For a few instants it seemed to respond to the warm air, flew through it as if finding lift, then it landed stalk-first amid the weeds growing along the high part of the bank. It stayed upright for two or three seconds, before wavering and toppling slowly to the side. Krystyna glanced at Torrance's face, perhaps to see if he was laughing at her. But he was not.

She said, 'All the girls I work with in the pool have the same dream. One or two of them have actually been given one to fly, but it does not happen often. We say the Spitfire is so sensuous, a kind of ideal lover, not a man, but something like a fine stallion that has to be tamed and ridden, a giant cat hunting at speed. The Spitfire is flown by men, but it was meant for women. We wear it like a close-fitting garment, an extra skin. I have a photograph of a Spitfire on the wall in my room, and I yearn to be inside it. Most of the ATA girls feel the same way, and although we joke about it and tease each other, underneath we are obsessed by it. Every now and then we go to the despatch office, and there is the order posted on the blackboard. It is like winning a big prize, and whoever is on the rota that day is like a film star. We all envy her.'

'Never you, though?'

'Not me, so far. I hope it is not never.'

'So is that it? A flight in a plane?'

'Not just a plane, and not just any Spitfire. It has to be one of the ones they are building now, the Mark XI. Do you know what that means?'

Torrance said inadequately, 'I work on bombers. We never see fighters, so I don't—'

'The Spitfire XI is the best, the most beautiful of all Spitfires! It is not a fighter. It is built for photo-reconnaissance, so all it carries is high-powered cameras. To save weight it has no weapons, and to give it range it carries auxiliary fuel tanks. It can fly so high it can never be seen, and it is so fast that no other aircraft can catch up with it.' She had stopped walking and was standing in the middle of the narrow lane, waving her hands with excitement. 'It is a work of art, Michael! To see a Spitfire flying overhead has the same effect as fine art: you feel altered, improved by being close to it. I sometimes think that even if this war is in the end lost to the Germans, everything will be justified by the fact that the British designed and invented the Spitfire. You think I am mad?'

Torrance said, 'No, because—'

'But *I* think I am mad! It is my madness, Michael. Forgive me, because I have come to this country and the only thing I can do to help this war is to fly, and to fly a Spitfire is the greatest of all acts. It is now the only thing I want, all I have left to achieve. Sometimes I lie in my bed and I imagine myself strapped into the cockpit of a long-range Spitfire, flying it high and fast, away from this war, far away, into the clouds and then above them, across the blue, scraping the roof of this world, flying forever, no Germans, no enemies, just the free air and the sky.'

She stopped then, staring at him. Her face was flushed, her hands were still raised. To Torrance she seemed at that moment to be beyond his reach, somewhere unattainable by him, above all daily concerns, free of the grim realities of the unfinished war. He glimpsed tears that had sprung into her eyes. She wiped them with a finger against her lids, and looked away.

'My god, I am sorry,' she said. 'I don't know why I am like this with you. I have never told anyone that before.'

He stepped towards her, put both his arms around her. No resistance – she held herself against him. He realized she was trembling.

'Michael, please – I want this over.'

'It's all right.' He tried to kiss her but she turned her face – he managed to press his lips briefly to her cheek. They stood like that for a while, but then gradually released each other. They walked on slowly.

'We speak of Spitfires,' Krystyna said, as they reached the entrance to the airstrip. The chunky tip of the Anson's tail fin could be seen from the lane. 'But this is what I must fly today.'

The workmanlike, distinctly non-sensuous plane was waiting

where she had parked it earlier. A young AC2 had been sent out to guard it, but as soon as Krystyna showed him her card pass he saluted her and went inside the command caravan. Torrance walked over to wait beside the aircraft while Krystyna went to the caravan to file her planned route, and to pick up the latest weather and operational data. When she came out again she had already pulled on her leather flying helmet, and her gloves.

14

The return flight to Tealby Moor took as long as the outbound trip, but to Mike Torrance it felt as if it was over in a few minutes. When the airfield was in sight, Krystyna circled the plane around the perimeter before landing, giving him a bird's eye view of the base he knew so well – he soon picked out the row of huts where he lived and slept, the hangar where he worked, and so on. He could also see the sea, surprisingly not at all far from the base, or so it looked from the air – normally, the ground crews' only awareness of its presence was the bitterly cold wind that sometimes scoured them from the east. There were more surprises from this temporary high vantage point: the rise of land that gave Tealby Moor its name, the western edge of the Lincolnshire Wolds, was all but indistinguishable from the air. The climb up to the airfield after a visit to the nearby market town of Market Rasen sometimes seemed a real challenge after an evening in the pub, but from the air it looked like no hill at all.

Staring down at the large field below the end of the main runway, Torrance looked for and found the still-visible trace of where H Henry had crashed after being shot down: the large black triangle burnt into the crops by the wreckage was starting to be grown through, and would soon disappear.

Krystyna levelled the Anson, throttled back the engines, and took the plane down to a gentle landing on the main concrete runway. She turned off on an access runway more or less at once, and taxied directly to Dispersal 11. She cut the engines, and an erk

Torrance did not recognize ran out from one of the buildings and chocked both the main wheels.

She ripped off her helmet and shook out her dark hair.

'So we say goodbye, Michael,' she said.

'I don't like goodbye,' he said. 'Too final. Anyway, you have promised.'

'I know. But I have to go. You do too.'

'The French say *au revoir*.'

'*Au revoir*, Michael.'

'I will contact you soon. I will write to you, I will telephone you.' He took a deep breath. 'Krystyna, I—'

'What?'

'I don't know what to say. What I can say.' The words of love were in him, and he was bursting to let them out, but here, in this cramped cockpit, in the late-afternoon sunshine, with a ground crew erk standing there, he could not say them. 'I don't want to lose you,' he said.

'Then remember me by my real name.'

'Malina.'

'Yes – don't forget our secret.'

She leant towards him and for a joyful moment he thought she was offering him a kiss. Instead, she was reaching across his lap to push open the cockpit door on his side. It gusted back in the wind on its hinges, banging against the fuselage. He freed himself from the seat harness, then turned and lowered himself to the wing and jumped down to the grass. Krystyna climbed down on her side at the same time.

The erk who had chocked the wheels was only a short distance away, staring at them.

The day with her had ended. She gave him her hand and they shook formally, then she walked swiftly towards the flight building. She did not look back. Torrance waited until she had disappeared inside, then walked over to where he had left his bicycle. Full of memories, dreaming impossible hopes, replaying snatches of conversation, remembering her face, he pedalled slowly back to the hut.

While he was still on the perimeter road the Anson accelerated down the main runway into the wind, its engines making an uneven roar. He halted the bike, propped it up with one foot on the ground and waved to the pilot. If there was any response from Krystyna he was unable to see it.

Ten minutes later he was back in the familiar and abrasive world of the Nissen hut and the other ground crew, but now he felt painfully distant from the men. They knew it too – some kind of coarse rumour about him had gone around the instrument section in his absence. He put up with the teasing and the ribald comments until lights out, then gladly sank into the peace and introspection of darkness.

At last he was able to think properly about Krystyna: the touch of her hands, her voice, the light brushing of her strands of dark hair against the side of his face, the glimpsing of the silent tears. Also her sheer, fascinating, unarguable foreignness. He was awake most of the night – he was utterly, hopelessly in love with her.

15

Torrance had only two ways of making contact with Krystyna afterwards. The simpler and cheaper was to write to her at the Hamble address she had given him. The trouble was that as everyone in the RAF knew all outgoing mail was censored before it was sent on. This made everyone circumspect by habit: no serving airman was allowed to give any hint of his exact location, or the type of work he was doing, or what his working hours were, or the exact days of upcoming periods of leave. Even letters kept to the dull minimum of information were prey to the black obliterations of the censors. Stories went around the huts about apparently harmless letters home, or to a girlfriend, arriving at their destination with so many arbitrary cuts and blacked-out lines that nothing was left that made any sense.

He was not even sure if he was permitted to make any contact at all with someone in the ATA – he imagined the possibility of some undefined secrecy about her work.

Whatever the reason, no letter that he wrote to Krystyna, in some of which he shyly called her Malina, ever received a reply.

Then there was the telephone. Aside from the prohibitive cost of a call, there were almost insuperable problems. Torrance realized that he must have been lucky when he first telephoned her about the purse. Long-distance connections were largely reserved for the authorities and the military staff. His first few attempts to get through after their meeting were thwarted by the operator telling him that the trunk lines were all engaged, and the one time he did get through someone else answered. It was a woman, who told him that 'Miss Roszca' was not at home. It must have been her room-mate Lisbeth, but the knowledge that she was the daughter of Air Vice Marshal Rearden put fear into him. He stuttered a message out, asking her to tell Krystyna he had phoned and that he would try again when he could. He hoped, irrationally, that Krystyna would find some way to return his call, but in reality the only telephone was the poorly lit call-box outside the NAAFI, which was usually in use when the ground crews were not working. Anyway, he had no idea how he could arrange an incoming call to it.

He was aching to see her again. He thought about her constantly.

He was not alone with such longing. Separation from loved ones was a normal state on RAF stations. Many of the men used their spare time for letter-writing, or for reading and re-reading the letters that came for them. Torrance knew his worries about Krystyna were not unique, but that did not help.

Meanwhile, the weekly toll of missing aircraft continued, and with those losses the unwelcome knowledge that another group of young men had at best been taken prisoner, or worse, injured when the plane was attacked, or worst of all, killed in the wreckage as the aircraft was shot down or when it crashed to the ground or into the sea.

Torrance knew his own life was not in any real danger, although everyone on the base had heard reports of occasional attacks on airfields by German intruders, and what had happened to the crew of H Henry was still a fresh and nightmarish memory. Unconcerned about himself, he worried about Krystyna.

The summer ran its course, turned to autumn, then dragged

slowly into winter. Torrance heard nothing from Krystyna. Bomber Command was mounting a winter offensive against the German capital, Berlin, with a long series of massed raids. From the point of view of the aircrew these were the most arduous bombing attacks of the war. The distance travelled to and from the target was at the limit of the Lancasters' range and involved hours of dangerous flying. The weather was almost always bad, with heavy cloud-cover and icing being constant problems, the German night fighters had introduced several effective new methods of attacking the RAF aircraft, and the city itself was well defended with powerful anti-aircraft guns. Casualties were inevitable every time there was a raid, and 148 Squadron suffered as many dead or missing men as every other operational unit at that time.

For Torrance, a feeling of numbness set in, partly as a reaction to the casualties, but also as a defence against the background feeling of disappointment about Krystyna. A part of him still clung to the hope that she would make contact with him soon, but in reality he knew that he was probably never going to hear from her again. Whatever it was that had existed, was gone.

On the first day of February, the squadron was particularly demoralized because of what had happened the night before. It had been a disastrous raid, with a total of thirty-three British air-craft lost in all. Five of them were 148 Squadron's Lancasters. Four were known to have been shot down, while the fifth had crashed during the long flight home. By this time the ground crews were accustomed to the tragedies these events involved, while never shrugging them off, but to lose five crews in one night was a ter-rible and discouraging blow. One of the aircraft that was lost was G George, which Torrance had been servicing for several weeks. He knew the aircrew well.

In the afternoon two replacement Lancasters were flown in, arriving at the distant dispersal at the same time as Torrance was heading back to the instrument section after lunch. As he walked along he saw a car speeding across the airfield. It came to a halt close to where he was walking and the passenger climbed out. He headed towards the squadron HQ.

Torrance recognized the uniform straight away: it was the royal blue of the ATA. He stopped dead, staring uncontrollably. The pilot was a man, a tall figure, slim, erect. He was walking slowly away.

Torrance could not help himself. He ran to catch up with the pilot, essaying a clumsy salute as he rushed along.

'Sir, sir!'

The man halted, and turned. He glanced at Torrance's well-worn fatigues, took in their meaning.

'You don't have to call me sir,' he said. 'I am not an RAF officer.'

'Sir, I know who you are!' Torrance said, feeling out of breath even though he had dashed no more than about twenty yards. 'I need to ask you something, please.'

'You say you know me?'

'I meant – I know you fly with the ATA.'

'Yes, I do.'

In the excitement of the moment, Torrance's mind was racing. He briefly recalled the bizarre stories that went around about the male ATA pilots, with their alleged crutches, glass eyes and wooden legs. This man appeared whole and fit, but he was silver haired, past middle age, well beyond the age of operational pilots, or even of administrative officers. Torrance became more flustered by these thoughts.

'I'm sorry!' he said. 'I don't know what—'

'You said you wanted to ask me something.'

Torrance took a breath, trying to steady himself, but he was tense all over and the sudden deep intake of the wintry air made him cough. Finally he said, 'I am trying to make contact with a – a friend, a pilot with the ATA. I don't know how to go about finding her.'

'She's one of our women pilots?'

'Yes, sir.'

'I don't have much contact with the women's ferry pool,' he said. 'We are based in different places all over the country. Can you tell me her name?'

'She is called Krystyna Roszca. She's a Second Officer, and she comes from Poland.'

'Poland – yes, I know there are several Poles flying with us. Where is she based?'

'At Hamble,' Torrance said.

'I'm at White Waltham. That's quite a distance from Hamble. I'm afraid I don't know of Miss Roszca. Have you tried the Polish government in exile?'

'No. I had not thought of that.'

'Well, maybe they wouldn't tell you what you want to know. I suppose you have a good reason for wanting to hear from her?' Torrance knew he was blushing. The man smiled. 'Would you like me to see if I can get a message to her?'

'Sir, if you would.' He stammered out a rush of words: please ask her to phone me, no, write to me, get to this airfield somehow, it's important, urgent, I must hear from her soon.

The man listened quietly, then took out a notebook. He asked Torrance for his full name and rank, and his service number, who the NCO in charge of his unit was, and the name of the senior officer. He wrote all that down. He told Torrance his own name: he was First Officer Dennis Fielden, and gave Torrance an address where he could be contacted – the airfield at White Waltham – and even the address of the ATA headquarters in London, which he suggested, 'if all else fails', might be the best way of locating Krystyna. He reminded Torrance that because of wartime security concerns it could be difficult to obtain exact information about personnel.

'Aircraftman First Class Michael Torrance,' he said, reading out what he had written down. 'Will she know your name and rank?'

'Yes.'

'Leave it with me,' he said. 'Sometimes these things can be found out. I joined the ATA at the beginning of the war, so I know my way around.'

When Torrance returned to work he felt more cheerful than he had for weeks, but for the rest of the base it was still a time heavy with sadness.

Three days passed, but because of Fielden's confident manner Torrance felt certain everything was going to be all right. On the afternoon of the fourth day he was summoned without warning to the Adjutant's office in the main block. He borrowed a bike and pedalled across there quickly – he had never been anywhere near the Adjutant's office before and when he reached the main building he had to ask the way.

Two men were standing in the corridor where he had been directed – one was Dennis Fielden, the other was an RAF officer he did not recognize, but he assumed it must be the Adjutant. As soon as he was noticed walking towards them, the officer nodded to Mr Fielden, then walked briskly away. Mr Fielden greeted him in the corridor, then ushered him into the office. Torrance noticed he was not wearing his cap, so he removed his own. Fielden closed the door. They remained standing.

He said without delay, 'Aircraftman Torrance, I have managed to trace Second Officer Roszca for you, but I'm afraid I bring sad news. Krystyna Roszca has been posted as missing and is believed to be dead. She was delivering a plane as a regular part of her job, when she appears to have diverted from her planned course. She did not arrive at her destination. No wreckage was found, so it is thought that she might have made an emergency landing in water somewhere. Part of the route she filed would have taken her close to the Thames Estuary, and the diversion she took from that course almost certainly led her out over the sea. It seems possible that she somehow lost her bearings, became unable to find her way back to the right course and was forced down when she ran out of fuel.'

Torrance had taken in only the first few words, the giddy sensation of bad news rushing through him.

They were both silent for a while, then Torrance said, 'Sir, when did this happen?'

'It was last year, towards the end of August. She was rota'd for the delivery on the twenty-seventh of that month.'

'Is it absolutely certain she is dead?'

Torrance had somehow sat down – he did not remember doing it. He was on a hard wooden chair placed behind the door of the office. The ATA pilot was standing beside him, leaning over with an expression of sympathy. He was calm, steady, tall. He placed a hand on Torrance's shoulder.

First Officer Fielden said, 'Michael, I am really so very sorry.'

'Thank you, sir.'

After Fielden had left, Torrance was unable to face going back to work straight away. He left the Adjutant's office, walked along the corridor and found an empty room at the end. Inside, with the door closed, he hid there alone.

16

In the summer of 1944 Mike Torrance was transferred to an RAF base in southern Italy, where he serviced P-51 Mustangs and P-38 Lightnings operated by units of the USAAF. He remained attached to this section until the end of the European war, when he returned to England. He was demobilized at the beginning of 1946.

In 1948 he met his wife, Glenys, and they set up home together in the south-east London suburbs, on the Kent side. They had three children, two boys and a girl. Torrance worked in a number of jobs after the war, but in 1954 began working for a medium-sized advertising agency in Bayswater Road, not far from Notting Hill. He was trained as a copy-writer, which was work he found stimulating and creative. He worked well in advertising for a few years and enjoyed what he was doing, but in the end he found copy-writing something of a blind alley. He was developing a taste for different kinds of writing. He transferred to the subsidiary of an American chemical company with an office in Bromley, closer to his home, and there he was appointed senior journalist. He was responsible for writing and producing all manner of printed material, from straightforward descriptions of products, to publicity handouts and the house journal, published every month.

Some years later, emboldened by both his enjoyment of the work and the belief that he was doing it well, he gave up paid employment altogether and started a new career as a biographer, working for himself as a freelance. He began modestly, producing short biographies of service personnel who had performed acts of exceptional bravery or gallantry in the Second World War, and these were commissioned and printed by a specialist military history publisher. Later he branched out into political and social biographies for the general market, where he was soon established as an authority in his field.

He rarely thought about Krystyna Roszca in these years – his professional life was full and he was absorbed in the experience of seeing his young family growing up. Eventually the age of retirement approached.

For Torrance this felt like a mere technicality of the calendar, because as a freelance the prospect of ceasing work was arbitrary and unnecessary. He was in good health, had active commissions for the work he was engaged in, and was planning more books as far ahead as ever. Even so, he was conscious of a general slowing down and he became more introspective than he had been before. He continued with his usual work as normal, but with increasing frequency his thoughts returned to the summer of 1943 and his brief romantic interlude with Krystyna, the flier from Poland, the girl, the young woman, who had cried and held his hand. He had not thought for many years of the secret she had imparted to him, her mother's love-name for her. Malina – it came back to him immediately. He said it quietly to himself, using Krystyna's own Polish pronunciation, with the emphasis on the long middle 'i'.

He thought about her with increasing interest and attention, quietly remembering himself at that time, at the age he had been: so shy, young, callow, inexperienced, unprepared for a worldly woman like her. He began to wonder – how had he seemed to her? He realized, belatedly, what she had achieved: that fierce independence and brave initiative that had given her a role in the defence of her country, the hours of dangerous flying while the Luftwaffe dive-bombers hit the towns and the fighter planes searched for any target they could find, the escape from the invasions, the nightmare overland journey to safety across Europe as war was erupting everywhere around. When he met her he had been not much more than a boy, uprooted from home, thrown into the hurly-burly of a wartime RAF station, just about getting by. Looking back, Torrance felt abashed by his memories of himself: his insular background, his unawareness of the wider world, his lack of experience with girls. At first Krystyna had seen in him, he knew, a reminder of someone else, her real lover, but somehow by the end of their day that was no longer so important. He believed she had been responding to him, not to her memory of someone else.

When the Second World War ended, Torrance, like many of the people who had been caught up in it, deliberately pushed it to the back of his mind. He had had enough of war, of life in the RAF. He almost never spoke of his experiences. Even when he met Glenys, six months passed before he mentioned he had been in the RAF, and even then he minimized his role and barely spoke of it again to her. With his work on the early biographies, corresponding with veterans and sometimes interviewing them, Torrance realized that what had happened when he met Krystyna was not at all unusual. So many of the war's participants were young, even the ones who had distinguished themselves in action. Nearly everyone was away from their families for the first time, thrown into the controlled chaos of service life. For many, the prospect of action and the fear of death heightened the need for friendships, for love, and the consequent separations, weeping, regretting, reunions, hopes, fearing not just their own deaths but those of the people they knew or loved or simply worked with. All those bereavements, families broken for so many reasons, so many liaisons and relationships and new starts and false hopes and tragic outcomes.

His meeting with Krystyna was the one wartime experience that had left a real mark on him. He recalled the account of her life in Poland, which he had written up from memory in 1953 while he was still working in unsatisfying jobs. At the time it felt like a way of making what happened coherent, something he could complete and finish. In this sense he had succeeded. He had not read his account or even thought about it for years. He searched his room, his desk, his cupboards, his old and inefficient filing – finally he found it, stuffed into a box file of papers which his wife had put to one side for possible recycling. He rescued it, read it.

It was full of memories, and it made him think about how he had heard of Krystyna's death.

There was something unexplained about the way she died, and it still nagged at him. While he accepted as true what the gentle ATA officer, Dennis Fielden, had told him, he felt from the first moments that it could not be the whole story. In the larger process of consciously leaving behind everything that happened to him in the war, Torrance had let this small mystery drift into the past. Millions of people had died, many of them in unexplained circumstances – it was in the nature of war, with its violent events, sudden deaths, guilty acts, secrecy.

But it still seemed unlikely to him that Krystyna would allow herself to get lost, or would divert from her planned route. It was of course possible she had crashed, through a mechanical failure of the aircraft, or by enemy action, or because of bad weather, but it was against everything that he knew about her that she would simply lose her way. No wreckage had been discovered, which he presumed meant that nothing had been found along her known route. He had seen her flying, admired her skill, her natural way of piloting – also her determination, the inner strength and individuality, all her hopes and wishes. If she had diverted from her route there would have been a reason.

Torrance decided he would try to find out what it might have been. He had learned a few skills of his own since becoming a writer. Notable among them was an ability to search and research, to explore boxes of dusty papers, to ransack newspaper libraries, to elicit half-concealed information from official bodies. He had many contacts, friends, ways and means. He knew it would help to be able to speak Polish, an ambition he had nurtured for many years, so he sent away for an audio course, then later took privately tutored lessons.

The facts were easier to find than he had at first expected, because in the post-war years many official papers and documents were released into the public domain, with many more becoming accessible after the collapse of the Soviet Union. This made the prospect of going to Poland much less of a concern. For researchers it became a matter not of trying to find out if the information existed, but of locating exactly where it was. In Britain, the aircraft manufacturers had released a huge amount of information about the serial numbers and marques of the aircraft they had built, when the planes were completed and where they were delivered. Among many other authorities the ATA had made their archives public and their pilots' logs and delivery schedules were available to be consulted. In a few cases, where the pilots had died in service or gone missing, personal effects were still on file, including some letters. Krystyna's file had several personal effects. Among the letters were two of the ones he had written to her himself, the ones that she had never answered. He started reading the first, but when he noticed the date, two days after she went missing, he was unable to go on to the end. In the same file Torrance found the little purse, the one that had started everything. It was now empty. The bright colours, which had so entranced him in that monochrome wartime world, had faded, and the red piping was coming unstitched. He held it for a while, consumed by memories, then sadly replaced it.

The first thing Torrance discovered about Krystyna was her full name: Krystyna Agnieszka Roszca. Foreign Office records revealed that she had been admitted to Britain firstly as a refugee, then accredited as a serving member of the Polish Air Force attached to the Polish government in exile. All this confirmed what she had told him about herself. He could find no information about her birth family. The rest of her story was corroborated in broad outline: certain elements of the Polish Air Force had escaped to Romania, their equipment was confiscated, and they were told to leave the country in the early part of 1940.

From the Polish Embassy in London he discovered facts about her he had not known. She had been given a rank in the Air Force, presumably by the general she had named: a temporary commission as Porucznik, or Lieutenant, Roszca. After living in Britain for some time she had eventually been given some back pay by the Poles, and a small stipend every week, but this was discontinued when she joined the ATA.

More interesting still was the fact that Sikorski's government had awarded her a medal for her flying duties during the invasion: the Cross of Merit for Bravery, or in Polish, *Krzyż Zasługi za Dzielność*. The citation read: 'Porucznik (Temporary) K. A. Roszca – for selfless bravery in the defence of national borders, and the life and property of citizens in especially difficult circumstances.'

In the background of Krystyna's story dark shadows hovered. The first was harmless and tragic, but it still had the power, decades later, to cause Torrance a pang of jealousy. She had not told him

– she had no obligation to tell him – that not long before their day together she had been involved with a young RAF pilot called Simon Barrett. In the ATA archive Torrance found Barrett's short letters to her, innocent and happy and joking, an outline of a brief wartime romance. In one letter Simon Barrett pleaded with her to 'put the past behind'. Later, Torrance discovered in the Air Ministry archives that Pilot Officer Simon Barrett, aged 21, had been captain of a Halifax bomber, returning in March 1943 from a raid on Stuttgart. The plane was shot down over the North Sea, with the loss of all the crew.

For Tomasz, the lover in Poland she had lost, the story was even darker. Sinister events had followed the collapse of Poland. It was not clear to Mike Torrance if Krystyna had known at the time what was happening, or had found out shortly afterwards. Possibly, she had heard enough rumours amongst the Polish exiles to have secretly feared it. The reality was that in April and May 1940, which was around the time Krystyna had travelled from France to England, the Soviet authorities in Occupied Poland rounded up the entirety of the officer corps of the Polish army and air force, some twenty-two thousand men in all, transported them to the Katyn Forest near Smolensk in Russia, and massacred them. Mass graves were discovered in 1943, at approximately the same time as Torrance had spent his summer's day with Krystyna. Most of the bodies they found bore a single bullet hole in the back of the head. News of this gruesome discovery did not officially reach Western Europe until after the end of the war.

Krystyna had managed to escape the atrocity, but what of Tomasz? Torrance began to feel certain that there in the Katyn Forest, unmarked in some mass grave, lay the body of the young aristocrat whom he had believed was his rival.

There was not much more that he could check definitively while he remained in Britain. From several ancestry websites devoted to the Polish aristocracy he elicited the information that the last known holder of the Lowicz title, from the family Grudzinski, was Rafal, son of Bronisław. Rafal Grudzinski was thought to have died in 1940, and with him the title ceased to exist. There was no reference to a son called Tomasz, nor to any other children.

A year went by after this initial sweep through what records Torrance could find while he was in England. Sikorski's government had left few traces or records after the war ended. He knew that to get more detailed information he would have to access not only army and regimental records in Poland, but also newspaper files and civic archives. Torrance had no idea how much of this sort of material would have survived the havoc that Poland endured during its years of Nazi occupation and administration, the rounding up and deportations, the forced labour camps, the extermination camps. A journey to Poland became essential.

A few months after his wife Glenys died, Torrance made the visit he had been planning for so long. He intended it as a working trip – as well as the research he always enjoyed travelling abroad, because it gave him indirect background experience that came in useful for his books. This time, though, he wanted to make best use of the time, and conduct a thorough search of whatever records were available. Part of him was nonetheless curious to see the country from which Krystyna had come. He travelled to Kraków at the end of 1999. He was then 76 and he knew that it was almost certainly his last opportunity to travel abroad.

His searches added little to what he already knew, but more alarmingly they made him question even that.

Firstly, there was Krystyna's birth family. Torrance went to Pobiednik, the village Krystyna had named – in fact there were two villages, Pobiednik Great and Pobiednik Small, a short distance apart. No trace of any family called Roszca could be found in either of them, and none of the present-day inhabitants he spoke to had ever heard of anyone of that name. Torrance was interested to see that Pobiednik had its own airfield: a small strip owned by an aero club. He was unable to discover whether or not it had been there in the 1930s, but the local people thought not.

Of Tomasz Grudzinski, or possibly Tomasz Lowicz, nothing could be found. Torrance searched libraries and databases without success. He spent two days in the civic archives in the Ratusz of Kraków, and although he found many references to land deals undertaken by Rafal Grudzinski, and the businesses in which he had an interest, and the taxes he had paid, and the woman he had married, and the noble titles he possessed, and the property and artwork of his that was seized by the Nazis, Torrance could find no reference to his children. As far as he could determine, Rafal Grudzinski had not had a family. The Lowicz line of inheritance was already set to be discontinued, even before the outbreak of war.

When he went to the records of the Poznań Uhlan Regiment, which Krystyna had specifically named, Torrance was shown names and details of every Hussar officer who had served between 1920 and 1939, when the regiment was disbanded by the German occupiers. There were many Tomaszes on the lists, and several Grudzinskis, but none with both names.

Although the Polish authorities had done years of work in establishing the identity of every victim of the Katyn massacre, Torrance could also find no reference to a Tomasz Grudzinski in the interminable catalogue, or at least he could not see any officer of that name, or one close to it, whose background was the same as the man he sought.

By the time he left Poland and returned home, Torrance was convinced that Tomasz, the man he had as a youth envied and feared so much, had either been eradicated from history, or, a much more puzzling conclusion, might never in fact have existed at all.

He made no more enquiries into Krystyna's Polish background.

However, he had at least worked out what must have happened to her at the end, and he had not needed to travel to Kraków for that. ATA records and logs were enough.

On 27 August 1943, approximately five weeks after the day she and Torrance met, Krystyna was rostered to fly a newly built Spitfire XI from the Supermarine factory near Southampton, to an RAF airfield in East Anglia. The Mark XI she flew was exactly as she had described it to him: it was designed for long range high-altitude reconnaissance, equipped with powerful cameras and extra fuel tanks. There were no weapons.

Her flight plan that day was uncomplicated: a more or less straight line across southern England, with an estimated flight time of less than an hour.

According to air traffic control records she appeared to deviate from her course not long after taking off, and headed towards

London. Her plane was routinely tracked on radar until it crossed central London, which it traversed at an altitude of more than ten thousand feet. The plane was picked up again when it left London airspace and began heading along the Thames Estuary and out towards the North Sea. When it was last observed the Spitfire was seen still to be gaining altitude, and had turned a few degrees to port, on a bearing of about 80 degrees.

There were no further sightings of the Spitfire, and, as Dennis Fielden had informed him so many years before, no wreckage of it was ever found.

Torrance believed that he alone could imagine what had happened. He pictured the slim young woman in her blue uniform, her distinctive dark-brown hair pressed inside the flying helmet, strapped into the narrow cockpit of the plane she considered the most beautiful ever made, flying it for the first time, wearing it like a second skin. She had probably given no conscious thought to what she was about to do. She followed her instincts, her mind spinning in a sort of ecstatic rapture. In this haze of happy completion she quickly took the Spitfire into the summer sky, flying it high and far, releasing herself from the bonds of war, through the white clouds, across the blue, scraping the roof of the world, flying without end, heading home, touching nothing but the free air and the endless sky.

PART 6

The Cold Room

1

THE SIXTH

The eye of TS Federico Fellini swept over the country from the south-west and now covered much of Lincolnshire and southern Yorkshire. The outermost rainbands stretched as far down as the Thames Estuary. Violent winds attacked the North Sea coasts, and on the far side of the sea Denmark reported mountainous waves and substantial damage to coastal defences. At Warne's Farm, Tibor Tarent's refuge, there was a brilliant electric storm followed by a brief period of bright sunshine and a misleading calm. The first main winds, on the leading edge of the storm cell, struck the Warne complex in the early hours of the morning. Tarent was woken by the noise as soon as the gale moved in over the buildings, shaking the walls and hurling rain and ice particles at the windows. He huddled under the bedclothes in the dark, terrified by the screeching of the gale and the many shuddering thuds as pieces of storm-driven debris crashed against the reinforced outer walls. By the time Lou Paladin left her own room and came to his, he was crying with fright. She stayed with him until dawn.

They spent the next day in close companionship, while the storm battered the outside of the building and the nervous exhaustion seeped slowly out of him. On the night of the main storm Lou slept alongside him in the same bed, but it was only for mutual comfort and reassurance. Once he had surrendered to the immense backlog of nervous strain, Tarent was its helpless sufferer and victim, no longer in control. A small part of his mind remained sufficiently detached to feel surprise at the intensity of what was happening, but intelligence was no match for fear. Most of the time he just gave in to it – he cried, he writhed with physical pain, he jabbered senseless words. He had the sense that he had become untethered from reality, yet he was too frightened by what was happening to fight for control. He lay awake for hours – when he slept it was a fitful sleep. He could not speak coherently, he could not keep food down, he could not think. He was daunted by memories of the savage violence he had witnessed in Anatolia, the illnesses of the small children, the mutilations the women had suffered, the insensible revenges taking place, the vast and intolerable heat, the brutality of militiamen, the indifference of uniformed soldiers, the smells of dying and death.

His cameras had captured images of everything. His memory was stronger, but his mind was under threat.

On the second morning there was a lull in the full ferocity of Federico Fellini. Lou warmed up some milk for him and he sipped it slowly. Thirty minutes later he was still managing to keep it down. Lou gave him two biscuits to nibble on, and they stayed down too.

Tarent knew he was almost certainly not losing his mind, but even so for the time being rational thought had deserted him. He could not concentrate on anything. He listened to Lou whenever she spoke, trying to disentangle her words from the chaos of his own thoughts.

'The storm will pass later today,' she said, into the silence around him but raising her voice above the constant roaring and howling from outside. 'It will intensify again soon. The trailing edge of the storm will pass over us, but it's not likely to be as bad as before. The storm has already been downgraded, but there's another system behind this one and it is heading this way.'

A broad metal strap, one of many visible from the window, ran down from the roof of the building, anchored somewhere on the ground. It whipped and shrieked when the wind caught it.

Lou said, 'We're safe here so long as we don't go outside. They claim the buildings can withstand cyclones up to and even beyond Level 5. Those straps hold the roofs on.'

She seemed to Tarent to be speaking slowly and pedantically, like a radio announcer conveying an important piece of public information. Even so, he had trouble following what she said. He was thinking about Melanie again, remembering the agony of realizing she was dead, but also Flo. What had happened to her when the vehicle was destroyed? Was it the same explosion that killed them both? He was no longer sure. Lou was stroking the side of his face.

Whenever he raised himself high enough from the bed to take a look at what was happening outside, Tarent was astonished by the amount of debris that had fallen into the wide quadrangle that lay between the buildings. As well as many branches and bushes, and other pieces of broken vegetation there were large pieces of metal, some of them bent or twisted sheets, beams of shattered wood and a thousand shards of broken glass. Often these wind-borne projectiles smashed against the rain-streaked windows. He pushed against the window by the bed, testing its strength.

Lou laid a calming hand on his arm. 'The windows won't break. That's why the glass is so thick, why the view outside is distorted.'

Tarent then remembered, in a glance of rational memory, the bottle-glass distortions of what could be seen from inside the Mebsher.

The Mebsher – he had remembered what it was called. He tried to say the word but it would not form.

Lou must have gone away while he slept, because he was alone when he woke. She returned not long afterwards. She gave him a drink of water and although he resisted the idea of being helpless and in need of nursing, he was reassured by her sitting beside him. He consumed the tinned soup she heated up for him. Somehow she had found fresh bread.

Something large bashed against the side of the building. For a moment the lighting in the room flickered. They both reacted, but Lou calmed him.

'There are three back-up circuits,' she said. 'The lights never seem to go out. I watched the news on TV just now. The only news channel I could find was from Helsinki. They said the next storm coming out of the Atlantic is TS Graham Greene and it's about two days behind this one. At the moment it's predicted to be Level 3, so although it's a full cyclone it won't cause as much damage. It might pass over more slowly, though. They also thought it was possible it would veer away from this part of the country. Not a big problem for us, anyway,'

'I need to get out of this place,' Tarent said, and realized he had formed a whole sentence.

'Don't we all?'

'I haven't read anything by Graham Greene,' he added. Coherent thoughts were forming for the first time in what felt like several days. It was an idea outside himself, the surrender he had made to the obsessions and fears and the loss of logical thinking. 'Yes, I have, I think,' he added, remembering an old book about Brighton.

'I've read a couple of his novels,' Lou said. 'And some of his short stories – I taught them a few years ago. But I've seen all of Fellini's films.'

'I can speak again.'

'You've never stopped,' Lou said. 'You ran a fever and you were talking for hours.'

'What did I say? Did it make sense?'

'No.'

'Do you mean you heard but couldn't understand, or that you don't want to tell me?'

'I heard. I couldn't understand most of it. It doesn't matter – I'm used to people recovering from shock. Years ago I trained as a nurse.'

'My wife was a nurse.'

'That was Melanie?'

'How do you know about Melanie?'

'You kept saying her name. I knew your wife had died, but her name wasn't on the database. I think you said she'd been killed by someone. Was that recently?'

'Last week,' Tarent said. 'Or perhaps the week before. I'm out of synch with the world. I've lost days, dates.'

'I'm sorry.'

'So am I.'

'You told me you were in Turkey. Was that where it happened?'

'There was some kind of terrorist attack, and Melanie was accidentally caught up in it.'

Tarent fell silent, trying unsuccessfully to remember what he might have said before, not only when he was delirious but also when he first met this woman. It was difficult to think like that, think back, because his memory of recent events was in disorder. He remembered Melanie with love and sadness, but he also remembered the woman who would only tell him he should call her Flo. Was that her real name? He could not remember if he had found that out. The disorder in his mind held a new kind of fascination for him, and he felt himself slipping back into it, a confusion he wanted to embrace.

Lou must have sensed something. She took his head in her hands, held him until he opened his eyes. He realized what had happened, breathed deeply a few times.

'Is nursing what you do now?' he said. An effort of will, an intent to sound normal.

'No – I told you. I'm a teacher. Nursing wasn't for me. I was coming out of my teens. I passed most of the exams, then I was employed by an agency for about a year before moving on. The only work I could find was abroad and I didn't want to leave the country. Is that why your wife went abroad?'

'Did I say that too?'

'Turkey.'

'My god, yes. I'm sorry. I keep forgetting what I've told you. Turkey was a part of what happened to me. I must have been out there too long, because now I'm home I feel as if this country has changed out of all recognition. I assume it's just the way I see it now. I feel stuck in the past, but in some way I find completely confusing it's a past I never actually knew. Or that's how it feels. No, Melanie wanted a change. She was a theatre nurse and after several years the job became too much for her. She was trying relief work. I went with her to Turkey because I wanted to be with her, and I thought I could probably take photographs for the syndicate I work for. Anyway, I was interested to find out what was happening, but then we both did find out and I think we wished we had stayed here.'

'How long were you away?'

'I lost track of that. We were travelling for ages, then several months went by when we were at the field hospital.'

'How do you think things have changed in Britain?'

'It's hard to say. When you're away from home for a long time you tend to build up a false memory of what you've left: you keep thinking about either the best, or the worst of it. The ordinary, everyday stuff, your normal life, is something you don't hold a clear memory of, because when things are ordinary you just do them. In Turkey everything was so bad for us, endlessly dangerous and depressing and threatening – Melanie sometimes worked a sixteen-hour day, which was too much for anyone. I shouldn't have been there with her. I ought to have realized that before we left. After the first few days I had time on my hands. I spent hours alone, day after day. I was bored, but life was dangerous and unpleasant. I stayed inside the compound most of the time. I used to think about being a child again, doing what I had done then, seeing the sea, walking in woodland, playing with other children, just being happy and safe. I know it sounds infantile. Although in reality my childhood wasn't particularly happy, and when I think back I can't find any memories of actually doing those things. So it's a sort of false nostalgia, something I must have made up or borrowed. Perhaps I saw it in a film once, or read it in books. My father died when I was very young, and although I took British citizenship years ago I'm half American, half Hungarian. My mother worked in London so I grew up in this country. I was in London most of the time – I don't recall a visit to the sea even once. Even though I did not have that particular childhood, it felt natural to look back and think how much better life was, or might have been, or perhaps might have been what I thought it ought to have been.'

Lou was sitting beside him, staring down silently at her hands. They were gripped together tightly, the skin on the back of each hand was corrugated by the pressure, her knuckles were straining under the skin.

'When I came back here,' Tarent said, 'I think I was unconsciously looking for that. Being in the field hospital was hell. It was hell to work in, for Melanie and the rest of the medical staff, but it was just as bad to be there, to experience it. Turkey has become a desert – the climate has changed more than anyone outside the region knows. The whole of the Mediterranean basin has become unfit for habitation. I don't suppose the people are suffering there any more than other places where the really hot weather has kicked in, but it's more or less unlivable now. I can't imagine what parts of Africa or Asia must be like. After Melanie was killed, the government transported me back to Britain straight away. It was like arriving in a different world. These storms – are they always as bad as this?'

'Recent ones have been. There were two or three late last year that caused a vast amount of damage.'

'Weather in Britain was always a joke, but there was never anything like this before. Is it just because of climate change, or is something else behind it? When I was being brought here I had to be transported in an armoured personnel carrier. I thought those were only used where there is an active insurgency, when you genuinely need to be protected. Aid teams routinely go everywhere in them. I didn't know Mebshers were in use here, that things had become that bad. When I was inside the Mebsher, trying to see outside, it was like being carried through a waste land. Buildings down, floods everywhere, most of the trees destroyed. Then London: I was in a car at that stage, before they put me in the Mebsher. I had to pass through London for some reason, but the officials blanked the windows of the car so I couldn't see out. Why do you suppose they did that? What I could see of the city had been transformed. The same in the country. Military everywhere, and police. And then this process of government devolution: every official function being moved out to the provinces.'

'There's an undeclared war in progress,' Lou said. 'People here say it's going to be the last war ever, the war that will end everything. They say the insurgents have some new kind of weapon – something we can't defend ourselves against.'

2

Another piece of blown debris slammed heavily on the roof and they both reacted as if something had physically burst into the room. Moments later a large branch skidded down past the window, half fell against the nearest metal strap and crashed into the yard outside. Tarent knew he was talking too much, as if some barrier inside had loosened. He concentrated on finishing the soup, which was cool now. Lou sat beside him, saying little. He kept thinking about Melanie, already a victim of this final war.

Later that day, as the winds at last started to abate, he began to feel as if he was regaining control of himself. Lou had returned to her own room. He looked at more of his pictures from Anatolia, but they depressed him. He could not carry on with that for long. He went online, searching for news channels or sites, but the government controls on the internet were as strict as those he had encountered abroad. All sites, channels and platforms were now graded according to security levels – the security clearance Tarent had been given for his journey abroad did not apply to the internet, and he had lost internet status when he went abroad. Almost nothing was accessible to him now. He went to find Lou, knowing he was becoming dependent on her, which was wrong, but needing to talk, which was essential. He felt guilty about that, but there was little he could do about it. She was all he had. His mind was starting to feel cluttered again.

As soon as she let him into her room he was overtaken by an irresistible desire to sleep. She let him lie down on her bed.

He woke up many hours later. There was the sound of wind, but it was quieter now. Lights were on in Lou's room and there was a smell of cooking. The door to the bathroom was open, but the light was off in there. The windows to the outside were blackened by night. Lou was on the far side of the room, seated with her legs drawn up in one of the chairs. She had a book on her lap, but her head was bent forward in sleep. Disoriented by this strange awakening, it took him a few minutes to leave the bed. He woke Lou gently, led her to the bed, made sure she was lying down.

He stayed with her for a while but soon returned to his own room. They were living in different time zones. He was wide awake. He showered, shaved and put on clean clothes, then tidied up the mess he had helped create in the room while he was ill.

The worst of his fears had receded again – he felt that he could remember them objectively but whenever he isolated one of the matters that had tormented him, brought it forward so that he could think about it properly, he found it unintelligible.

Later in the day Lou returned to him. He was pleased to see her. They embraced when she came to his door. She brought some food and a small bottle of red wine. She said that the vending machine had been replenished somehow, so there was more choice available at present.

'Lou, you told me you lived in Notting Hill,' he said. 'You said your whole life was there.'

'I lived in Notting Hill for many years. The last school I worked for was there. But then came the attack on May 10. My life there is over now.'

'Did you have friends in Notting Hill?'

'Some. The only one who really mattered was my partner. He was in our apartment on that day.'

'So have you been able to find out what happened to him?'

She opened her hands wide, despairingly. 'No one knows that. Everything in the area was totally obliterated. At first I couldn't see how he could have escaped, but no bodies were found after the blast. In some ways it might have been better if there had been, better to know the worst. I was already here at Warne's Farm when it happened and at first it was impossible trying to find out the truth. In one sense that's even harder now, because so many of the TV channels have closed, but people pass through here all the time, so I've been able to find out more from them.'

'You've been in this place since May?'

'I arrived at the end of April. I was about to take up an appointment at a government school in Lincoln when the attack came. Everything went into paralysis straight away, so I hung on, thinking that's what I should do, what anyone in the same position would do. I kept trying to contact Dumaka – that's my partner's name. I clung to the hope he might have been away from the apartment at the time, but I realize now it was almost certain he wasn't. He didn't have many friends in Britain, but the ones I could contact knew as little as I did. I soon realized he must have been caught up in it.'

'Can you tell me about him? About Dumaka?'

'He's a refugee from Nigeria – he's what some of the staff at the Home Office call an illegal. They wouldn't grant him permission to stay, and he absconded. At first I was frightened to ask about him, after May 10, because I knew that if he was still alive and they traced him they would deport him. You know what the rules are like now. He's been in Britain for nearly fifteen years but that wouldn't change anything. He came here with his brother but his brother has a visa, so he isn't at risk – I met Dumaka when he came to the school to talk about his work. He makes jewellery, beautiful, delicate pieces, and at the time he had exhibited some work in London. For the sake of staying out of sight he always had to work under his brother's name, but the brother didn't like that and neither did Dumaka. They hardly speak to each other now. The longer Dumaka stayed here the safer he felt, but I knew it wasn't the case. Anyway, we moved in with each other after we met. We were happy together for a year or two, but then things started going wrong. I don't mean between us. The collapse of the euro-pound meant no one was buying jewellery any more and then I lost my job at the school. You know the population of London has been declining for years? They closed several of our classrooms because of the fall in student numbers and I was one of the teachers they made redundant. That's why I started working for the government. It meant leaving Dumaka, but the idea was that it would be only temporary, a few weeks at most. As soon as I was settled in a secure position he was intending to follow me.'

She had turned her face away from him as she spoke. Her hands were clasped together again – Tarent could see the tension in her arm muscles. A tear had appeared on the curve of her chin. She brushed her hand over it. Tarent felt sad, and a realization of his selfishness swept over him. He had been so wrapped up in his own troubles that he had never wondered about this woman's life, what it was like, or what it had been like.

She took off her half-moon spectacles and wiped them with a tissue.

'You said you went through Notting Hill,' she said.

'Well, I told you I couldn't see—'

'Tell me again. It's the most important thing in my life.'

'There's hardly anything. I was in a car and there were OOR officials with me. I think part of what they were doing was making sure that either I didn't see much, or didn't ask too many questions. They blacked the windows so we couldn't see out, but at one point they were worried about a storm coming in. They made the windows transparent again so they could look at the clouds building up, and I could see outside. It was just a few seconds.'

'Where were you? What did you see?'

'I only know it was somewhere in west London because they were talking about that. But my wife had just been killed, I had been travelling for days, I hadn't had much sleep and I was disoriented. I had no idea where I really was.'

'But you saw something.'

'No – I saw almost literally nothing. It was all black outside.'

'Was it night-time?'

'No, it was coming up to the evening. There was still daylight.'

'So what did you see that was black?'

'Just, everything. I didn't know what I was seeing, so I had no reference points. You can imagine – I was in a car with the windows darkened, then they were lightened and everything I saw was black. Almost immediately the officials darkened the glass again.'

'Did you see if it had made a triangle, as they say?'

'I don't know. I couldn't see. I'm really sorry. I'd tell you more if I knew more.'

'I've heard it was an adjacency weapon. That was what killed your wife too, wasn't it?'

'Yes,' said Tarent. 'Melanie too.'

3

They went together to the vending machine, but before they used it Lou pointed out that the canteen further down the same corridor had re-opened. There were a surprising number of people there – surprising to Tarent because he had begun to assume that they were more or less alone at Warne's Farm. He realized there must be a quota of workers still in residence. Heavy rain was falling outside but the wind was no longer a destructive force. Lou acknowledged a few of the people as they passed, but she made no effort to introduce Tarent to any of them. He noticed the Frenchman he had met when he first arrived: Bertrand Lepuits. He seemed not to recognize Tarent, and glanced away as soon as their eyes met.

The canteen kitchen had prepared some basic hot food: a choice between a meat stew or vegetarian pasta – Tarent took the stew, Lou the pasta. There was no charge, but they were asked to pay for drinks. Tarent had no cash so Lou paid for them both.

When they went back to the residential block afterwards, the familiar feeling of isolation returned: the other people they had seen were presumably housed in the same sort of self-contained quarters, or worked in the other buildings. In the long, silent corridors of the residential block there was no sense of other people being around.

They spoke in the corridor briefly, but then Lou returned to her own room. Tarent went to his. She said she would look in later.

For a while he stared out at the debris that had gathered in the quadrangle, but even as he stood there at his window workmen in tractors began to clear the ground. The largest branches were moved away in one direction, everything else was lugged towards some sort of collection point beyond the buildings.

His view across the inner quadrangle was angled differently from the one at the window next to the vending machine, from which he had observed the helicopters landing. When was that? Two nights ago, or three? He had genuinely lost all sense of time. From his room the helicopter pad was partly hidden beyond one of the other buildings – he could see a pylon which carried floodlights for night landings, and a small section of the raised concrete platform that was the pad itself, but most of it was out of sight. If there was a chopper on the pad at that moment he would not have been able to tell.

He had, though, a clear view of the building across the quad from the helipad, the one to which he had seen the people wheeled on trolleys. This was a modern construction, institutional in appearance, single-storey, brutally made of concrete, an immense semi-cylindrical building, apparently designed to withstand the storm winds. It was not fenced off or placed behind barriers, but armed guards were pacing slowly to and fro in front of the only entrance that could be seen from where Tarent was standing.

As far as he knew there had been no flights in or out of the Warne complex since the storm broke, so presumably those people were still inside the building. It looked like it could be a clinic, or perhaps a small emergency hospital, but there was nothing outside to indicate its purpose. Tarent realized it was pointless to speculate about it. All he knew was that he had seen people taken inside on stretcher trolleys.

He was returning to his normal frame of mind – there was nothing by which to measure the improvement, beyond an inner conviction that it was happening. His mind felt clear. He moved back from the window, sat in the one large chair with which the room was furnished and for the first time in many hours thought about the woman he knew only as Flo.

She must have been one of the people he had seen removed from the helicopter to the clinic across the quadrangle. Hurt, injured – but how badly? He had seen that the people on the stretchers were quickly hooked up to oxygen supplies, which of course suggested that they were still alive. But he had witnessed the destructive attack on the Mebsher. He assumed from what he saw that everyone on board must have perished instantly. It was the same assumption he had made about Melanie.

4

Tarent heard a noise at his door – expecting Lou, he made no move to open it as they had adjusted the palm-reader settings on their doors to recognize them both. When the knocking was repeated he went across and with a welcoming smile he released the lock.

There was a man standing there. In his surprise Tarent took a moment or two to recognize him. It was Bertrand Lepuits.

'Mr Tarent,' he said. 'We have you registered in another room, but that is occupied by someone else. She directed me here. May I enter?'

'I suppose so.'

He held the door wider. The other man glanced along the corridor in both directions, then stepped through the door. He waited until Tarent had closed it before he spoke again.

He said, 'Mr Tarent, I need to be sure it is you.'

'But you have come here. You know who I am, and you found me.'

'Please – identify yourself. I am here on official business.'

Reluctantly, Tarent complied, pressing his ID card against the reader. A photograph appeared, the one taken by the OOR recording device before he left the country.

'Good, thank you. A mere formality, I assure you. Mr Tarent, I have come to ask you if you would perform a favour for us.'

'If you will perform one for me.'

'What would that be?'

'I'd like to know how I can get out of this place. You told me yourself I should not be here.'

'Yes, indeed. We are expecting transport later today, or early tomorrow. I could make it possible for you to be on that.'

'Good! And my friend – the woman whose room you went to. Louise Paladin.'

'You wish her to leave too?'

'Yes. She is desperate to get home.'

'I'll see what I can make possible.'

'No. If you want something from me, that's what I want in return. No vague promises. Is that clear and understood, Monsieur Lepuits?'

'I don't think you are in a position to demand anything at all. You should not be at Warne's Farm. This is a security-restricted site.'

'You said you wanted a favour from me. I'll be pleased to be out of here.'

'Very well,' said Lepuits. 'You and the woman may leave at the next opportunity.'

'Thank you. Would that be by helicopter?'

'Ah, no – it would be a personnel carrier. Helicopters are not used to transport members of staff.'

'A Mebsher, you mean? Would it take us to London?'

'London – is not possible at the moment.'

'That's where we need to go.'

'From here we can only take you to the DSG in Hull.'

'But I live in London. Louise Paladin also.'

'Mr Tarent – please! I have said you may leave here at the first possible opportunity, but first I need your help. I understand you are acquainted with Tebyeb Mallinan.'

Tarent shook his head. The man's slight French accent made the words sound to him like a blur. 'Would you say the name again, please?'

'I apologize. It is Tebyeb, or Doctor, Mallinan.' He spoke more slowly. 'It was Tebyeb Mallinan who sent a message saying that you had changed your plans, and that we should not be expecting you here.'

Tarent said, 'Is Doctor Mallinan a senior official in the Ministry of Defence?'

'I believe she is. So you would know her?'

'Yes – but if it's who I think it is, that's the first time I've heard her surname, not to mention the fact that she is a doctor.'

'Let me tell you what we require of you, Mr Tarent. There has been an unfortunate accident in which several people were killed. We believe that Doctor Mallinan is among them, but before we can release her body we have to obtain a preliminary identification. She will be properly identified later, probably by a member of her family, but for our internal purposes the Department needs to be certain that she is who we think she is. We are seeking an opinion about her identity. *Un avis*. Once we have that, we will be able to release her remains.'

'So she was killed?'

'Yes. I'm sorry to tell you she was.'

'This was when the Mebsher was attacked?'

'I don't know the details. She and the others were brought in here by an army helicopter.'

'I saw it arrive. But I also saw the staff treating the victims as if they were injured, still alive.'

'No – I assure you, the people who were brought in were dead on arrival.'

'All right.'

'Good.' Lepuits had moved back towards the door and now pulled it open. 'There is some urgency to this.' He indicated with his hand. '*Je vous prie, monsieur.*'

Tarent followed the man along the corridor and down the stairs. They walked quickly past Lou's room, where the door was closed. Tarent was trying to adjust to the knowledge, the now certain knowledge, that Flo had been killed in the attack on the Mebsher. Because of the lack of certainty, he had been unconsciously clinging to the shred of hope that she and the others had somehow survived. But, well, now that hope seemed to be gone.

They left the residential block and walked out into the open air. There was still a stiff wind, but nothing like the gale that had caused all the damage. All the larger pieces of wreckage had been cleared. In one corner of the quadrangle the tractors were still working, pushing everything away to an area beyond the buildings on that side.

When they reached the entrance to the building with the curved concrete facade, Lepuits showed an identity card to the two guards, then activated the door with another card, this one with an electronic stripe. He let Tarent walk past him and enter first. When the door closed against the outside, all was silent. No sound of the wind could be heard. The muffled acoustics of the place created a sense that all sounds had been muted. Lepuits switched on the overhead lights.

They were in what appeared to be an open-plan office, with several work-stations in orderly rows on the side nearest to them. Curtained cubicles were set against the far wall – these were open, ready for use, examination beds bare, metal bottles of oxygen and medical cabinets beside each one.

Lepuits said, 'You understand, this facility is maintained only for occasional or emergency use. We have a consultant A&E nurse on site, but no doctors. Since the recent crisis began we are treating it as a holding site, and anyone in need of anything more than first aid is transferred as soon as possible to a hospital in Nottingham or Lincoln.' He led Tarent away from this area, through a door, into a partitioned section. 'We don't have a mortuary, but there is a refrigerated room, so the bodies are being stored in there for the time being. It's extremely cold inside, but I don't suppose it will take long. Neither of us is dressed for this, so please let us be quick.'

There was a large insulated door which Lepuits pulled open, and led the way inside. The air inside was indeed freezing cold.

Most of the space was occupied either by cases of food, or by sealed drums of uncertain contents. Tarent took them in with barely a glance. The cold air was rasping in his windpipe. He had never known such cold in his life. A row of bodies lay side by side on the surface of a bench built against the side wall. Each was shrouded by a white sheet. The drums, boxes and other containers that had been stacked there before were now standing on the floor below.

Lepuits went to the figure in the centre. He leaned forward, having to balance himself because the boxes on the floor made close access difficult, and peeled down the sheet to reveal the face.

'This is the woman we have reason to believe might be Tebyeb or Doctor Mallinan,' he said.

Lepuits stepped back, and Tarent moved forward to take his place. He leaned over to see. He was already in shock, because of the news, the realization of finality as well as the awe-inspiring cold in the room, but there was Flo. She, the body, was lying with her eyes closed, but there were no injuries, no burns or scars or cuts to the face, no blast flares, no bruising, no disfigurement at all. He suddenly remembered what she had said in a completely different context, that she was beyond damage, that he would see what she meant. Now he was seeing, and it was as she had said. Whatever had happened to her when she died it had not marked her. Or it had not marked her face. Lepuits did not lift the sheet high enough for Tarent to see any more than her head and shoulders.

He did not feel repelled by her frozen appearance, nor by the fact of her death, nor even by a feeling of loss, because he had realized for some time that what had happened between them was a passing incident. But a sense of tragedy arose in him, the awareness of a life wasted, an intelligent and interesting woman, suddenly killed, pointlessly annihilated.

'Can you please identify her, Mr Tarent?'

'Yes. It's her.'

'You have to say her name.'

'I knew her only as Flo. Is that this woman's first name?'

'We need a more certain identification than that.'

'Do you know this woman's first name?' Tarent said again. 'If I say she was called Flo, and you know that, surely it would be enough?'

'Please identify her.'

Tarent gestured, partly with the frustration of having to deal with this man, but also as some way of physically expressing the despair he had suddenly experienced. 'I knew her as Flo. She told me she was a senior civil servant in the Ministry of Defence, that she was in the Private Office of the ministry and that she worked closely with the minister, Sheik Ammari. She and I were not close friends. We only met once and she would not tell me her full name. She even suggested that the name Flo was not her real name. But I do recognize her. This is the woman I knew.'

Lepuits lowered the sheet across her face, and tidied it at each side.

'Is that enough for you?' Tarent said.

'I can record it as an opinion.'

'But is that enough?'

'An opinion will allow me to release the body.'

'All right, then can we get out of this place? I can't stand the cold.'

'Would you able to identify the others?'

'I can't name them,' Tarent said. 'But if these were the people I travelled with in the Mebsher, then I would recognize them. The two crewmen's names were Hamid and Ibrahim, they were serving soldiers in the army, the Black Watch. They weren't officers, but I don't know their actual ranks. One of the men who was travelling as a passenger was called Heydar, but I've no idea if that was a first name or a surname. He was a colleague of Flo's. The other man was an American, but I know nothing else about him.'

'If you can recognize them,' said Lepuits. 'I will also record what you say as an opinion.'

Tarent moved awkwardly along the row, having to clamber around the boxes on the floor. He quickly looked at the next four bodies and confirmed that he recognized all of them. None of them showed any signs of physical injuries so far as he could see. They all had the waxy look of death, a horrid blankness, a lack of life-force, of existence: the two Scottish soldiers, Flo's colleague Heydar, the unnamed American. There was a sixth body, also shrouded, but this was at the far end of the shelf and the materials placed on the floor would have made it impossible to reach it without moving some of the large containers out of the way. Tarent's hands were shaking with the intense cold.

'There were only five people on the Mebsher with me,' he said, indicating the extra body.

'We do not need your opinion on the last person. He has already been positively identified. You and I are concerned only with these five people here.'

'You have everything you want from me?'

'Thank you, Mr Tarent. It is of great assistance to us.'

'Can we leave now?'

'But of course.'

To Tarent's relief, Lepuits led the way quickly from the cold room and pushed the door back into place.

'Is that all?' Tarent said, shuddering. His clothes were icy against his skin. He felt as if his eyelids had frozen.

'Thank you, again, *monsieur*. I have the opinion I need, so these remains can now be placed in coffins and the bodies will be released to the families as soon as possible. If you return to your quarters, I will inform you as soon as I know a suitable Mebsher transit will be available.'

'To London?'

'To the DSG in Hull,' said Lepuits. 'You will be able to make further travel arrangements from there.'

5

Tarent went straight to Lou's room.

'I think we can be out of here in the next twenty-four hours,' he said. 'I've been speaking to Bertrand Lepuits. Do you know who I mean?'

'Director of Operations. The Frenchman. I know him, but I've never liked him.'

'Can you be ready to leave at short notice?' Tarent said.

'You've really arranged this?'

'Lepuits hasn't given me a definite departure time, but he said we can be on the next Mebsher out of here. There's one expected soon. It's a bit late in the day now, so probably some time tomorrow. We can't get to London. It will only take us as far as Hull.'

'Anything's better than having to stay here indefinitely.'

'Once we're in Hull we can work something out. I want to go to London too, so we can travel together if you want to.'

'I want.' Lou unexpectedly went to him, and gave him a warm hug. 'You've no idea what this will mean to me, Tibor.'

'You have a lot of stuff in here,' Tarent said, looking around her room, which in layout was identical to his own.

'It doesn't matter – I can leave most of it behind. But I know how Lepuits operates. He'll give us hardly any warning, so to be ready I have to pack now.'

Tarent still felt himself to be in transit. Since arriving at Warne's Farm he had barely unpacked. He walked to the canteen for some food. Lepuits was not there. As soon as he had returned to his room he went to bed.

Then, in the dark, it hit him. Flo was dead. Just as suddenly, just as senselessly, as Melanie. He was deep in grief for Melanie, whom he still loved, but Flo had intrigued and aroused him. Both had been killed by an act of random violence, aimed not at them but in pursuit of some political or religious ambition or grudge. They had been murdered in a similar way.

The sense of loss was terrible. Not his own loss, which he felt like a dead weight in his gut, but their loss: both were still young

enough to have plans and future lives, both were already successful women. He knew for certain that if Melanie had not died he
would not have become involved with Flo, even for that one night,
that one brief liaison. He had always been faithful to Melanie.
Afterwards, as events swept past him, he felt a guilty conviction
that he must inadvertently have caused Melanie's death – the argument that led to her leaving the compound was largely his fault.
Now there was Flo too. Should he have tried to persuade her to
leave the Mebsher at the same time as him? It had felt at the time
as if she were immovable, locked into the demands of her work,
and on the contrary she had wanted him to remain in the vehicle
with her. She had unbalanced him – he was undecided about her
until the moment the Mebsher drove away. He remembered the
last seconds while the engine gathered full power, out there on
the escarpment, wondering which way he should go. Had he read
her correctly? Maybe things could have been different. It was a
part of grieving, he knew, for a surviving partner to feel blame for
the other's death, but even though he knew that rationally it did
nothing to reduce its impact.

He was lonely. All he wanted was to return to the old apartment
in London as soon as possible, deal with it somehow – sell it, reno-
vate it, clear out of it all their stuff and perhaps start again – but
essentially to be there and take his life back for himself.

It was difficult to sleep but in the end he fell into a fitful,
wakeful state, lying still but remaining aware of his surroundings.
Whenever he opened his eyes to look at the digital display on the
clock next to the bed he found that more time had passed than
he thought. It meant he was sleeping only lightly, but better than
he knew. As daylight broke, his restlessness turned to a kind of
wakeful impatience.

He showered, dressed and packed his bags. He wondered whether
to walk down to Lou's room to see if she was ready to leave, but he
knew she was probably still sleeping. It was a few minutes after 7
am – the sun had only just risen. Looking down from his window
he saw that the workmen had finished clearing the storm debris
from the quadrangle. There was no one about, although he could
see that the armed guard on the clinic remained. However, the

guards themselves were no longer standing or walking by the door. There was a guard point next to the entrance, a hut with a light showing from inside.

Tarent picked up his Canon Concealable, checked that the battery was fully charged, then walked down through the building and out into the quad.

He took some shots as he walked, knowing that the stabilizer would cancel any motion blurring. When he was nearly halfway across the quad he stood still, adjusted the camera properly, and looked around for the way in which the low sunlight was striking the buildings and making irregular shadows on the uneven concrete surface of the quad.

Both guards emerged quickly from the hut and without any hesitation raised their rifles and pointed them at him. Alarmed, Tarent stepped back, waved the camera high to show that he had understood the message and would not take any more pictures. The men were standing stock-still, aiming at him. They then lowered their weapons a little. One of them went back into the hut, and Tarent saw him pick up a telephone handset. After a moment, the other guard also walked to the hut.

There had been something unusual about the way the men moved towards him: there was a stiffness of movement as they emerged from the guard post, the raising of their rifles had been too quick, too speedily responsive. For a few seconds he had felt genuinely apprehensive of what they might do next, and he cursed himself for not letting them know immediately that he wanted to take photographs – normally a safe rule for his work, where local officials could be paranoid about people using cameras. He assumed the rifles were loaded. But then he thought again. The men had not shouted a warning at him, nor run across to him, nor challenged him in any way. They looked as if they were drilling, performing a ritual response.

He waited for a moment, holding the camera with his arm hanging loosely. Then he turned towards the building he had been intending to photograph, and raised his camera again.

The guards reacted exactly as before: they rushed out of the guard post, their legs almost comically stiff, they raised their rifles – but as soon as Tarent again lifted his camera to show that he would not take any pictures, both men lowered their weapons. One of them returned to the guard post and spoke into a telephone handset. Moments later the other one joined him.

Tarent moved back from them, to the side of the quad where the residential block was situated. He raised the camera but the men did not rush out of the guard post.

He took several frames in quick succession from that position, then turned around and took many more. The guards did not react – only when Tarent moved towards them, reaching approximately the centre of the open space, did they once again rush from the guard post and mutely threaten him with their rifles.

Tarent backed away again, but then by trial and error established how closely he could approach the clinic building before provoking the guards' reaction.

The presence of one building particularly interested him. It was on the southern side of the quad, next to the gated entrance to the compound. It was unusual because of its shape, size and physical condition, obviously much older than any of the others. It was a tall, brick-built tower, square and stout, but rising to at least thirty or forty metres. It was more or less derelict: several parts of the walls revealed that the mortar between the bricks had eroded away. There were high, narrow window frames, but no windows, or at least no glass in the frames. Towards the top, the outer walls had been rendered with concrete facing, but this had nearly all fallen away, revealing that the brickwork beneath was in even worse condition than the rest.

The building looked dangerous and unstable, as if it might collapse at any time, but it had apparently withstood at least the recent temperate storm and presumably several of the others that Lou had told him about. Temperate storms often recorded wind velocity in excess of a hundred miles an hour, or more than a hundred and fifty kilometres. TS Federico Fellini was clearly one of the more violent of the recent storms, to judge by the visible damage Tarent himself had seen in the quadrangle, yet this ancient tower had mysteriously survived in spite of the weather.

Staying within the zone he had worked out as uncontroversial Tarent took several shots of the building, fascinated by its appearance, the way it loomed darkly over the more modern buildings around it. He used the telephoto setting to capture close-up shots of the building's decrepit fabric.

The guards showed no interest in what he was doing.

By this time the sun had risen higher and the unique and subtle light that often accompanied a dawn was changing to a more usual kind of bland sunlight. The sky was clear, with no threat of storm clouds.

Tarent put away his camera and returned to the residential building.

6

There was a note from Lepuits' office on the terminal in his room. It said, *Transportation as requested to Hull DSG will be available at 1100 hours. Space restrictions apply. Limit: one suitcase, plus hand baggage. Office of B. L. – Dir. Ops.*

When he saw this, Tarent took his one bag and his cameras, and walked down to Lou's room. She had been sent the same information. She had completed her packing, getting everything into a single large wheeled suitcase. There were still some clothes in the closet, and she was leaving behind most of her cooking utensils. There was a long shelf of books, also to be left.

'I just want to get back to London,' she said. 'Most of this stuff was borrowed, or inherited from other people who moved on. I can leave it behind. None of it means anything to me.'

They went down to the canteen for breakfast, lingered over coffee, then returned to her room. There was still at least an hour and a half before the time they had been told the Mebsher would be ready. They sat together in her room, chatting to pass the time.

Tarent mentioned the old tower to her, wondering if she knew what it had been, what it might once have been used for, what it was used for now, but she did not seem to know what he was talking about. Now he was in her room he discovered that the tower could not be seen from her window.

'I'll show you,' he said. He took out the Canon, logged on to the remote laboratory and sent a coded request to view all of the frames he had taken that morning. Moments later the green light blinked. Tarent switched on the LCD monitor and held it so they could both see. He said, 'I was up early this morning, so I took these.'

He scrolled quickly through the shots he had taken: the quad as he first walked across it, the low shadows on the ground, the early sunlight, mist dispersing from above the roofs, then the sequence of trial-and-error pictures of the clinic building while he tried to establish how close to it he could go. After that: the residential block, the canteen, two other large buildings whose function he did not know, then finally the tower.

But the shots of the tower were not there. The sequence ended.

Tarent quickly checked the camera settings he had been using, then logged back on to the lab. He re-ordered the same shots, but when they arrived on the camera a second time the pictures he had taken of the tower were still not there.

'I took about a dozen shots of it,' he said to Lou.

'Which building do you mean?'

'The old tower, down on the south side. Close to the gate.'

She shook her head. 'I still don't know what you mean.'

Tarent felt frustrated with the camera – it was the first time it had ever let him down. So long as he kept the battery charged, or carried spares, the little Canon was a reliable workhorse. There were so few moving parts in modern cameras there was almost nothing that could go wrong, once the instrument had been passed by the manufacturers' quality control. The only possible cause of the problem might be that he had inadvertently pressed a key that suppressed picture-taking. He had been using the camera for months, though, and handling it was second nature to him. He could think of nothing he might have done to the controls that would have that effect.

Lou sat tolerantly beside him while he fiddled with the camera settings, trying to find the lost pictures.

She said, 'Could the tower have been part of the prison?'

'It didn't look like that. Would a prison have a tower, like something on a church? Anyway, I didn't know this was a prison.'

'It was for a while. An open prison. I researched its background once. Time hangs heavy when you're stuck here for months, so I started looking things up.'

Still examining and checking his camera, curious about how those shots had been lost, Tarent said, 'Tell me.'

'Well, it was farmland for years, probably centuries.'

'Is that where the name comes from?'

'No, that came later. The first real change came during the Second World War, when they built a bomber base here. It was called RAF Tealby, or maybe RAF Tealby Moor, I'm not sure which. Two operational squadrons were based here for most of the war. It remained as an airfield for a few years afterwards and still belonged to the Air Ministry, but no one flew from it. After about 1949 it was allowed to revert to farmland – the runways were broken up and removed, and within a few years there was no trace of them. At that time the farmer kept several of the old RAF buildings, including the control tower, one of the hangars and a water tower. They were used for storage, keeping animals, and so on, but they soon became dilapidated. I found photos of them on the internet, taken shortly before they were demolished.

'That was when it was renamed Warne's Farm. Probably the farmer's own name, but anyway it seems to have stuck. It was a mixed farm for many years, but in 2018 the area was bought back by the government and some of the buildings that are here now were put up. They used it then as a training camp for army recruits. By 2025 it had been converted again. That's when it became a prison. It wasn't a secure unit, but housed non-violent or long-term prisoners. There were more new buildings added and some of the older ones were modified. In 2036 the prison was closed and the Ministry of Defence moved in. They're still running it. It's partly an admin area for the north of England, but there are also closed buildings about a mile away, where some sort of experimental or development work goes on. I've never been down there. I think the building we're in now was one they put up for the army training camp, but the interior has been completely remodelled.'

Tarent returned the Canon to its protective case, without having worked out what had gone wrong with it.

'You can't see the tower from this room,' he said. 'I'll point it out when we're outside.'

'Could it be the water tower? From when it was a bomber air-field?'

'Is that still here? You said it was demolished ages ago.'

'That was what the website said. I thought the RAF buildings would all be gone by now.'

'I'll show you later.' Tarent stood up and paced around the room. It was after 10:30 and no word had come through from Lepuits' of-fice, or from the man himself, and in the quadrangle there was no sign of a Mebsher. He wondered if he should try to contact Lepuits, confirm the arrangement. He stood at the window, hands resting on the sill, staring down at the huge area of concrete.

'I think I'll take a walk,' he said. 'Will you come too?'

'No – I'll wait here. You're so tense it's making me nervous.'

'Sorry. It's just that I want to be out of here. I'll take my stuff down now. I'll come back for you when the personnel carrier arrives, or you could just meet me in the quad if you hear it. Mebsher engines make a lot of noise.'

He left the room, went out into the quad and dumped his case at the side. With his cameras slung over his shoulder, Tarent looked for the path he had used when he arrived at the Warne complex. He had to pass back through the residential building, then walk along a corridor through the next building. This led to the gravel-led walkway that went up towards the main fence. The gate he had used was locked with a security device, but his ID card opened it for him. He went through.

The last time he was here was in the immediate aftermath of what he had witnessed when the Mebsher was attacked. His in-tention, when he left Lou's room, had been to walk back up to the ridge and take another look at the site of the attack. What he saw that day already felt like an unreliable memory: it was sudden, inexplicable, horrific, and although he thought at the time he was keeping a cool head he knew now that the incident had helped tip him over into a state of delirium. It was tempting to go back for a second look at the scene of the disaster, but now there was a real prospect of actually doing so he suffered a strong but indefinite feeling of fear.

He paused just beyond the gate, which had swung closed behind him. He was surrounded by trees, many of which had been toppled by the gales, their root balls exposed. Most of the other trees had their branches broken off, leaves missing, splits in the trunks. Having experienced the violence of the last storm he was surprised how many trees had in fact survived, damaged as they were. At least they were to be spared the next storm: he had heard the radio news earlier in the morning. During the night TS Graham Greene had veered off unpredictably to the south-east, crossed the Bay of Biscay and almost immediately lost most of its strength as it swept on to the French mainland. No more temperate storms were thought to be imminent, at least in the British Isles, although there were advance warnings of heavy snow, with some drifting. It was still late September, but the winter, with its unpredictable and often dangerous moods, was almost upon them.

7

He heard then the deep throbbing sound of an engine, one that clattered noisily and was overlaid by the high-pitched whine of turbines. Tarent turned back immediately and presented his ID card to the scanner. After a long pause, which Tarent found worrying, thinking he might have shut himself out, the electrically powered gate swung open again and he slipped back into the compound. He looked across to the south, through the few trees that still stood there, past the first of the Warne buildings, and was rewarded with a glimpse of the huge dark shape of the Mebsher, heading slowly towards the main gate. Relieved to see it, Tarent hurried along the passages through the buildings and emerged into the quadrangle.

The Mebsher had already passed through the secure barrier and was coming to a halt. The driver, hidden behind the darkened, strengthened windshield, manoeuvred the vehicle close to the clinic building. The engine noise wound down, the turbines becoming silent, while the diesel power plants idled. The black exhaust smoke was swept back by the wind and across to where Tarent was standing. The familiar smell of the fuel, which he had breathed for so many hours on the long journey north from London, brought back the buried memories of confinement inside the Mebsher, the boredom of sitting still for so long, the lurching discomfort, and the mild distraction of speculating about the woman in the seat in front of him.

Several uniformed security men emerged from the guard post by the entrance to the clinic, and stood in a loose line. One of them, an officer, stepped forward and ascended towards the high cockpit area, using the crude steps welded to the side. A metal vane beside the windshield opened up, and a conversation took place. Soon, papers were passed out for examination.

While the check was going on, Tarent remembered Lou. He turned away, intending to walk back to her room to tell her the personnel carrier had arrived, but as he did so he saw her emerging from the building. She was tugging her large suitcase by the handle. She walked over and stood beside him.

On the Mebsher the guard handed the papers back through the vane to the driver, and the panel closed. The officer jumped down from the vehicle and with the other security guards walked quickly into the clinic building. The Mebsher's engine began to develop power, and in a moment Tarent watched the huge transporter manoeuvre to and fro, as the driver reversed it towards the clinic.

'Are you ready to leave?' Tarent asked Lou.

'Can't wait. How about you?'

'Yes.'

The crew hatch at the front of the vehicle opened, and one of the men who was inside clambered through the opening and levered himself up and out, pressing down on the rim. He climbed easily on to the housing at the front of the vehicle.

He was a tall young man with a narrow, athletic build. He was wearing camo fatigues, the sort favoured by the British Army on home duties: dark mottled green with specks of brown, black and a lighter green. A standard-issue lightweight automatic rifle was slung handily across his shoulder. Under his cap the young soldier's head was shaved, but he wore a long beard, wispy and dark. He was wearing shades. With his hands on his hips he turned to take in the view in all directions.

Tarent had his camera ready and took several quick photographs of the soldier, admiring the measured, self-confident way he carried himself.

Four of the security guards now emerged from the clinic, a casket resting on their shoulders. They marched slowly in step, heads bowed, and carried the coffin across to the cargo hold of the Mebsher. The hatch opened on its hydraulic rods – slowly, and with great care, the men slid the coffin into the hold. A second one was already being brought out of the building by another group of the security men.

The young soldier standing on the front of the vehicle monitored the process, and at one point leaned in and spoke to the other crewman, still out of sight inside the cockpit.

One by one the caskets were brought out of the clinic and placed on board. Soon all had been loaded, although the sixth had to be eased in carefully, as most of the space inside the hold was already taken. While this happened the soldier jumped down to the ground and helped the security men shift and relocate the coffins that were already there.

'I suppose this is why they said there would be restrictions on what we could bring with us,' Lou said, watching this slow and careful procedure. 'There's hardly any space left.'

'Put your case into the hold when you can,' Tarent said to her. 'I'll keep mine with me. I know how the passenger compartment is laid out and I'll be able to squeeze my bag in there somewhere at the back.'

He had been watching the loading of the caskets, which was done with outward respect and no false sense of ceremony, and as each of them was brought out he felt a sense of pain and distress growing in him. Inside one of those coffins, he knew, was Flo's body.

It was an uncomfortable thought, knowing that they would be travelling with the coffins beneath their feet.

Lou trundled her wheeled suitcase to the entrance of the hold and the young soldier, seeing her trying to push it inside, stepped forward to help. There was hardly any space left, which meant the case had to be placed on top of one of the coffins. The soldier took the case from Lou, managed it in one swift and muscular lift. He leapt down to the ground, and signalled to the other crewman to close the door.

The soldier straightened, glanced around, and for the first time looked directly at Tarent. The two men stared at each other.

It was Hamid, the young Scot who had been one of the drivers of the Mebsher that brought him here.

Instinctively, Tarent raised a hand in greeting, but in the same moment the soldier turned away. He returned to the front of the vehicle and climbed up to the position he had taken before, on the housing.

Tarent's hand fell to his side. He stepped forward, amazed to see the young man again.

'Hamid?' he called.

There was a security guard standing close to the vehicle. 'Keep back, please. This is a military vehicle.'

'I'm travelling on this vehicle!' Tarent shouted, annoyed by the intrusion, and swept his diplomatic passport from his back pocket and flashed the distinctive white cover in the man's direction.

'Sorry, sir, but I have instructions that no one must approach this vehicle.'

'I'm being picked up here. You can check with Mr Lepuits.'

'It was Mr Lepuits who gave me the instructions.'

Tarent gestured impatiently. 'Yes, but I have permission to travel on this vehicle. Ms Paladin too.'

Lou was again standing by his side.

'Wait there.' The security guard spoke into a handset, then waited for a reply.

'Hamid!' Tarent raised his voice.

The young soldier heard him then and turned in Tarent's direction. Again, their gaze met but he showed no sign of recognition.

Tarent was certain it was the same man. He moved away from Lou and approached the Mebsher. This time the security guard made no move to impede him.

'Sir?'

'Peace be unto you,' Tarent said. 'Weren't you the driver of the Mebsher that brought me here?'

'I've only just arrived, sir.' The Glaswegian accent was the same.

'Two or three days ago. I was in London at the end of last week, when I joined other passengers. The road was flooded and you helped me climb aboard the Mebsher. We ended up at a base at Long Sutton, but the next day you let me off the vehicle somewhere not far from here.'

'I have to follow a strict route, sir. We haven't come from London, and I don't recall being at the base you mentioned. Long Sutton is a closed unit.'

'Not this trip. It was just a few days ago. Surely you remember?'

'We are here to collect and transport materials. Two passengers as well. Inshallah.'

Presumably hearing the sound of their voices, the second crewman raised himself through the open hatch. He stared across at Tarent.

'Ibrahim!' Tarent said. 'Peace be unto you. Don't you remember me?'

He stared back at Tarent, but said nothing. He shook his head vaguely. The two crewmen spoke briefly to each other, a soft burr of slang, and then Hamid clambered quickly to the ground. Ignoring Tarent, who was now less than three metres from the side of the vehicle, he worked the outer mechanism of the main hatch. With a smooth mechanical sound the hatch raised itself on its hydraulic rods. The built-in steps also unfolded and lowered themselves to the concrete. Tarent had an angled glimpse inside, but because the hatch was too high above the ground he could see almost nothing of the interior.

The security guard approached them, putting away his handset.

'Mr Lepuits has confirmed these two passengers may join the personnel carrier,' he said to Hamid. 'They are to be taken only as far as the DSG in Hull.'

'Inshallah.'

Tarent said to Lou, 'After you.'

As she moved forward, Tarent also took a step towards the Mebsher's hatch. Now that he was as close as this he could smell the air drifting out from the passenger compartment. It was so familiar to him: the smell of people inside, recirculated air, bare metal, old seat fabric, bringing a mental image of the cramped conditions, the hard seats and the fluorescent lighting. Lou walked past him.

'You are coming too, aren't you?'

'I left my bag over there,' Tarent said, indicating the place outside the residential block where he had earlier dumped his luggage. 'I have to get that. I'll be back in a moment.'

Lou went up the steps, lowered her head and went through into the compartment. Tarent saw her come to a halt just inside. A moment later she turned and leaned back out, a glance around the Warne compound, one last look. She was smiling, and she looked at him.

'Thanks, Tibor,' she said.

Lou went on into the compartment but a moment later someone else came to the opening, leaned through the hatch and moved out to stand at the top of the steps. She glared briefly down at Tarent, but looked away again immediately. She was wearing a scarf over her hair, and her left hand was pressed lightly to the area behind her left ear. It was Flo.

To Hamid she said, 'What's the delay out here?'

'We'll be restarting shortly, madame,' he said. 'We have to pick up two passengers.'

'We are running late. I have a ministerial meeting in less than two hours' time.'

'Yes, Tebyeb Mallinan. There will be no more delays after this. We will depart soon.'

Flo then looked directly at Tarent.

'Have you been authorized to board this vehicle?' she said.

'Flo?' Tarent said, his heart racing.

She looked at him more intently. 'Why do you call me that? Who are you?'

She sounded as if she genuinely did not recognize him. Tarent

281

was staring at her, feeling shock, disbelief, even terror, sensing his own hold on sanity had been released. Only the evening before, in the clinic –

In the Mebsher hold below –

He said weakly, 'Don't you remember me, Flo?'

'Should I?'

'We met a few days ago. Travelling.'

'I don't – travel, as you call it. What business do you have here? Let me see your security clearance.'

Tarent was aware of the other people: Lou inside the compartment was probably hearing this, Ibrahim and Hamid were just behind him, the security guard was there. Flo was speaking loudly, authoritatively, dominant.

'Flo – you are Flo, aren't you? You wouldn't tell me your second name, but I know now it's Mallinan.' He still had the white-covered passport in his hand, so he held it up for her to see. 'I'm Tibor. Tibor Tarent. We know each other. You wanted me to—'

'Are you here on ministerial business?'

'No.'

'This is a government vehicle on official duties. You are delaying me.'

'I have been travelling for the government.'

'Why did you use my family name? Do I know you? Have we met before?'

'Yes, we met on the other Mebsher, before the attack.'

'What attack?' She looked around at the other men. 'Leave us,' she said in an imperious voice. 'This is a confidential conversation.'

She stood immobile, waiting. Hamid and Ibrahim went around to the front of the vehicle and climbed up swiftly into the drive compartment. The security officer retreated towards the clinic. Tarent looked back towards the buildings, half-expecting to see others coming to find out what was happening, but the quadrangle in all directions was empty of people. In a moment, the drivers' hatch closed and sealed itself.

Flo said, 'Let me see that passport.'

He handed it to her and for a fraction of a second their fingertips brushed against each other. She opened the passport, read the information on the front, then looked at the photograph of him inside the back pages, and simultaneously pressed two fingers to the hidden implant behind her ear. She raised an elbow to try to conceal what she was doing.

She handed the passport back to him.

'I don't know who you are, Mr Tarent,' she said. 'Nor what your business here might be. But you have been using that passport illegally. You have no diplomatic credentials and as far as I can determine, no legitimate business with either the Office of Overseas Relief or the Ministry of Defence. I have cancelled the passport, so if you wish to travel abroad you must apply for a new one. Now I have work to attend to.'

'Flo, please!'

'What is it you want?'

'May we speak privately?'

'This is a private conversation. I have never met you before. Under what circumstances were you issued with that passport? And you haven't told me why you are using my familiar name.'

'Do you really not remember me?' he said. On an impulse he raised his Canon, pointed it at her face and exposed three shots in rapid succession. She recoiled slightly. 'The quantum lens, Flo. You warned me about it.'

'You have no right—'

'That's what you said before. And Rietveld – he told me too, long ago. I remember now. He warned me that quantum adjacency was dangerous. You said I had met Thijs Rietveld, and you were right.'

A man moved behind Flo, taller than her, but he was inside the Mebsher compartment, so it was not easy to see who it was. He raised a camera above Flo's shoulder, close to where her implant lay, pointing it towards Tarent. A shutter opened and closed.

The man stepped back, and Tarent could no longer see him.

Flo moved her hand against her ear. She waited, then inclined her head slightly. 'If you don't hand in those cameras today, they will be confiscated.' She was shouting. 'There is nothing more to say.'

She turned away from him, ducked her head and returned to the compartment. On an impulse Tarent ran up the short flight of steps behind her, gripping the two support rails. Flo had already moved towards the front of the compartment and was leaning over to speak to the man Tarent knew was called Heydar. Lou Paladin was sitting on the row of seats beside the hatch. She was looking at Tarent with wide-open, panic-stricken eyes. She seemed to lean away from him, keeping a distance.

He realized then that he had forgotten his bag, still there on the far side of the quad. He would have to go back for it. The engine of the Mebsher was building up speed, and black smoke was pouring past him.

His mind was blurring, unable to interpret what he was experiencing, what he was actually seeing.

He saw –

He saw there was a man sitting next to Lou. It was the man who had come to the Mebsher door behind Flo. He had the straps of several cameras draped over his shoulder, and was holding a camera in both hands, a Canon Concealable. He pointed the camera towards Tarent's face, and held down the shutter release.

Beside the man, Lou seemed overcome by confusion and fright. She stared at Tarent, to the man who looked just like him, back to Tarent.

Tarent backed away. He felt the hydraulic door mechanism starting to move above him. He climbed anxiously down the steps, stumbling as he used the last one because it was already lifting away from the concrete and swivelling up towards its storage compartment. He felt something snag against the heel of his hand as he stepped hastily to the ground, and he winced with pain.

He half-stumbled across the concrete floor but as he recovered he grabbed one of the cameras strapped to his shoulder, and with trembling fingers held down the shutter on continuous exposure, taking three frames a second: the Mebsher, the shrinking glimpse of the dark interior of the compartment, the smoke, the hatch lowering on its hydraulic rods. As the door seated itself, a piece of torn, jagged metal was snagged by the weight of the hatch, but as it finally closed the sharp fragment jerked free again, standing out from the smooth metal of the Mebsher's outer skin.

The vehicle drove off. Tarent took no more photographs. The

Mebsher swung around towards the security gate and Tarent backed away.

He stood watching as the vehicle pushed through the entrance, lurching on the uneven ground. The tall, dilapidated tower loomed above it. Tarent sucked the blood that was flowing from the cut in his hand, a reopened wound, inflicted in the same place as before. The Mebsher had reached the access road, where the surface was smoother, and it began to drive away more quickly.

Tarent stared after it, finally realizing, comprehending and accepting, but still unable to believe, whose body it must have been, there in the cargo hold of the Mebsher, inside the sixth coffin.

PART 7

Prachous

1

FENCE

Like all the islands in the archipelago Prachous is neutral territory, but it is the most fiercely independent of all the island states. It has always been a closed island – the name means FENCE in island patois. Although visitors are allowed entry on strictly monitored short-stay visas, permanent immigration to the island is forbidden and for centuries Prachous has maintained a navy of its own to protect its borders. It is anyway a difficult island to navigate towards, because of a complex system of uncharted undersea reefs and shoals. Many unpredictable currents flow in the waters around Prachous and although there are some large areas of coastal swamp or tidal flood plains, much of the coastline of Prachous has high cliffs, with rocky outfalls. Along the southern coast of the island there are four major ports, two of which are reserved for use by the Prachous Seigniorial Navy.

To the north of Prachous lies the Glaund Republic, a belligerent nation on the northern continental mass, engaged in a war that has been fought for so long there is no one alive who remembers the beginning. No end to it is in sight. It is known as The War at the End of War, and both sides believe it is imperative not to yield. No truce or peace negotiations have ever been entered into. The hostilities are with the distant nation of Faiandland, which lies on the far side of the world, but is also a coastal state on the continent. Glaund and Faiandland each have an intricate array of allies, treaty states and co-belligerents, approximately but not rigidly divided between east and west. The hostilities do not directly affect life on Prachous, which is a peaceful place, although the proximity to Glaund does sometimes have an indirect impact on Prachoit foreign policy. Like all archipelagian states, Prachous is determined not to become involved in the war, and to a great extent succeeds in this wish.

A large part of the interior of Prachous is desert. In this, the terrain is similar to the part of the Glaundian coastal desert to which it is a neighbour. Because of the southern latitude, extreme high temperatures are common on Prachous, especially in the dry season. There are two large coastal mountain ranges, a high central massif north of the desert area, and along the north-western coast and all around the south there are extensive areas of fertile land. Prachous is more or less self-sufficient in food, although because it is a wealthy island many delicacies are imported from other islands, and also from Glaund.

There is no single seignior on Prachous, the land, mineral rights and tithes being divided between a number of Prachoit families, whose secrets are guarded as closely as the island shores. The economy is seigniorial in name only. Although constituting a closed feudal society, the leading Prachoit families are legendary throughout the archipelago for their business activities and commercial methods. Many of the big archipelagian commercial corporations are owned by Prachoits, and Prachoit families are the largest employers throughout the islands, with interests in mining, shipbuilding, shipping lines (including most of the inter-island ferries), construction, IT, internet and printed media, and many thousands of hectares of agricultural land.

Prachous is a secular island. Religious observation is tolerated but not encouraged.

Prachous is thought to be the second largest island in the archipelago, although it has never been properly surveyed or measured. Should cartographic drones venture into Prachous airspace they are invariably shot down.

2

THE SPREADER OF THE WORD

He left the desert encampment in the early morning, before the worst of the heat began, and walked south. He was accompanied by a woman missionary who was to guide him – she had made the same journey several times before. They both wore loosely fitting, lightweight robes as a protection from the sun's heat. These covered most of their faces, so Tomak Tallant did not even glimpse the woman's face until the second day. On the first day they were carrying supplies of food and water, enough for the first long section of the walk, but they were expecting to be able to obtain extra supplies on the way. They saw no sign of any settlement during the first day, nor did they come across any streams, water holes or wells.

The woman walked ahead of him, watching the ground as they traversed it. The only words she uttered for the whole of that first day were quietly spoken warnings about loose or buried pieces of rock on the track.

She held a scripture in her left hand. She answered no questions, nor did she ask any, and after the first hour Tallant gave up trying to make conversation. Breathing was anyway difficult in the constant, enervating heat. The sun glared down, bleaching what could be seen of the stony scenery, but Tallant made a point of taking several photographs whenever they halted for a rest. His cameras and attachments were as usual carried in their protective cases across his back, and although they were all made of lightweight materials they became a burden. The water flagon had to be held in his hand with the bag of his own possessions in the other. He changed them over frequently – the woman missionary was carrying only a flask of water and some food.

They rested in the afternoon – they found a ledge beneath an overhanging rock, which from the quantity of paper and empty food and drink containers lying about the place seemed to be a regular stopping-off point for travellers. Tallant spread himself in the shade, grateful to rest his aching limbs, but the woman sat with her legs crossed, holding the scripture before her. She kept her head bent forward under the cowl of white cotton, but if she was reading there was no visible sign of it. She turned no pages.

Tallant took some photographs of her with the shutter set to silent, but she must have somehow detected what he was doing, or noticed his movements. She waved her free hand irritably towards him.

He apologized and returned the camera to its case. She made no acknowledgement.

They continued their journey through the sweltering, scented air, the surface of the track now smoother and therefore easier to walk on. There were shallow hills to climb. At the summit of each Tallant felt the rising hope that some kind of destination might be visible from the brow, but the pallid, blinding landscape continued ahead without apparent break. Irrationally, he always looked for a glimpse of the distant sea. He craved a draught of cool air, sea air, wind from elsewhere.

The sun was beginning to lower towards the horizon when the woman increased her walking speed. Tallant assumed she knew of shelter ahead. In spite of his exhaustion he was relieved and kept pace with her. He had been fearing they might have to pass the night in the open.

Without much warning, and no signs, the track took a sharp turn to the right and the path led down between two rocky defiles. In continual shade at last, Tallant felt some of his physical energy returning. His feet skidded and scuffed on the loose pebbles and shale on the path, and several times he banged against the boulders that rose up on each side. The woman moved ever further ahead of him.

The path opened out into a deep gully where several trees and bushes grew. A coarse grass flourished. A dark pool of still water lay against a wall of white rock. Several well constructed wooden cabins were arranged in a semi-circle a short distance from the pool. The woman missionary was already lying full-length on the ground, her face close to the water, while she cupped handfuls to her mouth, and tipped it over the back of her neck and head. A printed sign warned travellers to drink only water from the well, but Tallant joined her, ducking his head thankfully into the cold, clean water, then sitting up to let rivulets run deliciously down his chest and back beneath the robe.

Darkness came on soon afterwards, following a brief period of twilight. Insects in the surrounding trees set up a raucous stridulation. Tallant and the woman each selected a cabin. Inside his, Tallant found a simple cot bed, a shelf of packaged food and sealed bottles of mineral water. There was no light inside, so he removed his robe and lay down naked on the cot. He woke only once in the night and that was when the desert chill fell on him. The thin robe barely warmed him, but he was exhausted by the long walk.

When he emerged in the morning the woman missionary was out of her cabin. Sunshine was beating down into the gully and the air was already hot. She had seated herself on an area of smooth rock by the side of the pool, her legs folded, her back straight, her head held erect. She was holding the scriptures before her face, which was no longer shrouded by the hood. Tallant stared at her with interest. She had a severe, handsome face, with high cheekbones, a sharp nose and a strong chin. Her eyes were dark brown, or almost black. She was reading intently.

He waited politely, but the woman did not acknowledge his presence.

'May I take some photographs of you?' he said. She gave no indication that she had heard him, so he repeated his question. This time she responded by raising her free hand and placing it slowly over her ear. At first he assumed she was shutting out the sound of his voice, but in fact her hand did not block her ear. Her fingers rested lightly on the mastoid process immediately behind the ear. He took this to be a symbolic gesture, asking him not to speak. She slowly lowered the hand and resumed her former position.

Tallant selected the smallest, quietest of his cameras and took a dozen shots of her, from a variety of angles and distances. At no point did she reveal any awareness of him, or, for that matter, a dislike of what he was doing, or pleasure at it.

'I am a professional photographer,' he said as he put away the camera. 'If you wish I will be pleased to let you see prints of these pictures. But I'll need an address where I might contact you.'

Her only response was to raise her free hand once again, press it lightly over her ear and continue reading.

Tallant returned to his cabin, ate a little of the food, then went across to the freshwater well and refilled his flask with clean water. He went to the far side of the pool and bathed briefly. He arranged the robe loosely about his head and body. The woman was waiting for him, and without any further discussion they resumed their journey southwards.

3

After walking for about an hour they came to a place where a vehicle was waiting to transport them down to the coast. It was an old and travel-worn passenger coach, with most of the windows along the sides either broken or permanently open. The seats were made of wooden slats, many of which were splintered or missing. Tattered remains of curtains hung beside some of the window frames. The floor was sticky with an accumulation of dirt and spilled liquids. The outside of the bus, originally painted in the silver which could still be glimpsed in places, had been over-written with many religious proverbs and sayings. The driver sat on a wooden box at the front and often stood up while driving. Sometimes he waved his arms in time with the loud music he played.

Tallant and the woman missionary were the only passengers. They were passing through a wide tract of unpopulated country. She sat apart from him, moving to the back if he chose a seat near the front, and similarly placed herself away from him whenever he changed his seat after a stop. Tallant relished the flow of air from the vacant windows, the relative relief from the endless heat. He drank one bottle of water after another, making free use of the crates which had been placed aboard the bus.

At intervals he leaned from his seat through the nearest window, taking many photographs of the scenery, but it was a landscape that did not much change, higher and more rugged in some areas, sandy or gravelly on the level. As they moved further south the temperature steadily rose, but the air felt more breathable: there was an increasing number of trees and low-growing shrubs, and sometimes high white clouds moved briefly across the sun. On some of the corners grit thrown up by the bus's tyres flew around him and he would duck inside, more to protect his cameras than his face and arms. He changed seats as often as possible, always believing that there would be more to see from the opposite side. He was constantly aware of the missionary woman keeping her distance from him, sitting calmly upright and swaying with the movement of the vehicle, facing ahead, her hands wrapped gently around her scriptures.

The third day came. They had stopped overnight at what at first sight looked like a large wooden shack on the side of the road, but which turned out to be a religious sanctuary for travellers. It was air-conditioned and temperature controlled. There were staff in attendance, who provided them with cooked food and cold drinks. They were currently the only travellers on this road, or users of the various refuges. Tallant slept alone on a bench in the main room – the woman was in one of the cubicles at the rear of the building. The driver apparently slept in the bus.

In the morning a wind was up and it brought a feeling of relief. The driver was edgy, though, saying he was anxious to get on with the rest of the journey.

For a few quiet moments before they drove off, Tallant was able to move away from the road. He stood alone, listening to the wind, thinking back, remembering. Somewhere in the distance he heard the bleating of goats. The insects were silent. The sun was still low when they left the refuge but the heat was rising.

Not long after they resumed their journey the road started a long, shallow climb through an area of hills. Gradually, the desert floor yielded to thicker and more profuse vegetation and a few flowers. The air was noticeably cooler than it had been the day before. Although the hills did not appear to be especially high the road as-cended steadily for more than an hour. Whenever a sharp turn was completed or a rocky outcrop was rounded, a new panorama was revealed, higher land still to come, distant mountains, glimpses of the narrow road winding steadily upwards. Tallant stared ahead of the bus, mentally urging it on, because he was certain the sea must soon become visible when they passed beyond the next barrier.

Instead, the final summit of the hill road revealed a plain below, the road snaking downwards. The hills on this side were heavily wooded. Tallant took many more photographs, relishing the difference in landscape, relieved to have left the seemingly limitless desert behind.

The bus moved ever lower, the road on this side of the hills much steeper. There were several precipitous turns with frightening descents from the unmade edge of the road. Tallant leaned out through his window, using the camera at every turn, discovering white-water rivers, trees, rocky slides, far below.

Eventually the road levelled out once more, passing through forest where there was evidence of much tree-felling. He saw areas reduced to stumps and undergrowth, broken branches discarded on all sides, with just a few remaining saplings standing slenderly in the ruins of the forest. Many stripped trunks were piled beside the road. Smoke drifted in the air.

The first of the shacks appeared inside the wood. Tallant assumed at first they were shelters used by the loggers, but he soon glimpsed inhabitants as the bus went quickly by. He saw men and women around some of the buildings, and children too. The road led out of the forest and entered another area of bush and scrub land. After crossing this they entered the main part of the shanty town.

At one moment they were driving through the open countryside, or what was left of it, then suddenly they were on a narrow, rutted, slightly raised track that ran past thousands of makeshift dwellings. These pitiful cabins were crammed up against each side of the roadway, desperate assemblies of temporary materials: canvas or tarpaulin shrouds, corrugated sheets of rusting metal, old planks, concrete slabs, vehicle tyres, pieces of broken branches. Anything, in fact, which could be found somewhere and dragged into use to build an improvised dwelling. Now there were hundreds, thousands of people in sight, and the bus filled with the stink of sewage, unwashed bodies, filthy materials, muddy ground, drifting smoke, animal droppings. The noise from outside – a kind of roar of rushing but unseen machinery, recorded music, things being struck or scraped or dragged, but above all loud voices trying to make themselves heard over the racket – entered the bus through the open windows, drowning the sound of the engine.

Both Tallant and the woman missionary were now staring out through the windows of the vehicle, half in fascination but also half in trepidation, because the shanty town appeared to be in a permanent state of imminent upheaval, with a likely outbreak of violence. Tallant realized that he had reflexively pressed the sleeve of his shirt over his nostrils as a kind of filter. He lowered his arm.

The passage of the bus, which because of the state of the road the driver had had to slow almost to walking pace, was a matter of intense interest and curiosity to the people of the shanties. Dozens of small children ran perilously close to the sides of the bus, stretching up their hands, shouting, begging insistently for food or money or cigarettes. Ahead of the bus, Tallant could see that two or three groups of men were forming in the road, as if to impede it. As the vehicle approached these groups moved to the side, so there was no real sense of threat about what might happen, but even so Tallant felt himself stiff with apprehension. He had starting taking photographs as soon as they entered the vast settlement, but he quickly realized that he was drawing attention to himself by doing this. He hid the camera on his lap, below the level of the window. He took only a few more shots, and then at intervals.

The missionary had also laid her scripture in her lap and for once was looking outward into the world. She too was obviously overawed by the sight of the immense slum. It stretched away interminably into the haze, no limit to its extent visible on either side.

The bus ground on, sometimes having to halt temporarily, reversing or manoeuvring from the main track. Once they were forced into a difficult diversion away from the main route and one that led between several of the shacks into a muddy stretch of rough ground. Here the bus almost became stranded. The strenuous efforts of the driver to extricate the vehicle drew a crowd of watchers as the bus lurched perilously from one water-filled pothole to the next, the spinning tyres throwing up sheets of brown and stinking spray.

Tallant had not realized until now that this settlement existed. His knowledge of Prachous hitherto was of the comfortable, prosperous towns that were built along the coasts, or close to the mountains, with no suggestion that anywhere on the island would there be a slum settlement of this appalling size and condition. He had, in fact, never seen anything like it on any of the other islands he had visited. He had been to only a few but temporary shanty towns were out of place in the archipelago, a realm of almost unlimited habitable space and untroubled living. He also wondered who these displaced people might be – how had they come to this island, the one place in the archipelago where the shelterate laws were rigidly enforced and were used as an absolute bar to entry? He himself had found it almost impossible not only to gain entry to the island, but to obtain his work permit for his relatively short stay. The conditions of his visit were difficult, and included having to register with the seigniorial police in every town he went to.

These were his memories.

Were the people of the shanty native Prachoits, or had they come to the island as immigrants? How had they passed through the border controls?

After their forced detour from the main track the driver increased speed, but even so they were still travelling barely faster than before.

Once, Tallant at last caught sight of the sea, or at least the silvery glistening of a reflected sky, away to the east of their route. Knowing that he was being taken towards the coast he wondered if this glimpse signalled an imminent end to the long journey. He silently willed the driver to steer towards it. Instead the bus ploughed on through the interminable spread of slum dwellings. Soon the distant sight of the sea was obscured by the buildings and irregularities in the land.

After some three hours the road widened slightly and the sheer pressure of the crowds of makeshift buildings began to ease. Not long afterwards the shanty town was behind them and the bus was once again driving at normal speed through farmland. Tallant was obsessed with the hope that this travelling might soon be at an end. However, there was a third night to come.

4

The place was a hotel, or so it was styled on a painted sign attached to the outer wall, but the front of the building was used as an open bar. When the bus arrived the sun had set and the area of levelled ground at the front was crowded with drinkers. Low floodlights covered the yard, but the illumination was fitful and not bright. Large winged insects swarmed around the lamps. There were tables and chairs but most of the drinkers were standing. The driver steered the bus in from the road and drove to one side to park, forcing a way past several groups of people.

Once inside the building, Tallant, the driver and the missionary woman were all allocated separate rooms and then offered a meal. The table was on an open verandah at the side of the building. An electric ceiling fan turned above them. Tallant ate slowly because he did not feel hungry, but he drank two glasses of beer from the bar. It was served so cold that his fingers almost stuck to the sides of the glass. Condensation ran into a pool on the table top, but soon evaporated in the warm air. The missionary, drinking water, said nothing, but he felt she disapproved of everything about him. Later, the driver went off by himself to drink at the bar. Tallant and the woman sat together at the table where they had eaten, but neither of them spoke. The woman, as was her custom, simply stared away from him with a vacant expression.

He sat through it, feeling that he was being adversely judged, that he was not living up to some moral or religious standard the woman adhered to rigidly, but he was determined to finish his beer and perhaps drink another.

The night was still and humid, but insects rasped on all sides. There was no wind and the thick smell of alcohol and tobacco smoke hovered around them as if in a closed room – the ceiling fan moved but did not clear the air. In the distance, far away towards the horizon, the sky was lit up by the glare from the shanty town, not so far away as he had thought. Tallant made a couple of attempts to start a conversation, but the woman cut him dead each time.

He finished his beer. In a final effort he said to her, 'Why do you never speak to me?'

She turned to regard him and looked straight into his eyes. After a long pause she said, 'Because you have not yet done or said anything that interests me in the least.'

'You never react! You don't seem to care about anything I say!'

'Then we agree.'

'What could I do that might in fact interest you?'

'I should like to know your name. That would change things. And you have not asked me mine.'

'My name is Tomak. Tomak Tallant.'

'You are not a Prachoit, then.'

'No. Are you?'

'I am liberated from nationality. I live only for the Word, which I spread.'

'That doesn't tell me your name.'

'I am a Spreader of the Word. That is all you need to know.'

Tallant stood up, having decided just then not to have another glass of beer. He stood beside the table, tall above her. He felt sticky with old sweat from three days of travel, itching from the bites of insects and the abrasion of the grimy robe against his skin, and now he was bored with and annoyed by this woman. There was an old shower cubicle in the corner of his hotel bedroom, and he thought how much he would enjoy just being alone for a long time, standing under a flow of cold water.

'I am going to my room,' he said, but she made no reply. Her expression did not change. 'Apparently that's something else that doesn't interest you,' he said, trying to control his irritation, but barely doing so. 'You have not even told me your name. You probably have weird reasons of your own, but I simply find you boring and discourteous. Goodnight.'

She did not respond, so he walked away.

Then, over the hubbub of the crowd of drinkers, he heard her say something. He stopped, turned back.

'What was that you said?'

'I told you my name,' the woman said.

'I couldn't hear you. It's too noisy out here. Tell me again – please.'

300

'I didn't mean to be discourteous, Tomak Tallant, and I apologize. I am sworn to modesty. I may speak my personal name in a public place only once, so I cannot repeat it now. I am merely a Spreader of the Word, and that is the only identity I allow myself.'

Tallant waved his hand with frustration, and left her. He pushed through the crowd in the yard outside the bar, then found the door that led into the hotel.

5

The room was unclean and dark, lit only by a dim electric bulb hanging in the centre of the ceiling. The bed was an iron frame with a bare and much-stained mattress. A single loose sheet, also discoloured, had been laid across the mattress, and a small towel was folded over the end. The floor was uncovered boards, with splintering patches. The walls had apparently not been painted or cleaned in many years and were grey with filth or mould or simply drab from untended age. At least the shower cubicle looked as if it had been recently cleaned, even though the faucet and pipes were loose and the shower head was buckled and dented. He ripped off his robe and let it fall on the floor beside the bed.

The water in the shower was, as he might have expected, tepid rather than cold, but it ran with steady pressure and seemed untainted. He stood under it for several minutes, face up to the spray, letting it run across his closed eyes, over his shoulders and chest and legs, into the channels of his ears, in and out of his open mouth. He was blinded by the water, deafened by the running of it in his ears. Finally, with some reluctance he turned the tap and the spray ceased. He wiped his eyes with his fingers.

Only then did he realize he was no longer alone. The missionary woman had entered his room unheard and was standing by his closed door, staring at him. Tallant grabbed at the inadequate piece of towelling he had found on the end of his bed and held it over himself.

'There is no shower in my room,' she said. 'I hoped I might use yours.'

She continued to stare at him, undisguisedly looking his body up and down. He was embarrassed by the candour of her gaze, tried to rub himself dry by bending double and trying not to move the towel too far.

He said, 'I'll be finished in a moment. Then you may use the room without me being here.'

'I have been watching you. You might as well watch me.'

'No, I'd prefer—'

'I should like you to stay.'

Giving up his futile efforts at modesty with the towel, Tallant flung it aside and grabbed the robe he had been wearing for days. The woman was already pulling apart the sash at the front of her robe, letting the loose garment fall open.

'I don't want to embarrass you,' Tallant said. 'You are a devout woman—'

'I am not a priestess, or a nun. The vows I have taken are personal ones. I am a lay field worker. I travel alone and the only text I shall ever read is contained in the holy book I carry with me. I am a true Spreader of the Word, which I shall never deny or renounce. But I am also a woman in good health and I have physical needs. Sometimes those needs become urgent.'

He had his robe on now but because much of his body was still wet the thin fabric was sticking to his legs and arms, his back and chest, and it hung at an angle on him. She pushed past him, went straight into the shower cubicle and turned on the tap. She stepped into the spray still wearing her robe, then turned and leaned beneath the flow of water, holding out the fabric to cleanse it. When it was soaked through she pulled it from her and allowed it to lie on the floor of the cubicle, crushed under her bare feet as she turned around in the spraying water, raising her face and arms, scraping her fingers through her hair, soaping herself between her legs, over her breasts, under her arms. She kept her eyes closed against the spray, apparently uncaring about his presence in the room.

Tallant watched her and moved closer so that he was standing beside the open door to the cubicle.

She had brought no towel with her so Tallant handed her the small one he had used, still damp. She wiped it over her face and hair, then tossed it aside. She went to Tallant, pulled his robe open with a brusque movement and pushed it away from his body. They made love on the bed.

She seemed to fall asleep after that, or at least lay still and calm, breathing steadily with her eyes closed. Her skin was shiny with perspiration.

'I still don't know your name,' Tallant said, lying beside her with his hand cupping one of her breasts. He was wide awake. Her soft flesh felt fervent beneath his fingers, and he toyed with her nipple, which was at last becoming soft and seeming to shrink from him. He watched a teardrop of sweat forming on the side of her brow, running down to her shoulder, then plopping on to the filthy mattress. He was eagerly breathing the sweet scents of her body. The window was a glassless circle in the wall above them, and the raucous sounds of the drinkers in the yard outside drifted into the room. Over and around their own body aromas he could smell strong spirits, smoke, the unwashed sweat of others.

'I have told you once.' Her eyes did not open, but she sounded fully awake.

'And I could not hear what you said. It was too noisy out there. We are in private now.'

'My name is Firentsa, or that is the name by which you should know me. You must never address me as Firentsa when anyone else is around. I told you that I am sworn to modesty, but that was merely a simple promise made to the people who send me out on my missions. The Word demands that every promise made should be honoured.'

'You didn't mind me taking photos of you.'

'They were irrelevant to me at the time.'

'Don't photographs threaten your modesty?'

'I am modest in word, not deed.'

'What if I were to photograph you naked?'

'I am modest in word, not deed. You may do with me whatever you wish, in any depraved circumstances you choose. I know noth-ing about physical modesty because my body is simply what I have

303

been given. There are some people who consider me shameless. But they are wrong, because I cannot for example speak the vulgar words that describe what you and I have just done together. But physical action is one thing, while silence is a judged option. That is my choice. What I cannot say out loud I exult in doing.'

'Yes,' said Tallant, thinking back.

'Many of the people who follow the same calling are alike.'

'You spread the word.'

'I do.'

She opened her eyes, turned against him so that as her position changed his hand slipped from one breast to the other. He held the nipple lightly between two extended fingers.

'Do you know where we are?' he said.

'Do you mean where we are emotionally, or do you mean physically?'

'I mean – where are we? Where on Prachous have we reached? Are we near the coast yet?'

'We'll reach the sea tomorrow. Where we are at the moment – I'm not sure exactly.'

'That shanty town we passed through, the settlement, the slum. I have never seen anything like it before.'

'It's the largest settlement on the island.'

'Have you been there before?'

'I took the Word to Adjacent last year. I would not attempt it again.'

'Were you threatened?'

'Ignored would be a more accurate description.'

'How long were you there?'

'I persevered for a whole year. I would not return.'

'I thought Prachous City was the largest on the island.'

'It's the capital, but Adjacent is more populous.'

'What is that name you are using?' Tallant said.

'The shanty town is known as Adjacent.'

'Adjacent to what?'

'I have no idea.' Firentsa shifted position again, easing her back on the uneven mattress. 'Would you like to do again what we did just now?'

304

'For which there are no words?'

'There are words, but I don't want you to say them. Well, would you do it again?'

'Yes, but not yet.'

'I thought you would.'

'Soon. Tell me about Adjacent.'

'There's nothing I can tell you. It's a social problem for which no solution has yet been found.'

'How big is the shanty town?'

'You saw today how long it takes to cross it. The settlement spreads over a large part of the south-east corner of the island. More people constantly arrive, so it's almost impossible to estimate the total population. When I was there last year it was thought there were about a million inhabitants, but it must be larger than that now.'

'Who are they?' Tallant said. 'Where have they come from? It's supposed to be impossible to get past the border controls.'

'The people in Adjacent have found a way. In theory they are all at risk of deportation.'

'So how do they do it?'

'I've no idea.'

'You said you were there. Didn't you ask them?'

'I heard many answers, none of which I understood, and anyway I think none of the stories was true. Ask yourself, Tomak: how did you get to Prachous? Where were you before we met?'

Tallant felt a cold, familiar inner fear, something he habitually shied away from. He slid his hand away from her body, sat up. Someone outside in the yard was shouting, followed by several more yelling back. The music suddenly increased in volume. He heard laughter. The noises from the drinkers seemed remote from him, hidden behind a transparent screen. For the first time in weeks he felt chilled. The woman, Firentsa, did not sit up beside him, but she turned her face away so that she was gazing up at the ceiling. He saw the strong jaw, the high forehead. She was in repose, waiting for him to speak.

'Why did you ask me that?' he said.

305

'Because you don't know the answer and neither do I. You are here, I am here. We are much the same.'

'I have always been here,' he said.

'So have I. How far back do your memories go?'

'All the way.'

'As a child?'

'No. Not then.'

'So it was later than that,' she said. 'How old were you when you arrived on Prachous?'

He swung his legs around and sat upright on the side of the lumpy mattress. He felt rationality was being tested by memory. He knew he was not a Prachoit but he had always been here on Prachous Island. There were times in the past when he had not been here but his memories were textureless, uninterrupted, a smooth continuity. He felt an agony of uncertainty, memory being tested by rationality.

He stood up.

'You do not know where we are,' she said. 'You have never before been to Adjacent. You do not know Prachous City, because if you did you would not call it that. You are not even sure in which the direction the sea might be. All these would be familiar to islanders, which tells me you have recently arrived. I think I have too.'

'But you were here last year, working in the shanty town.'

'I was spreading the word in Adjacent. That is true. I am certain of that as you are certain of your own memories. You seek inner peace. I know how I could offer you that. I have words that I love to speak.'

'I don't want them.'

'Then ask me the same as I asked you.'

'How did you come to this island?' he said. He was back beside the bed now, standing naked beside her, looking down at her. He could see his shadow thrown across her breasts by the single light-bulb in the ceiling. 'You are not a Prachoit.'

'I am a Spreader—'

'Come on, that's just an evasion. What are you really, Firentsa?'

'You're evading it too. We are both refusing to accept that our lives are not what we think they are. Come and lie down beside

306

me again. We are here to do that together and my needs are still urgent.'

'Say the words.'

'I won't.'

'Then say again what you said about memory. That felt true.'

'Do you remember how we met?' Firentsa said.

'We were walking together through the desert, heading south.'

'But before that? Before the desert? Where were you and what were you doing?' The weak, shadowed light from the bulb did not reveal much of her to him – now she further shaded herself by raising a knee. He could see all of her face, and some of the light from one of the floodlamps outside was reflecting back from the wall behind her. Her body interested him, but there was something about her he could not comprehend. 'Before that, Tomak?' she said again.

'My wife. I was with my wife, at that place. The one in the desert you and I left together. If we were together then you must have been there too.'

'No. I wasn't there. It was an army post. Soldiers everywhere.'

'You're as unsure as I am. I think it was a hospital, a field hospital. My wife was a nurse. Is a nurse. Something happened to her. Do you remember my wife?'

'There were no nurses when we left, or doctors. No one ill. Just soldiers.'

'I don't remember soldiers,' Tallant said.

'They were militiamen, I think. A bit of a rabble.'

'But who were they? Prachous is a wealthy island, heavily regulated. There's no need for private armies.'

'Didn't you take photographs while you were there?'

'Yes. They're still in my camera.'

But all three of his cameras were in their cases, now inside his bag, lying against the wall on the far side of the room. To get them would mean turning away from this woman who wanted him, fiddling with the luggage and the closures and fasteners, checking through the three cameras to remember which one he had used, and when.

'Tomorrow,' he said. 'I'll show you tomorrow.'

'Still evading, then. Come and lie beside me, Tomak.'

Briefly, he glimpsed in her expression the same sort of uncertainty he himself was feeling. There was a gap in his memory, like a period of amnesia, but in fact it was the opposite of that. Not a gap but a *presence*, an infilling. He had too many memories, but none of them was precise, or more exactly his own. They weren't real – they were just good enough narratives. All he knew for sure was the experience of the last three days he had spent with this intriguing woman, and more exactly still, the last several minutes.

'Will you stay with me here tonight?' he said to her.

'I could.'

'Will you? Do you want to?'

'I no longer wish to be alone.'

As he lay beside her she reached for him, stroked his belly, stroked the top of his legs. He did not need her to encourage him, but as he placed his arms around her and they both stretched across the old mattress, he felt her hands go behind him. For now, reality was the sensation of her strong hands on his backside, her fingernails pressing into him. He let the noises from outside drift away into the background, he ignored the squalid room in which they lay. One of his hands was lightly holding the back of her head, his fingers buried in Firentsa's short, curly hair, while he pressed his lips to hers – the other hand held and caressed one of her breasts. He was lost in the moment. Ahead would be an arrival at the coast, perhaps tomorrow, somewhere by the sea, with a prospect of winds, the taste of salt on his lips and the sound of the waves, the famous reefs and lagoons that fenced this difficult island. He dreamed of finding a harbour, a ship that would carry him away, or a beach to lie on in idleness, or an apartment to rent in a harbourside village, or a reunion with his wife, who was somewhere here. He wished he could remember her name.

6

The five leading families of Prachous are called Drennen, Galhand, Assentir, Mercier and Wentevor. The names are known to everyone living on the island, but few ordinary people are ever likely to meet any member of these families.

Although by reputation the five families have always been involved in deep and vicious feuds with each other, in modern times they have come to an accommodation and have arranged matters to suit themselves. Some of the family members live permanently on other islands, many of them travel in pursuit of their extensive business interests, but most of them stay within their family Keeps: these are immense family estates situated in the more inaccessible parts of the island. The leading families have little contact between themselves, or so it is believed.

The background of these families has to a large extent created the code of criminal justice for which Prachous is notorious throughout the archipelago.

Because Prachous is a feudal society, private property does not exist. All land, infrastructure, services, businesses, homes and even individual objects are ultimately in the ownership of one or other of the ruling families. Use of them is paid for by tithes. These are collected annually under strict rules of enforcement, through a system of collection agencies administered by professional specialists. The civilian policier force has wide and repressive powers of arrest, detention and prosecution, but few Prachous residents are foolhardy enough to break local laws, except inadvertently or in trivial matters. Prachous is an unquestioning, subservient, materialistic society, where acceptance is rewarded and authority is rarely challenged.

Of course there are many small offences, most of which are committed because of personal disputes, bad behaviour when drunk, minor breakages or, most frequently of all, traffic or driving offences. These are inevitable in any society. On Prachous they are not dealt with under the criminal code. The traditional means of dealing with offenders is for the aggrieved to take revenge.

In some cases the aggrieved is of course an individual, but more often the grievance is said to be felt by the community at large, when civic retribution is allowed. For example, there is no law prohibiting anyone driving around under the influence of alcohol or drugs, so if anyone is arrested for that the policier treat it as a civic matter. The driver is then handed over to his or her neighbours.

All Prachoits know, understand and abide by the principle of proportionate revenge. Retaliation must be in proportion to the offence – if the revenge oversteps that proportion, then the right to revenge is passed back.

Schoolchildren in Prachous are always taught that one of the patois names of the island means REVENGER.

Prachous is therefore a conforming society regulated by apprehension. Prachoits enjoy their lives – few of them ever emigrate to other islands, or even try to. The tithe regulations discourage emigration, but the will is not there. Life on Prachous is benign. Most of the island is scenically beautiful, especially in the mountainous regions. Although the interior of the island is hot, the tropical climate is tempered in all the main areas of coastal settlement by cool sea currents and the prevailing winds. The cities are clean, safe and prosperous. There are sports and leisure facilities everywhere. Prachoits are free to travel anywhere on the island, except of course within those parts reserved for the leading families. They enjoy an uninhibited freedom of speech and expression, of assembly, of opinion. The internet is controlled and monitored by the family representatives, so it is not widely used. The day to day effect of the feudal system brings easy access to almost any material possession. Prachoits are comfortable, contented.

Prachous is a secular island. Religious observation is tolerated but not encouraged.

Culturally, Prachous is something of a backwater. Although sponsorship schemes for Prachoit artistes do exist, funded anonymously by the Galhand and Assentir clans, few artistes appear to take advantage of them. Most of the available funds are handed over to local amateur dramatics groups, evening classes and self-publishing ventures. Prachoit writers, musicians, painters, composers and so on are encouraged not to emigrate, but many of them do. Most

Prachoit books or films, produced on other islands, depict Prachous in an unfortunate light, which because of the revenge laws makes returning to their home island a problem. The performing arts are well supported, although conventional in form. Experimental work is not encouraged.

7

THOM THE THAUMATURGE

Thom the Thaumaturge was born in the Prachoit town of Waalanser, a dull and workaday place on the north coast. The main industries in Waalanser at the time of Thom's birth were fishing and associated activities, such as the smoking, canning and freezing of fish, and a number of manufacturing and mining industries which grew up around the valuable mineral wealth buried in the surrounding hills. For Thom, it was a place to escape from and this he did at the age of seventeen. A touring group performed an evening of live dance, mime and magic, which fired Thom with the urge to become a performer. The show was closed down by the authorities after only one performance and the troupe left town, but they had done enough to change Thom's life.

As soon as he could Thom set off in pursuit of the travelling players, believing, wrongly as it turned out, that they were touring the coastal towns of Prachous. He headed west along the scenically dull northern shore of the island, turning south with the curving of the coast after Ryneck Point, seeking news of the band of players in every town he came to.

It was not long before he came to realize that either he had set off in the wrong direction or the troupe had dispersed after their hostile reception in Waalanser. He never saw or heard of them again. By this time he was beyond disappointment. He had already developed a taste for the freedom of the road, for moving on and around, scraping a living doing whatever casual work he could find. Occasionally, he was able to find temporary or seasonal jobs with one of the theatres, music halls or cinemas he came across, but most of the odd jobs he landed during these early years were on construction sites or in kitchens. He learnt the rudiments of a dozen trades as he went along, but most of all he discovered that Prachous society had little interest, at best, in the entertainment arts.

However, he was happy and contented, teaching himself theatrical skills as he went along. He learned to dance, to recite, to work marionettes, to play acceptably on half a dozen musical instruments. He learned mime, fire-eating and modest acrobatics – he could ride a unicycle and juggle wooden clubs, and for a while both at the same time. For a few blissful weeks he found work in a travelling circus, but the circus came from another part of the archipelago. The circus management's visa forced their stay on Prachous to be short. Thom parted company with the other performers when they told him they had booked a steamship passage to the distant island of Salay.

By the time Thom was in his mid-twenties he had become an accomplished magician, not so much through inclination as the gradual realization that the conservative burghers of these bourgeois Prachoit towns did still enjoy the sight of live magic.

As the years went by he had become more skilful and adept at the art of conjuring, able to match the expectations of different audiences. What would thrill the members of a business seminar seeking diversion was not the same repertoire as he would perform for retired people in one of the seaside towns.

His itinerant life gradually lost its appeal and after his twenty-fifth birthday he found an apartment in the east coast town of Beathurn, surrendered his least-used magical apparatus as a depositing tithe, and became permanently resident at an address for the first time since leaving his parents' home.

Living in Beathurn turned out to suit him. It came close to having what Thom considered to be civilized values, not the least of which was the presence of a working theatre – *Il-Palazz Dukat Aviator*, or 'The Grand Aviator Palace'. This oddly named venue was a well-equipped theatre, which the management insisted on filling with an apparently endless stream of pop tribute bands, evangelists and celebrity chefs. Once or twice a year there was a general variety show, but the acts were unimaginative and repetitive. There was also a cinema, an extensive lending library, a music store and a bookshop.

For a while Thom worked part-time as a licensed pavement performer: singing, playing, sometimes juggling and always performing street magic. He became well known in the town, but he was constantly frustrated in his attempts to be given a booking at the theatre. Every now and then he would earn a gig in one of the neighbouring towns: a party or an event, sometimes guesting in private drinking or gambling clubs, and once or twice even given the chance to perform on a stage, but *Il-Palazz* remained persistently out of reach.

One day, though, when Thom the Thaumaturge was thinking at last that he might retire from performing, he saw a letter printed in the local newspaper. It gave him an idea.

8

The letter was from a man who had spent some time travelling around the Dream Archipelago, and during his journey had seen something he described as a true and baffling mystery.

On the island of Paneron he and his family had witnessed what they considered to be a miracle. He had seen a shaman or a fakir, or some other kind of wild religious zealot, make a young boy disappear from sight in extraordinary circumstances. The letter writer was imprecise with detail, but said it had taken place in the open air, on a patch of recently mown grass, with no assistants and with scores of spectators on all sides.

The letter closed with an appeal to anyone who might have an explanation for what had happened to make contact with him care of the newspaper.

Thom, sensing that this man had seen a skilled illusionist at work, knew that one of the invariable conditions of illusionism was that the audience only saw what they were intended to see, and that they would contentedly assume the rest. What was in fact going on was something else entirely. There was enough description in the letter to convince Thom that this was such an illusion, but annoyingly the details of the performance were lacking.

Subsequent issues of the newspaper carried letters from other readers. Some were just as intrigued as Thom, but others had their own anecdotes to tell. Finally, someone sent in a letter saying that he too had watched this illusion on Paneron – he was also baffled by it, but unlike the first correspondent he included a description of the performance.

With this extra detail Thom was able to make an intelligent guess about what the illusion might have been. All stage magic evolves gradually, tricks adapting as society changes or as new technology become available, but every illusion is based on a handful of principles that have not changed in centuries. What appear to be fresh concepts or innovations are in fact the result of showmanship, or novel ways of presenting old ideas.

Thom immediately set about designing the apparatus he would need for the performance, and sent off to a mail order supplier in Glaund City, on the mainland, for the one crucial piece of equipment he could not make for himself. This was a specially manufactured industrial hawser, mainly used in undersea exploration, but which would be ideal for his purposes.

Two or three weeks later he began his preparations. He rented a function room above a restaurant to use as a rehearsal room and workshop, and every day, working with the blinds drawn and the inner door locked, Thom went through the creation and rehearsal of his new stage act.

9

It was around the same time as this that Thom began to feel that he was being watched or followed. For all its bland character, Prachous could be a place of suspicions, of doubts, of interference. Most people pretended to be absorbed in their own lives, but in reality all Prachoits were nervously curious about what their neighbours might or might not be doing. It always paid to be careful if you had something, no matter how harmless, you wanted to keep to yourself. In Thom's case, because he was a magician, a feeling of secrecy about what might be involved in his preparations was habitual.

Every morning when he walked across the town centre to his rehearsal room, Thom normally stopped at a particular pavement café in the central square of Beathurn. He would buy a pastry or a small piece of cake, drink two cups of coffee, and while he sat alone at a table he would read the day's newspaper. Around him, many other people were doing much the same. It was pleasant to sit there under the shade of the big trees in the square, listening to the sound of other people's chatter and the traffic going past, and harmlessly watching the passers-by as they headed for work, or home, or to the university on the opposite side of the square.

He rarely took much interest in the other customers, but one morning he realized that a certain young woman was once again sitting at a table not far from his own. He had noticed her before – although she was young, looked interesting and always dressed well, there was some kind of deep stress apparent in her expression and bearing. She seemed never able to relax, but always sat forward, slightly hunched, staring out across the street. She was often frowning. In a town of contented people, she looked like an outsider. She always arrived at the café after Thom had ordered from the waiter, and she was still there when he left. Whenever the right table was available she sat at the same distance from him: not too close, not too far away. She always sat at an angle towards him – neither facing him nor with her back turned.

She never looked directly at him, but on the morning when Thom took a special interest in her he glanced up suddenly from his newspaper and his eye happened to fall on her. She was staring at him then, but the instant she noticed him looking she turned her gaze away. Until then, Thom had given her no more thought than anyone else he saw in the café, but after that he was more aware of her.

It became, for Thom, a sort of mild game without rules. He started choosing a different table every day, but each time he did the young woman would contrive to sit at the same general distance away from him as always. One morning he deliberately chose the only free table in an area that was crowded – the young woman had to sit on the far side of the café area. Another time he chose a table inside the café – she took a table outside, but one close to the window with a view towards him. She never seemed to look directly at him, though.

A few days later he realized that she often followed him when he walked the rest of the way to his rehearsal room. She was adept at it: she shadowed him at a great distance, and it took some time for him to be certain that following him was what she was doing.

Not knowing who she was, and feeling sure that her behaviour was not some odd way of showing she was attracted to him, and not himself being interested, at that time, in forming any new relationship, Thom began to wonder what might lie behind it all. Just about the only motive he could ascribe to her was that she trying to find out what his plans were, what he was preparing in his rehearsal room.

His work a year or two earlier as a pavement performer had given him a valuable lesson in the ways this town had of dealing with unconventional activity. The first few times he stood on a street corner and busked his guitar, policier officers had courteously but firmly moved him on. He had soon acceded to the inevitable and applied for, and was quickly granted, a street performer's licence. After that, he was left alone.

One afternoon, when the woman's behaviour had for some reason bothered him more than before, Thom went to the local policier office, applied for and was quickly granted another licence. This was for Live Performance and Rehearsal. In the part of the form where he had to enter a *Performance Description* he wrote the word Magician. Then, thinking that he should cover all possibilities, he added Illusionist, Conjuror, Prestidigitator, Thaumaturge, Wizard, and many more synonyms. He looked forward to being left alone by whoever was instructing this woman to watch him.

But a week later she was still shadowing him. By then Thom had another problem he had to solve.

10

He could not perform the new illusion without an assistant. Indeed, the assistant was the essence of the illusion. What he required was a boy or a girl, or a very young man or woman, who was not only willing to work under the unusual directions of a stage magician but who above all was strong, lithe and athletic. Most of the magical effect of the trick would be gained by the acrobatic performance of the assistant.

He advertised. He tried asking among the people he knew in Beathurn. He approached model agencies and actors' agents.

Applicants were few, and none of them turned out to be suitable. He waited, advertised again, asked around again. He had taken his own rehearsals of the illusion as far as possible – nothing more could be done until he had an assistant to work with. Once again he began to wonder about the wisdom of trying to pursue a magical career in this place.

One morning, when he happened to be sleeping late, he was awakened by someone coming to his door. Dishevelled and barely dressed, Thom was greeted by a man who introduced himself as Gerres Huun. The Huuns were one of the better-known families in Beathurn, managers of several seigniorial tithe agencies in the town.

Huun had arrived with his daughter, an eighteen year-old scholarship girl who was about to attend the Beathurn Multitechnic University, where she was to take a degree course in Body Tension Applications. Her name was Rullebet. She stood quietly beside her father while the two men discussed what she would be required to do if she was given the job. The father said, and Rullebet quickly confirmed, that she lived for athletics and other kinds of physical activity. She had seen Thom's job when he first advertised it, but it was only now that she had managed to persuade her protective father to allow her to apply for it.

Thom was of course eager to explain that the work she would be asked to do, although unusual, was perfectly safe, that the hours expected of her were not long, that he would fulfil any special conditions her parents requested, and of course that she would be remunerated regularly and promptly.

Pleased in every way by Rullebet's appearance and personality, he offered to show them the rehearsal room immediately. After Thom had hastily dressed, the three of them walked through the sunlit streets towards the restaurant building. On the way they passed through the square by the university, where he would normally stop for his morning coffee. It was a little later than his normal time. Thom wondered if he would see the woman who was shadowing him, but he saw no sign of her as they passed.

The high-ceilinged rehearsal room was cool, the windows shrouded with wooden blinds.

'Would you please climb this metal pole,' Thom said, when they were inside with the door locked. The pole was firmly mounted, connected to the floor and one of the ceiling joists. Before Rullebet was allowed to start her father checked it thoroughly to make sure it had been properly secured.

She then shinned up the pole in a matter of seconds. Her body movements were smooth and elegant and when she reached the top she contrived to swirl around it, arm raised in a graceful salute.

'Is that all she will have to do?' said Gerres Huun.

'I require her for rehearsal,' Thom replied. 'That will take several intensive days, with warm-up practice before every performance.'

'Full reward for rehearsals?' said Huun.

'Naturally,' said Thom. 'I will make credit available either to Rullebet herself or to you – or, if she prefers, I could pass the credit to the Body Tension department at the Multitechnic. I'll also credit her with a bonus for every performance in front of the public. The first one of those is yet to be arranged, but I am eager to mount my illusions. I'm certain that now Rullebet will be working with me I can obtain a firm booking in the theatre, here in Beathurn. After that – who knows?'

'I shall be expecting Rullebet to concentrate on her studies.'

'I understand. And I want you to appreciate, sir, that I shall take the greatest of care with her, so that everything she wants of life will be possible. I hope this will even contribute to her studies at the Multi. And of course she will be paid well.'

While they were speaking, Rullebet slid down the pole with a gracious circling movement, and landed lightly on the floor. She acknowledged an unseen audience with a wave of her hand, a radiant smile and an easy curtsey.

11

The management of the community-run theatre was reluctant to put on Thom's new show. He underwent a discouraging interview with the woman in charge. She had avoided him for days but when he finally tracked her down she told him with evident bad grace that their audiences were tired of magic shows. She said that the last magician who performed at *Il-Palazz* had been released from his contract halfway through the week's run.

Thom knew the magician she was meaning – a conjuror of the old school, whose repertoire consisted entirely of tricks with playing cards, handkerchiefs and lighted cigarettes – but Thom's enthusiastic pitch that he had devised an exciting new illusion was to no avail.

Later, he went around to see the editor of the newspaper and invited him to visit his rehearsal room to see a performance for himself. The man's memory of the brief correspondence in his letters column had faded, so Thom had to remind him several times of the intrigue that so many people had expressed.

The elderly editor, a true Prachoit who had made his career reinforcing the cautious views and outlook of his readership, missed his first appointment and sent a trainee reporter to the second, but did manage to turn up after Thom had gone to even more lengths to persuade him.

Rullebet, now exotically clad in the glittering costume she and Thom had chosen for their performances, clambered up the special rope he had imported from Glaund, and at the sound of Thom's mystic incantations disappeared into thin air.

'Do that again,' said the ageing journalist, as the smoke of her disappearance drifted through the large room.

'A good magician never repeats a trick,' Thom replied.

'Where the devil did she go? And where is she now?'

'You have seen her disappear. For that reason alone I could not repeat the illusion.'

Grudgingly, the man said, 'All right. It is astonishing.'

'Thank you.'

Thom clapped his hands loudly. Rullebet ran lithely from the cloakroom at the far end, her arms spread wide, a beaming smile on her face. She bowed deeply to the editor, then without saying a word hurried back to the cloakroom.

Thom had to restrain the man from going after her. He wanted to interview her, wanted to know how she felt about being transported invisibly from one part of the room to another, but Thom led him firmly to the door.

'Sir, do you agree that what you saw just now is amazing?'

'I suppose.'

'Then if you were to write a review of what you have seen, pleading perhaps with the management committee of *Il-Palazz*, maybe our townspeople might have a chance to share the experience? This is only one of many illusions I can perform.'

'I'll see what I can do,' said the editor, but not encouragingly.

12

The write-up did not appear until two weeks later, just as Thom was beginning to despair of the whole matter, but once the article was in print it could not have been better worded. It spoke of mystery, skill, amazing impossibilities, a dazzling young lady, a fiendish sorcerer, one shock and stunning sight after another.

Thom was about to hurry around to *Il-Palazz* with a cutting of the article, and plead with the woman manager to change her mind, when she appeared in person at his door.

Not long afterwards, luridly coloured posters appeared all over the town: An Evening with Thom the Thaumaturge! A month later Thom enjoyed his triumphant opening night.

He was given the two prime spots in a programme of general varieties. He closed the first half before the interval with a series of relatively straightforward illusions, and he came back at the end of the second act for the finale, saving his vanishing trick with Rullebet for the climax. The shows went well all through the week.

Once he was inside the building and using it regularly, Thom felt less happy with the physical state of the theatre. The auditorium itself would have benefited from a general updating and re-decoration, but much more concerning to him was the condition of the theatrical machinery. In particular he discovered the electrical wiring was antiquated. Most of the stage lights appeared to work, but there were worrying intermittent flickers whenever the main spots came on. Touching the microphone stand during a techni-cal rehearsal, Thom received an electric shock – afterwards, one of the tech crew wrapped some insulating tape around the stand and declared it to have been made safe, but Thom could still feel a tingle of static whenever he touched it. He did so as infrequently as possible after that.

One of his illusions in the first half of the show required the use of the stage trapdoor, but during technical rehearsals it jammed several times. Again, the tech crew came to his rescue and quickly claimed to have solved the problem. Watching them work, Thom came to the conclusion that these apparently keen technicians were the cause of many of the small problems. Most of them were unpaid volunteers, enthusiastic enough, but that was the best that could be said of them. There were two men in charge of the gang who said they had worked in theatres all their lives, but they were both elderly and every day the marginally younger of the two was drunk by mid-afternoon. After the trapdoor was allegedly repaired Thom could still not make it work reliably, so he dropped that particular trick from his repertoire.

As unobtrusively as possible he went through the rigging loft and checked the hemps and lifts. No magician should ever leave anything to chance. His first technical rehearsal cast him into gloom because so many things went wrong, but the second one was better.

Then the week of performances began and all was well. There

was a good audience on the first night, a smaller one after that, but as the week went by the numbers steadily increased.

After the first few variety acts – a television comedian who had been famous some years earlier, a chanteuse, a troupe of dancers, some piano duettists – his simple but puzzling tricks went down well. He began with card tricks, then performed a trick known as the Pejman Illusion. This involved a curtained litter, pushed on to the stage on wheels with its compartment concealed by drapes. When the curtains were opened it was shown to be empty, but as soon as Thom closed them again, they would be thrown open from inside and Rullebet sensationally appeared. He then carried out a series of acrobatics-cum-legerdemain stunts on his unicycle, and finished with a more complex illusion which involved an escape from a metal cage under the threat of an array of deadly-looking knives poised to fall across him.

The main attraction was of course the illusion with which he ended the show.

For this, Thom assumed the identity of a sorcerer and appeared on stage in a flowing gown, his face painted to make it seem sinister or inscrutable. When he moved about the stage he did so with a sinuous gliding motion, keeping his arms folded and his head tilted back.

After some exaggerated descriptions of the wonders of ancient magic he would reveal his main prop: a large basket placed in the centre of the stage. From this Thom pulled out a length of thick rope. Two members of the audience would be invited on to the stage to examine the rope, and they would, inevitably, confirm that it was in every way normal. It was not, of course: it was the technologically sophisticated hawser he had imported from a specialist marine industrial supplier. The rope, reinforced with metal and carbon fibres, undetectable by the untrained eye, had a self-rigidifying property – when it was used in a certain way it would become as strong and solid as a steel rod.

With the volunteers departed from the stage, Thom embarked on what was for him the most difficult and physically demanding part of the illusion. He threw the rope upwards towards the rigging loft in such a way that it would self-rigidify. He had rehearsed this for weeks and could count on a successful throw at least two times out of three. Even so, for effect he always contrived to get it wrong a few times. This would underline the 'normal' properties of the rope, as well as providing the theatrical spectacle of a heavy rope collapsing down on top of him, apparently with great hazard to himself. Finally, though, he would succeed and the rope would magically stand upright. What the audience could not see was that the base of the rope was mounted securely inside the solidly constructed basket, so that once the rope was erect it would not again collapse until he wanted it to.

Rullebet was of course concealed inside the basket throughout all this. He would magically cause her to appear, and she would rise like a beautifully plumed bird from the basket. Thom would place her in what seemed to be an intense trance, and she climbed the rope towards the top. Not to the very top, but as high as possible so that she could be seen by everyone in the audience.

Once she was there, Thom would cause her to vanish, with many flashes and loud bangs, and the rope, now secretly controlled by Thom from below, collapsed down on to the stage again, most of it falling into or around the basket.

After the audience had been given the time to marvel at what they had seen, Rullebet would mysteriously appear in some other part of the auditorium, and she and Thom would take their final bow.

They performed this six times during the course of the week, and all went well. Then came the final performance.

13

The house was not full on the last night, but every seat in the stalls was taken. Latecomers were moved to the upper circle. Word of mouth about the show was positive and people were curious to see Thom's act.

In the afternoon he and Rullebet rehearsed the illusion once more, adding small flourishes wherever possible to enhance the effect.

Just before the show began Rullebet told him that her father was going to be present. He had been determined to find a seat as close as possible to the stage. Thom experienced a feeling of disquiet – for a performer the belief that an audience is anonymous can enhance the illusion of rapport. Knowing people in the audience could be a distraction.

When the show began Thom watched the early acts from the wings, trying to get a feel for the audience. They were responsive to the performers, which had a mixed effect on Thom. Prachoits made undemanding spectators, but their generous laughter at the comedian's unfunny wisecracks was disappointing. Thom had worked hard on his act and wanted to feel that any applause he received was properly earned.

Then it was his turn. His sequence of tricks to close the first part of the show went without a hitch. When Rullebet appeared unexpectedly inside the Pejman cabinet the audience clapped loudly – he saw Rullebet's father standing to applaud them. Thom then escaped dramatically from his deadly cage of knives, and that was the end of the first part. The applause continued after the main tab had come down, signalling the interval.

During the break Thom noticed that two of the tech crew were working on one of the junction boxes – this sent power to the winch that raised and lowered the main curtain. The two men were making hasty repairs. One of them rushed away, returning a few moments later with a roll of insulating tape.

Thom wandered over.

'Anything wrong?' he said.

'Nothing that affects you.' The man was struggling to get the tape around a section of exposed cable. 'Leave it to us. We had to lower the main curtain manually at the finale, but we've fixed it now. Is that all right with you? We know you're the expert.'

Feelings between him and the tech crew were already strained by his earlier criticisms, so Thom backed off. He went to his dressing room, sat alone and thought for a while, then started to apply the heavy sorcerer make-up for his big illusion. He knew that Rullebet would also be preparing, along the passage in her own dressing room.

At last it was time. While a close-harmony quartet sang before the front curtain, he made sure that his basket was positioned correctly on the stage, that it was secured properly and that the mechanism for the rope stabilizer was working. He went about the stage and placed the explosive caps which would be detonated remotely for effect. Then he helped Rullebet lower herself into the cramped space inside the basket and made sure she was safely in position before the trick began.

The music swelled up, the curtains swept back, the lights picked him out. He launched into his sorcerous speech more confidently than ever before, being sure every now and then to address the more distant faces he could dimly see in the upper circle.

He brought out the rope, handled it expressively to show that it was as flexible as any normal rope. The volunteers from the audience were found, they came on stage, they convinced themselves of the rope's conventional type, they returned to their seats. Thom made the first attempt, deliberately bungled, to throw the rope into a vertical position. It collapsed down on the stage around him.

When he picked it up, coiling it around his arm, he was disconcerted to feel the faint irritant of a static electrical charge. He pushed the thought to the back of his mind. He glided across the stage from side to side, declaiming about wizards and necromancers of the past who had tried and failed to make this illusion work, how dangerous it could be as well as difficult. The faint tingling sensation continued whenever he touched certain parts of the rope.

He threw it up a second time – again it fell back to the stage. He tried again, this time intending to make it work, but his luck was out. The rope fell alarmingly around him.

When he collected up the rope he felt the burr of static electricity once more. It seemed harmless, because the only electricity used in the illusion was in the rope stabilizer and he had wired that himself, double-checking its insulation. He braced himself, concentrated on the broad swing necessary to elevate the rope to its full height, but also into such a position above the basket that the dozens of tiny rigidifying relays buried inside the fibres would click into place and hold the rope stiffly.

It was his fourth attempt and this time it worked. The musicians in the pit picked up the cue with a triumphant chord.

The rope stood stiffly vertical, swaying slightly from side to side. Applause broke out spontaneously from the audience. With sorcerous arrogance, Thom ignored this reaction and instead strode disdainfully about the stage, throwing violent gestures towards the pyrotechnic capsules he had placed. Each one exploded as designed: bright orange and white and yellow bursts of sparkling flame, loud bangs and plenty of smoke.

Within this swirl of smoke and diffused lights he went to the basket and raised Rullebet magically from within. Another exultant chord from the pit orchestra. The spotlights found her and her dazzling costume sparkled brightly. She ran prettily around him and acknowledged the audience.

Adopting his most fearsome and villainous look, Thom placed Rullebet in a trance. Soon the young woman was standing before him with her head leaning forward, her arms dangling limply at her sides. Thom mimed an instruction for her to climb the rope. Rullebet turned, clambered up on to the lip of the basket's opening, then with her familiar easy grace shinned slowly towards the top.

She paused twice during her climb. Holding on to the rope with a hand and an entwining lower leg she allowed herself to turn around the rope, her free hand waving aloft, slowly slipping down just a little. Two thirds of the way to the top she repeated this – both times the audience applauded her loudly for her skill and poise.

At last she reached the top and once again she balanced herself away from the rope as the audience applauded her.

Thom braced himself to make his magical gesture, to cause her to vanish, or at least to appear to vanish. He raised his arms, tilted his head back. He was immediately beneath her.

As the music became louder, more urgent, Rullebet raised her hand again, and in the instant of that moment disaster struck. There was a terrible blue-white flash and a hissing explosion. Rullebet's body jerked in agony, her back straightening in an extreme reaction, her grip on the rope lost. In her spasm of involuntary motion she flung out her hand and another flashing discharge of electricity consumed her.

She fell.

Thom leapt back in panic as Rullebet landed violently on the stage beside him. He realized she must have touched something in the loft, most likely an uninsulated cable. She fell heavily on her head and shoulder, but other than the crash of her body against the stage boards she made no sound. What he could see of the skin on her hands, her arms, one leg, the back of her neck, flared an angry red. A thick miasma of smoke was about her. A panicky instinct made Thom look upwards.

A black spiral of smoke showed the trace of her horrific fall.

The music from the pit orchestra died. Many people in the audience had risen to their feet in shock. Thom glanced desperately towards them, then knelt beside Rullebet's contorted body. He tore off the ridiculous head-dress he had been wearing, pushed the voluminous sleeves of his robe up his arms. The house lights came on, flickering. An alarm bell was ringing. Three men dashed on the stage, one carrying a chemical fire extinguisher. Everyone seemed to be shouting.

Thom leaned over Rullebet, laid a hand on her face, tried to turn her head so that he could see her. She had fallen so that her head was somehow too far over, curved at a horrible angle towards one side of her chest.

He felt no breath from her on his fingers. Her flesh was crisp, hot to the touch, charred. The men who had just arrived pulled him backwards and away from her body, yelling at him to move out of the way, give her space to breathe. They struggled to resuscitate her. One of them rolled her forcefully on to her back, began palpating her chest. Her head lolled back, rolling as if it had become loose on her neck. Her eyes were opaque, unfocused.

One of the man's legs, thrusting out behind him as he punched Rullebet's chest with increasing force, caught the edge of the illusion's basket. The rope above, still until that moment erect, swung to the side. The hidden relays relaxed. The heavy rope came tumbling down, fell across them all, an unyielding deadweight, an immobile black serpent.

Thom was struck hard on the back of his head by part of the rope. He half crawled, half staggered away, then fell forward, lying face-down next to Rullebet's body.

14

'It was an accident,' Thom said, in desperation. 'The theatre is responsible. There must be an uninsulated power cable above the stage. No one warned me about it. The building is not maintained properly. Ask the management to show you their safety certificates, their fire certificates.'

'Be quiet. You're under arrest.'

Thom was standing in the centre of the stage, facing the auditorium. The remains of his illusion apparatus lay on the stage behind him – the rope sprawled across the boards, partly covering the basket. Thom had removed the outer layers of his costume, the sorcerer's gown with its huge sleeves and baggy trousers, and these lay on the floor in a heap. Thom stood in his stage underclothes: an off-white vest, pants held up by braces. His face still bore the vivid blue and bright-green flashes of the sorcerer's make-up.

Most of the audience had hurried away out of the theatre after Rullebet's body was removed, but more than a hundred people remained, clustering near the orchestra pit, close to the stage. Rullebet's father was among them. He stood against the low, curtained wall of the pit, his face distorted by fury and pain. There were others Thom recognized too, but who in the urgency of his situation, and because of the waves of unhappiness and sorrow that were flooding through him, he could not properly identify. They were people from the town, his neighbours, others he must have seen from time to time, some perhaps he had spoken to during his years in Beathurn, or even longer ago, in his days as a traveller. They were anyway a blur on the edge of his ability to comprehend what was happening.

Two policier officers arrived with the ambulance that had been called to take away Rullebet's body. One of them now stood beside Thom, handcuffed to him – their wrists hung together side by side in a perverse parody of companionship. The other officer was standing on the edge of the stage, his back to the people below, facing Thom and accusing him.

'The law says that there are precautions that must be observed at every theatrical performance. Were you aware of them and did you abide by them?'

'I was aware of them,' Thom said weakly. 'But the theatre apparently was not. Everything here is maintained badly.'

'Are you claiming that you had no idea there were live electrical cables above the stage?'

'They shouldn't have been there. No one warned me.'

'But you were seen in the rigging loft.'

'I was checking the hemps, the ropes. The tech crew were responsible for the electrics.'

'They say they told you there was a fault.'

'They said there was a problem with the curtain winch.'

'But they warned you there was a fault?'

'No.' Thom was struggling to remember exactly what had been said during that brief encounter in the interval. 'I asked them what the trouble was, but they wouldn't discuss it with me.'

'They say you complained about their work.'

'Yes. They are incompetent.'

'You still went ahead with the show, though. You put your young assistant's life in danger.'

'No. It's the theatre's responsibility to provide a safe working environment.'

'So you admit you didn't make your own safety check. Is that because you didn't know how to? Or couldn't you be bothered?'

'I signed a contract. A standard agreement. That agreement contains warranties about safety and public liability.'

'You are not a member of the public when performing.'

'No.'

The questioning went on, frequently going over the same ground as before.

The officer was a local man, a serjeant in the Seigniorial Policier, thought to be a reliable, community-oriented man, liked by Prachoits. Thom was a Prachoit too – he knew what was happening, what was likely to happen next. In his terror of this dangerous situation, and his inability to influence it in his favour, he felt total despair. Above all there was an aching sense of guilt and misery about the violently sudden way in which Rullebet had died. She was so young, so pretty, intelligent, full of life and fun, certain of what she wanted to do. Thom genuinely adored her. His incursion into her world was intended to be temporary. It was unnecessary to her, a brief distraction from whatever other plans she might have had, but it was he who had brought about her death. How could a young woman's life end like that, so randomly, suddenly, definitively? None of it was her fault, nothing of it was anything to do with her real life.

'Have you anything more to say?'

Thom looked up. He tried to see past the policier serjeant's bulk to the group of people who stood beyond.

'I'm sorry,' Thom said. 'Desperately sorry. It was an accident. I couldn't have foreseen it happening. I took every care. Rullebet was a lovely girl – I would not wish her any harm. I did what I could.'

The officer standing beside him reached down and unlocked the handcuff on Thom's wrist. He moved away, walked briskly across the stage and climbed down to the auditorium by way of the wooden steps at the side.

The serjeant said, 'This is outside policier jurisdiction. It has become a civic matter.' He turned towards the people clustered around the edge of the stage. He added, more quietly, 'The law requires that no policier officers may be present during civic retribution.'

He followed the other officer, walking quickly down the steps. They marched together up the main aisle between the audience seats. Thom was left alone on the stage under the bleak, fitful lights, surrounded by the wretched debris of his magic act.

He saw the two policier officers disappear through the curtained door at the back of the auditorium, and moments later it closed with a loud thud.

The reaction in the crowd was instant.

Several people shouted, 'He's got to pay for this! Get him now!'

The crowd shoved forward, some of them, including Rullebet's father, climbing over the low wall around the orchestra pit, coming directly towards the stage. Many more moved towards the short flight of wooden steps at each side. Terrified of what they were going to do to him Thom backed away, looking anxiously into the wings. Several of the backstage technicians were there, deliberately blocking his escape.

The first of the crowd reached the stage and started striding aggressively towards him. Thom raised his hands defensively, already knowing there was no hope, there was nothing he could do to the prevent them taking the traditional remedy, nothing he could say to plead or argue with them, reason with them, apologize to them again.

A young woman was the first to reach him, pushing her way quickly and determinedly in front of the others and rushing across to him. Thom instantly recognized her: it was the woman he had seen every morning in the café in the square, the one who was for some reason shadowing him.

She turned back to face the others, raising her arms as they pushed forward. She leaned back defensively against Thom.

'Please!' she cried. 'Not now. Don't go on with this!'

'Get out of the way!'

'No – listen! You saw what happened. It was a terrible accident!'

She could hardly be heard over the noise of everyone else. Thom could hear her, but he realized that few others could. They were all around him now, pushing the woman against him. A man behind him barged Thom with his shoulder. Some had their fists raised. Everyone was shouting at once. They were working themselves up, the madness of a crowd.

'Let's hear what he has to say!' the young woman shouted. 'It's only fair!'

'We've heard his excuses!'

'Kill him now!'

Someone else was pushing towards him, thrusting people aside with great force. It was another woman. She was strongly built, and her face had prominent features: high cheekbones, a wide brow. Thom had never seen her before. She was having an effect on the crowd, because she was pushing many of the people away from Thom. The crowd behind him were kicking at his legs, and one punch landed painfully on the back of his head.

'Calm down!' she shouted. 'Leave him alone!' She raised her right hand high, and for a moment Thom glimpsed a leather-bound sacred text. 'The Word demands peace and forgiveness!' she announced.

Now Thom and the first woman were rammed hard against each other by the pressure of bodies. Her face had been pushed against his chest. She seemed unable to turn away. Some of the men closest were jabbing their fists past her at his face. The woman with the scripture somehow managed to fend them off, partly by blocking them with her arms, but mostly by pulling Thom away from them. They were all shuffling in a shambles, backwards across the stage, towards the backdrop.

Thom shouted at the young woman pressed against him, 'Why are you helping me? Who are you?'

'I'm Kirstenya. I love you, Thom—'

Another hard blow to the side of his head dazed him. By some feat of strength the other woman had managed to force her way through the affray and was using her broad body to block attacks coming from one side. Some of the people she had pushed past had fallen to the floor, but were quick to regain their feet. Her face was directly in front of his. She wheeled around, knocked one of the men aside, but he was holding something metal and hard, and immediately struck her with great violence on the side of the head. She reeled sideways, blood flooding from her head and nose.

There were too many assailants, the odds against Thom were too great. He was surrounded. The two women who had inexplicably taken up his cause were pinned against him, kicked and shoved and punched as much as he was, and as hard.

Everyone was shouting, pushing and jabbing their fists. Thom had taken several painful punches to his face and head, and many more to his body. He tried to duck away, tried to fold his arms over his head, but two men shoved him hard and he fell backwards to the floor. Part of the thick rope lay on the stage under his spine, an extra source of pain. The people around him started kicking.

The two women also fell, and they sprawled on the floor beside him. There was no longer anything they could do to protect him and they were now, like him, huddled on the boards of the stage, trying vainly to protect their faces and necks with their arms. The woman with the scripture was facing him and she was intoning something – it was inaudible in the clamour of shouts, some words spoken, a kind of prayer, a hopeless appeal to those who refused to listen. The younger woman had fallen so that she was turned away from him, and as Thom's consciousness faded he saw that people were stamping all over her in their eagerness to reach him. A booted foot came straight into his face, hard and with full body strength behind it.

15

Thom died on the stage that night, according to the Prachoit traditions of civic revenge. He was fortunate, in relative terms, in soon losing consciousness after the first violent kicks to his head, and was therefore unaware of what followed: the angry and selfish disputes about priorities, the shouting, the arguments about who should finish him off.

The kicks against his inert body became token, symbolic, ritualistic. Several of the women shouted Rullebet's name as they took their turn. He was almost certainly dead, or on the point of death, when the *coup de grâce* was delivered: a messy decapitation with a knife, carried out by Gerres Huun, Rullebet's father.

Thom died without knowing who the women were who had tried to help him – the one who tried to fend off his attackers with a spoken Word, the one who called herself Kirstenya, who had been watching and following him. They were not known to each other.

Both women were badly injured in the assault: they suffered broken limbs and ribs, cuts and severe bruising, damaged internal organs. They were unconscious when the ambulance crews arrived, but in the end they survived. After prolonged stays in hospital they recovered sufficiently to be allowed to go home. They needed long periods of convalescence and when well enough sought and were given compensation, under the regulations covering disproportionate revenge.

After the evening at the theatre these two women had no contact with each other again, both assuming the other had died during

the affray. They each found ways of leaving Prachous forever, and
eventually they did.

16

Prachous has only one airport capable of handling inter-island
or intercontinental aircraft. It is situated on the outer edge of
Prachous Town and is operated by the seigniorial families, who
carefully restrict its use. The island is well defended with batteries
of anti-aircraft missiles, and unwelcome incoming flights get a
hostile reception. Most of the large aircraft allowed to land or take
off are cargo flights. The airport tithe is set at a high rate, forcing up
the price of the food delicacies and electronics and other consumer
goods being brought in. Passenger flights are rare, and all civil
flight plans have to be negotiated in advance with the authorities.
Certain categories of passenger are allowed more or less unimpeded
use of the airport – these include members of the diplomatic corps,
military chiefs of staff, assayers of the rare-earth minerals which are
mined on Prachous, and of course all members of the seigniorial
families, their deputies, staff and representatives.

All other travellers are required to use the seaports, where inter-
island ferries provide regular services. The restrictions on travel are
similar, but the border officials who oversee the rules at the ports
are given extensive discretion about whom they will allow in or
out of Prachous. This pragmatic loophole in the border controls
does allow a certain amount of interchange between Prachous and
the islands in the seas around it.

The Prachoit compulsion to maintain controls on movement
of the population is traditional, and can be traced back through
the centuries. Before the invention of air travel the seaports were
much more tightly controlled and the penalties for trying to enter
illegally, or to escape, were extreme. For this reason, the name
Prachous means in certain patois contexts CLOSURE. To modern
Prachoits, closure has become a definition of how they understand

their island society and explains the attitude to strangers, the rejection of cultural influences from other islands, and the constant need for social reassurance encountered at every level.

There are many recreations open to the Prachoit population and because of the overall wealth of the island these are popular and well used. The mountain areas, in particular, contain a multitude of resorts and spas, open the year round. Sailing is enjoyed along all the coasts except the eastern one. Although Prachoit children are taught seamanship from an early age, the lagoons and tidal reaches in the east are considered too dangerous to navigate. All sailing is required to take place in river estuaries, closed lagoons or within five kilometres of the coast. Deeper water is said to contain defensive mines.

Team sports are enthusiastically followed.

Perhaps the most popular pastime of all, though, is club flying. The island is dotted with many small, privately run airfields and almost all are unregulated. At weekends and during holiday periods the skies are busy with dozens of single- and twin-engined aircraft. Traffic control is becoming a problem for the authorities, although the more experienced pilots claim that self-regulated airspace makes the most sense and has worked well on Prachous for many decades.

There are few attempts to fly out of Prachous. Fuel supplies at most airstrips are limited, and in any event all aircraft licensed to fly from Prachoit landing strips are equipped with fuel tanks of restricted size. There are exceptions to this – for example, aircraft used for agriculture or crowd-control purposes are given many freedoms.

Prachous is a secular island. Religious observation is tolerated but not encouraged. No churches, temples or other places of worship have been built in the new town of Adjacent, or in its general area. Aircraft are banned from flying over Adjacent or anywhere near it.

17

THE NURSE, THE MISSIONARY AND THE REEDLAND

I spent most of my first few months on Prachous trying to locate a close friend of mine called Tomak. We had lost contact when war broke out, when as a reservist he was commissioned and sent to the front. Before we parted, Tomak told me everything he knew which would enable me to keep in touch with him. He told me the name of his unit, the rank he had been given and the likely part of the country to which he would be posted. We both knew that as a cavalry lieutenant, in an army confronting a heavily mechanized enemy, he was likely to be kept in reserve and not be involved in front-line action, and we both welcomed the news that he had been posted to guard duty at a top-secret base, which Tomak understood was a scientific research station of some kind. I had therefore temporarily stopped worrying about him.

However, the power of the enemy was overwhelming, our country was subdued and occupied, and all the surviving commissioned officers in the armed forces were rounded up. At the time I was a civilian attached to the air force, so my position was ambiguous, but I managed to escape before anyone captured me.

I later learned that Tomak had been injured during the fighting and evacuated to a hospital somewhere on Prachous. His life was said to be in no danger but he required surgery and extensive post-operative therapy. If this was true it would mean he had fared better than many of his fellow officers. After being rounded up they had been transported en masse to a small, uninhabited island called Cahthinn, and there, it was rumoured, they had been shot. No one knew this for sure but it was a persistent rumour, given credibility by the known disappearance of so many young men.

Because I was not a Prachoit, the people I met almost always treated me with polite suspicion. I later found out that this was normal on the island, not just aimed at me, but at first I felt it was an unwelcoming place. Because of the way I arrived on Prachous – I had flown in and landed at a small, privately owned airstrip near the south-east coast, not realizing until later that by doing so I had broken several local laws – I always found it difficult to explain who I was or what I was doing there.

For the first few days I was lost, not just in the sense that I was unable to find my bearings, but also in trying to understand the unwritten rules, customs and expectations of the place I had arrived in. I have rarely felt so foreign, so much an outsider. At first, exhausted after my long flight, I tried to find a hotel or guest house, or anywhere I could spend the night, but no one I met seemed to understand what I meant. Hotels turned out to be almost unknown on the island, because there were so few visitors from abroad. Prachoits have instead devised an informal system of room barter, for when they travel around the island. I had no knowledge of this at all. I not only needed somewhere to stay but I was hungry and thirsty. Later I would need to rent a car or buy some maps. Their polite suspicion and complete lack of understanding made such things seem impossible to achieve.

On the first night I returned to my aircraft and slept, or tried to sleep, in the cramped cockpit. The next day, as soon as the airstrip opened, I was told by an official that my plane was going to be impounded. The plane was wheeled to a bonded hangar and I was handed a mass of paperwork. This would commence the procedure by which I might be allowed to have the aircraft returned to me. I was told to complete the first two pages immediately.

On the top line of the first page I had to write my name. This was a problem I had foreseen, because I knew my name would look and sound foreign to the people of this island. I wrote 'Kirstenya Rosscky', seeing no alternative. If I was asked to identify myself, all my papers, including my solo pilot's licence, were in that name. I handed over the required basic information expecting objections, but the official accepted it without comment.

I managed to find a guest house on my second night – in reality it was a refuge or hostel for walkers – and began to learn at last the ways of this island. Money, as I understood it, did not exist. Residents of the island have to surrender tithes, while visitors like myself can either pay a tithe like everyone else, or exercise the option to take out a long-term loan, which need only be settled when leaving the island. I immediately decided on a loan, as the alternative would have been to give up my plane.

More paperwork followed but this was easier: it was the sort of form you would have to fill out when applying for a job, or opening a savings account. The loan was drawn up on the spot by a clerk who happened to live close to the hostel, and from then on I was able to charge all my expenses to a numbered account.

Those early days now seem remote to me. After I had been on Prachous for a few weeks and learned to blend in, I discovered it was an easy place to live. There were dozens of apartments or houses to choose from, food was plentiful and inexpensive, and most people were polite once they were used to me, but they were always incurious, rarely open about themselves, always closed off, never likely to invite you to their homes, these materially endowed citizens, all of them profligate consumers.

18

As soon as I had found a small apartment in which to live, and arranged for the use of a car, I set about the legal process of changing my name. It was protective colouring – I had no wish to draw attention to myself or what I was doing. I already knew the severe way the Prachous authorities dealt with people they considered to be illegal immigrants. A change to a commonplace Prachoit name was a first step as a harmless, simple disguise. I chose a name I had seen written down and heard spoken many times, one I hoped would blend in and that to me sounded attractive: Mellanya, Mellanya Ross.

I began to make a few friends, mostly people who lived in the same apartment block as me. They behaved like Prachoits – I tried to copy them. This meant we were always friendly towards each other, but it never went further than that.

All this gave me an increasingly safe base for what I wanted to do on Prachous.

The search for Tomak was still my only reason for being on

the island. There were several immediate problems to tackle. For instance, if he was in hospital I had no idea which one it might be. Every town of any size had its own hospital. If he had been discharged, where was he now, and in what sort of physical condition? Then there was the immense size of the island. Getting around was clearly going to be a problem, even with the use of a car. There were trains, but these tended to follow the developed parts of the coastlines, making the vast interior inaccessible except by road or air. I discovered that some of the aero clubs would arrange short internal flights, which might be a solution. It reminded me of how much I wished I still had use of my own aircraft – so many small problems would be solved if I could fly wherever I wanted, as I was used to doing at home.

But perhaps the greatest task would be finding out how to penetrate the bland bureaucracy that functioned in every walk of life on Prachous. I realized that if Tomak, a casualty of war and an army officer, was receiving hospital treatment on this fiercely neutral island then the records would not be easy to find. Whenever I asked any neighbour or acquaintance for information or advice, I usually received the familiar Prachoit comment that it was better, always much better, not to ask questions and better still to stay put. Officials were unfailingly courteous to me, especially when I told them that Tomak was my wounded lover and I wished to find him and care for him, but at the same time they were routinely, infallibly unhelpful.

As soon as I felt settled in my new apartment I began the search for Tomak. I went first to the hospital in the town where I had chosen to live, a place on the coast called Beathurn, and then went to similar hospitals in other towns close by. I soon discovered that there was little chance of Tomak being in one of these, as they mostly dealt with accident and emergency, maternity, day surgery, and so on. All the major illnesses, injuries and traumas were transferred to one of many specialist campuses, which were situated in a number of different parts of the island.

I located the specialist burns unit at a place called the Nekkel Campus. It was a three-day drive across the island, passing through some of the wildest, most barren terrain I had ever seen. Tomak was not there at the Nekkel, never had been there, and no one on the staff would give me any further information about how I could trace him, I was not of course a blood relation, nor was I married to him. The system was closed against me.

When I had recovered from that trip I tried again, this time to a place called SATU, which I understood had a unit specializing in gunshot and other traumatic wounds. Again, travelling to SATU involved a major and difficult journey of several days, in this case skirting around a huge area of virgin forest. Once again, my search produced nothing except an awareness that Prachoit rules on privacy and confidentiality were almost impenetrable. At its highest my relationship with Tomak, in Prachoit terms, was only as a friend of the family, and this was not enough.

My long drives across the island awakened me to the picturesque and varied scenery of Prachous. Although much of the island is covered by desert, and a large part of the remainder is buried in subtropical forest, there are many areas of natural beauty: open fertile countryside, magnificent ranges of mountains, and a thousand different views of the turbulent seas and the spectacular wave formations. Even though I was on my single-minded quest to find my lover, I stopped the car many times to look at the view.

On nearly all the highways there were allocated parking places to see the best scenery. I particularly liked breaking my journey at the sites high in the coastal range of hills, where broadleaf forests provided some relief and shade from the ferocious daytime temperatures. As I drove along I began to look forward to the next stopping place, as the road climbed through and over the thickly wooded hills, sometimes skirting beaches and bays, at other times ascending by way of dizzying viaducts and corkscrew mountain roads to the heights. From so high above the coastline the scenery was of an ocean constantly in motion, a fabulous ultramarine in colour, but flecked and broken everywhere by the white explosions of surf against the rocky barriers. I never tired of staring. My one regret was that I could not fly over it in my plane, make a flying tour of the entire coastline.

Many other people were using these viewing positions, but the sites were large and well laid out, so there was never any sense of being crowded. It was always possible to walk away from the central area and follow narrow paths or steps to different vantage points. I also discovered that most of these places had a choice of restaurants, and some of them even offered overnight stays. On my outward journeys I travelled fast along the wide main roads, concentrating on my need to find Tomak, but when I was returning without news of him, and with no clear idea of what I might try next, I deliberately dawdled, making the most of the trip.

19

It was the beginning of my slow habituation into the Prachoit way of life. It was an insidious process in which the unobtrusive ease and comfort of everyday life felt like a freeing from all responsibility. It was the way Prachoits lived, and by not resisting it I found it suited me. I settled in Beathurn, and soon was feeling safe and happy for the first time in my life.

My inner compulsion to find Tomak was lessening. I had never thought it would happen, but the daunting practical problems that had to be overcome, and the uncertainty of what I might learn, coupled with the bland congeniality of everyday life, soon had a sedative effect. I left long gaps between each excursion, and as the months went by the gaps grew longer and my resolve became weaker.

This diminishing of my intent began after a chance remark from the woman who happened to live in the next apartment to mine. Her name was Luce. Like most Prachoits, Luce was superficially friendly if we happened to run into each other, but she never made any attempt to make herself known to me. I did not even learn her name until later. If we passed in the hall we always smiled briefly to each other, but nothing more.

One evening, though, I was walking into the building after a long day of driving. I had been enquiring about Tomak at a hospital far away along the southern coast, with the same lack of success as before. I was exhausted after a long day behind the wheel of the car, driving most of the way beneath an unrelenting sun. Luce happened to be entering the building at the same time as me.

My obviously weary state gained a sympathetic comment from her. I told her how I had been driving all day, mentioned the hospital and my hope of finding a friend there. I told her about previous attempts. She seemed interested, concerned. She told me her name, and I told her mine. Once I started talking to her about Tomak I could not stop. I was so alone on this island, with so few people to talk to.

She said, suddenly, 'Have you been to Adjacent? Your friend might be there.'

It meant nothing to me, so she explained. She spoke quickly, softly, with many a glance around, as if to be sure no one could overhear what she was saying. She said, 'People are always trying to enter Prachous illegally, so the authorities have built a large camp where the incomers are sent. It's possible your friend might be there.'

'How would I find it?'

'It's somewhere on the coast, to the north of Beathurn. It's a long way. There's an estuary with what was once a huge area of marsh. It used to be called the reedland, but that's all gone now. They drained it, put up temporary buildings. I've never been there myself, because it's a closed area. Members of the public aren't allowed to enter it, and anyway it's nothing to do with me.'

'So how would I discover if he was there?'

'I don't know.'

'You say the place is called Adjacent?'

'I'm not sure why.' A door on the floor above opened, and footsteps crossed the landing. A moment later a man came quickly down the stairs, passed without acknowledging us, and went out of the main door. 'I've probably said too much,' Luce said, once he was gone. She was speaking more quietly now. 'We're not supposed to know about Adjacent.'

'But they couldn't keep something like that secret.'

'I think they try. I shouldn't even have told you that name. It's officially called something else, but that's a seigniory secret too. Please forget I said anything.'

'Tomak isn't an illegal immigrant,' I said. 'He was involved in the war, he was injured. He was brought here because of the hospitals.'

'Then he won't be there – where I said.'

'In Adjacent?'

'I'm sorry – I'm in a hurry.'

She moved away from me, clearly regretting having said what she had. I rarely saw her again after that, and I began to understand that she was probably avoiding me.

That was in fact the only direct mention I ever heard made of the camp. Because of the possibility that Tomak had been sent there, I naturally tried to investigate, but in a way that I was quickly learning to identify as habitually Prachoit my enquiries were met with vagueness, denials, evasions.

I once even tried to locate the place myself, driving north from Beathurn along the coast. Nowhere called Adjacent, or anything like it, showed on any maps. All I had to go on was Luce's vague description. There was indeed a large area of swampland by a river estuary, roughly where she had described it, but it was either left unmarked on maps or described as undeveloped land. It was impossible to get to it by road, as I discovered when I tried. Barricaded warnings about floods, subsidence, fallen bridges, and so on, blocked the way, and after trying one or two of the roads that looked as if they might lead there. I soon gave up.

For all the time I remained on Prachous, the place called Adjacent was a kind of vacancy on the island – there but not there, a non-place that everyone knew about but that no one had ever been to, and certainly would not discuss with me.

It was an early step on my way to becoming more able to fit in with life on Prachous, although there was a part of my outlook which would never let me surrender entirely to it. My parents were peasants – we lived on a humble farm deep in poor and unyielding countryside, but my father and mother were strict and idealistic, disdaining bourgeois values. Some of that rubbed off on me, but even so I admit the generous life in Beathurn came easily to me. After several months I knew that my search for Tomak was becoming an excuse, a way for me to justify remaining on Prachous long after it was necessary.

One day, walking along the high reinforced harbour wall in Beathurn, enjoying the dazzling sunshine and the cooling sea breeze, relishing the bright colours of the yachts and motor boats, the glistening sea and the endless distant roar of breaking waves, I had one of those moments of self-reappraisal that, in their suddenness, can transform your outlook.

So much time had elapsed since I had last seen Tomak, even longer since we had been able to speak intimately, and even beyond that much longer since we had spent any time alone together. We had been close since we were in our early teens, and were still young when the war tore us apart. I had spoken to him only briefly as the invasion was erupting around us, in a chaos of fire and explosions and collapsing buildings. Tomak had gone to face that war – I had escaped it.

Many months had passed since I landed my aircraft on that grassy Prachoit airstrip, the engine coughing and misfiring as the last drops of fuel were pumped into the carburettor. I had grown, matured, changed, experienced much. It was not that my love for Tomak was immature, but the person I had been then felt distant, remote even from me. The world I knew and had lived in with him no longer existed. Maybe Tomak too would never again exist for me.

20

I moved house and found more friends. A house on a hill became available so I negotiated for it and took it over. I began to fill it with the sort of furniture I liked, put paintings on the wall, stacked the shelves with books and records and started the long task of re-landscaping the overgrown garden. The balance on my numbered loan account grew steadily larger.

I looked for and soon found a job. I had never had a proper job in my life, but for most of the wealthier Prachoits finding work was an option, not a necessity. It was one way of bringing down the tithing debt, but otherwise there was no material advantage. I had found out that the type of loan I was using could be extended indefinitely. If I chose never to pay it back then it would only become payable if I wished to leave Prachous, or it would be seized on my death, when the Seigniory would take whatever assets I had in settlement.

It was fairly easy for me to find a job I could do. I worked for a while as a secretarial assistant, light duties, three days a week, not because that interested me but because I thought it would help familiarize me with some of the ordinary commercial life of Beathurn.

The job hardly ate into my free time, and I continued to make my sightseeing expeditions in my car. I discovered the unique network of cable-cars that had been put up on the tall range of mountains that lay to the north of the town. These high and slightly nerve-racking rides were popular with everyone in Beathurn, because of the sensational and breathtaking views they offered of the town, the coastline and some of the surrounding countryside. I rode on the cable cars most weekends, particularly relishing the cool air close to the summits of these mountains. I also enrolled in a local gymnasium and in my spare time worked out three times a week. A colleague gave me a bicycle which would fold down and fit in the back of my car, so that I could drive out to the less accessible areas of the island and ride across the wild terrain. I joined a local book-readers' group, I took up dancing and I became a patron of our local theatre, *Il-Palazz Dukat Aviator*, the Grand Aviator Palace, which I loved because of its logo, a stylized airman in leather cap and goggles, with a racy propeller-driven aircraft in the background.

As a volunteer patron of the theatre I was one of several who took it in turns to carry out routine tasks behind the scenes. My own duty was to work with the wardrobe department, arranging for the costumes to be collected and cleaned after a performance. There was a contract laundry in the town – all I had to do was drive the costumes across to the laundry, then either wait while the cleaning was carried out, or return to pick them up later.

One afternoon in the warmest season I went to *Il-Palazz* as usual to collect that week's laundry. After I had parked my car at the back of the theatre and was walking around to the side entrance, a tall

345

young man in dark clothes and with a tangle of unruly hair came out through the door into the narrow alleyway. The theatre is a deep building, reaching back a long way from the road. As I had only just entered the alley from the car park we were a distance apart. He did not look in my direction at all, but everything about his appearance sent a thrill of recognition through me. He turned away and walked quickly towards the front of the building, where the main entrance was.

I stood in shock, staring after him, frozen into immobility by seeing him. It was Tomak!

I called his name at once, then hurried after him. He was too far away to have heard me so I called again, much more loudly. My voice cracked with excitement. He turned the corner, walking down the road away from the theatre. It seemed to me that he had heard me because for a moment his head turned in my direction, but almost at once he passed behind a tall hedge. I had glimpsed him face-on! As I walked quickly down the alley I expected him to pause, or look back at me, but he did not.

I ran the remaining distance but as I turned to follow him along the road I saw him opening the passenger door of a car, preparing to climb in. He was speaking to the driver. I called his name again, this time fearful that he was for some reason deliberately ignoring me. Once again he looked back at me, but then he lowered himself into the car and slammed the door. It drove away at once.

In the confusion, the sudden rising of excitement, I hardly knew what to do. I desperately tried to remember what I could of the car, but it was a neutral grey colour, a popular model – there were thousands like it on the streets of Beathurn. There had been a licence plate of course, but I had not thought to look properly. The grey car was already far away – I could see that it had halted at the junction where the road leads down towards the port, but then it moved on, heading away from the shore. I could no longer see it.

I hurried inside the theatre, hoping someone might know who the man was and how I could contact him. There was no matinee performance that day so much of the building's interior was darkened. The tech crew were away from the theatre until the evening show. I found the front-of-house manager but he had not noticed anyone going in or out. Backstage I came across two scenery riggers – they were just returning from lunch and had seen no one they did not recognize. The same was true of Ellse, the wardrobe manager, whom I worked with regularly. She said she knew that Madame Wollsten, the community manager, was interviewing someone, but had no more details. I found the manager straight away but all she would tell me was that a magician from the town had called in to try to obtain a booking from her. Would that have been the man I saw leaving the building? She shrugged her shoulders, losing interest.

I completed my errand with the laundry, dropped off the clean costumes at the theatre and then returned home. My thoughts and emotions were still running wild. That young man had been Tomak! But it couldn't have been Tomak. He looked just like him, but the information I was given before I arrived on this island was that Tomak had suffered burns to his head and shoulders. It was this knowledge that had lent an edge of urgency to my search for him. The man I glimpsed outside the theatre showed no sign of injury.

And if that was the magician Madame Wollsten had told me about, then of course it could not be Tomak. Unless Tomak and he were one, unless Tomak had for some incomprehensible reason become a stage performer, an illusionist – it was too fantastic to consider.

After having been pushed into the background for a long while, Tomak became my obsession again. The thought that he might be living in the same town as me, not only alive but apparently un-harmed, was something I could not ignore. That night I lay awake for hours, wondering what I should do, while an entirely separate part of my mind was arguing that it was a coincidence, that he was someone who only resembled Tomak, who was not him, who could not be him.

The next day I walked into the town, wandering through the most populous parts, scanning the face of every man I saw. I walked slowly through the streets for hours, sweltering in the heat, desperate to see him.

The only thing I knew, but then not with total certainty, was

347

that the man I had seen leaving the theatre was almost certainly the magician. He must be living somewhere in the town.

I started to ask around, trying to find out if anyone I was in contact with knew or had ever heard of any magicians in Beathurn. None had. Later I contacted a conjurers' professional organization in Prachous Town, but the only member they had in Beathurn was now elderly and semi-retired.

I made a habit of walking through the centre of town most days, sometimes even diverting to one of the outer suburbs, always hoping to find him. Several weeks went by with nothing, but then at last I saw him again.

21

Close to the centre of Beathurn there is a pleasant, tree-filled square, set aside for pedestrians and people who want to relax over a quiet meal in the open air: there are several restaurants fronting the pedestrian area, and a couple of café-bars. The square is virtually closed to traffic, which is confined to a narrow road running along one side. This peaceful and attractive place is in front of the main building of the Multitechnic University and is a natural meeting area, not only for the students, who congregate there in their hundreds, but for everyone else too.

While making my regular forays in search of Tomak I almost invariably went through the square, thinking it was one of the more likely places he would be.

And so it turned out. One morning, while walking to work, I passed through the square, not in fact at that moment thinking of Tomak or trying to see him. Then I did: he was sitting alone at a table for two, a newspaper spread out in front of him, a pen in one hand while he solved some kind of puzzle, and a cup of coffee in the other. Next to his hand was a plate with the crumbs left over from something he had eaten.

Of course I came to a halt, staring across at him. He was unaware of me, reaching forward with his pen from time to time to mark a square of letters printed in the newspaper. My first instinct was to approach him, but since I saw him at the theatre a few weeks had passed. I wanted to be careful.

I walked past the café, turned around, walked back. He was ordering something from the waiter, so I stood still until he had finished, thinking he might glance around, notice me. He did not. I waited until the waiter brought him his order, a second cup of coffee, then went to one of the empty tables. When the waiter came across I ordered a coffee for myself.

If the man I thought was Tomak noticed me, he did not act on it. If it was Tomak surely he would recognize me? I sat still at my table, trying not to stare, but being constantly aware of him. Who could he be? If not Tomak he looked identical to the young man I had lost when the war broke out. A magician? It stretched credulity, but all I knew was that this man reminded me in every way of Tomak – apart from the facial resemblance, which was uncannily close, he had the same hair, the same colouring, sat hunched over his newspaper in a way that was completely familiar to me.

He settled his bill, folded his newspaper, which he tossed into a waste receptacle beside the main door of the café, then walked out into the square. He did not pass directly by my table, but he was close, so close.

I was thrown by this encounter to such an extent that as he walked off into the busy square it did not occur to me to follow him. By the time I thought about it he had disappeared into the crowds.

The next morning I went to the same place at the same time, and to my relief he was there again. I took a table on the far side of the café's concourse, from where I could look at him without feeling obvious about it. I ordered a croissant and a cup of black coffee, and while I toyed with them I thought again about the dilemma presented to me by this man. I now understood that the conflict was between heart and head.

If it really was Tomak, the man I had known and loved, why did he not recognize me? Why did he show no trace of the injuries about which I had been given such explicit, shocking and authoritative information? Of course, he might be pretending not to know me, but I could not think of a single reason why he should do that. Or another possibility: the injuries he received might have been different from the ones I had heard about: maybe he had suffered traumatic amnesia, so that much of his past life was forgotten?

On the other hand, my calm head told me that it was not Tomak at all, that it could not be him, that it was an amazing coincidence. A coincidence of his dark and often untidy hair, of his wide eyes, his high cheekbones, his broad shoulders, his easy way of sitting. When the man smiled I saw Tomak smile and I went rigid inside, uplifted by remembered happiness, laid low by a sense of abandonment.

I knew there was only one way to find out. I had to resolve it by speaking to him directly. I signed for what I'd eaten, then stood up and started across the café concourse, my heart thumping with sudden nervousness. As I did so a young woman made her way quickly towards him across the square, waving her hand. She wound her way sinuously through the tables, went directly to him and leaned down to kiss him on both cheeks. Laughing, she sat down on the chair opposite his. He squeezed her hand across the table, smiling.

I halted. I backed away.

I stood by the edge of the café area, staring across. Who was she? She was young – I guessed she was still in her teens. She was barely out of childhood, on the brink of womanhood. A student at the university? She had come across the square from that direction. She was glowing with youth: she had a slim, agile body, long delicate hands, her fair hair was drawn back in a pony-tail. She was wearing tight white jeans and a loose jacket. Sunglasses were propped up on her brow. As she sat with Tomak, she crossed and uncrossed her legs, spoke vivaciously, made him laugh. She rarely looked away from him. He was her first love, the one she would remember just as I was remembering, for the rest of her life, for the rest of mine.

The waiter brought her a soft drink with ice, which she sipped, staring at Tomak across the rim of the glass. He was telling her something, waving his hands expressively. I knew that gesture. I knew all his mannerisms.

She was too old to be his daughter – or he was too young to have a daughter of that age. But could they be lovers? She looked as if she was at least seven or eight years younger than him. They were acting together as if they knew each other well, were close or intimate friends, but once she had sat down opposite him he let go of her hand and seemed to be content just to chat casually with her. They were both smiling a lot and the girl was leaning towards him with her elbows on the table, holding her drink in both hands.

I was incapable of moving away. I stood there at the edge of the square, where the paths crossed the grassy parkland and the tables belonging to the restaurants and cafés spread out across their allotted areas. I knew that I was probably making myself prominent by standing so still, staring so obviously across the café concourse, but I felt paralysed by the discovery of this young friend of his.

Tomak sometimes glanced around expressively while he spoke to her, and once or twice his gaze came in my direction. He must have noticed me there, yet somehow he still did not recognize me.

They left the table, scraping back their chairs, then straightening them before they walked away. He let her go first. They walked past me, as close to me as Tomak had been when he left the café the day before. Once they were in the open he walked beside her, his arms swinging at his side. They did not touch each other.

I let them get a long way ahead of me, then I followed. I maintained the distance, but because they were walking slowly, sauntering, wrapped up in each other's company, I was soon catching up with them. I went more slowly. I dawdled behind them for a long time, certain they must realize they were being followed, but they were preoccupied with each other. I was confused, anguished, but also full of a kind of awkward happiness.

I knew I should turn away, walk home, leave these carefree and infatuated young people to each other, but it was just not possible. My rationale for being here on this island was Tomak, and in some mystifying, unsatisfactory but undeniable way, I had at last found him. Walking away was not a decision I felt I could take.

They walked slowly past the shopping area of the town then entered a narrow street, a place of deep shade created by the tall houses on each side. He led her to the door of an old building, where there had once been a restaurant at street level, with several storeys above. The windows were all bricked up. Tomak unlocked the door and she went in before him. He followed, slammed the door and I heard the lock turn.

I hurried home, collected my car, and when the couple emerged from that secretive-looking building some two hours later I was parked unobtrusively at the far end of the street.

By keeping them at a distance, driving deviously, watching, following, I eventually discovered where Tomak lived.

22

What then followed was a sequence of events which I am not proud of, and was not proud of at the time, but such were my intense feelings about Tomak that I could hardly have acted otherwise. Every spare moment I had I devoted to trying to solve the deeply personal mystery that this man presented. I had to come to some kind of understanding of the turbulent feelings he aroused, and the enigma that surrounded him.

I soon learned his regular movements about the town: there were certain bars or restaurants he favoured, houses or apartments he sometimes visited. He walked everywhere, having no car or other vehicle. Once I saw him being driven again by the friend who owned the small grey car I had seen outside the theatre.

I followed him whenever he went to meet his young companion. He saw her once or twice every week, always in the café in the square by the university, and after a relaxed conversation they would walk to the large old building and lock themselves inside. I had to wait for them to emerge, fighting down my feelings of sadness and jealousy. I envied what appeared to me to be their unworried life together.

In the evenings, when he appeared never to meet her, I regularly went to watch the entrance to his apartment from the darkened streets outside the building.

On one evening of intense humidity, in a wave of hot air flooding across the town from the simmering interior of the island, I took up what I believed was a secure position close to his apartment.

Thunder rumbled out at sea. I was in a shadowed place from which one window was visible, often uncurtained at night. I could also see the main door to the apartment block. I could observe when he left or arrived. The lighted window did not give on to a room – it was a hall or passageway of some kind. I rarely saw him there, except when he moved to and fro between the rooms, but it was enough of a view to prove to me, more or less beyond doubt, that he never took his young girlfriend to the apartment. But I was more obsessively interested in the man who had been Tomak than in the girl.

I was aware of the torpid stillness of the town. The oppressive weather was bearing down on the houses, keeping people inside. The storm seemed to be approaching no closer to the shore. Sometimes I saw lightning flickering far off to the east. Traffic moved in the distance but there were no cars in the streets around me. The normal noises of the city seemed hushed, muted. The birds were still. Leaves rustled above me as the hot, slow wind blew. I heard insects stridulating in the trees and bushes. Wherever my bare arms touched the side of my body, I felt the burning of inescapable heat. The town was waiting for the storm to break, relishing the prospect of a cleansing downpour.

'Who are you, and why the hell are you following me?'

He was there without warning. He must have left the apartment block by another door, approached through the gardens or yards at the back of the buildings. He had emerged from a gated entrance close to where I always stood.

I was shocked into silence. Embarrassed by being caught. Frightened of what he might do. But above all electrically aware of his closeness to me.

'You're stalking me. Why?' His voice was raised, angry.

I stumbled back, away from him, but there was an ornamental shrub behind me, bulging out into the street, above the containing wall. I normally depended on its foliage to conceal me as I waited but now it was blocking my escape.

A light came on, dazzling me. He was holding a battery torch, shining the beam into my face.

'Let me have a look at you!'

I said at last, but feebly, 'Tomak? It is you, isn't it?'

'Has someone sent you? Is it blackmail? Is that what it is?'

At last I was hearing him speak. Although he was angry his voice was the same as I remembered it, but now he was speaking in the Prachoit demotic, the popular language of people who were born on the island. I understood demotic but found it difficult to speak, unless I had time to think ahead about what I wanted to say.

Now I just said, 'Tomak! Please! Don't you remember me?'

'You look harmless enough. Why are you following me? Is it Ruddebet's father? Has he put you up to this? Is he paying you? What are you trying to find out about us?'

'I can't see you with that light in my eyes!' I cried. I was dazzled by the flashlight beam – he was just a dark shape. 'I've been searching for you, Tomak. I heard you had been injured, suffered terrible burns. I came to find you. You must remember what we promised each other.'

'What you're doing is illegal. You probably think I'm not aware of you, but you've been following me all over town. Ruddebet too. What are you up to? She's just an innocent girl. It's a crime – you know that? Stalking is dealt with by populace vengeance. Do you want me to call my neighbours?'

'Please listen to me. My name was Kirstenya when we were together. I've had to change it since I've been living here, but I was Kirstenya. Don't you remember? Kirstenya Rosscky. We were brought up as brother and sister, but when we grew up we fell in love with each other. War was breaking out around us, and I flew back home to find you. I did find you, close to where we lived. You were with a squad of your troops, trying to rescue people trapped in their houses, and dealing with the fires. Shells were landing everywhere. There were awful explosions and aircraft were above us. Dive bombers! Don't you remember those terrifying bombers, Tomak? It was as if the whole city was on fire. I wanted you to escape with me, but you advised me to flee while I could, while I still had an aircraft. You told me there was a plan for the army and air force to regroup. You told me to go there, to a city a long way south of the invasion.'

'What's your name? I'm going to report you.'

'I flew to the other city, but although I waited as long as I could

354

you never arrived. I had to move on, keep moving. I left messages for you everywhere I landed, because I was told I had to escape. I'm a qualified pilot – you knew that. They needed me, the generals in charge. It doesn't matter how, but I got away. Then when I was safe, weeks later, I heard that the enemy had rounded up most of our army officers and they were taken to an isolated place, a forest somewhere, or an uninhabited island, and then massacred. I was terrified you were among them.'

'I'll give you one last chance. If you promise to stop doing this I won't report you to the policier.'

'I just wanted to see you again. Don't you remember me?' I shouted the last words, losing control. 'When we were children, then later as we grew up. The flying! You must remember that? Your father was a flying ace. We went together to races and festivals.'

'Keep away from me. You understand? And if you see Ruddebet's father, tell him to mind his own business too.'

'Don't do anything, Tomak – please! I'm sorry. I meant no harm.'

He still had not touched me, and he kept his distance from me. He switched off the torch at last.

'How do you know my name?' His voice was suddenly much quieter, less hostile.

Now I could see his face, half-lit by a street-lamp somewhere behind me. It was Tomak, it was not him. The physical resemblance was astonishing.

'I'm sorry. I shouldn't have done this. I won't do it ever again.'

I began to retreat from him, pushing around the ornamental shrub, but I was scared of turning my back on him. Thunder cracked suddenly, much louder and more frightening than before. It was like a physical blow. Tomak had become a stranger. He could not be the man I was hoping to find. Yet the dilemma remained, head and heart, heart against head. It *must* be him! Everything about this man was strange, threatening, but the threat came from my own foolish actions, not from him. Tomak was always gentle with me.

I was overcome with a sorrowful guilt, a realization of what I had done, seeing myself as he must be seeing me.

Something lay between us. It was intangible, inexplicable: we seemed to be shouting to each other across a divide. It was as if we were in sight, physically close, adjacent to each other but separated by misunderstandings, different lives, different memories. How could Tomak have forgotten me? That was impossible. Who was this man, if not my lover?

He was making no effort to detain me, so in a rush of rising shame I turned away from him and began to run, hurrying away from him down the dimly lit pathway. I looked back once – he was standing where we had been, a tall figure in the dark. I was so sorry, so overcome with guilt.

I went down the road, took a side turning, ran down that, then another. A terrible flash of sheet lightning, flickering blue-white four or five times, lit the road and the houses around me. I was alone in the night, running and stumbling, frightened of the dark, frightened now of the ferocity of the storm. Thunder again thudded deafeningly above me. I finally came to the main road and from there was able to work my way back through the silent streets to find the place where I had left my car. The rain broke about me as I arrived there, but I wrenched the door open, scrambled inside. My dress was already soaked through, my arms and legs were wetly glistening. I sat in the car for several minutes before I felt able to drive. I was trembling and shivering, and alone in a violent storm. Hard rain fell, swamping visibility and drumming like huge beating hands on the roof of the car. Cascades of floodwater poured down the street outside. I was terrified the car would be washed away. I started the engine, moved the car to the centre of the road where the flood was not pouring so deeply. I felt the welcome relief of the breaking weather after weeks of torrid heat, but my inner life was as suffocated and undecided as ever before. I knew I had lost everything, that my quest had ended. I had made the search for Tomak central to my life but now I had to put that behind me.

Eventually, I put the car in gear and drove slowly back to my house. The roads were littered with fallen leaves and branches, rain continued to fall, the streets were awash. The storm moved on as I drove up the hill to my house, the thunder rumbling away in the distance. I parked the car, then walked through my garden to the house. I felt the blessed relief of the rain-washed air, the temporary cool of the dripping trees and the puddled earth.

23

The next day I changed my car in case Tomak recognized the old one. I began to wear different clothes, I made superficial changes to my appearance: I arranged my hair differently, wore dark glasses, tied scarves around my neck. I felt ridiculous, and constantly in danger of him carrying out his threat to report me, but in spite of what happened during the night of the storm I could not let it go. I knew I was edging down into something more psychologically dangerous than obsessive curiosity, but I was trapped in a dilemma of my own making.

Then something happened that brought closure for me. It was perhaps a timely intervention, saving me from myself.

I was in my new car, watching the old restaurant building Tomak and his young girlfriend went to whenever they met. A few minutes earlier I had noticed them meeting in the café in the square, so I guessed where they would be next, and not long afterwards I saw them entering the tall building. Once they were inside I left the car where it was and went to a small café a couple of streets away, where I bought a cold drink. I knew that they always stayed inside the building for at least two hours, so I had time to kill. I sat at a table under the canvas canopy and browsed the daily newspaper. After an hour I strolled back to the old restaurant building, intending to stand at the intersection where the traffic turned, and where there was a clear if distant view of the door to the building. I took up position beneath a tree and opened a book to read.

I became aware that someone was approaching me in a deliberate way, crossing against the traffic, waiting for cars to pass then stepping forward quickly. I kept my eyes on my book. My heart leaping, I assumed it must be Tomak, but when I looked up I saw it was an older man, dressed in casual shirt and shorts, striding towards me. His manner was anything but casual. He raised a hand towards me, pointing a forefinger at me.

'Are you waiting for my daughter?' he said. His manner was forthright, but unthreatening.

I shook my head, uncertain what to say. 'No – a friend.'

'That magician, the illusionist. I've seen you before, hanging around him. You keep following him.'

I felt it was none of this stranger's business, so again I simply shook my head. He was close beside me. He took my arm in a gentle hold.

'I don't know your name,' he said. 'But you and I have interests in common. We need to speak. Shall we go somewhere that we don't have to shout over the traffic?'

There was a park beside the intersection, so I allowed him to lead me, not discourteously, through the wrought-iron gate to the area of mown grass and flowerbeds beyond. We walked to the shade of a grove of trees planted on a shallow slope. A brook ran down through the trees towards the edge of the park.

I made sure that where we stopped was a place from which I could still see the door to the building. We were now much further away, but it was in sight.

'You should know who I am,' the man said. 'My name is Gerred Huun. The young woman who is currently inside that building is my child, my only daughter. Her name is Ruddebet.'

In the Prachoit custom he removed a plastic ID card from his pocket and let me see it. I responded with my own.

'I am Mellanya Ross,' I said.

'I'm concerned about the effect your friend might be having on my daughter. I need your help.'

'I know nothing at all about your daughter,' I said, mentally thrusting away from my mind the hours I had spent obsessively imagining and worrying about what her relationship with Tomak must be.

'If you've seen her with your friend, you know that she is barely more than a child. In fact she is just eighteen years old and in a couple of months she will be starting university. She's an intelligent, talented girl. She has been accepted for a degree course that is academically demanding and yet will allow her to develop her love of sport. I was once a sportsman myself, as was my wife. My wife, unfortunately, died three years ago. Ruddebet is now the only family I have, and I am concerned that she should not be led astray. This man, this idle magician, is several years older than her, and I don't know what he's up to.'

'I don't see how I can help,' I said, but a sympathetic understanding was starting to grow in me. Interests in common, indeed.

'You could tell me what you know of your friend. He moved into the town only recently, and has kept himself to himself.'

'It's complicated. I thought he was a friend, but I was wrong. I thought he was someone else, someone I knew in the past. I made a terrible mistake. It's not the same man. I'm not even sure what his name is.'

'I can tell you that. He calls himself a thaumaturge, and his name is Tom, or perhaps Thom.' He pronounced it with a soft 'th', but then corrected it.

'Would that be short for Tomak?' I said.

'No, I've never heard a name like that. It's Tom or Thom. But he doesn't even use a second name. Few people seem to know anything about him. Who is he? Where has he come from?'

'Those are questions I can't answer.'

'It was my own fault,' Gerred Huun said. 'I was the one who suggested to Ruddebet that she might be suitable to apply for this job.'

'Job?' I said.

'As his assistant on stage, when he performs his magic. She has to wait a few weeks before starting her course, and I thought she might find it interesting and make a little credit. I had no idea she would become emotionally involved with him.'

'Are you sure that's what has happened?' I said, surprising myself with the quickness of the thought, but I was remembering what I had seen of them when they were together. They were affectionate to each other, but it was the affection of friendship, not of lovers. This was what had puzzled me, because they went to a place where it was obvious they would be alone together. That implied something much more physical was taking place. But their behaviour outside was not at all suggestive of that. 'Do you know what the job involves?'

'I was shown the apparatus once. He had it set up in that building in the street across there.'

'So they're using it as a rehearsal room?'

'That's what Ruddebet calls it.'

'They are rehearsing while they're there? Why do you think that means they have become lovers? That's what you fear, isn't it?'

'It's just the way she acts now. She's become secretive, she is angry with me if I ask too many questions. I'm losing her, I can't do or say anything right any more. We used to be so close all the time, but now it's becoming difficult.'

'If she's eighteen,' I said, 'then she is an adult, no matter what she is doing.'

'Yes, but she's my daughter and she is still living with me.'

I sat silently for a while, thinking how I too had misunderstood what was going on. In my single-minded need to find Tomak I had been making a lot of assumptions. It had not occurred to me they might be working together. I liked Gerred Huun – he seemed a decent man, over-protective of his daughter, but perhaps it was only that his concern for her was greater than it needed to be. Our brief conversation had already made me see the young woman differently, and now I began to imagine how Ruddebet herself might feel. We sat down on the grass together and spoke for a long time. Gradually, we became more relaxed in each other's company, speaking frankly. I tried to describe from a woman's point of view what his daughter might well be seeing in this slightly older man. As I spoke I realized that I was no longer thinking of him as Tomak, that I had somehow accepted it was someone different, Thom or Tom, Thom the Thaumaturge. My head was at last resolving the dilemma of the heart. I pointed out that when Ruddebet started at the university their relationship, whatever it was now, would certainly come to a natural end and that in the meantime no harm was being done.

'You understand, Ruddebet and I find it difficult to speak openly to each other.'

'She's growing up,' I said. 'A lot of fathers find it difficult to adjust as their daughter becomes an adult woman. Things have to change.'

'He said he will make her disappear in some way.'

'Does that bother you? He's not going to run away with her.'

'I don't think so. But yes, I'm not sure why, but it does make me nervous I might lose her.'

'But he's an illusionist, isn't he? Nothing he does is real. That's the way magicians work.'

'Yes, I suppose.'

I was still keeping a watch on the door, far away beyond the perimeter of the park, but it remained closed. I was looking covertly, but while I sat there with Gerred Huun I was thinking that already it was more from habit than from any real need to keep watch. I was defending Ruddebet, accounting for the relationship with the magician, almost accepting as fact what in reality I had never been able to understand. Perhaps until now. I had been alone too long, my quest to find Tomak was too one-sided. I had never confided in anyone before, but now, when the chance arose, I found that the role had unexpectedly reversed and Ruddebet's father was confiding in me about his own fears. It strengthened me, gave me a distance from myself.

'Maybe they are merely rehearsing, as you've been told,' I said. 'You said he showed you the apparatus once.'

'Yes. But you've seen them together. You know how they behave. He is obviously infatuated with her.'

'And she with him. That wouldn't change the fact that they are working together. Is he paying her what he promised, when it began?'

'Ruddebet told me he was.'

'Magicians normally rehearse in secret, don't they?'

Later we parted, suddenly rather awkward with each other, as if we had opened up too much, in a non-Prachoit way. We had both exposed something of our inner fears, Gerred Huun more than I, but our meeting was a revelation to us both. I saw Tomak, or Thom, differently, understood Ruddebet more, even realized that my own behaviour had been extreme and unwarranted. I was ashamed of myself. I said none of this to Gerred, as I now knew him, but perhaps he had noticed a change in me, even during the time we were sitting on that shady hill looking down at the door, locked against us.

For me it was closure, a freeing from my own compulsive behaviour. I returned to my car, drove straight home.

That evening I made enquiries of the airfield where my plane was impounded, trying to find out what I was required to do for the aircraft to be released, how long it would be before I could fly again.

24

A few days later Gerred Huun mailed me a ticket for a show at *Il-Palazz*. Thom the Thaumaturge had succeeded in obtaining a booking. A programme of magic was announced, to commence the following weekend.

Such was the transformation in my feelings that when I opened the envelope and saw what was inside I wondered briefly if I should bother to visit the show at all. Gerred enclosed a publicity handbill describing in vague but enthusiastic terms the marvels that were about to be performed.

Gerred had also written a note to me: *I shall be going to every performance during the week, but I thought you would like a ticket to the final show.*

I was to spend much of the week of the performances trying to establish the condition of my impounded aircraft, in particular finding out if it was still airworthy, or at least might be considered so. It had performed perfectly on the flight out, but for most of a year it had been lying unused. By now it would require a thorough technical check-up. It was still under official seal, meaning I was not allowed to go to the hangar where it was being kept.

A new difficulty had arisen without my knowledge, while I was obsessing over the man I thought was Tomak. Because of what was perceived to be my lack of interest in the plane, some bureaucrat in the Seigniory had ruled that because it appeared to be a warplane, albeit of an unidentifiable type, it was in breach of the island's neutrality and must therefore be seized. In practical terms, it meant that the plane was still in the same hangar, but was now buried under one more layer of obstructive officialdom. I had to prove that the aircraft was properly mine. Once I had done so I would then have to attend a formal neutrality hearing in court to explain what I was doing bringing a warplane into Prachoit airspace.

The only documents I had with me were my original written orders for the flight – after much argument these proved to be sufficient to establish the fact the plane was properly mine, but the neutrality hearing still hung over me.

However, matters started to improve in small ways. Unexpectedly, the people at the airfield forwarded to me a letter from another seigniorial department confirming that the plane had been inspected and was judged to be airworthy. That seemed positive at first, but when I looked more closely I saw that the letter was dated not long after I arrived on the island. I knew I should need a more up-to-date airworthiness certificate before I would be allowed to take off. The letter gave me the contact details for a second official inspection, so I set that in train immediately. The plane was almost new, and apart from early proving flights at the factory the only flight undertaken by the aircraft was my own long one to Prachous. I had made sure after I landed that the lubricants, cooling and hydraulic fluids were all drained, so these would have to be replaced, and the engine and the control surfaces would need to be inspected.

In preparation, I requested that the engine should be serviced and tested, and that the main fuel tanks as well as the auxiliaries should be filled with 100-octane aviation spirit.

I was concerned that the aircraft had been declared a warplane. Although basically a fighter design, the plane was essentially a long-range high-altitude reconnaissance aircraft so it had no armaments. There was, though, a valuable camera positioned in its belly. The camera was of no use to me but I did not want to be responsible for it if someone removed it. I had to assume that in the absence of any guns it was the powerful camera that made the officials realize it was a warplane.

I had let several months drift by without paying too much

attention to the problem of my plane, but all that was changing quickly. I suddenly wanted to leave Prachous as soon as possible. I had convinced myself that the man I saw with Ruddebet was not Tomak. The island held nothing more for me and it was time to leave. I had lived the unnervingly calm and comfortable Prachoit life long enough. I had no idea if the war that drove me and Tomak apart was even still going on, but I wanted to return home.

While I made the practical preparations to take possession of my plane once again, I also started to look for someone who could move into my house, perhaps take over my car, keep the garden. I also had to dispose of the personal possessions I would not be able to take with me. Gradually, I was reducing my involvement in Prachoit life.

There was still the evening at the theatre, a performance of stage magic by the man who looked so uncannily like Tomak. I was curious about this, more so as the week went by. I was hearing that the show was excellent, the illusionist performing inexplicable marvels with great skill. It's possible that if Gerred Huun had not sent me the ticket I might have left Beathurn without going to the theatre, but that was not how things turned out. I thought it would be one last chance to watch the man whose existence had taunted me for so long, and who had driven me to the brink of a kind of madness. I decided not to make my flight home until after the performance.

25

The theatre was full for the show – live magic was a novelty in Beathurn. Because I worked for this theatre I had grown to love it, so I was thrilled to see the number of people thronging the foyer, the bar, the staircases, the corridors. I knew that the ticket sales had enabled the management committee to order replacements for some of the outdated technical equipment still in use, and that the manager was talking about redecorating the auditorium during the months of the quiet season. A pit orchestra had been hired for this show. The auditorium was alive with the audience's excitement and anticipation when I went in. The band was already tuning up.

After I was seated, Gerred Huun hurried in and took the place next to mine. We greeted each other in a friendly way.

'I'm pleased you could be here for this, Mellanya,' he said.

'Thank you for sending me the ticket.'

'I think you'll enjoy the show. I have no doubt seen it too many times this week, but I still enjoy what Ruddebet and the magician are doing. I can't imagine how he manages those tricks. Every night his act is slightly different, but each time I'm left amazed by it.'

Not long after that the orchestra started the overture, the curtains opened and the stage filled with dancers and singers. I settled down to watch. After the dance routine a comedian opened the show, introducing each of the acts in turn. His jokes were unfunny and loud, and he went on far too long. At one point he tunelessly sang a song. Next to me, Gerred was enjoying himself, laughing noisily at every joke. When a group of singers came on later, he hummed along with the tunes – when an acrobat juggled plates and knives, Gerred cheered with enthusiasm.

Around us, the rest of the audience appeared to be enjoying the acts every bit as much as Gerred, to judge by the laughter and clapping. I sank low in my seat, waiting for the magician.

He was billed to appear twice: a short act to close the first half of the show, then the finale. The other acts in the first half felt as they were going to run forever. Even though most of the turns were noisy with music or singing or acts of physical exertion, and made attempts to provide a spectacle, I felt uninvolved and started to drift mentally, thinking about how much I wanted to depart from this island, return to my own life.

I was worrying about the flight I intended to take as soon as I could: would the plane still be safe to fly? How would I navigate? How could I obtain an accurate weather forecast before I departed? And what about this neutrality hearing in court? I did not like the sound of that, knowing what the Prachoit authorities could be like about real or imagined breaches of their neutrality. Assuming I could take off without too much trouble or interference, and could make the flight safely, what conditions might I return to if the war was still going on? It frightened me to think like that, but it was now obvious that I could not stay on Prachous much longer. I bitterly regretted the time I had spent, and wasted, searching for Tomak. I also regretted what it had done to me, the way I acted. I felt I had betrayed myself, even that I had betrayed the trusting and loving relationship I once had with Tomak. I realized now that my quest was largely caused by denial: when I heard the news about the army officers and the massacre, I had simply not allowed myself to believe that Tomak was probably among them.

Time to put an end to all this.

Musing, I missed the announcement of Thom the Thaumaturge's act. He was on the stage almost before I realized it was him. He was heavily made up and was wearing a voluminous costume, brightly coloured and made of shiny material. A bandanna was wound around his head, partly covering one side of his face.

I watched with fascination as he swiftly performed a few card tricks, then brought on a wheeled cabinet with curtained sides. It was possible to see beneath it, and when Thom walked around to the back of the cabinet his body was visible to the audience between the narrow legs of the apparatus. Indeed, he then opened the curtains at the rear, span the cabinet around so that we could see inside, and opened the curtain which was now at the back, revealing the whole of the interior. He leapt up into the cabinet, crawled through, and stood beside it. With swift movements he then spun the cabinet around again, snatching the curtains closed once more as they went past. The whole cabinet was still rotating as the curtains billowed out from inside and Ruddebet appeared.

She leapt down on to the stage. She was dressed in a costume of glittering sequins, which flashed and shone in the spotlight. She bowed deeply, and ran into the wings while the applause still rang out. Beside me, Gerred was on his feet, clapping his hands above his head.

Thom next performed a few acrobatic tricks while cleverly riding a unicycle. Then Ruddebet returned. This time she was wearing a different costume: a voluminous dress, with flounces and wide sleeves. Thom dragged a large wicker basket to the centre of the stage, and helped Ruddebet insinuate herself inside it. The dress made this difficult, as it billowed up around her, seeming to fill the entire space, but in the end she was contained inside and Thom placed a lid on top. He plunged several long and apparently razor-sharp scimitars into the basket through small apertures at the front and back, and at each side, culminating with a long broadsword, thrust down through the lid. He turned the basket around so that we could see how the blades ran through every part of it. Swiftly he removed each of the swords, throwing them aside with thrilling clattering noises. We were in no doubt of the sturdy manufacture of the blades. As the last one came out, Ruddebet pushed up the lid from inside, and gracefully stepped out on to the stage. Not only was she completely unharmed but she was wearing a totally different dress.

Gerred was on his feet again as she took her bow, and this time many other members of the audience stood up too.

The curtain came down, and now it was the interval.

As soon as I could I left the auditorium. The antiquated cooling system could barely cope with the presence of so many people on a warm evening, and it was a relief to move out to the small balcony at the rear of the building. This overlooked the car park and afforded a glimpse of the sea. Lights were sparkling on the dark ocean. In the town, towards the port, I could see many people out and about, the nightly promenadá, the leisurely stroll through the wide and brightly illuminated boulevards where the restaurants and night clubs were situated. It was another hot night but the sea breeze made it more bearable than staying inside.

I was trying not to see Gerred during the break but he followed me out. He pushed past the people on the balcony behind me and handed me a glass of cold beer. I was in fact grateful for it and I drank it in two deep draughts. We stood side by side, looking down at the closely parked vehicles below. Gerred was trying to tell me about the variations Thom and Ruddebet had worked on the basket trick during the week: a different dress, flaming torches instead of swords, and so on, and also how horrified he was at first to see his daughter apparently placed in such peril, but how proud of her he had become when he saw the professionalism of the act.

I tried to filter him out, because I was thinking, almost wistfully, that this place would soon be in my past, it would represent a finite period, a transition from one way of life to the next. I wanted it to end now – I was restless to be away. I stared around at the night-dark town, now so familiar to me, the air heady with the fragrance of night-scented flowers. I was thinking that one day I would miss this place. I listened to the constant sound of the traffic, music coming out of an open door somewhere close by, and behind everything the constant rasping of the insects.

A bell rang inside the building, requesting the audience to return to their seats. Gerred placed his glass of beer on the parapet of the balcony. He had drunk less than half of it.

'Doesn't Ruddebet look beautiful on stage?' he said as we turned to walk back inside, moving along slowly with the other people.

'She's a lovely girl,' I said.

'It feels strange to me that Ruddebet should be somewhere inside this building at the moment. I can't see her, speak to her – she's a star. This morning we sat side by side in the kitchen, eating breakfast together.'

'Has she said anything to you about the show?'

'Not very much. But since you and I spoke – it's been easier. I don't ask her about it, and although she still doesn't say much we're a lot friendlier now than we were. Almost like the old days. I'm really grateful to you, Mellanya.'

'And I'm grateful to you too,' I said. 'For different reasons.'

He would never know what they were. We followed the crowd down into the warm interior of the building and took our seats again. We were close to the front of the auditorium, only a few rows away from the stage. I fanned myself with the programme booklet. Gerred was close beside me, his arm resting against mine, soft and warm. I tried unobtrusively to ease away, but the seats were narrow and I too was pressing against the person next to me on the other side.

The second half of the show began with a loud roll of drums and a brassy fanfare. The dancers returned and then the comedian. I was interested only in seeing the magical act and I began to feel impatient. All around me other people were fanning themselves in the airless heat. There was a monologist, some piano duettists. A close-harmony quartet came on, performing in front of the curtain.

368

Behind it I could sense movement as the next act was made ready.

The comedian returned, and thankfully without attempting jokes announced the second appearance that night of the act we had all come to see: Thom the Thaumaturge!

As the curtains opened there was a loud bang and a flash, and a cloud of orange-coloured smoke mushroomed above the stage. Thom emerged from the smoke, waving his arms and hands in a mystical way. He launched straight into a series of tricks, producing flames, handkerchiefs, candles, billiard balls and bouquets of paper flowers, all seemingly from nowhere. One trick made the audience roar with laughter: a lighted cigarette appeared from inside his mouth, the smoke bursting out around his head. He worked swiftly and expertly, soon filling the top of his table with all the colourful materials he had produced. He performed in silence, occasionally fixing the audience with a non-committal stare. He always smiled at the completion of the trick, as if communicating to the audience his own delight at what he was doing. We clapped enthusiastically.

He was costumed as we had seen him before: he presented a dazzle of bright colours with glints of reflected light from his shining, bejewelled clothes. Although his face was made up with heavy streaks of coloured greasepaint, it was easy for me to see beneath. He looked so like Tomak! I did not dwell on the thought.

We were not kept waiting long for the climax of his show. Two stagehands appeared and moved the table of effects offstage, then at Thom's bidding a half-curtain upstage was raised, to reveal the wicker basket we had seen earlier.

The stagehands scraped the heavy basket forward, placing it centre-stage, exactly at the point Thom indicated. The men left the stage.

Now alone, Thom strode to and fro by the footlights, eerily lit from below, the chiaroscuro of coloured lights making his appearance mysterious and sometimes sinister as he prowled across the stage. He made a speech describing what he was about to do – he gave away no details but emphasized the years of concentration and meditation required of him as preparation for what we were about to witness, the dangers inherent in the presentation, the uniqueness of the illusion. He asked the audience to remain silent throughout the performance, so great was the need for exact movements and physical balance.

In the orchestra pit the drummer began a quiet, continuous roll. You could sense the tension spreading through the audience, the anticipation, the curiosity about what was going to happen.

Thom reached down through the top opening of the basket and pulled forth a strong-looking rope. It was obviously heavy, but by looping it around his forearm Thom showed that it was just a normal rope. When he had pulled most of it from the basket he held it in both hands, then with an expansive gesture of his arms he threw it upwards with great strength.

He backed quickly away, protecting his head and neck as the heavy rope snaked down.

As he collected it up again he made a self-effacing remark to the audience, about how tricks sometimes don't work the first time. There was a nervous laugh in response to this, almost an expression of relief, but Thom raised a warning palm, reminding us of his need for silence and concentration.

He made a second effort to throw it upwards – again it fell.

On this third try the rope briefly took on a rigid, vertical appearance, wavered for a moment but collapsed once more to the stage.

At a signal from Thom to the orchestra pit the drum roll grew more urgent, louder, then subsided again. He made a fourth attempt and this time the rope, by some magical means, remained vertical. It swayed slightly but stiffly in the lights shining down on it from above.

Thom moved swiftly about the stage, gesturing towards the mysteriously rigid rope, bowing towards the audience, beaming as we all applauded the astonishing sight.

As our applause died away Thom returned to the basket, and again reached down through the opening at the top. Ruddebet rose up from inside, her slim body unfolding sinuously as she stood upright. Thom helped her step out of the basket. As he held her hand they went towards the footlights and took another bow.

The drum roll took on a more urgent note.

I was able to see Ruddebet closely and clearly for the first time ever, and I was stunned by the unexpected flow of intense emotion

370

her appearance induced in me. I could not help the feeling – I saw her as the young rival who had snatched my lover away from me. It went against everything I had thought through in recent days, but I could not help that. She seemed to me to embody all that I thought I was not. She was so graceful, lithe, beautiful, filled with life's bounty, smiling and enjoying the blaze of lights and the rising sound of the music. The drum was now accompanied by a throbbing double bass note, a heartbeat. Ruddebet ran lightly around the stage, one hand constantly reaching towards Thom, a happy smile on her face. I envied her but I also admired her and wanted to know her, perhaps grow to like her, discover whatever there might be that we had in common. I could not stop watching her.

The illusion moved into its next stage. Thom took hold of the stiffly vertical rope, leaning forward, using both hands to try it, gripping it low down close to the neck of the basket, the other hand reaching higher. He flexed the rope, testing its solidity. The top of the rope rotated in a tight circle.

Ruddebet tossed some white powder on the palms of her hands, clapped them together, then blew away the surplus in a cloud that drifted into one of the beams from the spotlights.

With a confident, athletic motion she strode across the stage, leaned down so that she could pass Thom's hands where they gripped the rope, then seized it with both of her own. Gracefully, she took her weight on her arms and raised herself.

Within seconds she was halfway up the rope, already above Thom, holding it with both hands. One knee was crooked tightly around it, with the other leg swinging up to raise her to the next position.

Thom released his hold and moved back from the rope. Now Ruddebet was unsupported. I knew that Gerred was tensing beside me, his knuckles protruding whitely. I laid my free hand on his, felt the slick of perspiration on us both, the uncomfortable warmth of our skin.

Maintaining her poise, Ruddebet raised herself in small stages, allowing her body to twist around the rope, but managing by turning her head swiftly to keep her attractive smile flashing towards the audience.

Thom stood beneath her, almost directly below, next to the basket, both his arms raised and his fingers extended, as if exerting some kind of magical influence on her. In fact it was obvious that the young woman was a natural athlete, agile and strong, entirely without any need of sorcery to help her climb.

The music was growing steadily louder – now there was a sharp, eerie note playing from the synthesizer. The colour of the stage lights changed suddenly – while Ruddebet was still picked out by a brilliant white spotlight the rest of the stage was illumined with a green glow.

Thom moved away from her, turned towards the audience and for a moment had his back towards Ruddebet. It was in that instant that the disaster happened – something went wrong with the stability of the rope. It buckled and collapsed beneath her, snaking down. Ruddebet crashed to the floor of the stage, landing hard on her head or shoulder, her body twisting around. She made a horrible involuntary shout or cry, loud over the music, and lay still.

The music died away. The drum roll ceased.

You could hear the shock searing through the audience – first a sudden mass intake of breath, then groans and shouted words you could not pick out. I stood up, as did many other people, and pushed in haste past the two or three people between me and the aisle.

I saw Thom rushing across to Ruddebet's unmoving body, bending over her, reaching down with his arms.

I yelled, 'Don't try to move her! Leave her!' Thom did not appear to hear me, so I shouted again, 'I know what to do! Don't touch her!'

Other people from the audience were already moving towards the stage, but I was suddenly steeled with unshakable determination. I elbowed people aside, headed for the side of the orchestra pit, where a short flight of steps gave access to the stage. Two men rushed on to the stage from the wings. I clambered up, shouted at them not to touch her. I reached the stage, stumbled on the last step, and in a clumsy staggering motion I reached Ruddebet's prone body.

Thom was holding one of her hands.

'Stand back!' I shouted. 'Let me do this! I'm a nurse.'

I shoved myself in front of him, trying to block him. I bent over Ruddebet's body – she was still breathing. I called her name and her eyelids fluttered. She clamped them tightly closed again. People were already pushing around me. Again I yelled at them to give me space. Ruddebet's head was slightly tipped to one side, but it did not seem as if her neck was broken. I could see no blood, no obvious injuries.

'Please call an ambulance now!' I said to the people clustered around.

'I called one already,' someone said. 'It's on its way.'

Then a voice said, 'I'm a doctor! Make way, please!'

I glanced up – it was a tall woman, strongly built, with a prominent jaw and a high forehead. She was wearing an all-white garment.

'Move back, please!' she said to me.

'I'm a nurse,' I said.

'Good. Let me see her.'

The woman doctor knelt down alongside me and ran her hands lightly over Ruddebet's head, neck and shoulders. Then she carefully tested her arms and legs. Ruddebet gasped with pain, saliva spilling from her open mouth.

'Everyone else, please move off the stage!' the doctor said. She continued her examination with deft and careful movements of her hands.

'I believe she has fractured her hip, but there is no sign of concussion.' The doctor was speaking softly to me. 'She has a dislocated shoulder, and perhaps a broken arm. Her ribs might have been damaged. I don't think there is any internal bleeding. Do you agree?'

'Yes,' I said, although my own examination of Ruddebet had been much more superficial.

'Bring a blanket,' she said to one of the stagehands. 'No one must touch her. Is there any morphine in the building?' she said to me.

'In the first-aid cabinet. It's locked, but I have the key.'

I stood up, turned towards the wings. Gerred had pushed his

way through the crowd of people, and was heading for Ruddebet.

'Please stay away,' the doctor shouted. 'Move back!'

'This is my daughter,' Gerred said.

I said, 'It's true. I know the family.'

'All right,' she said to him. 'Your daughter has been badly hurt but I don't think her life is at risk.'

I was already on my way to find the first-aid kit. The key to the locked cupboard was still on my own ring, and somehow I had taken it out without realizing I was doing so. I rushed into the darkness of the backstage area, found the cabinet, took out the sealed carton with the emergency morphine.

Thom was standing by the side of the stage as I hurried back. He had thrown off much of his stage costume, but his face was still covered in the garish stage make-up. He looked desperately at me, but I brushed past him.

I gave Ruddebet a shot of the morphine and she cried out with agony. It was terrible to hear, but soon she was breathing steadily again. The paramedics arrived then. I stood back to let them get on with their job. Under the watchful eye of the doctor Ruddebet was placed on a wheeled stretcher and taken away. Gerred went with them, his hand resting lightly on the side of the stretcher. He did not look back at me. Ruddebet was sleeping.

26

The doctor asked me to wait on the stage, close to where Ruddebet had fallen, then went away to telephone ahead to the casualty department at the hospital to inform them of her diagnosis. Thom had disappeared. The theatre staff had ushered everyone away, and now the auditorium was empty. All the stage lights were extinguished, replaced by the house lights high in the ceiling. The cooling fans whined somewhere above or behind me. I was alone on the dimly lit stage, looking down at Thom's wicker basket, the fallen rope. I could not help feeling responsible for what had happened, as if my obsession over Tomak and his relationship with

Ruddebet had somehow led up to the accident. Of course I knew that Ruddebet had already taken the job with Thom before I was aware of her, that this show, this illusion, this accident, all would have taken place whether I was there or not. But I still felt complicit.

The doctor returned and I could see her face was shining with perspiration. Her simple white garment was damp, adhering to her body under her arms, across her chest. She gave me a questioning look as she approached, apparently trying to read how I was feeling.

'Are you all right?' she said, with surprising warmth.

'Yes,' I said. 'I'm glad her injuries aren't dangerous. It always makes it harder if you know the patient.'

'You reacted remarkably quickly.'

'The training kicks in when it's needed. I'm relieved you were here too.'

'I was at the back of the audience, so it took me longer to come forward.'

'Do you think she will be all right?'

'She's in a great deal of pain. Her hip will take a long time to heal, but I don't think there will be any long-term damage. She landed badly, that's all.'

'Has anyone told you she's an athletics student?'

The woman looked pained. 'No. That could turn out to be a problem for her. But – she's young, she's strong. If she gets the right treatment, and therapy afterwards, she should make a full recovery.'

She took my hand, trying to reassure me. We stood there together, the aftermath of an emergency. I was still upset, not especially because of Ruddebet's accident, but because I continued to feel irrationally responsible for what had happened. I found the doctor's presence comforting but also intimidating – she was an imposing woman, and in spite of the softness of her tone she rarely smiled. I exhaled suddenly, and was not able to prevent myself from making a sobbing noise.

Then she said, 'I think as a precaution you and I should exchange names and contact details. Someone might take it upon themselves to seek justice for what happened to the girl. We could become involved.'

'But it was obviously an accident. Who would take revenge?'

'You said the man who came forward was her father. He might.'

'Not Gerred! He's not like that.'

'No one ever is, until they find out how the law works. The rules about accidents at work are complex. The father might not want revenge, might not even consider looking for it, but there are firms which offer a proxy service. They can start an action, then have the other parties joined later.'

'I want nothing to do with that,' I said.

'Neither do I. But we don't have much choice if someone starts an action. What is your name, and where do you live?'

'Mellanya Ross,' I said. 'I live here in the town, but I'm planning to leave in the next few days—'

'My name is Mallin, Firentsa Mallin. I live in a village just outside Beathurn.'

'Doctor Mallin?'

'I never call myself doctor. Since I moved to Prachous I have stopped practising medicine and become an adherent. I'm not from Prachous and I wouldn't be allowed a practitioner's certificate without re-training. I work as a missionary now.' She glanced around at the remains of Thom's illusion. 'If they found out, I would probably get into hot water with the medical council for doing what I just did. What about you? I sense you are not a Prachoit either.'

'That's right.'

She regarded me with her deep-set eyes, still clutching my hand.

She said, 'If we meet again you should call me by my first name only. I'm Firentsa. I hope nothing more comes of this incident, but on this island you never know what might happen.'

I wanted to explain that I was planning as soon as possible to leave Prachous forever, but I became unsure. I did not know how some act of revenge might be carried out. Against Thom the Thaumaturge? Could I be forced into becoming a part of that? How might I, or this woman, be involved? As witnesses to an accident, or as responsible parties because we performed first aid on the young woman?

I was wondering what to say, when suddenly Firentsa Mallin turned directly towards me and we embraced. I felt her strong arms wrapping protectively around my shoulders. The sides of our faces briefly pressed against each other. I could feel her jaw working with emotion. We stepped back from each other and for a moment I glimpsed a trace of tears filling her eyes. She turned away without another word, then walked down the steps from the stage and exited the auditorium through one of the curtained audience doors. I stood alone.

The trick rope that had caused the accident was still lying in curves and loops across the floor of the stage – part of it ran between my feet. The hidden end still lay inside the wicker basket. There was no sign of Thom. The quiet noise of the ineffectual cooling fans, venting above me, cut out.

27

I closed up my house for the last time and drove to the airfield. The journey took about four hours, which meant that even if the problems of officialdom were to disappear it would be too late to start my flight. I needed all the daylight hours possible.

The airfield where I had first arrived was in an area of hilly pastures, not forested but well covered with mature trees. It was in the south-eastern quarter of the island. I had found it by chance as I flew across Prachous in the gathering twilight, running low on fuel and desperate to find anywhere at all that I could put down the wheels.

Following my arrival, learning about the everyday life of Prachous, and especially my search for Tomak, had absorbed me. The adventure of the long flight soon dimmed. There had been so many other flights in my life before that one, unique though it was. As my intention to leave the island became certain, I returned several times to the airfield, trying to work my way out of the maze of difficulties I had made for myself. The staff there now knew me. They were fully aware that once the aircraft was released from the bond I would want to fly in it.

The height of the hills above sea level gave the area a pleasantly temperate climate. I relished my visits, because they provided an escape from the humidity of the town. I enjoyed watching the local people flying their light planes in and out of the airfield, envying them a little, but also knowing that locked away in the bonded hangar I had one of the most beautiful and powerful aircraft ever built. I ached to fly it again.

During my visits I would lie in the long grass at the perimeter of the field, soaking up the familiar sounds and smells as the aero engines revved up for take-off. I longed to feel the vibration of the aircraft engines and the pressure of the slipstream pouring back violently from the propellers. Safety regulations meant I could not approach too close. On one visit I was invited into the flimsily built control tower, actually erected on top of the hangar where my plane was being kept, and listened with painful familiarity to the curt, polite conversations with the pilots, about wind bearing, altitude and approach paths.

When I arrived at the airfield the news was good: the tithing agency had been looking into my finances. My loan account had established a credit rating equivalent to twelve per cent of the estimated value of my aircraft. I had no idea how any of this was worked out, but the commodore of the air club sat down with me and explained the calculation. I was none the wiser, but it did mean that as far as he and the authorities were concerned I could guarantee the tithe value of the impounded plane. This, it transpired, was one of the main reasons the aircraft had been impounded in the first place. I asked about the breach of neutrality, but the man knew nothing about that. He told me that provided I did not attempt to leave the island's airspace and surrendered the aircraft again on my return, it should not affect the outcome of the hearing.

What it all amounted to was that the tithe bond would be discharged at midnight, and I would be allowed to take my aircraft up for a short proving flight first thing in the morning.

I was allowed into the hangar where two mechanics were conducting a final check of the instruments, wiring, and control surfaces. The engine, they told me, was in good working condition, or so they believed. It was unfamiliar to them, and they asked me several questions about its technical specifications, none of which I could answer. I wanted to touch the plane, even put my arm across its slender fuselage, but the mechanics had clearly been told to keep me away from it.

There were more questions to answer about the quantity of fuel I had ordered. 100-octane aviation fuel had been obtained specially, and was available, but the maintenance crew had of course discovered the auxiliary tank in the rear of the aircraft. They were concerned about the sheer quantity of fuel I was asking for. I needed both tanks filled to capacity for my main flight, but I did not want to arouse suspicions about my destination. I said that at first I would need only enough fuel for the short proving flight, but if that went well I intended to make a longer flight around the coast of the island. That was why I needed the extra fuel.

I went to a house where I had stayed on earlier visits to the airfield, slept well in spite of my feelings of excitement, and in the morning I returned to the airfield as early as I could. Several of the ground crew were already working but I was the only pilot there. I went to the met office for a weather report – it was expected to be another fine day with a high pressure system stable over the eastern part of the island. There was a seventy per cent likelihood of storms in the north and west of the island. Visibility was excellent. There would be low winds at all altitudes. The storm warning did not concern me – I was planning to be far away by the time it arrived.

I collected my flying jacket and helmet, then walked across to the bonded hangar. I noticed at once that the main doors were open. The official tags of tithe bondage had been unclipped from the aircraft's propeller, undercarriage and fin. One of the mechanics gave me a cheerful wave, which I took to mean all was clear. After a short wait, the plane was pulled out by the club tractor and turned around. The wheels were chocked.

I climbed into the cockpit, trying to act as if I had done it a hundred times before, although in fact I had only ever been inside this Spitfire twice: once when I began the outward flight, then again after arrival, when I had nowhere to stay and was forced to go through the night in the cockpit. Now I eased a leg over the edge of the cockpit with the canopy pushed wide open, lowered my backside on to the hard seat, pushed my legs around the joystick, found the rudders, wriggled and shifted to get into the right position.

Was it the plane that was going to be proved, or was it me? I was aware that what I was doing was attracting attention. All the ground crew had followed the Spitfire out of the hangar, and were now watching to see me start up. When I craned my neck and peered up towards the control tower I could see that a handful of people were standing at the window, looking down at me. I began the cockpit check, trying to appear calm.

The sequence was the familiar one – all pre-flight checks are similar, and I had memorized the Spitfire variations the previous year. Undercarriage: locked down, confirmed by the green light. Flaps: up. Lamps: up. Fuel cock levers: both on. (I had to search quickly for the second fuel cock.) Throttle: a finger-width open. Next to that, the mixture switch: rich. This cockpit check was starting to feel natural, habitual. Airscrew control: back. Radiator shutter: open. All OK. Next was the priming pump, on the starboard side. I tipped my head out of the cockpit on both sides, making sure no one was standing by the propeller, switched on the ignition, pulled the priming pump handle, pushed the starter.

The prop turned, the engine fired. I held in the starter button until the engine was running smoothly, then screwed down the priming pump.

My hands were shaking with relief. While the engine warmed up, I looked at all the instruments, checked they were working and zeroed. No one had changed the seat position, so my legs naturally reached down to the rudder pedals.

Now that the engine was running my nervousness was cured. I ran through the normal warm-up procedure. Brake pressure correct. Canopy locked open. Throttle opened on weak mixture, propeller pitch working OK. Throttle back, select rich mixture, throttle to maximum boost. Magnetos checked. All working. All ready.

I spoke to the control tower and was cleared for take-off. I waved a hand through the open cockpit and two of the mechanics scrambled forward and pulled the chocks away.

My Spitfire began to move forward. I eased the throttle open, and the plane taxied at normal speed.

When a Spitfire was on the ground it was always at a nose-up attitude because of the low tail-wheel, which meant there was no forward visibility, and because of the low wings there was only a restricted sight-line at the sides. When visiting this airfield before I made a point of learning what I could of the landing strip by walking up and down alongside. It was a grass airfield but the grass was kept short and there were few bumps or sudden inclines that could throw the plane into the air before it had gained enough airspeed.

I checked the wind direction once again, then taxied the plane out to the strip. As soon I was in position, the final check: elevator one click down from neutral, rudder full starboard to trim for take-off, mixture rich, propeller pitch fine, fuel on, flaps up, radiator shutter open.

I opened the throttle and the Merlin engine ran smoothly up to full power. The plane accelerated forward.

Moments later I was flying. The ground fell away, trees and fields at an angle below, white clouds above, the fabulous roar of the Merlin, the rush of air through the open canopy. I closed the canopy.

28

I flew the Spitfire carefully in a long circuit of the field. I was high enough to be able to catch sight of the ocean far away to the south, and even gain a glimpse of part of the great central desert, not so far away but beginning beyond a range of hills to the west. I was not up there to look at scenery – I took the plane through a sequence of basic flight tests: a climb, a turn, a dive, an incipient stall. I raised and lowered the undercarriage and monitored the reading of each of the instruments as I changed speed, direction and height. I looked at the instruments as if they were old friends: the artificial horizon, the altimeter, the air speed indicator, the fuel gauges.

Everything was working normally on the superb aircraft. As I realized what this day might hold for me I was briefly almost giddy with excitement. I radioed my intentions to the tower, was given permission to land and had the approach bearing confirmed, then I headed down towards the airstrip. As I passed over the field towards the turn-in point I could not resist testing the potential of the engine. I opened the throttle, felt a brief kick of acceleration. The countryside of this part of Prachous was passing swiftly below, a blur of green and brown – all I wanted now was to be done with the island, to be in the air, heading home.

I landed, waited as the staff recorded the necessary details of my flight, and while I went across to the control office they drove forward the fuel bowser and started to fill the tanks.

I filed my flight plan, which was a decoy to my real intentions: I drafted an extended flight along the coast, up to Beathurn, then briefly out across the neutral sea – a knowing concession to the law, as to continue up the coast from Beathurn would take me into the zone around the officially non-existent place called Adjacent. This route then made a return across the coast further north, a flight across part of the desert, down to the southern beaches, and a high-altitude dash across the sea before curving back for the last leg of the return flight to the airfield.

Although it is dangerous and illegal to file a false flight plan, I needed to justify the full load of fuel I was taking. I would never be given permission for what I really intended. The flight plan was calmly accepted and recorded. I was authorized for take-off.

I went to my car, collected my personal belongings and crammed them down into the spare spaces inside the narrow cockpit and behind my seat. The sun was climbing high, the heat beating down on my back as I stood on the Spitfire's wing and leaned into the aircraft. My hands were sweating, my heart was racing. With an effort I stayed outwardly calm. I shook hands with the crew on the ground, waved towards the tower, then at last climbed down into the small cockpit, my elbows pressing against the sides of the fuselage. I ran through the cockpit check again and taxied down to the end of the runway. I left the canopy partly open. I wanted to feel the rush of the air, hear the sublime roaring noise of the Merlin engine. How many times again would I enjoy the unique experience of flying this plane?

A minute later I was in the air, the engine racing, the slipstream beating against my head through the open canopy, the dome of the sky above, the slipping green of the land below. I climbed quickly. I turned the Spitfire towards the north and east, my first departure from the flight plan I had filed. Already the airstrip was a long way behind me.

I was flying at the same altitude as the cloud base. Great white cumuli were billowing up on the thermals from the rapidly warming land below. I closed the canopy, adjusted the pitch of the propeller, selected weak mixture, held the speed at an indicated two hundred knots. I was in the loveliest aircraft ever built. I had become part of it, joined to it, flown by it. I felt the relentless thrust of the engine, its roar now a steady drone because I was cruising. There was hardly any vibration inside the supremely trimmed machine. I skirted close to a white cloud, dived deliberately into the next, felt the kick of the internal turbulence, emerged into the blue, still climbing steadily. I soared past the other clouds, wanting to leave all trace of the land beneath me. With the canopy securely closed I switched on the air pressurization. I stared bewitched at the open sky around me, the land far below, a distant glimpse of the ultramarine sea and a clutch of islands, white-fringed.

29

I reached the height of about six thousand feet, which allowed a good view of the ground but was also above the rising clouds. I trimmed the plane for the best range at this altitude: engine speed of 1,750 r.p.m., weak mixture, coarse pitch, which gave me an indicated airspeed of about 160 knots. It was going to be a long flight, but I needed to conserve fuel – the distance the plane could cover mattered more to me than how long it might take. I was following a heading of 35 degrees by dead reckoning, a clumsy and often unreliable kind of navigation forced on me by the inferior maps that were the only ones I could find in Beathurn. The lack of maps was a constant problem on Prachous. If I had wished to find picnic grounds, beaches where there was safe swimming, or historic buildings where I could admire cultural artefacts, then the mapping of

Prachous was first-class. But for any serious navigation, by car as I had discovered many times, or by air as I was now experiencing, technically reliable charts or maps simply did not exist, or at least were unavailable on the open market.

I watched the ground as well as I could, seeking the rough navigational landmarks I had identified. I had noted them during my many car journeys across the island, in preparation for this flight without maps: certain lakes, rivers, an estuary, mountains, a conglomeration of tall buildings. The Spitfire's compass aided me in maintaining a steady course, while the known distance to the part of the coast I wanted was soon eaten up by the speed of the aircraft.

As I scanned the ground ahead of me I saw the coast coming into sight: that brilliant blue streaked with the white of Prachous's troubled waves. The sun was now much higher, casting a golden halation across the distant deeps. While I was living in the town I had searched the hinterland of Beathurn for markers, and I picked out two headlands to the south. These indicated a particular group of offshore islets, and contained a bay with an almost geometrically precise half-moon curve. From this I would of course be able to pick out Beathurn itself, whose overall shape and layout I had measured and mapped for myself.

Not long after I had located the coast and was flying offshore, parallel to the beaches, I saw one of the headlands and knew at once where I was. I corrected my course marginally and headed swiftly along the coast. I came to the sprawl of Beathurn itself. The air was so clear in the morning light that almost as soon as I spotted the town I was able to distinguish local landmarks: the central park, the estuary where the port was built, the area where my house had been, even the *Il-Palazz* theatre.

Now that I was certain where I was I headed directly towards the mountain range to the north. When I lived in Beathurn these mountains had seemed from street level to present a solid barrier, a termination of the town's territory, but from the height I was flying the same peaks appeared insignificant, passing beneath the Spitfire with at least a thousand feet to spare. I could see the full extent of the range – the first slopes were far inland, at the edge of the desert. The peaks closer to the sea were higher and more rugged.

I flew across them, glimpsing the large houses and estates on the lower slopes, the extensive system of cable-cars that ascended to the heights. The Spitfire was buffeted by strong updraughts from the windward slopes. The plane stabilized itself, almost as if it had a machine intelligence that relished coping with the irregularities of the sky and the climate.

Once past the mountains I was looking as far ahead as I could, anxious for my first glimpse of the closed zone containing the shanty town called Adjacent. What I was seeking was another estuary, much wider and more complex than the one that ran beside Beathurn, with several distributaries comprising a small but intricate delta. Alongside this, on the northern bank, would be the area of reedland I had seen on the old maps.

I eased the plane lower. I was passing over an area of farmland, with small fields marked out by hedges or stone walls. Ahead was a river plain. As I approached I could see the shape of the delta, a wide arrangement of sandbanks and channels flowing out into the shallow sea. I slowed the Spitfire to just over a hundred knots, which was above stalling speed with the aircraft so full of fuel, but without much margin of safety. I did not like the way the Spitfire handled at such a low speed, but I wanted to be able to take a good look at whatever there was on the ground.

I crossed over the delta and beyond was a huge area of marsh and undrained flood-plain. It was a forest of tall reeds, pale beige in colour, with dark seed pods clinging to the top of every stem. They waved constantly – the wind carved patterns in all directions, as the stems flexed to and fro. I stayed at about a thousand feet. Any lower than that was a risk. At a low height I could not be able to count on the altimeter giving an accurate reading, and the moving reeds were already making it difficult for me to estimate height by eye alone.

I could see no sign of habitation. In fact it did not seem possible that this land could ever be made habitable without major drainage schemes and tidal barriers. I flew for about five minutes, constantly aware of the fuel I was using up even at this slow speed, but the presence of the Adjacent zone on Prachous was the one matter I had never entirely understood.

I flew across the blackened ground almost without realizing what it was. I had been trying to see ahead, and I passed an area on the starboard that appeared suddenly, but seemed to flicker and disappear as I looked towards it – I was aware of a sense of something missing, a black absence.

I circled around, gained a little altitude. As I headed back I saw the full extent of what I had somehow missed when I flew past. There was an area of deep blackness on the ground – black, as if everything had been incinerated to the point of total destruction. It did not look like burned vegetation or the wreckage of something that had been there before. It was an annulment, an absence, a piece of negative terrain.

I flew across it, deeply disturbed by the sight. As I once more reached the plain of reeds, I gained height and circled around for another look. This time, as I flew towards the blackened ground I could see its full extent. It was immense, spreading out far to my starboard, less so on the port side. There I could see the terminator between the black impression of absence and the edge of the reed bank. It appeared to be a precise line, as straight as if it had been carved out with a massive knife.

I increased speed – I was feeling exposed while flying so slowly. I gained another five hundred feet of altitude, circled around again. This time I was high enough to take in the whole area of blackness. I could now see that it was an exact and regular triangle, carved out of the reedland. It spread for miles.

I headed towards it, but something about it gave me fright, and I shied instinctively away. There was something horrible about that negative sight, as if to venture too close would lead to my being drawn inexorably into it. I banked the aircraft, turning away, but then I changed my mind and held the turn, went back yet again for another look.

The triangle had disappeared.

I immediately thought that I had lost my bearings, but I had been flying by the compass and I knew that I was now heading back directly towards where the mark had been.

There were buildings ahead of me.

Where the triangle had been there was now what looked like

part of a town. I saw houses, streets, an area of green parkland, a church spire. There was no movement, no traffic driving along the roads, no people in sight, just the buildings, the roads, the solid exoskeleton of a modern city. I could see the shadows thrown by the bright sunlight.

The townscape also took the shape of an equilateral triangle, carved out of the reeds. It was the same size: each of the equal sides was at least two miles in length.

I flew across it, banked, turned through a hundred and eighty degrees, went back. How could I have missed it before? This time I saw tall buildings, concrete and glass, rising up above the ordinary houses and streets. I saw long terraces, cars parked outside. Many of the roads were lined with mature trees. The piece of park, which ran as far as one of the straight-line sides, also had many trees, a small lake, paths laid across the grass.

I flew away, banked again, headed back.

The town had disappeared. The triangle of black nullity had returned in its place.

I began to feel frightened again of what was down there, as if it were unreal, a decoy or a trap, something that was dangerous to see or know. Yet the aircraft in which I was flying gave me a feeling of immunity from what was outside. I took control of myself, tried to decide what to do. While I thought about this I had once again crossed the zone, and was on a bearing towards the sea. I made a decision.

I put the Spitfire into a steep turn and flew back towards where the triangle had been. This time I made no attempt to fly across it, or above it, but I set myself a circular course, skirting around all three of the furthest extremities of the immense triangle, close enough that I could see, but not so near to it that I became subjected to the deep fear it invoked in me.

I flew an anti-clockwise course, the dark triangle on my port side. I maintained a steady speed, a safe distance, the plane was cruising. I stared towards the triangle as I went around my circuit.

It changed.

At some points, from some angles, the triangle contained the buildings of a city – from other views it became once again that terrifying place of zero colour, black non-existence. Whenever I was close to one of the apexes, the sixty-degree angle at each of the triangle's corners, the image began to flicker with increasing rapidity. As I banked around that angle, the shift between the two became so rapid that it seemed for a moment that all I could see was a part of the reedland, but then, as my course took me along the next side of the triangle, the shifting between the two began to slow, and at the halfway mark what I could see was a steady view: from some sides it appeared as the black triangle of nothingness, from the others it would again be the image of the city.

I circled the zone four times, trying to work out whatever logic there might be in this incomprehensible vision, but as I started a fifth circuit I felt a certain jolt of reality. I had a larger purpose for making this flight, and I was critically wasting valuable fuel.

I made one last crossing of the zone. This time I knew that for the rest of the long flight I had to take the Spitfire to the operating altitude at which it had been designed to fly, and where I could burn what fuel remained more economically while flying faster. I made a last turn, opened the throttle to gain the best speed for a climb, then flew directly across the zone called Adjacent. As I did so I leaned forward, pressed the switch that until that moment I had never touched, the one that would start the powerful reconnaissance camera installed in the belly of the aircraft. I set it to run automatically, with one picture being taken every two seconds.

I heard the servo motor begin to run, felt its vibration, as I crossed the closest edge of the dark triangle, and moments later I saw the signal light on the operating box flicker on and off, as one frame after another was exposed.

I left the camera running as the great Merlin reached its full power, and the Spitfire climbed at speed to the familiar heights of the open sky.

30

An hour later I was on a bearing of 260 degrees and had long ago passed safely out of Prachous air space. I was in a sky of high, billowing clouds. Below me was the sea with many islands in sight. Increasingly I saw larger pieces of land pushing out towards the islands, and I knew that before long this course would take me over the continental mass for most of the remainder of the flight. I was at just over twenty-five thousand feet, much lower than the operating ceiling at which the Spitfire reconnaissance pilots normally flew, but at this altitude the plane was cruising at high speed on a weak mixture. Because I was flying without maps, I needed to be able to see the ground from time to time. The aircraft's cockpit heater blew warm air gently across me.

An immense column of heavy cloud lay ahead, blinding white at its anvil-shaped crest, but a thunderous dark below. I knew what it was, knew I should avoid it, but I had been trying to dead reckon from looking at the ground. The long trailing shelf of the anvil was already above me and a stinging shower of hail was falling. It drummed terrifyingly on the Spitfire's wings and fuselage, crashing against the canopy. The cumulonimbus stretched across the sky in front of me. My only option in the time left to me was to attempt to climb above it. Once again I raised the nose of the aircraft, but I was still climbing when I rushed against the wall of the cloud and slipped headlong into the turbulent darkness within.

31

I struggled through the dense cloud for nearly half an hour. Lightning streaked around me and violent up- and down-draughts battered the aircraft. The constant hailstones sounded like the impact of bullets. I was repeatedly thrown against the canopy or the fuselage – once the Spitfire acted as if it had rammed headlong into a solid obstruction. I was jerked forward in my seat against the control column, causing an unwanted dive. Any hope of maintaining my bearing was lost the moment I entered the cloud, because the internal currents were so violent and unpredictable that I could only hope the aircraft would stay in one piece and the engine would not fail or overheat. Sometimes it was impossible even to be sure the plane was still upright. This was the first and only time in all my solo flying that I felt out of control and in danger of crashing. Several times I was convinced I was going to die. The best I could do was cling on to the joystick, nursing the throttle with one hand, trying to keep the aircraft safely in the air.

I escaped from the cloud as suddenly as I had blundered into it. I flew out, more or less straight and level, moving in a few seconds from the terrifying up-draughts into calm, still air, blue and blue and blue around me. I was dazzled by brilliant sunshine.

I immediately checked my instruments, looking for any clue that the plane might have suffered critical damage, to the engine, to the flying surfaces, or to the hydraulics and fuel lines. All seemed well but it was impossible to be certain. I adjusted the mixture and the engine resumed its reassuring droning noise. The plane was still flying and it responded to my movements of the stick and rudder pedals. From the altimeter I discovered that we had ascended nearly five thousand feet while we were inside the storm cell. I let the plane descend to the former altitude. I checked my bearing, adjusted the direction, flew as calmly as I could, although I was feeling badly shaken up by the experience. From that point on I kept a wary eye open for any more storm clouds of that sort.

The long day continued. I was flying blind, depending entirely on my compass. I had no idea where I was. The land below me was unbroken countryside, impossible from this height to pick out any features. As far as I could see in any direction there were no distinguishing marks, no mountains, urban conglomerations, coastlines, not even a river whose shape or position might tell me something. All I could cling to was the 260 degrees bearing, my only route, my only way to the place I thought of as home.

Something glinted in the sky to starboard. It happened so quickly that it vanished by the time I turned towards it for a better look. I flew on. Then it happened again and this time I saw that it was a single-engined aircraft, dark against the bright sky, but the sun was glinting from its wings as it kept swinging from side to side – that was how fighter pilots kept a watch below them. Fear gripped me again. A second fighter plane had now joined the first, zooming up from below. Were the fighters friend or foe? They were too far away for me to identify them definitely, but I knew almost beyond doubt that they must be German. I was in the most distinctive British warplane of all but it was unarmed – in any event I had no idea how one went into combat while flying, so a fight was never an option. They were backing off, taking up a position somewhere behind me, presumably gaining height so they could launch an attack on me.

Moments later a fiery trail of bullets passed above my canopy, disappearing somewhere ahead of me. Something impacted on the Spitfire, behind the cockpit. The plane lurched, but although it had been wounded and it felt less responsive to the elevators, it continued to fly. Then one of the attacking planes zoomed past me and for a couple of seconds it was clearly in sight. I recognized it at once – I had been trained to spot every aircraft known to be flying, allied or enemy. This was a Focke-Wulf 190, the only German fighter that could match the high performance of a Spitfire. I glimpsed the spotted dark green camouflage on the upper surfaces, the black Luftwaffe cross clearly visible, the swastika sinisterly painted on the fin. The Focke-Wulf roared low above my plane, and I swung the stick to one side to avoid it. The German plane then banked away from me. The second Luftwaffe plane followed it, without seeming to have fired at me.

Unable to fight I could only try to evade. The one advantage I had was the advanced flying performance of this Spitfire XI, increased even more by the fact I was now light on fuel, and of course it lacked the deadweight of heavy machine guns buried in the wings. I threw the nose down, flung open the throttle and dived towards the ground. I turned, levelled out, dived again. My indicated airspeed was greater than 400 knots.

I lost sight of the German planes but I knew they must be somewhere around. I kept scanning the sky, but the sun was lowering in the west and the sky was too dazzling for me to see with any certainty. I saw two more aircraft – it might have been the original two, but it made no difference. They were flying at me from dead ahead and slightly to the side. I briefly saw the flickering flash of the guns embedded in their wings, but our combined speeds meant that these planes were only in sight for a couple of seconds. They swooped up and past me, one of them flying so close to my Spitfire I was certain of a head-on collision. It went just above me, though, kicking the Spitfire with the violence of its wake.

I flew on without sustaining any more damage.

The ground came closer, so I levelled the aircraft while trying to maintain the fabulous speed. Never before had I flown such a fast plane. The sheer thrill of that outweighed even my fear of being shot at by more German aircraft. High speed made me safe, made me feel safe. I went on and on, now so tired after hours at the controls that I was flying almost by instinct alone. I loved this aircraft more than I could express, even to myself. It seemed to anticipate my moves before I made them, sometimes even before I thought of making them, a sort of instinctive extension of me, a part of my consciousness that had been equipped with wings. I was still on the same bearing, somewhere over Europe, probably over the German homeland or perhaps a part of the occupied territories.

I was alone in a hostile sky, the sun sinking towards the horizon ahead of me. I wanted to be home, away from this, away from the past. I had a life ahead of me. The shore appeared suddenly and I flashed across the breaking waves. I was now flying low, at about two thousand feet. Anti-aircraft guns mounted on a ship moored offshore opened up on me as I streamed past. I saw the tracer bullets bright in the evening sky, curling up, nowhere close to me. Within seconds I was out of their range. It was getting dark – I guessed that in this summer evening there would be about an hour of subdued daylight left that would be good enough to let me fly safely. All I would need was the sight of a runway, straight and level. I took the plane down even lower, until I was only about two hundred feet above the surface of the sea. I could not maintain this height by instruments so I watched the sea ahead as it seemed to dash towards me, hypnotic in its steadiness and sense of unstoppable rush. I was yawning. My mouth was dry, my muscles were exhausted, my eyes were sore from constant straining through the brightness of the sky. I flew on, with no idea where I was, where I was going. If I was over the wrong sea, or had drifted away from my course, I might fly forever above these waves until the last drop of fuel had been used. But then, ahead, low on the horizon, a sight of land. I took the plane up to about a thousand feet, stared ahead, saw the flat coast hurtling towards me, dark, unlit, almost unprotected. It looked so harmless, the edge of a small island at war, vulnerable in the declining twilight. I closed the throttle a little, and the Spitfire slowed. I was almost at the coast, saw the white of the waves fringing the beach, the quiet shore of Great Britain. This was the place I thought of as home, the island that had taken me in when I had nowhere else to go, the island country I had grown to love and wanted to defend. I crossed the English tideline, saw below me an area of dunes, a small town nearby, beyond there were silent fields, mature trees. I slowed my beautiful, wounded aircraft even more and flew carefully across the crepuscular countryside, looking for an airfield where I might safely land.

PART 8

The Airfield

1

THE RETURN

Tibor Tarent waited until the Mebsher was not only out of sight, but also until he could no longer hear the distinctive high whining of its turbines. The personnel carrier had been driven away towards the east, which was the direction for the time being from which the wind was coming. For several minutes the sound of the Mebsher's engine came intermittently to him, as the cold wind bore it across the high Lincolnshire Wolds. The further it travelled the more distorted by the wind, and to Tarent the increasing distance lent the sound an eerie, other-worldly quality. It was close to midday in full daylight, and the sun was breaking fitfully through the racing clouds, but that far off wailing made him think of night. In particular, of those nights in Turkey when people had come to the field hospital too late to be treated, had been forced to wait outside the locked compound overnight, who howled in pain as they died in the dusty, enervating heat of the Anatolian night. It was a regular task in the morning for the orderlies to retrieve the bodies of those who had not survived the hours of darkness.

The Mebsher, its turbines howling into the distance, had become a carrier of human remains, of people whose image had been doubled by death. He thought of Lou Paladin trapped inside the grey steel compartment, accompanied by people he knew were dead. Who was that she was sitting next to? That man who had the same cameras, the same face and no doubt the same name? How could he ever explain to her what had occurred?

Tarent could not think of it, or try to imagine it, because there was no verbal or visual vocabulary to describe it.

The Mebsher finally moved out of earshot. Silence followed, the partial silence of the outdoors: wind, movement, foliage and branches. There was no birdsong in this place. The wind was edged with a deep chill, a harbinger of the early winter that threatened. Tarent felt the cold, not only from the wind.

He was alone in the quadrangle of Warne's Farm – even the men who had been guarding the closed building were gone. With no one now to stop him, Tarent took several photographs of the concrete building where he had identified the bodies. He switched cameras, putting aside the Canon he was most attached to and taking out the Nikon. He immediately took a series of shots of the dark tower by the main gate, checked online that they were in memory at the lab, then went towards to the building and took a few pictures closer up. Pigeons had invaded the building and were squatting on the sills. Moss grew in the many crevices in the brick-work and render. For the first time, Tarent noticed that a placard had been placed on a door at the base of the building, warning that the structure was unstable and that no one should try to enter it. The area immediately around it had been designated as a hard-hat zone.

Again he checked online for the confirmation that the Nikon's images had been received and were archived.

He walked across the quad to where he had left his bag, then moved it to a less exposed position inside a doorway. His name was shown prominently on the label, following OOR regulations.

He decided he should not attempt to leave Warne's Farm until he had finished what he planned to do before the Mebsher arrived. Taking all three of his cameras he walked back through the lower corridor of the residential building, then followed the gravelled walkway that led to the fence. At every door or barrier he passed he made sure that his ID card was still functioning – the cavalier way in which Flo Mallinan had suddenly invalidated his passport made him wary of being locked out, but his card still worked.

Tarent passed through the main gate, checking and double-checking that his pass still functioned, then went through to the outside. He turned back, took some shots of the gate, the fencing, the notices and warnings attached. He also photographed the general view of the Warne's Farm compound, seen from this slight rise of ground, visible through the trees.

As he climbed up the slope towards the ridge he thought at first that someone must have been out with tractors or heavy earth-moving equipment, because the fallen trees he remembered from before, up-ended by the storm, were not there. There had been one particular root-ball which hung over the pathway. That tree alone, a huge beech, would have taken a team of men several hours to chainsaw up and clear away.

Tarent tried to remember how long it was since he had been up here. It was before the Mebsher arrived, while he and Lou were waiting. An hour or so? How could all those felled trees have been removed in that time?

As he approached the top of the ridge he had to leave the pathway, because it curved down and away, so he scrambled up the slope through the undergrowth. There were many clumps of brambles and rhododendrons, and towards the top a tangle of gorse. He pushed through the branches and prickly bushes. Maybe he had climbed a different part of the ridge, because he did not remember so much dense undergrowth up here.

However, when he finally forced his way out he realized he was in much the same place as before, and for the same reason – he had clambered up to the ridge from the highest part of the path.

He looked down at the wide field where he had witnessed the adjacency attack on the Mebsher, where the triangle of annihilated earth had been scorched into the surface of the ground. Two days ago, before the storm? Three or four? He had lost count of those days. But however long it was, there was no longer any sign of it. He clearly remembered the place where the attack had occurred – it was more or less in the centre of the field, and the black triangular mark left on the ground could not be missed. But the crops were growing uninterrupted.

Baffled again, Tarent stared for a long time, wondering what he had seen, or even if his memory had failed him. There were so many contradictions he had to absorb, so much to try and make sense of.

An idea came to him. He switched on the Nikon and selected

the infra-red view, an option he rarely used because it caned the battery. With the quantum lens set to telephoto he slowly scanned through the viewfinder the part of the field where he felt certain the Mebsher had been just before the adjacency attack. Most of the image came through neutrally, but there was one spot, slightly to the side of where he expected the adjacency mark to be, that gave a positive register.

It was an area of the ground beneath the growing wheat and it was roughly triangular in shape, perhaps ten or twenty metres across at most. He turned up the gain – the image became clearer. There was something there, even if it was not what he was seeking. He had seen similar traces before, usually when images were taken from above by aircraft or reconnaissance drones – they often revealed historical workings, or the foundations of ancient roadways or buildings, or most commonly areas of violent impact, such as traces of explosions or the sites of crashed aircraft.

The Nikon's battery failed after that so he took out the Olympus Stealth, keeping the Canon in reserve. He took several photographs of the field, including a few telephoto shots of the area of the old trace, but the central mystery of the adjacency scar remained.

He turned to walk back to Warne's Farm. He was feeling warm in his jacket, which he had put on when he went out to find the Mebsher. In the erratic current climate sudden temperature shifts were not unusual, but normally they involved unexpected cold snaps. The air was much warmer about him, the sort of feeling he remembered from childhood, the calm evening after a sweltering day, when the air stayed warm long after the sun had set.

The light too had changed. It was around midday when the Mebsher had been at the Farm, a cool but bright day, with broken clouds, a stiff wind. He had walked up through the trees, in their shade. The air was now still, and it was evening. There was a glow in the sky towards the west: high cirrus clouds lit by a setting sun.

How much time had passed? And in what manner had it passed?

Tarent removed his jacket, pulled his camera holdall on over his shirt and pushed his way back through the gorse and rhododendrons to find the path below. Once under the trees, where swarms of midges hovered beneath the branches, he wondered if somehow he had blundered into another place entirely. The shallow hillside was thickly wooded, with trees of all ages and sizes, and a thick, loamy soil below, rich with leaves and twigs and other pieces of vegetation. He vividly recalled the wretched damage caused by the storm, so many fallen trees and broken branches, so much chalky soil and clods of earth bared to the elements.

He continued down the slope through the gathering twilight until he found the path, which at least looked familiar and as he expected it to be. He walked back towards the Warne's Farm complex, looking for the gate and the fence. A heady smell, sweet and almost intoxicating, drifted up towards him through the trees: gasoline.

2

In the half-light of the evening he passed the place where the gate had been before he realized he had done so. He was walking down through the trees, looking ahead to see the Warne's Farm buildings, thinking in a confused way about the trees – where had they come from, hadn't they all been blown down? He realized he had reached the lowest point of the path, where he would cross the compound to go through the corridor of the residential block, but none of that was there any more.

When he looked back he could see no sign of the fence, nothing at all of the gate. The light was failing rapidly, but there was enough for him to see that all traces were gone.

He walked out of the trees – none of the now-familiar buildings were there. The Warne's Farm compound had disappeared. Tarent, already in a state of mental disequilibrium, did not panic, did not try to find an explanation, did not try to understand. He was still perspiring after his climb up to the ridge, and confused by the changes he was experiencing, but for years he had trained himself to limit his activities to seeing and observing. Photography was only incidentally to do with the camera – real photography began with the eye of the photographer.

It was as Melanie had said. Photography was a passive art – not an art of creative intervention or making, but of creative receptivity. Tarent had learned as a photojournalist not to become involved: he had been present at street riots, fights outside nightclubs and bars, he had been surrounded by surging crowds at political rallies, he had run alongside desperate people in times of war or natural disaster. A photographer's work was never about what he did, it was about what he *saw*.

The world he was moving through now was one that had changed in ways he did not understand, but even in spite of the fading daylight it was one he knew he had to see, and to keep seeing. Nothing else made sense – his cameras were his only hold on reality, or at least they represented a reality he felt he could comprehend.

He clicked the Olympus light receptor to night sensitivity. While he looked around at what was before him, he reached down to the Canon inside its case, and by familiar touch alone switched that also to night use.

Ahead of him there was a small piece of lawn, enclosed by white-painted cobblestones. Beyond that a tarmac path, an expanse of concrete, some young trees recently planted, and two or three nondescript two-storey office buildings with flat roofs. There was another similar building to his left. They all reminded him of the elderly MoD buildings he had seen during his overnight stay at Long Sutton. He took several shots of them, digitally enhanced by the camera. There was a road running down between the two buildings, with a view of another road crossing that one further along, and more buildings in the same functional architecture. Three cars were parked along the road, but without exception they were models he did not recognize. They were cars of a boxy, outdated design, probably from around the middle of the previous century. They were all the same colour: unpolished black paint, or possibly, because it was none too clear in the twilight, dark blue. They were unoccupied, except for the one closest to him – in this a young woman in a military cap was sitting behind the steering wheel, staring ahead. He took more night pictures, using a long focal length – the woman in the car did not react to being photographed, or she chose not to, or she had not noticed him.

Two young men in work clothes came out of the building beside him, carrying mugs of what looked like hot drinks in both hands. They passed close to him – Tarent took several more shots. He smelled tea made with milk, which he found unexpectedly appetizing. They walked on, went into the next building. As the door opened, Tarent heard loud voices inside, someone hammering, something else being drilled. Once the door had closed he photographed the building itself.

He looked to his right. There stood the only familiar remnant from Warne's Farm – the tall dark tower, vaguely similar to a church tower. It was silhouetted against the evening sky, making it appear darker, but Tarent could see that whereas before it had been in a bad state of repair, in danger of imminent collapse, now it looked solidly built, four-square on the ground, a recent construction. The tall window frames, three on each of the two sides he could see from this angle, contained glass.

He walked towards the tower, intending to take more photos, but suddenly he became aware of a deep-throated roaring noise, getting louder or coming closer, and in the next moment an aircraft swept low overhead, black against the sky. It was a four-engined propeller aircraft, heavily built with a deep fuselage and sturdy wings. Gun turrets were mounted fore and aft. Its wheels were down. The engines made a concussive roar that Tarent could feel throbbing against his face and chest. Then the plane was gone, sliding down towards the ground, too low to be seen, beyond the buildings and trees.

Tarent recognized the aircraft – it was a bomber from the period of the Second World War, a Halifax, perhaps, or a Lancaster. It passed overhead too quickly and unexpectedly for him to be sure which, but when he was a boy he had gone through a period of obsessively learning to identify all the British warplanes of that period.

Using the LED screen on the back of the Olympus, Tarent quickly looked at the shots he had just taken, then pressed the upload key. Almost at once the camera showed a red warning light. Familiar words, always unwelcome, appeared on the display: *Network unavailable or offline*. He never felt his pictures were secure until they had been uploaded to the lab's archive so he tried again immediately, with the same result. It reminded him of the worst days in the field hospital in Anatolia: being isolated from everything, including his archive.

He made a third unsuccessful attempt to upload, then decided to change cameras. All three of the cameras used the same archive, but sometimes one of them accessed the lab more reliably than the other two. Or it seemed that way – it varied, so there was probably nothing in it. He tested the Canon and quickly received its own version of the error message.

The sunset was over and the darkness was now almost complete. Although the buildings and paths and roadways were unlit, there was still some light in the sky, presumably from the moon, at present too low to be seen or perhaps because for the moment it was covered by cloud.

Tarent walked towards the building where he had seen the men entering. He paused on the way, regarded it through the nightsight of his camera, which was able to display its enhanced image in colour. From this, Tarent discovered the building was an aircraft hangar. It had been camouflaged in a way that he found familiar from films and TV shows set in the Second World War: great rounded waves of dark green and brown were painted across its walls, and the huge steel doors at the front.

He cautiously pushed open the access door he had seen the men using, and walked inside. Bright lights were glowing down from above, illuminating a great deal of purposeful activity. At least twenty airmen were at work. Notably, the main floor of the building was taken up with two of the four-engined aircraft, which Tarent was this time able to recognize as Lancaster bombers. These were both partly dismantled and the focus of much work. One of the aircraft had all four of its engine nacelles open, while some kind of testing or parts-replacement was going on. The other aircraft had obviously been damaged by gunfire, or by a near-miss from an anti-aircraft shell – the covering of its wings, tailplane and part of the fuselage were in tatters. The rear turret had also been removed and a new one was on the floor of the hangar, presumably soon to be mounted as a replacement.

He was standing there, staring, trying to understand, trying to continue to act as an observer rather than a participant, when one of the men turned sharply towards him, then strode angrily towards the door.

'Who left the bleeding door open?' he shouted, and slammed it closed. 'Was that you, Loftus?'

'Don't think so, Sarge,' one of the airman replied, in a deep Birmingham accent. 'I thought I'd shut it behind us.'

'Mind the blackout.'

A mumbled chorus from two of the men: 'Sorry, Sarge.'

Work resumed.

Using the ambient light in the hangar, Tarent took a series of rapid shots of the two Lancasters, expecting at any moment that he would be shouted at, or manhandled, or threatened with some breach of the regulations covering this place. But it was as if he was not there. Everyone ignored him. He moved towards some of the men as they worked, took close shots of what they were doing. They continued to ignore him. The plane, standing high on its main undercarriage and tailwheel, was at an angle to the ground. Most of it was painted matt black, but the narrow strip at the top of the fuselage visible from below was painted in dark-green camouflage. The tall letters P D and S were painted on the side of the fuselage, aft of the wing, with the RAF roundel between them. Below the cockpit canopy drawings of bombs were stencilled on the black paint, indicating the number of sorties it had so far completed.

Tarent took detailed close-up photographs of everything he saw.

Finally, he retreated and went to stand by the door again. The network was still down, so he switched off the Canon and slid it into its protective pouch.

It was against all reason, against all logic, against everything rational, but Tarent knew that in some fashion he had wandered on to an operational RAF base, in wartime, an old and mostly forgotten war of a hundred years before. How was that possible?

It was beyond his ability to comprehend. All he could do as a re-action to what had happened was to look, to see, to watch, to take pictures. That damned passive attitude that Melanie had criticized him for, unfairly but accurately, had become his only resort in this time of unreason. To try to think or do anything different was a risk that for the moment he did not know how to take.

He expected it to end suddenly, this vision, this experience, this glimpse of a distant past, this dream, this hallucination – he still could not describe it, even to himself. Until it came to an end, until the unreason was reversed, he had to hold on to what he knew.

He again took out the Canon, his talisman of known reality, switched it on, routinely glanced at the battery level to be sure there was still enough charge, checked the default settings for taking pictures in extremely low light, watched as the automatic dust-cleansing of the processor chip was swiftly carried out. The whole procedure took less than two seconds, and was completed by the familiar electronic beep, confirming the boot-up was correct.

He played back the photographs he had taken since he arrived in this place. They were all there in camera memory. The network and therefore the archive lab continued to be inaccessible. He tried again, twice.

It was hot inside the hangar so Tarent returned outside, this time being certain to secure the door behind him. The mild evening air, with its taints of gasoline and rubber and paint, but also of recently cut grass, was still warm after the day. Thinking that being in the open air and away from the immense metal doors of the hangar the network signal might have been restored, he tried once more to access the lab, but without success.

He waited for a few moments for his eyes to adjust to the darkness after the lights inside the hangar, then set off towards some of the other buildings he had noticed earlier. Although they were obviously blacked out so that no bright lights showed, there were in fact many doors, windows and other apertures where glints of light shone through.

After a short walk he came to one of the two-storey brick buildings he had noticed when he first arrived. He could hear the sound of many voices. Inside, there was a short corridor, which then turned to right and left. Before that he saw a double door, with a sign attached to it: *Crewroom*. He went through, closing it quietly behind him.

It was a long room, packed with airmen, the air thick with cigarette smoke. Tarent's first breath made him reel back, gasping. He turned away and re-opened the door, seized by a bout of helpless coughing. Never before in his life had he been in a place so full of smokers. His eyes were watering. He returned outside, breathed the evening air until he felt better. Then, more cautiously, he returned to the room.

The airmen were all wearing flying suits, lounging around in dozens of armchairs or standing in small groups. Cups and saucers, and large ashtrays filled with cigarette ends, littered every tabletop. A radio was playing dance music, but no one appeared to be listening. The mood in the room was not jovial, but noisy and friendly, most of the hubbub coming from conversation rather than anything else. Many of the men were standing, carrying extra items: flying helmets, maps, life jackets, Thermos flasks, pairs of leather gloves. At the far end of the room was a huge map of northern Europe: part of Great Britain was visible at top left, but most of the map showed mainland Europe, from France in the west as far as Czechoslovakia in the east, and Italy in the south. Two long ribbons, one red and the other blue, had been thumb-tacked over the map, showing two routes from Lincolnshire across the North Sea into Germany. The red route ran a track slightly to the south of the other, but they ended in the same place: a town in the north-west of Germany.

Tarent began taking photographs and once again no one took any notice of him at all. He was becoming bolder, so he took several close-ups of the men's faces. He was shocked to realize how young they were – most of them were barely out of their teens. He worked quickly, catching the men's expressions, the way they used their hands when speaking, their bulky uniforms, the mannerisms with cigarettes and angles of caps which looked as if they had been copied from movies.

He was moving towards the end of the room where the map hung against the wall, when two officers walked out of a side door and took up a position on a low platform in front of the map.

Silence fell, and all the airmen stood up. Someone switched off the radio. At a signal from one of the officers, they resumed their seats.

The leading officer spoke, addressing the room.

'You've been fully briefed,' he began, 'so I won't repeat what you already know. Your navigators have the route in detail and tonight's recognition codes are inside the aircraft. The target for tonight is a tactical one, a plant that manufactures synthetic oils, which the Luftwaffe and the German Army are increasingly dependent upon. Any questions?' No response. Tarent walked forward, went up to the officer, began to take photographs of him and the other man. They both wore medal ribbons on their breasts. 'All right. You know what's expected of you. We need precision bombing tonight, so the Pathfinders will be there a few minutes before you. Weather conditions over the target are expected to be cloudy, but not so much that you won't be able to bomb accurately. You don't need me to tell you what to do when you get there, but let me wish you all the luck you deserve, and a safe return.'

He saluted, then turned away quickly. He left the room and the airmen all stood up again. The other officer indicated the clock, and told the airmen to synchronize their watches with it. When this was done he too then walked briskly away. The airmen began to shuffle around, picking up their equipment and heading for the door.

Tarent looked closely at the map. The indicated target was the town of Sterkrade, in the northern part of the Ruhr. He had never heard of the place before. Since no one seemed aware he was there, Tarent took several photographs of the map, and the view of the room from the platform.

There were many newspapers left lying around on the chairs, on the tables, so Tarent walked over and picked one of them up. It was a copy of the *Daily Express*. The date on it was Friday, 16 June 1944. He took photographs of the front and rear pages. He did not stop to read the pages then, but he noticed that the main headline concerned a new kind of weapon the Germans were launching against London: unmanned aircraft filled with high explosives, designed to crash randomly on the city with devastating effect.

As the last of the men left the room Tarent followed them

outside. A number of trucks were waiting to transport the men away. One by one these drove out across the airfield, with the men standing or squatting in the back. Some of them sat by the tailgate, their legs dangling.

The moon had appeared while Tarent was inside the building, and it was easier to make out the shape of the buildings and the extent of the airfield. The trucks carrying the airmen were speeding away in several directions, and in the moonlight he could just make out the distant shapes of one or two of the Lancasters, parked close to the perimeter of the field.

Unexpectedly, there was a loud bang fairly close at hand. Tarent snapped around to see what it was. He saw what appeared to be a fiery rocket shooting up into the sky. At the peak of its flight a bright red flare of light appeared, throwing a distinct reddish glow on the ground.

It was directly above his head, a coincidence that immediately triggered a feeling of alarm. Flo had said that adjacency attacks invariably involved a bright overhead light.

But this one, fizzing and spluttering, continued on, moving down and away from him on the wind, probably destined to burn out before hitting the ground somewhere in the middle of the airfield.

Two airmen had emerged from another building, and were walking close to Tarent. He heard one of them say, 'What was that Very for?'

'Not sure. But someone came on the phone from Scampton just now. The radar there picked up a couple of what they thought might be intruders.'

They walked directly past Tarent, so close to him that he could see the features of their faces in the dimming red glow from the Very light. They were both young men, as youthful-looking as the aircrew he had seen. Once again they revealed no awareness that he was there. He decided to walk along with them and listen in to what they were saying.

'They don't usually fire a flare just because Scampton sees something.'

'Maybe one of the intruders is headed this way?'

'A Junkers came in one night before you were posted here. He got one of our Lancs.'

'Did you see it?'

'No, but I had to help clear up the mess the next day.'

'I heard a single-engined plane come in about an hour ago.'

'That was a Spit. I heard it too, and went out to watch it land. Whoever it was must be lost, coming in here.'

'So it wasn't a German?'

'Not that one.'

In the distance, at the various extremities of the airfield, the Lancasters' engines were starting up. The two young airmen paused. Tarent stood beside them in the dark.

'I'm going down to the NAAFI for some grub. You coming too?'

'I thought I'd walk out to the end of the runway and watch the lads take off again.'

'OK. See you in the morning, then.'

'Probably not,' said the other. 'I'm leaving first thing in the morning. The posting came through a couple of days ago.'

'I'm sorry to hear that, Floody. You going to another squadron?'

'I'm being retrained, then I'll be sent to Italy. Yank planes, apparently.'

'I bet they're crappily built.'

'Just because they're American?'

'Of course. Not half as good as ours.'

'OK, see you after the war, then!'

'Yeah, OK. Good luck, Floody.'

'You too, Bill.'

3

The man called Floody watched his friend walk off in the direction of the main group of buildings, then he turned away, walking quickly back towards the hangar. Tarent stayed where he was. In a moment, Floody re-appeared, throwing his leg across a bicycle as he mounted it. Tarent saw him dimly in the half-light of the moon, pedalling erratically along the footpath. It looked like a hazardous thing to do in this low light, but presumably he knew the way.

The Lancasters' engines were now making a great deal of noise and several of the huge planes were taxiing slowly along the perimeter of the airfield. Tarent had never before seen anything like it, this ungainly procession of heavily loaded bombers in the dark, proceeding around to a distant take-off point. Floody was bicycling in that direction, so Tarent followed. More of the bombers moved away from where they had been parked, and set off down the airfield. The noise increased.

Another Very light went up, fired from somewhere out in the centre of the huge field. Once again, to Tarent it seemed that the flare was sent in his direction, bursting into its full glare when it was directly above him. This second Very, which had been fired against the direction of the wind, did not describe an arc, but remained above Tarent, falling slowly towards the ground, guttering and spitting out a trail of bright red sparks.

Tarent felt no fear of it – everything that was happening on this air base had for him, increasingly, a dreamlike feeling of unreality. In a moment the flare sputtered out, and whatever was left of it fell to the ground invisibly and harmlessly. Tarent felt immune from it, as he felt immune from everything else. No one was able to see him, no matter where he went or what he did. Yet he was not imagining any of this: he could enjoy the warmth of the summer evening, feel the light pressure of the breeze, savour the smells and scents in the air. He could touch, hear, see. He was capable of opening and closing a door, he could choke on the cigarette smoke filling a room, he could hear the sound of the Lancasters' powerful engines, he could bend down and pluck a few blades of the coarse grass on which he was walking. He could take photographs and the images were recorded on the microchip. In every sense except one, what he was experiencing was real.

The one exception was that none of it could possibly be happening.

Tarent held his camera in one hand, almost as if it defended him somehow from the unreality of the situation. He was not afraid of what was happening around him, nor did he have any understanding of it. He sensed that his presence, his half-presence, had no influence on the events he was seeing, nor had been arranged for his benefit. He was here, he witnessed, he saw events unfolding. If he were not here the same events would still be taking place.

Floody had wobbled away on his bicycle out of sight, lost in the darkness of the evening. Across the field, Tarent could see the squadron buildings, but at this distance, in this imprecise light, they could be seen only as dark shapes, or as an overall presence. He walked on, heading in the same general direction that Floody had taken.

A few minutes later lights came on suddenly. They were on the ground, a couple of hundred metres to the side of where he was walking, placed in two parallel rows. They were not bright and were widely spaced. They ran for most of the length of the airfield. As Tarent wondered what they might be for, their function was almost immediately made clear: in the far distance a Lancaster suddenly opened up its engines and with a great roar began to accelerate along the runway, which was marked out by the flare-path of lights. Tarent watched while the enormous bomber thundered towards him. As it passed by it was still in contact with the ground, but its tail was raised. Moments later the heavily loaded aircraft lifted away from the ground, its engines straining with the weight. The sound of the engines now battered against him, a thrilling, awe-inspiring sound of immense mechanical power.

The Lancaster was barely flying when the engines of a second plane at the distant end of the runway emitted their full-throated roar, and that bomber too began its take-off run. Entranced by the experience, unlike anything he had ever known, Tarent remained where he was, daunted by the sheer physical presence of these cumbersome and deadly warplanes, but which were also somehow elegant.

This second Lancaster had already struggled into the air as it passed where he was but was still low above the runway. Gradually gaining height, it flew away in the direction taken by the first plane. It was soon almost invisible to Tarent.

The flare-path lights were quickly extinguished.

Around the perimeter of the airfield, other Lancasters were taxi-ing down towards the end of the take-off runway. The sound of their engines reached him intermittently, on the vagaries of the wind. Tarent walked on, hoping that he would be able to reach that point in the airfield before the last aircraft left. He wanted to experience the start of the take-off run from close quarters.

After another minute or so, the flare-path lights were switched on again, and in quick succession two more Lancasters thundered down the runway and took off. Tarent again stood still to watch them.

The flare-path turned off, and more of the Lancasters taxied towards the distant take-off point.

The lights came on again, ready for the next take-offs, but almost immediately another Very light was shot high into the sky. The flare-path lights were instantly extinguished.

Again it seemed to Tarent that the exploding flare of red light was exactly above him. Once or twice might be a coincidence, but three ...? He watched nervously as the spluttering flare drifted down towards the ground. This time he could smell the remains of its smoke – a childhood memory of fireworks swept through him.

The waiting Lancasters remained in two lines, converging from both sectors of the perimeter road towards the end of the runway.

There was another engine sound. This had a different pitch from that of the Lancasters, a sharper, higher sound. It came from an aircraft that was low in the air, fast-moving.

Without warning, a ground-based machine-gun, mounted at the far side of the airfield, opened up. Its tracer bullets arced across the sky. The intruding aircraft's engine noise increased, and for a moment Tarent glimpsed a twin-engined aircraft with a bulky body, banking low above the ground, swinging away from the airfield. As it swiftly flew across the perimeter towards the east, a second anti-aircraft gun started firing from the ground. Its tracer bullets crossed with the others, too high, too far away to have any effect.

The flare-path lights remained off – in the far distance the Lancasters waited, engines running.

Another Very went up – again, it burst in the sky directly above

Tarent's position. He stepped briskly to one side, beginning to feel that these things were somehow being aimed at him, and not wishing to have the hot remains of the flare container fall on him. However, this flare had a serious purpose – as the latest Very tumbled slowly earthwards, the twin-engined intruder reappeared. It roared over the airfield again, this time flying fast and low above the take-off runway the Lancasters were using. It was heading directly towards the point where the bombers were queuing for take-off. Tarent could see a deadly flicker as cannons mounted in the stocky wings fired towards the waiting aircraft.

The anti-aircraft machine-guns at the sides of the airfield started firing, and tracer arced low above Tarent's head, directly towards the intruding German plane. As the intruder rushed past him, no more than a hundred metres away from where he crouched in the grass, Tarent saw the tracer from the AA gun behind him make violent contact with the side of the plane.

The reaction was instant. The engine on that side made a screeching noise, the German plane banked sharply to one side, and lifted dramatically away from its attack run. With the damaged engine still shrieking intermittently, the intruder levelled out and flew away towards the east. Tracer from the airfield machine guns followed it, but it was already too far away to be hit again. It was obvious in any case that it no longer presented a threat to the Lancasters on the ground.

When he felt certain there was to be no more shooting Tarent stood up. He continued to walk towards the far end of the main runway. In a while the flare-path lights came on again, and two more heavily loaded Lancasters made their lumbering but successful take-offs into the summer night.

4

Ahead of him, Tarent saw the dark outlines of two small buildings. They were to the side of the airfield, close to the perimeter track. He planned to walk across the long grass as far as the buildings, then continue the rest of the way by following the perimeter road itself. Although the moonlight still shone, slightly brighter now that the moon had risen further, Tarent stumbled two or three times on small but unseen obstacles on the ground. He was holding the Canon in his hands, and was all too aware of the risk of tripping over and damaging it. It would have been safer to slip the camera into its protective pouch, but for him the Canon still felt like a token of reality – so long as he held it ready he was in control of at least that part of his life.

He came closer to the buildings and two more Lancasters went roaring past on their way to the raid on distant Sterkrade. Tarent briefly wondered if any of the airmen aboard had, before this raid, known the name of their target town. The flare-path flipped into darkness again, and at the end of the runway two more bombers moved slowly into position. He was now close enough to the take-off point to hear clearly the sound of the engines of the waiting aircraft.

He walked on to a concrete apron in front of the two buildings. Parked there, partly blocking the way he was intending to take, was a small aircraft. It was a single-engined plane, streamlined, low-winged. After the sheer bulk of the heavy bombers it looked almost like a miniature. Tarent paused, raised his camera, and used the night-sight to take a clearer look at it.

He quickly took three shots of it, trusting to the digital clean-up of underlit subjects.

The plane had RAF roundels on the wings, which otherwise were painted in drab green-brown camouflage. There was someone standing beyond the aircraft, leaning against the wing. Through the night-sight, Tarent could make out only a leather flying suit, thickly lined, crumpled brown.

He lowered the camera. The figure was a woman.

As he walked around the plane, the woman turned towards him. She was wearing a leather flying helmet, which she swept off and threw to one side.

'Is that you, Tibor?' she said. 'What are you doing here?'

Her voice was familiar, completely recognizable, but it could not be –

'Melanie?'

They were facing each other, unbelieving, almost afraid. Neither of them moved, preserving the shock.

'I thought you were dead,' she said.

'I thought you had been killed.'

'No – that's not what happened. They said you had been blown up in a Mebsher.'

'Who told you that?'

'What?'

They were having to raise their voices. As he moved around the aircraft, yet another Lancaster was accelerating along the runway. It was so close the noise was deafening.

'I can't hear you!'

'Come here.'

They stepped towards each other then, their arms outstretched. Gently, cautiously he reached out for her. He expected to feel the thick leather flying jacket under his hand, but he touched a bare arm, then the thin dress she was wearing. He could feel her back, her spine, through the fabric.

'How did you get here?' he said.

'How did you?'

'I don't know.'

'Neither do I. My god, I've missed you!'

'Melanie!'

He held her close to him, feeling her arms around his back, squeezing hard. She was pressing the side of her face against his, that familiar touch, just as he remembered.

She said something, a soft word or two into his ear, but the second Lancaster went down the runway, drowning out all other sounds.

As it moved away, its tail lifting from the runway, she said, 'Tibor, where are we?'

'I'm not sure. I really don't know.'

Somewhere behind them there was a loud bang, and another Very light was fired into the sky. He had become so used to the sound that he barely glanced up, but Melanie arched her head back to see. Then he did too. At the top of its flight, the red flare was burning brightly.

Again, it was directly above him. It was falling towards them, spitting bright sparks.

Then it turned white. It brightened. It became a point of light so brilliant it was not possible to look directly at it.

It was casting a shaft of brilliance across a large area of the ground. Tibor and Melanie were at the centre of it.

Tarent turned, sensing a movement, somewhere towards the perimeter, away from where they were. A tall young man went by on a bicycle, head down, pedalling hard, watching where he was steering. He was unaware of them, did not react to the intense light coming down around them. He passed on into the darkness, freewheeling.

The light above brightened. It descended towards them. On the ground the patch of light grew smaller, and was cohering into the shape of a triangle.

Incredibly it intensified yet again, blinding, searing them, annihilating them.

Then it went out, leaving only blackness.

Tarent was holding his wife in his arms. It was so strange to do, yet so right, so unquestionably right. She was folding herself against him as she used to, as she always had, right at the start when they were young, and even later on, whenever they found the time to be alone together, and still loving.

Daylight had broken around them. It was early morning, cool and sharp. They were standing on tussocks of grass, long and damp with dew, wetting their ankles. The sun was low in the east, already clear of the horizon and too bright to be looked at. In the near distance was a line of trees, but their trunks were masked with a light mist, so that their green foliage spread above, making it look as if the trees were floating above the ground. There were cows in the field – some were sitting on the grass, chewing slowly, while others were already up and grazing. One was close to them – it regarded them with wide eyes, while it continued to chew.

'Where are the planes?' Tarent said. 'It was night. I was on some kind of airbase. It was in the year 1944 ... I saw a newspaper.' He clutched at the camera hanging on its lanyard around his neck. 'I took a photo of the front page, let me show you.'

He fumbled with the switch, to turn on the Canon, something he had done a thousand times in the past but today, this time, his fingers felt clumsy and incapable. Melanie reached down and gripped his wrist.

'Not now. Show me later, Tibor.'

She turned, keeping her arm around his back, and they began to walk slowly across the field, feeling the damp grass, blinking their eyes away from the brightness of the morning sunlight. The meadow signalled an innocent past, a summoning of a collective wish, a simple shared experience. But Tarent could still hear, as if hearing a memory, the Lancasters taking off, the sights and smells of the airfield at war. A dark, real and deadly war. He knew he had been there, but in what way, by what means, and for why?

'Do you know where we are?' he said. 'This is not where I was. I came back from Turkey, I was taken to a government place—'

'I came here because I was told that this was where I would find you.'

'But how did you travel? I thought all travel had been—'

'I came by car. Someone lent it to me. It's parked down at the farm.'

'The farm?'

'I thought you knew. This is a farm in Lincolnshire, in the Wolds, not far from Hull. I had no idea why you would be here, but they were right.'

'Who is they?'

'At the hospital. The admin staff told me you were back in England, so I came here to find you.'

'On this farm in Lincolnshire?'

'Yes.'

'Warne's Farm?'

'Yes, of course.'

They walked on, came to a gate, which Tarent opened and then closed again, making sure the beasts in the field could not escape. Beyond was a road, a narrow country lane. The grasses here on the verges were long, the hedges above thickening as the leaves broke out for the spring. He could smell soil, dampness, grass, mud. The air was so still.

'What date is it?'

'Some time in March, I think,' Melanie said.

'You think?'

'I'm not sure of that any more.'

'Do you happen to know what year we are in?'

'No.'

'Why not?'

'Tibor, I don't know. I'm not certain of anything. Just this. Isn't this enough? Why do you need to ask about dates, years?'

'I keep losing days and dates.'

Ahead of them the farm buildings were coming into sight, nestling against the side of a hilly ridge. Prominent among them stood a tall, brick-built tower, church-like. He took up his Canon again, switched it on, waited while it booted, then zoomed the quantum lens to its maximum focal length and focused on the tower. It looked dilapidated, unstable, a dark and unsafe relic from an earlier age. He clicked the shutter release. Melanie moved forward so that she was standing between him and the farm buildings. She was an unfocused blur in the viewfinder, so he let the automatic lens readjust and she came into sharp focus. He had never stopped loving her but he had forgotten how beautiful she was, forgotten how much he liked to look at her, liked to photograph her. He clicked the shutter release, then, because she was smiling, twice more again.